Armed, Cute, and Dangerous

Zeppy Cheng

Dedicated to the person who came up with the concept of 'Magical Girls.' They're awesome.

Copyright © 2015

Zeppy Cheng

Table of Contents

August the Monster Slayer 6

August and Elyse Get All Mixed Up 16

Zombies? No, Monkeys! 26

Elyse: Genius Inventor Extraordinaire 34

Attack of the Magical Girls 50

These Ones are Overage 56

General Stysh: Smart, Cute, and Very, Very Dangerous 64

Yeah! Save the World! So, Where do we Start? 70

It's a Dress! It's a Fairy! It's a Dress Fairy! 73

Politics. Little Girls. Need More Be Said? 81

Beat Up By a Buncha' Little Girls 87

Secretary of the Gods 93

You Have Learned a New Spell 98

Science! 102

Meanwhile 113

It's Got a Gutter. On Its Back. 116

This is Going to Take a Whole Lot of Paperwork. 124

Ice Cream Kiss 131

Are They . . . Edible? 137

Whalegirls' Doing Some Wranglin' 140

Sing to Me, Softly 148

Just Being Careful 151

The great escape 155

Little Girls Alone in the Forest 161

Armada of Blue Steel 166

Old Man + Little Girl = ... 169

Burial at Sky 172

The Little Girls are Coming! 175

A fix 179

You Don't Gotta Look Tough to be Tough 183

A short swim 186

How do you pronounce it? 192

Wait—Did You Say Dress Fairies!? 197

The Baron is a false person 207

More evidence that Denyse is awesome 215

Firing Up the Ol' Tower Defense 219

Trouble Aboard the Nonelstch 222

A Divine Slip-up 229

It's Drifting. Alone. In the Middle of Nowhere. Sure, Let's See What's Inside. 234

A Reason to Start the Hatin' 240

Theory of Relativity as Projected in a Fantasy World 244

Little Girls Lost in a Cave, Alone. 247

It Might Have Been LSD. Who Knows? 251

I. Am. God. 255

Say I Love You 260

Shoot the Shrooms! Aim for the Shrooms! 266

Pep Talk 272

Last Line of Defense 276

Emeralda Saves The Day 279

Getting warmer 284

She's fine 287

Hello, I'm a Serial Killer Who Likes to Torture People, and I'll Be Your Guide for Today.. 289

Breakneck Speed 291

Arrival of Team One 293

Arrival of Team 2 294

The Big Bad 296

Plans of Mice and Men 298

Armies Are for Fighting With 303

It's Just Chance. 305

A Hard Choice is Made. 308

Stress... 312

All Part of the Plan 315

Attrition 317

Extraction 318

I Don't Want To 320

A True Hero 322

Boom... 323

Epilogue 324

August the Monster Slayer

    There were always monsters for August to slay. No one knew where they came from, but, just like the rocks in the fields, they would seemingly pop out of the ground, start terrorizing any good citizen that happened past them, and generally make life in the countryside miserable. For most people, they were a nuisance at best, and a terror at worst. For August, they were his livelihood.

    Everywhere he traveled, whether in the forest, mountain, or plains, he carried his monster slaying kit. It consisted of a battered but serviceable sword, a suit of chain-backed leather armor, and a shield that had seen more coats of paint than August had seen years. With it, he traveled the land, going from village to village, looking for jobs, and things to kill.

    One day, on the path from one tiny village to the next, when the sun shone strong and beat upon the back of his cloak, and the trees rustled in the cool breeze, he sat down to take a nap in the shade of a trunk. It had been a long day, and he expected to reach the next village by sundown, but he wasn't in such a hurry that he could pass up a rest on the tranquil path.

    Soon, he fell asleep. When he woke up, he jumped up in surprise. There, leaning on him, sleeping, was the most peculiar girl he had ever seen. Shock white hair flowed down past her eyes, over which she wore black tinted spectacles. A black coat covered her entire body, from toes to fingers to the tip of her nose, so only the skin around her cheeks could be seen. And what skin it was, pearly white, almost ghostly, translucent, giving off a glare in the sunlight.

    August marveled at her. *Who is she?* He thought to himself. After considering a few options, he chanced to look up.

    "Ah . . ." he said. The sun had already sunk low in the horizon. "Time to get going . . ." he muttered. He got up, and stole one last glance at the sleeping girl. *Should I wake her up?* But she was sleeping so peacefully, at rest with the world. August hated the idea of waking her up. She did look beautiful, as she slept, the setting sun casting her pale face in sharp contrast against her coat. August sighed. The girl needed to wake up. It was getting late, and it was dangerous outside at night time. August knelt down and pushed her shoulder.

"Hey, you there. Wake up."

The girl stirred. She shifted from one shoulder to the other, leaning against a tree. August pushed her again.

"Wake up. It's dangerous out here."

The girl opened her eyes. August could barely see them through her sunglasses. She pushed them up, rubbed her eyes, and slid them back down. August watched her. The girl said nothing, only gathered up her coat and stood up. August stood up with her. The girl turned aside and began to walk down the path. August looked at her go, and then shrugged. The girl looked over her shoulder.

"Thank you."

August scratched the back of his head. "No problem."

The girl turned and walked away, in the direction opposite the village. August turned around and headed towards the village. The sound of his sword clanking against his shield gave him a comfortable feeling inside. Still, the thought of the girl troubled him, until he reached the walls of the village.

"August!" The gateman called. "You're back!"

The village was called Numerville by its inhabitants. Inside the wooden palisade, a collection of a dozen hovels sat scattered about. August sensed something off, as he walked into the main square: a frown here, a sulking mother there. The town elder came out to greet him. He was a greying man, leaning on a cane, with a crooked back and a lumpy forehead.

"Anything I need to take care of?" August asked.

The town elder's face was one of gravity. "A witch."

August didn't respond. Instead, he surveyed the village. Now, he could see. That sulking mother was sick. The frown was followed by a cough.

The town elder bowed his head. "She has cursed our water for more than a month now. There is nothing we can do, we have tried everything."

August shook his head. "No." He let the word sit for a moment. "I don't do humans."

The town elder raised his head. "You must help us. We have no other solution. You are our last hope."

A crowd had gathered around them. A bulky man, with woodcutter's arms, stepped out. He had a square jaw and dull eyes. "She's not human," he said.

The town elder seemed as surprised as August.

August furrowed his brow. "What do you mean?" He asked.

"Its eyes," said the woodcutter. "They're like fire, red and evil. I saw them for myself."

August considered this for a moment. The town elder gave him a hopeful glance.

"Do you swear this is true?" August asked.

The woodcutter nodded his head, his chin bobbing.

There were many monsters that took the form of humans, and some might have even been said to have red eyes. But a witch . . . *Perhaps they are mistaken,* thought August. *Though I should at least check.* In any case, it wouldn't do to stand where he was all day. He turned to the woodcutter. "Where did you see it?"

"Up at the top of the hill nearby," the woodcutter pointed, "In that direction. I was cutting down wood to fix Gender's barn after the fire..." The woodcutter trailed off. "You can kill it, can't you?"

August shrugged. "I can certainly try." He turned to the town elder. "Let's discuss payment."

The elder tensed. His eyes grew shifty. "Sixty coppers."

August shook his head. "That's what I usually get for killing a marsh-rabbit. Three silver pieces, no less, for this 'witch'." At 'witch' the elder cringed.

"Fine, fine, I'll make it two pieces." The elder said. "We need to keep some money, you know. We can't have you gutting us dry."

"I'll go down to two silver and fifty copper. Only if they're Capital mint."

"Fine, gouge us if you must, but we need that witch gone. You'll get your money when the job is done."

August considered this, then nodded. "Fair enough." He adjusted the shoulder on his pack, and prepared to leave. As he walked out the gate, a young girl chased after him, a green rag doll in her hand, bouncing in lockstep with her footfalls. Her name was Penny. She looked to be perhaps nine, with a serene face and pigtails that could be called childish.

"Uncle August! Uncle August!" She called, her small voice carrying out across the courtyard.

August stopped, and waited for her to come to him. When she did, out of breath, dust on her forehead, August hoisted her up onto his shoulders, placing her in the spot between his sword and his neck. "How have you been, Penny?" He asked.

"Hmm..." Penny said, as she considered. "I got a new doll. Do you want to see?"

"Sure. What's her name?"

The doll's dirty green cloth covered his eyes. It smelled like mud, and faintly of perfume. "It's a he, not a she, dummy."

August walked around the courtyard, making sure to duck under awnings so Penny didn't hit her head. "Ok, fine. What's his name?"

"Henry." Penny stated, simply. "He's my new best friend."

In the distance, a woman's voice called. "Penny! Dinnertime!"

August turned towards it. In the doorway of a hovel, a pretty woman in a simple apron stood holding a broom. Penny waved to her, and the woman waved back.

"Go on, now." August said, as he let Penny down. "Your mother is waiting."

Penny huffed, and looked back up at August. "You'll come back, right? After beating that evil witch?"

August looked into the distance. "If she really is evil, I'll beat her, and come back." He looked towards Penny, and only saw her back, halfway across the courtyard, the green doll trailing behind her. A smile crept across his face, as he turned to leave the village.

Once outside, August switched gears. He called upon his Greenblood ability, which allowed him to communicate with monsters, and spread his consciousness out into the world. The ability ran in his family. Its origins were a mystery.

August walked along the path towards the spot where the monster witch had been sighted, running over in his mind what it might be. His plan of action would differ depending on the type of monster. *It could be a Metherwerry,* he thought. They looked like humans, and even had red eyes. *No, no, no. If it was, I would already have known it.* Metherwerries broadcasted their presence with an unmistakable screech. Plus, the woodcutter had come back from his encounter alive, which would have been very unlikely had the monster been a metherwerry. *It could be a false person.* False people were monsters that could take on the forms of humans, and could even talk like humans. They were shape shifters, and it was said that they were the most intelligent of all monsters, perhaps even more so than humans. It was good that they were few and far between, and that they preferred taking the form of trees and snakes and other more devious creatures. *But can they have red eyes?* August asked himself. *Surely they must be able to . . .*

August stopped. He stood at the top of a hill, in the center of a moonlit glade. There was a tree only half-cut down at the edge. August was sure that this was the place the woodcutter had spoken of. He calmed himself, and let his Greenblood ability flow. His heartbeat drowned all other noises. Deep inside of himself, something stirred, something that pointed . . .

Nowhere.

There were no monsters nearby, and there hadn't been for some time. *Could the woodsman have been lying?* But no, there was his axe, laying abandoned, shining in the moonlight. *Something must have scared him.*

August checked his surroundings. He began a thorough search, as if he were hunting a deer, instead of a monster. He looked for tracks, and didn't have to go far. There, in the middle of the glade, were footprints that were definitely not the woodsman's. They were light, as if the walker had weighed no more than a kid, and soled with strange patterns that August could barely make out. *Writing?*

August followed the tracks down the hill, the other side from the village, to the riverbank that passed by the village, and up the river. He came upon a cave, hidden in a jumble of rock. A flash of white stole his attention, and he looked up. There, hanging on a branch drying, were clothes, and a robe—a heavy one that drooped down like a curtain. August narrowed his eyes. *Monsters don't wear clothes.* He had a vision of coins slipping out of his palm.

He glanced at the cave again. *Perhaps . . .* He walked closer, and peered inside. It was dark, too dark for him to see. He calmed himself again, and checked for monsters, allowing the beating of his heart take over.

Clear. He ducked his head under the cave's entrance. The world shimmered, and he popped into in a brightly lit room, a large one, that looked like the inside of an alchemist's shop. A table stood in the center, piled high with books, ingredients, gadgets, and all sorts of paraphernalia. Around the edges hung shelves topped with ornate glassware that ran in tubes all around the wall. Colored smoke drifted around, flowing up a chimney, assisted by a wooden fan that ran of its own accord.

In the corner, hunched over a bottle, a black robed figure made busy. August tried to do something, anything, but before he could, the figure swept around. Her red eyes were what caught August first. They were fair, and wise, and not evil at all. The girl had a nice nose, freckles, and a slim mouth at the moment curved down into a scowl. Her skin glowed pure white skin, white as the moon on a summer night.

"Oh, it's you," she said. She wrapped her robe tight around her body, possessively.

"I . . . I . . ." August couldn't speak, he was so surprised. *She's a witch?* "You . . . You don't look much like a witch."

Armed, Cute, and Dangerous. | 12

The girl moved closer to August. "How nice of you to come visit me. Let me ask, how did you get in here? My house was supposed to be invisible." The girl stood toe to toe with August, and looked up at him. The top of her head perhaps reached his chin.

"Are you a witch?" August asked, his mind still too muddled to do anything.

The woman raised one eyebrow. "You haven't answered my question. How did you get in here?"

"There . . . There were clothes outside, hanging. So I decided to check the inside of the cave."

The girl frowned. "Oh. That." She put her hand to her chin. "I knew it was a bad idea. But my clothes were wet. Maybe I should have used that drying spell." Her eyes clouded over, lost in another world. They roved over and stopped at August's sword. They lit up. "Can I see that?" She held out her hands.

At a loss for what to do, August nodded. He took his sword and handed it to her, hilt first. *Idiot!* He thought immediately. *You just gave away your weapon!* He reached to grab it back, but stopped before taking hold of it. The girl held it in both hands, cradling it like a baby. The folds of her robe dropped away from her hands, giving her the air of a scholar. She held her hand over the blade, a small purple ball of light on the tip of her forefinger. Up and down the metal she ran it, her face rapt with concentration.

August stared into her eyes. They really were red, more on the pink side than the evil side. They certainly didn't look like anything natural. August dove into his Greenblood ability and checked her for a monster. She wasn't a false person. She wasn't a metherwerry, either.

"What's your name?" He asked, wanting to break the uncomfortable silence.

The girl waited a few seconds, continuing her examination of the sword, and then flicked out the light on her finger. "Elyse." She said, curtsying. Somehow, it looked . . .

Proper. August thought. *Like a princess. Or a famous person. Though she's certainly not one I've ever heard of before.*

Elyse scowled, and handed August his sword. "You're staring at me."

August blinked in surprise. "That's because, well . . ." He hesitated.

"You can say it." Elyse twirled a piece of her hair around her finger. They were almost the same color, her skin, and her hair.

"Your eyes," August continued. "They're red."

Elyse smiled. "I like to think of them as rose colored."

August paused again. He looked around the room, at all the alchemists' tools, at the bottles and the books and the racks of stuff. "You're that witch, though, aren't you?" he asked.

Elyse tilted her head. "What witch?"

"You're not a witch?" August asked, surprised.

"No." Answered Elyse, definitively. Her red eyes crinkled at the edges, and she chuckled. "You really thought I was one?"

"Well . . ." August answered. Now he was embarrassed, though he didn't know why. "The townspeople . . ."

"What townspeople?" Elyse asked. Her reaction was natural, as if she hadn't known about them.

"The townspeople, over the hill, they said that their water was cursed." August was confused, now. He had first expected to see a monster, and then seen a witch, but the girl who looked to be so young in front of him couldn't be a witch. She didn't look like one at all.

Elyse's face became serious. "Take me to them. Now." She pulled her cloak together so that it covered her entire body. She gripped a small piece of metal near her waist, and pulled up on it. A zipping sound cut through the room, one that sounded simultaneously like the tearing of cloth and the buzzing of a bee. The cloak wrapped around her, almost magically, and soon, only her two red eyes could be seen above her cheekbones. Lastly, she reached into a pocket in the cloak and brought out her black spectacles. But, she didn't wear them. She draped them over her neck, attached to a pin in her cloak.

When she was done, she turned to August. "Lead the way," she said. "I need to clean up my mess."

August and Elyse Get All Mixed Up

As they walked thought the forest, up the hill, August in front of Elyse, the moonlight shone bright through the leaves and made dappled patterns on the forest floor. Elyse's hair shone, mixing with the moonlight, blending with it, until it was hard to tell which was light and which was her. Her posture was hunched.

August looked at Elyse. "When you said clean up your mess, what did you mean?"

"I didn't know there were people there," Elyse answered, almost to herself. "It's been a month, at the concentration I was dumping it at."

"What? Concentration?" August stopped. He turned to face Elyse, and looked into her rose colored eyes. "I think you should tell me everything."

Elyse's eyes flickered to the right, and then to the left. "I suppose we have time. It's already been a month." She stopped, and sat on a root.

August sat down on the pine needle floor, across from her. "Tell me everything."

Elyse seemed to decide something. She looked up longingly at the moon. "I'm an Alchemist. Not a witch. I make potions, brew concoctions, and do chemistry, that sort of thing." She held on to the edge of her black spectacles, rubbing her finger back and forth across the frame. "I've been working on a special potion, in my lab over there. The byproduct is . . . A nasty thing. A bluish substance, that I'm pretty sure causes kidney failure and necrosis, but I'm not positive." She looked up at the moon. "I picked this place because I thought it was deserted."

August raised his eyebrows. "You didn't notice a whole village just a few miles away?"

Elyse looked down, and August could see how fragile her features looked, with her almost translucent skin. "I just checked the riverbank. I didn't see anybody, so I thought it would be okay."

"I see." August said. He got up. "Let's go."

Elyse got up with him. She walked beside him along the forest path. August looked over at her. "Why do you wear that coat?"

Elyse seemed startled. She fingered the hem of the coat. "I wear it because I have to. The sun hurts me, because my skin is so pale."

August examined the coat by reaching out his hands, and took a piece of it between his fingers. It was of a heavy fabric, pure black, seeming to suck in the moonlight around it. August let it go.

"Are you sure you're okay?" he asked. "I mean; you look kind of distressed."

Elyse pulled her cloak tighter to her body. "I didn't mean to. I really didn't. The thought that . . . that people could be suffering because of me is . . . I don't know how to think about it. Am I really that bad? I screwed up, didn't I?"

"I mean, when I looked," said August, "There didn't seem to be any deaths among the villagers from you. Otherwise, they would have been more adamant when they asked me to find you. For now, I think it's just sickness."

"Even so," said Elyse, "It's my fault. I have to go diagnose them, and fix it."

August tensed. Deep inside of himself, there was a grating sensation, from within the Greenblood part of him. It was a monster, close. A dangermuff. August reached out to it. *Hello, friend.* He thought. *Why are you here?*

He got nothing in reply, only tensed static. Dangermuffs hunted their prey by using their minds like a weapon, entering their thoughts and swirling them around until the prey wanted to become food, and gave itself to the dangermuff willingly. They were frustratingly hard to find, which meant that the only real defense against them was to counterattack with one's own thoughts. Only Greenbloods had this ability.

August stood on guard. He felt the presence of the Dangermuff, all around him, its mind searching for prey. *Careful,* he thought. He rallied his mental defenses, preparing for the worst.

The dangermuff attacked with a river of images, all coming at once, that August blocked with ease. Then, they stopped. August could hear nothing, only the wind in the trees.

Elyse screamed. She fell to her knees, and held her hands to her ears. "No, no, no, no!"

In a flash of comprehension, August dropped right down to Elyse's side. He gripped her as tightly as he could, and held on to a root. Elyse needed his help, and it didn't matter who she was, August was going to help her.

Elyse began to struggle, her eyes glazed over, her mouth drooling. "Let me go!" She pounded at August's chest. "I have to go!" Her voice sounded frenzied. "It needs me!" She cried, full of longing and despair.

August only held on tighter. As he did, he prepared a counterattack. All it took to kill a dangermuff was a simple paradox, a phrase like "This statement is false." Their brain locked down, and they could no longer operate, and died once their physical form decayed. The problem was getting the paradox in. Their minds were whirlwinds of activity, and even the slightest mishap could result in destruction.

August tried a frontal assault, but couldn't muster the concentration through Elyse's kicks and scratches. *Too dangerous,* he thought. He tried an underhanded assault, leaving himself as bait, and then counterattacking once the dangermuff had penetrated his own mind. No dice. The dangermuff already had prey.

He thought for what seemed like an eternity, with Elyse scratching him through his chain leather armor, kicking him, latching on to his glove with her teeth. Once, he almost let her go, after she slammed her head into his jaw. He could taste blood on his tongue.

This won't work, he thought. *I can't do this for much longer. Elyse . . .* And then, he made a discovery. *Her mind! I can feel it!* It was like that of a monster's, only more thoughtful, tame, and much more lively. He had only heard legends of Greenbloods with the ability to sense human minds.

Using her mind as a relay, he launched himself into the Damgermuff's consciousness. There was no resistance. He spoke three words. *I always lie.* All motion stopped. Elyse hung limp. In the distance, August could sense the Dangermuff, mulling over what he had said. Over, and over, and over again. *I always lie.*

And then, an explosion of emotion, that knocked him out cold.

In the dream that he had, he was Elyse, walking down a deserted alleyway in the middle of the night. A cat stared at him with moonlit eyes, and slunk off with a purr.

Where am I? Asked August. He got no reply. All he could sense was a torrent of emotions, a train of thought, at the back of his consciousness, as if he were suddenly learning a tremendous amount of information. The alleyway disappeared, and then scenes flashed by, one after another, containing memories that were not his own, both from the Dangermuff, and from Elyse.

After what seemed like an eternity, he woke up, just in time to see the light of dawn peek over the horizon. Elyse lay in a pile near him, her coat covered in pine needles and twigs. There was something different about her now, though. Where there used to be shock white hair, pure as moonlight, there was now a stripe of red, bright as a ripe apple, about the width of August's hand. August rubbed his eyes, and tried to make sense of it.

What had happened? All of the images that he had seen, all the memories, came flooding back. *Elyse's?* Thought August, confused. *Is that even possible?*

Elyse stirred from her resting place on the forest floor. She got up sleepily, and rubbed her bright pink eyes. The look she gave August said "Who are you?"

"Do you remember anything?" Asked August, concerned. He waited for Elyse to reply.

Elyse took a moment, and then seemed to gain her bearings. "You..." She said, and then dropped off, staring at August intently.

August stared back, unsure of what to do. *Somehow, this feels... Intimate...*

Elyse recoiled, her eyes wide, questioning. *What do you mean, Intimate?* Her voice sounded in August's head, clear as day. Along with it came emotions, embarrassment, confusion, fear.

August backed up on his hands, his fingers pressing into the moist grass that was just beginning collect morning dew. He kept his eyes on Elyse.

Elyse narrowed her eyes, and then opened them even wider than before. "Ahh!" She pointed. "You can . . . Hear me!" The words resonated in August's mind, as well. She noticed the red streak in her hair, and cradled it, as if she did not know what to do. August felt her surprise.

"I don't know what you did," she said. August could feel the turmoil inside her. He knew she could feel his own turmoil as well.

Elyse's memories shot through August's mind. She was young, and happy, and ignorant. On the street one day. A group of boys surrounded her. They wore cruel expressions on their faces.

"Monster!" They cried. "Demon!"

Elyse curled up inside of herself, promising herself that she would stay there. That no one would be able to come close to her. They didn't deserve it, and she wouldn't give it to them.

Elyse held August's gaze, her rose red eyes piercing his own.

You can't just barge in here, she said. *This is my world. What do you know of me?*

August offered up no defense. *I'm sorry. I did what I had to.*

Elyse's emotions rolled over August like a wave. They were raw, surprisingly so, quite different than the outer emotions of the woman that August had met the night before. It was Elyse, pure and simple, reduced to her basest components. No one was ever supposed to see her that way, August saw. August hung his head, offering up one of his own memories.

His father stood over him, a burly, big man, with a strong sense of presence and of responsibility. He put his hands on his hips.

"August, be sure to always understand. Whenever you talk to someone, make sure that you know where they are coming from. Respect them, and they will respect you. Keep what they want private, private. Then, you will be a strong man. You will be able to make friends, and keep people with you."

Elyse shook her head. *That means nothing. I don't want you in here. It feels . . . wrong. Why are you looking at me like that? You're not going to start calling me a monster, too?*

August shook his head. *No, I respect you. I'll respect your boundaries. If you don't want me to look inside your head, I won't, if I'm able to. But I don't think I'm able to. Not look, I mean.*

Elyse grabbed August by the shoulder. *I wasn't supposed to know someone like this. I didn't want to. I barely know you. What did you do?*

I saved your life, August said.

Elyse sat back, and put her hands over her face. *Even so, I don't like this. This feels too intimate. I don't like this at all.*

August took Elyse by the hand. He felt a sudden attachment to her, and he knew that she felt it too. She looked up into his eyes.

You're not fair.

August got up, pulling Elyse with him. *None of this is fair. Let's roll with the punches, and see where we go.*

Elyse smiled, despite herself, and faced the trail. Now that the sun was up, she pulled her coat close to her body, and put on her black spectacles. *We still have a job to do.* She looked ahead, to where the village was. *Lead the way.*

As they got closer to the village, something felt wrong to August. It was if a tickling sensation resided in the back of his head, annoying him until he could figure out what it meant.

Elyse sensed it. *What's wrong?* She asked.

August kept his eyes on the trail. *I've been thinking. Why was a Dangermuff in this part of the world, at this time? There shouldn't have been any monsters, let alone one as dangerous as that.*

I don't know. Elyse said. *Perhaps it was just a coincidence?*

August shook his head. *It couldn't have been. I remember now, I found something in the Dangermuff's head, just as it was about to die. Something about a directive.*

A directive? You mean, like an order? Elyse ducked under a branch as she hastened to follow August.

Yes. I didn't get more than the foggiest idea, but I think it had something to do with other monsters, and, a little girl? August felt the itching grow bigger in the back of his head.

Suddenly, Elyse grabbed onto August's pack. *Wait.* She stood stock still, her entire body tense. *I sense monsters.*

You do? August was surprised, but he could feel that it was true. He felt the monsters as well. *I wonder why I didn't notice earlier . . .*

It doesn't matter now. Elyse stepped in front of August. *We're close to the village. They might be in trouble.*

Then we have to save them! August quickened his pace, and followed Elyse down the deer trail, until it met the main road. They both broke out into a run.

They might be perfectly fine, thought August.

Or, thought Elyse, *they might all be dead. We have to hurry.*

As August approached the village, he could feel the tickling sensation inside of him grow stronger. *So many monsters!* Something was wrong, something was very, very wrong.

Black smoke drifted over the treetops in a sooty column. Faint red streaks could be seen underneath.

The village! Now sprinting as fast as they could, August and Elyse came around a bend in the road, and ran straight into the midst of a crowd of monsters.

There were great wigglers, worms the size of people that burrowed through the ground and had razor sharp teeth; ganglers, monkey-like monsters with a propensity towards crude tools; and Alazoths, razor-backed alligators that could fly as well as swim. They faced the direction of the village's wooden palisade, but turned around in an instant when August and Elyse came around the bend. It was obvious that they intended to attack.

August wasted no time in drawing his sword. Through his connection with Elyse, he tried to communicate as succinctly as possible the best way to kill the three monster types that they had met. Elyse, wasting no time, brought out a ball of fire from the tips of her fingers, that twisted and curled into a flaming lash.

August paused, stunned. *Is that . . .?*

No time! Elyse sent August an image of a book, and a name. *Instrator.*

Somewhat satisfied, August turned to face his first assailant, a reptilian alzoth, flying low, aiming straight for his chest, the barbs on its back bristling with menace. August looked into its scaly eyes, and saw only malice.

I'm sorry. At the last minute, before the alzoth could collide with him, he stepped aside, and swung down hard with all his might. The giant flying crocodile was defenseless, and August's sword tore it in two.

The rest won't be so easy. A rumbling came from below him, resonating up his legs and into his chest. August fought to control his breathing. *It's okay. It's ok.*

On the other side of the road, Elyse engaged a pack of the monkey-like ganglers, who poked at her with crude stone spears. They wore clothing, barely mentionable: ragged loincloths that looked to be where they put all the filth that they collected, wherever they lived. Even though her weapon was quite a showpiece, it fought with deadly efficiency, almost as if it had a will of its own. August could feel the heat even from where she stood.

A gangler monkey pressed too close to Elyse. In one smooth move, she jumped over it, and, lashing out with her whip as she fell, pulled an in-air turn around, culminating in a fatal drop kick. Her hair splayed out in all directions, moving as if in slow motion, and the sun glinted off the carapace of her black spectacles.

I'm glad she's on my side, August thought. He turned his attention to his fight. The wiggler that burrowed under August took its time. August took his time too, noting the frequency of its vibrations, and calling upon his instinctual Greenblood knowledge to correctly judge its intent.

It's going to attack . . . The rumbling shifted ever so slightly. *Now!* August flung himself to the side, and just as he did, the wiggler burst through the ground like a sprouting tree trunk, jaws open wide, slime mixing with dirt and flinging off its teeth in little balls of mud. August aimed an attack at its heart, but was stopped by a massive force that plowed into him from behind. *Elyse!* He called, not knowing what else to do. A flurry of thoughts passed between them. August could feel hot breath down his neck, a drip of saliva on his ear.

Elyse rushed to his aid, and smashed into the side of the beast behind August with a yell that resounded though the forest. August felt the pressure on his back disappear. Before he could recover, though, the wiggler that he had been fighting split the ground underneath him, bringing him straight into its massive gaping jaws. Dirt and mud flew everywhere.

The jaws snapped shut. Pain lanced through August's body like a coating of fire, concentrated on the punctures ripped into his side by the monster's teeth. He could feel himself falling, falling . . .

A light shocked him out of his stunned stupor. *Elyse?*

Don't give up! Her voice called. *I'll save you!*

August couldn't help but smile thought the symphony of pain that was his body. *Then we'll be even.*

At that moment, his thoughts melded with hers again, and the two became one. She felt his pain. He saw through her eyes. The lash cutting through meters of dirt, the ground rumbling, the worm bursting forth, black and green blood spraying out of the slash that appeared across half of its body.

August fell out of its stomach, covered in blood, acid, and gore from head to toe. Elyse ran to his side, and reached into her coat, her mind a frantic hive of activity. August wasn't sure who gave the potion, and who drank it. In the end, though, he returned to himself, and saw Elyse leaning over him, her face a twist of a hundred emotions. Her black spectacles hung at her neck, her coat flapped in the breeze, a great rip all down the side.

I got you, Elyse said.

And then he blacked out.

Zombies? No, Monkeys!

When August came to, at first, all that he could see were wooden planks and a thatch roof above his head. Slowly, his senses came back to him. He heard a pounding, someone trying to break down a door, and Elyse grunting in an effort to keep it shut. He felt a rumbling through his entire body. His mind filled with fear and adrenaline. He smelled burnt wood, and singed flesh.

Are you ok? Elyse asked. She didn't turn from her position at the door.

I think so. August replied. He lifted his arms, and was surprised to see that the holes where the wiggler's teeth had punched into him were gone. So were the cuts and scrapes from fighting. The only thing that showed of combat were his torn clothes.

Then help me. Elyse's body strained, fighting to keep the door in position.

Without hesitation, August got up and braced the door with her. There were no windows, and the walls were made of thick pieces of raw timber. The floor, made of crude concrete, would keep out wigglers indefinitely. The most effective way in was the door, and judging by the sounds from the other side, the monsters knew this.

Do you have a plan? Asked August, as he strained against the force hammering the other side.

Elyse shook her head. Her face showed determination. *I don't know.*

August pushed harder against the door. It seemed that more monsters gathered by the second. *If I had known a group of monsters was coming, I would have stayed here at the village.* He thought about all the villagers, and Penny, but quickly pushed that thought out of his mind.

But you didn't. Elyse stated it as a matter of fact. *And in any case, what would you have done against so many?*

August strained against the door. *True, this is the biggest group I've ever seen. And three species, no less.* Something did seem off about all this.

At that moment, a split in the wood of the door cracked forwards, all across its length. The door would not hold out much longer. Light streamed through from the other side, as well as the nasty stench of the gangler monkeys. A stone spearhead lodged itself in the gap.

We need to get out, August decided. He looked around the room. In the corner of the roof, above a shelf lined with medicinal herbs, the thatch sagged in, black with rot. *We can probably go through there.*

He transmitted his plans to Elyse. *I'll hold the door,* he said. He had a better grip on the boards.

Elyse let go without comment, and turned to the corner. The door surged forwards against the decreased resistance, pushing August to his limit. Sweat beaded on his nose. The stench of ganglers grew nastier. Another spear point jammed through the door, an inch from August's arm.

Hurry up! August thought. He didn't know how much longer he could hold.

Done, said Elyse. The room filled with light. *Now hurry!*

August picked up a loose board and jammed it across the door. He pushed a table against it, as well. *That will buy me a few seconds.*

He turned to the corner, just in time to see Elyse's legs disappear into the hole in the roof. August followed, using the shelf to climb up the wall and out. A jar of herbs fell to the floor, splintering, just as the door cracked open. The board that braced it flew across the room, the table twirling behind it.

The triumphant howls of the ganglers soon turned to fury, as they discovered that their quarry had escaped. August escaped just as a spear embedded itself in the wall below him. The shelf he had been standing on broke, the supports snapped, and it all clattered to the ground. August barely made it up.

On the roof, Elyse lay facing upwards, breathing with all her might. Both she and August felt exhaustion seeping through their bodies, but Elyse felt by far the worst off.

How long was I out? Asked August. He lay down beside her. His breath came in short gasps, enough so that speaking out loud would have been a problem.

Elyse felt the same. *A few minutes,* she answered. August brought up his head, and looked around the town. Some of the houses burned in bright blazes that brought up sickly clouds of black smoke, twisting in the breeze. August could feel the heat on the side of his cheeks, when the wind blew right. He didn't hear any screams, and assumed it was because the villagers were either evacuated, or dead. He hoped it was the first.

From the roof of another house, an alzoth took notice of the humans laying out in the sun. Bristling its tough spines, it unfurled it wings, like those of a bat, and took to the sky. Two more alzoths followed, their snapping jaws hanging open, swallowing the wind.

It looks like we're not out of it yet, said Elyse. She wearily got to her feet. A ball of fire appeared from her fingertips, and again unfurled into the deadly fire lash Instrator. Its flames reflected off her black spectacles, combining with the fires all around to breed a deadly, vicious glare. In contrast, Elyse's skin glowed almost soft pink, where it peeked out from under her coat.

August decided to ask her where she had got the weapon, when he had the time. He got to his feet as well, and turned to face the alzoths. Their green skin, scaled like a dragon's, glinted in the early morning sun. Each serrated claw was painfully visible against the light, each tooth glistening with mottled spit.

Here we go. August braced himself, and reached for his sword, and his shield. It seemed that Elyse had at least managed to find them while he had been unconscious. *I should thank her for that.*

You can later, Elyse said to him, *after we're out of this mess.*

The alzoths circled around and around, judging their prey like professional swordsmen in a duel. August judged them too, but couldn't help but be surprised. *They're using tactics.* Monsters were supposed to be dumb, except for a small few, but those always worked alone or in pairs, nothing of this sort.

The sun glinted in August's eyes, blinding him. He had come around to face it while tracking one of the alzoths. Elyse stood with her back to him, also tracking an alzoth. At that moment, the giant lizard dived. The one facing Elyse did so as well.

Too late, he realized his mistake. *The sun!* It was at the alzoth's back, so that he couldn't judge its position well. It was almost as if a two-dimensional shadow were bearing down on him. August almost jumped, but then realized something else. *Elyse is right behind me!* If he jumped, the alzoth would plow right into Elyse's back, claws ripping, teeth slashing. *I'm trapped!*

Just as he thought that, he received a parcel of information from Elyse, slightly jumbled, but still understandable. In a split second, he knew what to do. Just as the alzoth in front of him was about to hit, as far as he could tell in the glare, he spun around, swinging his sword up. Elyse did the same with her whip. For an instant, they faced each other, his sword raised, her whip slicing the air above. August trusted her to watch his back. With her black spectacles, Elyse could see as if there were no glare at all. The other alzoth heading for Elyse turned to the side, surprised to see August's sword raised in defiance, attempting to dodge his sideways slash.

It succeeded, but plowed into the roof of the house, breaking through and catching its wings on a splintered timber. Behind, August felt a whoosh of air as Instrator sliced the alzoth that had attacked him in two. The two halves split to either side of him, singed black and smoking.

For a second, nothing happened. Then, without warning, the third alzoth dropped out of the air, crashing straight into Elyse. Insrator flew out of her hands, dissolving into noting but air the instant it left her grip.

The alzoth opened its jaws wide. August slashed at it, cutting it almost in two, but the jaws still did not stop closing over Elyse's neck.

And then, in a burst of bright purple, the flying crocodile's head disintegrated, a quarrel sticking out of its remains. Nothing happened for a second. Then, a great wind picked up, and a shadow fell over the entire village.

August looked up, to see the bright wooden hull of an airship, coming out of high altitude.

A rope ladder dropped down over the edge of the ship. From his position, all August could see was the hull, a railing, and the tip of a great mast above. Elyse stood up, shaking off pieces of meat, her coat splotched purple, just like August's clothes. August grabbed the ladder first.

Wait. Elyse stood and peered up at the ship. *We don't know if they're friendly or not.*

August began to climb. *We'll find out once we get there.*

Elyse followed him, still full of suspicions. August couldn't help but agree, as those suspicions bled into his mind.

As it turned out, the ship's sailors were friendly, a merchant vessel that had seen the burning village and decided to investigate. August and Elyse soon stood aboard the plank deck. Below, over the railings, more alzoths circled, smart enough to stay out of range of the marksmen that pointed at them with crossbows.

The captain approached them, stepping down from the forecastle and around the main mast. He was a thin man, in a leather cuirass, with a blade dangling at his side. His face showed kindness, but also a sort of shrewd judgment. He wore no ornamentation.

"Is there anyone else alive?" He asked, showing his concern.

August paused, as he tried to communicate to him like he did with Elyse. Then, he realized what he was doing. "I don't know" he said, his voice hoarse.

The captain peered over the side, his face lit by the flames that had even begun to lick at the house that August and Elyse had been rescued from. The smell of thick smoke, and burning flesh, wafted upwards with the wind.

A scream cut through the silence, unmistakably human, and the flying alzoths that circled the ship dived down towards the point. The captain, wasting no time, turned to his crew.

"Full to port! Get us over there!" He stormed off in to do his duties as a captain. The ship didn't have to move much, as the town was small. The scream had come from a house that looked like hell's inferno, flames flinging into the sky, reaching for the sun.

The door to the house opened, and a small figure ran out, trailing behind her a little green object. Monsters from all over closed in on her. It was clear she would not survive long.

Penny! August knew it at once. He turned to Elyse, who thought the same thing.

A pair of sailors threw a ladder over the side, and two began to clamber down. Elyse and August wasted no time in following them. As they drew closer to the ground, Penny stopped, in the middle of the town's courtyard. An alzoth tried to take a dive at her, but didn't go more than a few feet before one of its wings buckled, shot out by a marksman. It plowed a furrow in the courtyard.

Elyse and August hit the ground, right behind the two sailors. August drew his sword. Its blade was pure skysteel, so that in the heat from the fires, it had become light, its edge thinning and beginning to glow. In his other hand, he gripped his battle-worn shield. Elyse drew the fire from her fingertips and brought out the crackling red whip Instrator, again. August still hadn't gotten used to it. The two sailors also took out their swords, but not before stopping to marvel at Elyse.

A pack of ganglers had surrounded Penny, who darted in and out of their grasp for the moment. Their whoops and cries made it known that they were having fun, and August could feel their excitement radiating outwards.

Disgusting things, thought Elyse. August couldn't help but agree.

They both exchanged glances, and soon a strategy was born. Elyse cracked her fire whip over the heads of the ganglers, the flaming tendril sizzling in the cool morning air. The ganglers paused, unsure of their surroundings. At the same time, August moved to the other side of the pack, to the opposite side of Elyse. He made sure to escape notice, heading for where Penny now lay curled against the ground.

The ganglers, seeing the new, more dangerous target that lashed at them with living fire, abandoned their pursuit of the little girl. Elyse backed up, and shouted to the sailors behind her, who had until now been staring at her whip like amazed children. "I'll distract them. You kill them." They quickly responded to her commanding tone.

August wrapped his arms around Penny and, picking her up, draped her over his shoulders like a freshly killed deer. As Elyse and the sailors handled the ganglers, August ran back around the engagement, ducked behind a cart, and grabbed hold of the ladder that hung down from the airship.

At that moment, quite stupidly, he wondered what the ship's name was. He spent a precious second to check: the *Lady Lass*. The words filled a six-foot high panel near the ship's stern, letters painted in green and pink.

The smell of burnt flesh became stronger. Instrator crackled like a demonic torture device, as if it were actually enjoying the taste of singed monster monkey meat. For all August knew, it might have been a demonic torture device.

Absorbed in his thoughts, August climbed up the ladder, one-handed, adjusting his grip on Penny with each rung he grabbed. Soon, the sound of battle faded, replaced by the sound of another battle, between the reptilian alzoths that circled around the ship and the human marksmen in the rigging. August chanced a look down. Elyse had disengaged, leading the two sailors with her. They headed towards the ladder, a whole troop of ganglers chasing them, leaving behind several monkey corpses. Furrows in the soil, further back, told of the wigglers closing in.

Are you all right, Elyse? August asked, as he turned back. The deck was almost before him.

As well as I can be, answered Elyse. August felt her concentration. Overhead, the *Lady Lass's* marksmen kept up the furious battle with the flying crocodile lizards. One man, in the rigging near the end of the ship, took the full brunt of an alzoth's dive. He flew upwards, now between the beast's great jaws, his arm dangling by a thread. It broke off after a few seconds and twirled back to earth in a shower of blood.

One saved, one lost. August hurtled over the railings and onto the deck of the ship. The two sailors who had gone down followed, Elyse bringing up the rear. Instrator coiled away to nothing in her palm.

Soon, the *Lady Lass* went underway, taking full advantage of the brisk northeastern wind. The captain plotted a course for the Capital, yelling out navigation corrections over the snapping of the sails. The last of the monsters fell behind, returning to the village to do whatever it was they were doing before. August hoped that that didn't mean eating people.

Elyse: Genius Inventor Extraordinaire

As the village disappeared behind the rolling hills, leaving only smoke in the air to tell of the carnage within it, the captain came down from the forecastle to speak to August and Elyse.

"Who are you?" He asked. During the frantic battle there had been no time for introductions.

August bowed. "August Cerulean, monster slayer and freelance Greenblood, at your service."

Are you always so formal? Elyse asked him, shooting him a glance.

It's part of my job, August answered, although he did wonder why he had gone all the way, considering the situation.

The captain noticed the pause in which they conversed. Raising his eyebrows, he turned his gaze to Elyse. "And who, my lady, do you happen to be?" It seemed he knew enough politeness to not comment about Elyse's black cloak and blacker spectacles, or her white skin, or her silver hair with the red streak that ran through it, or even the fiery whip which she had so effectively used against monsters. The captain addressed her as if he were addressing any other lady.

August could feel the relief that Elyse felt about this. The other members of the crew did not possess as much tact, as evidenced by their unhidden stares. Their questions would have been more and worse, if not for Elyse's stunning, and intimidating, fire whip show.

Elyse considered the question for a moment. "I am Elyse Marigold, alchemist and tinkerer and lady lasher," she finally stated, with an air of certainty. She curtsied.

And you scolded me for being formal, August thought.

I didn't scold you, Elyse answered, *I made an . . . Observation.*

Observation, thought August, sarcastically. *Right.*

Again, the captain noticed the pause, during which Elyse and August stared at each other. It wasn't as long as it would have been if the two had been speaking out loud, but it still managed to be substantial. Enough to seem weird, as the captain's eyes clearly showed.

He made no mention of it, and then introduced himself. "I am Captain Zephania Yuseph, commanding officer aboard the *Lady Lass*." He pointed to the forecastle, where a man held the wheel that kept the shyship steady. "That is first mate Relwin." He pointed to a large shiny area in the center of the ship, where metal plates formed a sort of housing, in which all sorts of beams and gears and cogs and levers cluttered together around a single chunk of metal in an indescribable shape. A greasy man stood in the center of it all. He held his arms out, hands on the levers, watching dozens of dials as they flipped all around.

"That is engineer Davis," said Captain Yuseph. "Talk to him or first mate Relwin if you have any questions. You may stay aboard until we reach the capital, but that is as far as we can take you." He took one last look at Elyse, and then turned back to his ship.

On the starboard side, a group of men had gathered, mourning their fallen comrade. Over near the prow, several men sat polishing their crossbows. At least two men climbed through the rigging, carrying out the captain's orders.

August felt tired, as if he were carrying a huge weight. Penny, her mass made insignificant by adrenaline, now felt as if she were twice her size. August almost dropped her as he sat down. He placed on the floor as gently as he could, and then leaned against the railings. Elyse followed suit.

I must have looked stupid when I bowed, August thought. He stared off at the distant horizon.

Not as stupid as I did when I curtsied, thought Elyse. August felt a soft laugh within her, softer than any laugh could be out loud. *But we made it,* she thought. *And in one piece.* Now, she began to laugh out loud. *What did we start out to do? Clean up the water supply?*

August couldn't help but chuckle, himself. *Well, we did manage to do something.* He looked at the unconscious form of Penny, right beside him. It seemed that sometime, during August's escape, Penny had passed out from fright. August didn't envy her, seeing her home go up in flames, perhaps her parents dead.

Only perhaps, Elyse added. *We didn't see any bodies in the main square, and there were no screams other than Penny's.*

Maybe, August thought. There was a long pause, in which nothing happened, the whistling of the wind in the rigging the only sound in the clear morning air. *There are other things we need to talk about,* August finally said.

Right, thought Elyse. *This whole mind-meld thing.* August felt, more than heard, her description of the event. It was like a rushing torrent, silent, but at the same time louder than anything in the real world.

I suppose we can find out more about it in the capital, August thought. *I'm sure that someone will know something. Maybe someone in the Green Blood Guild, or the Academy of Royal Sciences.*

The Capital . . . Right . . . Elyse tried to hide her emotions behind her featureless spectacles, and would have succeeded if it had not been for their mental link. As it was, a wash of emotions passed over August: embarrassment, regret, fear, confusion.

What's the matter? August asked. He could pick up some things just by reaching out his mind, but it was swirled and garbled with other things.

I guess there's no hiding things from you, is there? Elyse thought. August couldn't help but pick up a slight amusement, which surprised him, considering her reaction from before.

It goes both ways, was all August replied. He waited to Elyse to begin.

Elyse waited as well, formulating something in her mind, a sort of plan. When she finished, she presented August with an odd sensation, like a world being pressed upon his consciousness. *It will be quicker to show you,* she said at last.

And then, August felt aware of another world, like a daydream, but not of his own control. Behind it he could feel Elyse's consciousness. The world was cluttered with all sorts of unrelated things: a house, a cat, some barrels floating around in a rack, bottles and potions. In the center of all of it stood Elyse, but not Elyse, the version that presented her as she saw herself. August could see that she thought herself far less pretty than in real life, her coat bigger and her spectacles almost the size of goggles.

Through this, Elyse and August sat motionless against the railing by the side of the *Lady Lass*, eyes closed, moving nothing. Penny lay in a heap between them. The sun glinted off Elyse's spectacles and fell into her deep black coat.

Inside the dream world, Elyse and August faced each other. It was not like facing another person in real life. It was as if all of their superficialities had been stripped away, only to be replaced by their own vicious self-criticisms. August knew that he must look the same as Elyse, a jagged shadow of his real self. All in all, it felt quite strange.

Elyse began. *I'll start with the beginning. I was a genius, see. A child prodigy.* The dream world changed, to show a memory. August saw it from her perspective, felt her emotions, processed everything as if he himself were remembering.

A big, open hall. Thousands of people. Expensive clothes. Bright lights. Elyse standing on a massive stage, made all the more massive by her tiny child stature. Beside her, a device that bristled with cogs and pistons—a skyship engine, a novel and crazy one. August knew everything about it, just as Elyse did at the time, because, of course, she had created it.

Elyse folded her arms behind her back like she had been taught. Her black coat, small to fit her size, wrapped itself around her like a protective shield. In the stadium's indoor light, her spectacles hung at her neck.

"This is my engine," Elyse said in the memory, gesturing towards it. "It harnesses the power of magic to heat and cool skysteel, generating more lift than conventional steam engines."

The audience hall was silent, incredulous. *Such a little kid?* They all seemed to ask.

Elyse then launched into an hour of technical explanation, taking apart the engine piece by piece, and explaining it all. August only understood with Elyse's help, relying on her to fill in the gaps in his knowledge. Once he got basic understanding, he truly understood how magnificent her invention was.

August opened his eyes, just to check. Sure enough, in the cabin where engineer Davis worked, covered in soot, Elyse's engine glowed brightly like a hot poker.

August closed his eyes, and dropped back into the memory. Elyse had finished her explanation, and now stood facing the audience. Nothing happened for a good minute. And then, someone clapped. Another joined him. Then, the entire audience erupted into thunderous applause, that lasted for a long while, until Elyse cut the memory off. August felt her satisfaction, but at the same time, he felt a sort of longing, and a deep sense of regret.

Elyse started another memory. She stood on the same stage again, a little taller this time. The room was even more packed with people than the time before. Men stood in the aisles and hung over the balconies. But, something was wrong. The admiring atmosphere, the sort of incredulous feeling, was gone. In its place seethed a dark emotion visible on every face in the room. Jealousy? Anger? August couldn't quite comprehend.

Beside Elyse, there stood a table with a series of bottles full of colored liquids. Wasting no time, Elyse began her presentation.

She explained what all the liquids were, one by one. One was a healing potion. One was a potion of death. Another was a potion of major strength. All of them were imbued with magic, as every potion was. Elyse was about to prove what that really meant.

A fourth bottle, full of a mysterious green liquid, sat apart from the others, underneath a complicated distilling apparatus. Elyse poured the potions into glass bulbs that hung over the setup, one at a time. When she was finished, four bulbs hung full, each with a pipette leading down into a central mixing chamber. Elyse began with the mysterious green liquid. She turned a knob, and it dripped down into the mixer. When the bottom of the mixer had been coated, she turned the knob for the first potion, the potion of health.

The liquid coursed down, into the chamber. After that, it flowed through the apparatus, being heated and cooled alternately, all while Elyse held her arm over it, her hand glowing bright hot. She recited a complicated spell that no ordinary person could ever hope to understand.

Soon, it was finished. At the bottom of the glass maze, in a small flask, there rested a droplet of pure light. It had been separated from the rest of the health potion, which now seemed to be much darker than before.

The audience, seeing this, held their collective breaths. People leaned over chairs, over railings, and even over each other to get a look at the little droplet of light.

Elyse repeated the process systematically with the other two potions. Each bottle of liquid gave another little droplet to the flask, leaving only dirty water behind. When she was finished, Elyse turned to the audience.

"And so I have disproved Farlsman's theory of magic immateriality, and concluded that magic, indeed, has a physical form."

Unlike the last time, there were no claps. None at all. The audience simply glared at her, as if they wanted to kill her. August could feel her confusion, her wounded pride.

She began to pack up her setup without another word, but was stopped when a man stepped onstage. "Ms. Marigold, if you will leave your apparatus behind for further study."

Elyse paused for a moment, shocked and hurt, and then turned away without complaint. She mumbled, almost to herself. "Don't take the magic out of the bottle…"

Later, as she walked down the street, tall houses rising to either side, an explosion from behind rocked the ground and pushed a front of warm air past her.

Elyse ran away, her feet pounding the cobblestones, tears streaming down her cheeks and burning her eyes.

She left the capital, pursued by an angry mob of magicians and alchemists. Soon, the entire city knew about her, and wanted her captured.

And that, Elyse concluded, *is why I am as you see me now. Give or take a few years of wandering, of course.*

When August opened his eyes, he looked over the other side of the ship, and saw the same hill he had seen before gliding past the mast. He realized that the whole exchange had lasted under a minute.

Beside them, Penny stirred. Her eyes fluttered open, and she stretched out her arms as if she were just waking up from a good night's sleep. She froze halfway. Her eyes went blank, and she stared down at the plank floor. "Mommy..." She said, hugging herself.

Elyse traded a glance with August. *I'm bad with kids,* Elyse thought. *You can handle it, right?*

August nodded his head, and turned to Penny. "Are you ok?" He asked, cringing as he thought about how stupid the question was.

Penny nodded. "I'm ok."

August paused. Either the girl was seriously tough, or she had some major problems inside. She had just seen her entire home destroyed, been chased around by disgusting ganglers, and seen who knows what happen right in front of her.

Penny looked around the airship, her eyes glazed over. "I'm ok." She said, again. Any trace of youthfulness that might have been left inside of her vanished with those words. She looked to be much older than she really was. Again, August wondered what she had seen. Where had the little girl who carried about her doll gone?

August looked back up at Elyse. The two of them talked for a while, thinking about what to do. In the end, they decided to leave her alone. They didn't know anything about that kind of thing. They decided to just wait, and see what happened along the way.

And just like that, the *Lady Lass* headed towards the Capital, carrying a freelance monster hunter, a genius outcast alchemist, and a traumatized little girl. After sixteen days, the *Lady Lass* finally arrived at the port of Charduke, just outside the Capital.

The Capital was a city in perfect proportions, a circle concentric to the world itself, a city inside of a great glass dome, just like the real world, for the real world was flat and inside of the dome of the sky. It was even possible to reach the edge and touch the side of the sky itself, at the point where the circle met the inside of the sphere. Not many people had done that, of course, because the journey was long and perilous, and took one through monster infested territory, as well as other dangers, more sinister.

The Capital mirrored the world. A magic sphere surrounded it that projected day and night down at its own pace, set by the guild of clock workers. At any one point, it was impossible to tell whether night or day would be longer, for the ever-changing politics underneath regulated its position. Some years, it never stayed dark for longer than an hour. And some years, the opposite was true. Those were the years in which the necromancer's guild, the vampire's guild, and the nocturnal creature's guild resolved their disputes and forced the lighter sides away. Thankfully, that happened quite seldom.

August looked up in awe at the bright towers that held up the day-night sphere, the magic runes that covered their incredible height readable even from the distance of the docks. He, Elyse, and Penny left the ship together, walking out onto the great bridges that connected the Capital to the outside world. Each bridge ran though one of the great supporting towers, heading underneath it to come out on the other side, inside the capital.

As August passed underneath, he looked up. The tower seemed so huge, this close. Even back at the docks it looked big, but here, underneath, August couldn't help but feel insignificant. He knew Elyse felt the same way, if not more, and assumed that Penny felt it the most, being a third his height.

As they stepped out of the gate and into the Capital itself, throngs of noise assaulted his ears while smells unaccounted for perked up his nose. All around, things moved. Not just people, but animals as well, trained monsters that carted things and carried things and kept things in their bellies as they moved about.

In between the monsters, there were the contraptions, magical gizmos that walked and flew and rolled about just like the monsters they mimicked. August knew, after a pained exposition from Elyse, that they were only made possible by the discovery of solid state magic. That is, Elyse was effectively the mother of modern machines. It made August feel even more insignificant than he already did. Elyse got further and further away, the more he knew about her.

"Where are we going?" Asked August. For Penny's benefit, they had agreed to talk normally unless talking silently was needed. They still shared information, though, which was more efficient, and less conscious, than talking.

"We're going to go meet a friend of mine," Elyse said. Her walk was a little furtive, her eyes suspicious looking. August couldn't blame her, what with what had happened.

The streets grew larger as they walked, and more and more machines replaced the tamed monsters. The houses grew more ornate, more splendid. They were nearing the center of the city, where the great domed academy of magic, alchemy, and mechanics dominated the skyline. Its mechanisms created the light that brought day to the city, reflected off the inside of the magic sky capsule. Now, in the daytime, a single focused beam of light hit the curved ceiling right where the sun would be at 3:00 pm precise. August had seen the sun before he entered the city, though, and could have sworn it was 11:00 in the morning.

Elyse noticed his confusion. "Time here has no relation to the outside world," she explained. "People operate by their own rhythms."

August wondered where the energy came from, that powered the massive beam of light. It must have some source, he concluded. However, it didn't seem like he would find out anytime soon.

Penny stared upwards at the beam, her little mind churning and her eyes burning with an indescribable fervor. She followed August and Elyse without a single word.

Elyse took a side street off the main road, one of the many that circled the center of the Capital, growing ever wider as they banded the straight spokes of the avenues. They stopped in the middle of a city wedge, next to a shop that looked a little less splendid than its neighbors.

"I'm already risking myself to bring you two here," she said, "So I want you to be as inconspicuous as possible." To August, she sent an image of a bumbling man of about thirty, with a paunch and a careworn face. She glanced at Penny, who still stared at the bright beam of light that replaced the sun. Then, she knocked twice on the door, and kicked it once.

August understood that it was their secret code.

"I'll be there in a minute", a voice said from inside. Clinking sounds followed. Soon, the door cracked open a bit. A man, who August knew right away was the man Elyse had showed him, poked his eyes out. Upon seeing Elyse, his eyebrows raised, and then the door shut with a snap. August heard locks clinking and the rattle of a chain. Then, the door opened fully, to reveal the man in his entirety. He looked a little older than Elyse had remembered, his hair a little greyer and further back, his paunch a little bigger.

"Elyse!" The man said, his voice betraying his surprise. "I thought you had gotten everything you needed the last time you came." He ushered them in with a hurried wave. "What brings you here?"

"This is Dex," Elyse said, before she answered his question. Penny and August both nodded. Then she spoke. "I need your help, Dex. I got into a little bit of... trouble."

Dex raised his eyebrows, and then looked over at August, and then the red streak in Elyse's otherwise silver-white hair. "Trouble?" He finally said. "I see a stranger and a kid, and a new hairstyle, but I don't see anything that might be troubling. But of course," he added, "I'm talking purely magical. Your aura seems fine, just a little... different."

Elyse shook her head. "Trust me, it is trouble. I wouldn't have come to you if it wasn't."

Dex seemed to perk up a little at that. August frowned, not happy about being labeled trouble, as if it were his fault.

"So then, tell me about it." Dex sat down at a cluttered desk, and motioned to a set of chairs behind it.

Penny climbed onto the arm of one of the chairs and sat with a glazed expression.

Upon seeing this, Dex leaned forwards to examine her, his entire countenance changing. He looked as if he were seeing Penny for the first time. "But first, tell me about this girl."

August frowned, and Elyse drew a blank. They exchanged a glance.

She has been a little weird, August admitted.

And she did experience a lot of magic . . . Elyse added. She looked at Dex. "We don't know." She said.

Dex frowned. "That's odd, her aura is very . . . developed." He reached into his desk and pulled out a device that bristled with antennae. It beeped non-threateningly. He gazed at the panel in its front for a minute, and then attached a little clip to Penny's wrist.

The machine beeped, and then beeped again, and then again, this time very threateningly. Dex seemed taken aback. He stared at the machine as it continued to beep, the rhythm growing frantic, like a man out of breath.

Through this, something changed about Penny. It was as if something had been released, like a key had been turned in a lock. Her features relaxed. Her eyes lit up, although something was still off about them. "That will be all," she said, her voice just high enough to capture the idea of a little girl, but yet level, like that of a professional soldier. She took off the clip with grace, placing it back on the desk. The machine's beeping subsided. "I trust you know enough already," Penny said.

Dex's expression voiced his agreement. He turned to Elyse like nothing had happened. "In any case," he said, his voice a little thin, "I want to know what happened."

Elyse and August exchanged glances. August stared at Penny for a moment.

Penny shook her head slowly. "Carry on."

August looked at Elyse. *Should we?*

Elyse nodded. *It looks like we have to.*

Dex noticed them talking to each other. "It seems you managed to get your auras all tangled up." He looked between August and Elyse. "And also managed to tangle other things up as well."

"Other things?" Elyse asked. Both she and August were curious.

"Yes, it seems like . . . Bits of a monster aura, perhaps?" Dex put his fingers together to form a steeple. "In any case, you two are certainly the most tangled I have ever seen. Would this be the problem you mentioned?"

Elyse nodded, unsure of what else to say.

"What does it mean?" August asked. "I mean, what happens when people get their auras tangled?"

Dex leaned back in his chair. "I'll give you the full explanation, because it seems you might need it. I assume you already know about auras, right?"

He only looked at August. Of course Elyse knew, genius that she was.

She quickly filled August in, telling him everything he needed to know. Auras, or souls, as they were commonly called, were the magical manifestation of the brain, where all a person's thinking took place. It was sort of like a magical footprint left behind by the energy of thought.

August did his best to try to understand, but could only handle it so far. He was lost after magical footprint and how it affected the real world and other magical footprints.

Dex began to explain. "Aura entanglement happens when contact with another person's aura is severed before it ends. This can happen any number of ways: death, unconsciousness, deliberate but very difficult severance. When this happens, the pieces of aura that left their person to interact with the other are trapped, unable to return or to even give information. After a very short time alone, the pieces integrate with the mind of the creature that they inhabit in order to avoid death." Elyse nodded the entire time, absorbing the explanation without the slightest hitch. August, unable to keep up, relied on Elyse's understanding to support his own. Essentially, August had left a piece of his aura in Elyse's mind when he had jumped in to save her, and then gone unconscious from the explosion of the dangermuff. It had then gotten stuck.

"And so," Dex continued, "if the connection is reestablished, the aura bits that are trapped and now part of the other person's mind return to the original owner. However, because they were part of the other person, or creature's, mind, they retain their connection. Two auras become one and a half, sort of like a Venn Diagram." Here Dex brought out a piece of paper, tattered and covered with ink splotches, and drew two intersecting circles. They crossed each other in the center, creating a third, ovular shape.

"This is you," Dex pointed to Elyse, and then to the circle on the right. "This is you," Dex pointed to August, and the to the circle on the left. "And this is both of you." Dex pointed to the oval in the center. He put the paper down, and then sat back, satisfied with his explanation.

August understood, after the trick with the circles. It made much more sense now. However, it didn't tell him how to fix it. In fact, he wasn't sure he wanted to fix it. Having a genius partner who shared his every thought made things a lot easier to understand.

Oh, so is that all you see me as? Elyse prodded August good-naturedly. *In that case, you're to me like an extra arm. Really nice for reaching those high places.*

August grinned despite himself. He had since gotten used to sharing thoughts with a sassy alchemist, if not learned to enjoy it. Elyse nudged him in the ribs. August held up his palms.

Penny reached forwards from her seat on the arm of August's chair. She picked up the pen and began drawing. When she was finished, she presented it like a trophy. "And that's me," she said. The picture was in between the two circles, a stick drawing with a fiendish smile and dangerous looking weapon.

When no one said anything, Penny looked around as if to say, *what are you looking at?* She climbed down from the chair, the arm reaching up to her shoulders when she stood. "I think it is time we should be going, Mr. Dex sir."

Dex raised his eyebrows at the address. "I take it you have something to attend to?" He spoke to her with a deferential tone, almost as if she were his superior.

August and Elyse, completely baffled by the exchange, followed Penny out the door and back into the street. The door closed behind them with a clunk.

It was dark out, a crescent moon and stars projected from the same beam that produced the sun in the day. However, August didn't remember spending more than fifteen minutes inside of Dex's shop.

It's politics, Elyse explained. *The night guilds probably bought another one of the clock worker's seats.*

August shrugged, glad that he didn't live in a world where the time was decided by politics.

At the end of the alleyway, Elyse stopped. Beads of suspicion built inside her mind. She turned towards Penny, who had also stopped. "I think you're not telling us something," Elyse said, her voice a mix of command and request. She looked straight at Penny with her rose red eyes, having taken her spectacles off in the dim light of the artificial moon.

Penny stared right back at her, holding her gaze. "It was my choice," she stated. She turned away for a moment, her eyes betraying some sort of insecurity. "And anyways, I promise not to . . ." She looked back at Elyse sheepishly.

August felt as if he were being left out.

Hold on a minute, was all Elyse told him when he asked for help. He couldn't figure out what was going on in her mind, either. It was too jumbled; he suspected Elyse barely knew herself.

"Not to what?" Elyse asked. She seemed to be prodding Penny.

Slowly, August began to make connections. A guild he had heard of. A certain . . . strange property that manifested itself in preadolescent girls.

Penny thought for a moment, and then gave in. "Look, I don't know anything more than what they told me. What it . . . told me." At the word "it", August saw a mixture admiration in her face, and—

he couldn't believe it—adoration, like what she had once held for her doll.

"You don't know? Than why did you accept?" Elyse seemed certain of something now. It colored her words and thrummed against August like a minor chord.

What is it? What? What? August couldn't bear it anymore. He looked at Penny one more time, and then, it hit him. She looked like a certain famous person, with her air, and her stature, and her age: the international chief of magical and mystical police, Emeralda Stysh. August had seen her photo in a newspaper once. It was rumored that she had her own force of peacekeepers, which, unbounded by any law, magical or otherwise, turned up enough ruckus to keep every country on its toes.

That force was none other than Disciplinary Force of Female Magicians, open only to females of the ages 7-11, granting magical power rivaling that of an adult master, as well as immortality and a charm that played proper adults like butter. It was somewhat of a mystery as to why the entry requirements were so specific, but it had something to do with the magical power produced by pure, innocent thoughts. Everything made sense, and August found himself looking at Penny with awe and respect. Elyse felt the same as he did. The organization was one of the great forces in the world.

"I wanted to rescue my parents, but I couldn't," said Penny. Penny looked down as if she were still remembering what had happened. "You didn't see them, they . . . they died a few hours before you got there. It came to me then, when I was hiding underneath a table. It promised . . ." Penny's shoulders slumped. "It promised to save me, but I said, no, it was too scary, and ran away."

She straightened herself up now, as if adjusting a heavy burden. "That's when you found me, and brought me on the ship. It came back last night, though. It said that I had a chance to save the world. I don't know what it meant, but I had been crying a lot, and hated myself for it, and I wanted really bad to do something, and so I accepted." Penny dropped off, finished.

August stood for a minute. Elyse stood across from him.

Penny stood between them, looking alternately from one to the other. "But I'm still cute, right?" she asked. She seemed to be trying to lighten the mood.

August chuckled a little. She was cute, much more than he remembered. In any case, he didn't really know much about the Disciplinary Force, and so he couldn't make a judgment. Neither could Elyse.

"I have one last question," August said. "What's 'It'?"

Penny looked to be thinking up an answer. "Kind of a cross between a rabbit and a bird, that can talk," she finally said.

August shrugged. Not the most ridiculous thing he had heard, and believed, recently. "Well, take me to him . . . It . . . the next time it comes."

Penny nodded, and then broke out into a huge yawn. Her eyes watered, and her small form leaned back a little. August felt as if he were watching a kitten. The same sense of the adorable pervaded her actions.

"You certainly do have a sort of magical quality about you," Elyse said, her face softening. "But in any case, it's dark and I'm tired."

August could feel that it was true. They hadn't done much that day, short as it was. What they did do, however, drained him more than walking between villages and slaying monsters could.

"I know a good place to sleep," Elyse said, and led the group out into the main road. Even at night, it bustled with feverish activity. They walked out and soon lost themselves in the frantic hive.

And so the magical girl, the monster hunter, and the lady lasher alchemist ended their first day in the great Capital City.

Attack of the Magical Girls

That night, as the three shared a room in a cheap dive inn, Penny told them about her meeting with "it".

"Its name is Koko, and it's a he" she said. "He told me that I had a chance to save the world. I don't know why. I really wanted to help my parents, though, and the pictures that he showed me of the magical girls when he called me made me really want to be one." She looked down sheepishly. "He said he would come to me tonight for my first mission."

August and Elyse exchanged glances. Truth be told, they really didn't know anything about the Disciplinary Force. It was more of a legend than a real existing thing. After a little bit of debate—Elyse wanting to leave Penny alone, and August wanting to stay with her—they both decided that a compromise could be reached. They would stay until she received her first "mission" from Koko, and then see what happened afterwards.

They told Penny, who agreed with them. And so they waited, long into the night, for the messenger of legend to arrive.

As the moon rose above the top edge of the window, and the sounds of the city died out like a drying up waterfall, a little figure perched on the windowsill. August saw it first, and shook Elyse's shoulder to wake her from her doze.

"Look" he said, and pointed. Elyse looked, and stared with interest. They both turned to Penny.

She faced the figure, walking up to meet it eye to eye. "I'm ready," was all she said.

The figure, who really was named Koko, nodded his assent. "I will tell you now." His voice was sweet, pretty, accented by the fluffy motion of his twitching nose and the fanning of his wings. "You must repair the chain of command."

August, Elyse, and Penny all stared. Koko acted as if he didn't notice. "I have high hopes for you, Penny Sharp." He lifted off the windowsill, hanging by his big floppy wings, that sprouted from his head, and looked like bunny ears. With amazing speed, he disappeared into the fake night sky.

"I don't understand," August said. "What did he mean by 'chain of command'?"

Penny shrugged, and Elyse only stared at where the monster (was it really a monster? August couldn't tell) had flown off into the distance.

Something happened down below the room in which the trio stood, a commotion like people fighting. Loud voices, young and sweet, carried over the sound of banging furniture. One word sounded again and again, distinguishable even through the thick floorboards. "Where!"

The commotion stopped. August and Elyse held their breaths, straining to listen. Penny shuffled around the room and twitched nervously. Her frilly dress, burnt, tattered, and dirty as it was, gave her a magical aura that enhanced her motions and drew others towards her. It was as if she were drawing strength from her clothes.

The footsteps came up the stairs. August tensed up, Koko's words echoing in his head. *Fix the chain of command.* The people coming up had something to do with the mission, August was sure. He clenched his fist and waited for them to come. Elyse felt the same way August did. Penny paced back and forth across the room.

She stopped, just as the footsteps arrived at the door. She turned to face it. "Back up," she said to Elyse and August. They did so without question.

The door glowed, faintly at first, and then grew brighter, until it seemed as if the entire room were a single color of white. With an ear-shattering smash, it flew off of its hinges and slammed into the opposite wall. The bed that stood in its way cracked in half, straight down the middle, then busted through the outside wall and poked into the night air. Dust floated down onto the street below.

In the doorway, three girls of about Penny's age stood side by side, the shortest one in the lead. She was pretty, in a cute, girlish sort of way. Her eyes burned with a fiery intensity, giving her a beautiful, exotic aura, that conflicted with the rest of her features. She wore a green dress, ornately embroidered, shimmering in its radiance. She cut an imposing figure, her small stature paradoxically adding to the effect.

The two girls to her side also resembled her, albeit in a more ordinary way. One of them kept a comically large sword over her shoulder, and another brandished a beautiful carved staff. The leader held nothing in her hands.

"I'm Ruby Grandsham." She stated, in a powerful voice. She motioned to her sides. "This is Denyse Lilly, and this is Justle Lin." She raised her hands into a stance that coiled with aggression. "You have gotten too far ahead of yourself. I will now eliminate you."

Her tone brokered no negotiation.

That sure was fast, August thought.

Elyse drew Instrator, cutting it off halfway. The remaining whip coiled around her fist and created a swirling gauntlet of fire.

Ruby raised her eyebrows, and then held out her palm. Water condensed out of the air in a cloud, and then weaved itself around her fingers until the shape of a hammer appeared, mottled light giving it a ghost-like appearance. Then, it froze into solid ice.

"Two can play at this game, my dear stranger," Ruby said, her voice dripping with ire. "You are no concern of mine, and neither is your friend." She glanced at Penny with hunger, and then pointed her icy weapon. "The girl is all I need."

The fiery gauntlet around Elyse's hand jumped and sparked, as if Instrator was excited to face another of its kind.

Penny turned to August and Elyse. "You go," she said. "This is my mission, my problem."

Ruby took a step back at the word 'mission.' "What did he tell you?!" she cried, her voice pretty as a lullaby even under stress.

Penny frowned and held out her arms. "It's none of your business," she said, and then she transformed.

Bright light filled the room, Penny lifting up from the ground at the center, her face upturned, placating some higher power. Her clothes unraveled about her. After only a second, a new set of clothes materialized out of thin air, attaching to her in pieces from the top down, swirling as straps adjusted and bows magically tied themselves into pretty knots. The whole attire looked as flowing as the wind but retained at the same time an air of steely strength.

When she was finished, the room returned to dimness for the second time that night. Major Ruby had watched the whole thing with an increasing look of irritation, and now she seemed about to burst.

"You have just crossed the line, private Sharp," she said, tapping her ice hammer against her knee. She brought it up and held it ready to strike. "You die now."

Penny now held in her arms a staff, ornate, like the one held by the other girl in the doorway. It sparkled as it met Ruby's ice hammer in mid-strike.

"Ha!" Ruby exclaimed, staring straight into Penny's eyes. "Your movements are unpracticed. Your instincts are raw. But," She seethed with anger now, and Penny's hold faltered for a moment. "Why?!" She pulled back and swung down again hard. Penny blocked. "Why!?" She hammered Penny, surrounded her with a flurry of solid icy wind. They fought across the room, tearing it up, through the center and then the sides. Ruby attacked again and again, but was battered away by Penny's staff. Everyone, including Penny herself, looked surprised as she deftly deflected even cunning hammer blows. The room filled with the clunk of ice on wood.

"Why!?" Ruby said, one last time. Her attacks faltered. Penny stood back for a moment, her face coated in sweat, obviously tired. She seemed to have given up protesting against the strange things that were happening to her.

Ruby knelt down on the floor. She looked up at Penny, her face covered in tears.

Throughout the exchange, the four other people in the room barely moved an inch. Elyse held Instrator ready, but did not move in to assist. August exchanged glances with Denyse and Justle. They simply shrugged when he motioned to the combat in the center of the room.

Penny lowered her staff, her face a bright shining star. She looked so serene, compared to Ruby's explosive countenance. The two stared hard at each other, having a conversation without words. Penny's eyes were sad, full of sorrow, reflecting the rage that Ruby unleashed upon her straight back from where it came.

August sat down on the bed, carefully at first, relaxing when he saw no one notice. The air in the room became decidedly less tense, outside of the two little girls locked in combat. The magical girl with the sword leaned against the doorframe, and the one with the staff placed it over her shoulders and hung her arms on it.

Elyse chuckled first. August felt it coming beforehand, and yet it still surprised him. He couldn't help himself, though, and soon he chuckled along with her. The two magical girls opposite them also cracked smiles. Soon, the chuckles turned to laughter on all sides. Penny and Ruby, in the center of the room, noticed it only after it had taken root and sprouted. At first, they both seemed confused, looking about like they were in a room full of crazy people. Then, they looked at each other.

"This isn't funny!" Ruby cried, stomping the floor like a kid having a tantrum. Penny smiled, and then began to laugh herself. The room soon filled to the brim with loud guffaws, everyone but Ruby rolling about with tears in their eyes. Ruby seemed to break inside. Or rather, it was as if something were fixed.

"You just looked, so . . ." The girl with the sword wheezed while holding her side.

"Serious!" The other girl completed, also fighting hard to breathe through her laughter.

Ruby looked at her arms, and her ice hammer dissolved back into vapor in a twirl of mist. Instrator followed suit, Elyse disarming only after Ruby had sheathed her weapon. The two magical girls in the doorway put their weapons away as well, the sword returning to its sheath and the staff dissolving into light.

Penny was the last to put away her staff, after helping Ruby to her feet. Ruby leaned on her, having given up on whatever vicious spirit that had possessed her with such anger. She seemed suddenly more fragile, like a china doll, pretty and yet untouchable. "I've busted my skirt for two hundred and seventy years, trying to do my best," she said, her voice hollow, yet charming even in regret. "Now you come along, and the whole world says that you'll be better than me." She hunched over, as if hit by a roiling wave of internal pain. "Better than I ever will be."

The two girls, who had until now simply been spectators, stepped forwards. They surrounded Ruby, forming a circle with Penny.

"You've always been the best to me," said the one with the sword. "You're my number one friend, remember?" She looked kindly, and reached out to grab Ruby's hands. The girl with the staff did the same.

Ruby looked as if she were about to cry, tears of relief and regret rather than tears of pain, like before. "I . . ." She looked down at her hands. "I don't know what came over me. I think I . . ."

She turned to Penny, her attitude changed to the point where August's first impression of her simply didn't compute. "I think I needed that, Penny Sharp." She stood up straight like an officer, like the person that she should have been. "I apologize for my conduct, private, and I sincerely hope that we may have better relations in the future."

Penny could only nod, mesmerized by Ruby's transformation. "I'm glad I could help," she said, and then pulled Ruby into a hug. Ruby's eyes widened, her face showing surprise, and then her cheeks reddened.

"Just don't tell anybody, ok?" Ruby asked, as she relaxed into the embrace.

These Ones are Overage

August decided that he should get the names of the two other girls straight. However, he couldn't think of a way to pose the question without sounding awkward. He had heard their names from Ruby: Denyse Lilly and Justle lin. He didn't know how figure out which belonged to whom, either. Did the sword wielding girl, with the fiery red hair and pretty mouth, look like a Denyse, or a Justle? Did the last name Lin indicate a certain race? If so, August couldn't tell. They both looked similar in every way, except for the sword girl's fiery red hair.

The one with the red hair and sword is Denyse, and the one with the blue hair and staff is Justle. Elyse had noticed his confusion, and answered the question for him.

Blue hair? August felt confused for a moment, but then noticed it: a slight sheen in the hair of Justle that, when seen in the right light, appeared blue.

In any case, August thought, *how did you know?*

Nah, I just know, said Elyse, smiling smugly.

The heart to heart in the middle of the room between the four girls wound down about then. Penny turned from the huddle. "You've been talking to each other, haven't you?" She sounded inquisitive, and a little defensive. Something about her new dress had perked her up. "Is it something about us?"

"As a matter of fact, it is," answered Elyse, who was quick on the draw. "We were discussing your rankings, and I cleared up a little confusion August had about Denyse and Justle's names."

Hey! August thought. *Why did you tell them?*

You were the one that mixed them up, Elyse said, nudging him with her consciousness. It was eerily similar to how it would feel if it had happened in real life. *The least you can do is own up to it.*

It's not my fault that I don't know magical girls, or whatever, and that I'm not a genius that knows everything, August replied.

Elyse smiled at that. *You do have a point.*

"You're doing it again," said Penny, who crossed her arms with a pout on her face. "Let me in on it too."

August was reminded that Penny was still nine years of age. Even though she looked the same age as the officers that had barged into their room. If what Ruby had said was correct, then the officers had been living for quite some time. Ruby had mentioned serving for 270 years, so she must have been at least 280. It made August feel a little weak inside.

"August wants to know how old you all are," Elyse asked, chuckling good-naturedly.

"No, No, wait—" August said, but he was cut off by Ruby.

"I'm two hundred and eighty-one." She seemed not at all put off about the question. Perhaps it was because of her immortal pre-adolescent appearance.

"I'm one hundred and seventy-six," added Justle. Her blue hair shone a little more when she said it, as if it had absorbed all those years and was pound of it.

"I'm fifty-three," Denyse followed, looking a little embarrassed. It was true, though, that at less than a fifth of the age of her superior, Ruby, she would feel a little small, August imagined.

A charming voice called everyone's attention, from the windowsill. All heads turned at once, to see Koko, the flying rabbit, perched like an inquisitive pigeon. "I knew you could do it, Sharp," he said, looking at Penny. "You've done a marvelous job, to be expected of one with your presence." He then addressed Ruby in a different tone, without waiting for an answer. "Ruby, take your girls and report to General Stysh, immediately."

Ruby seemed to know that it was coming, but flinched anyways. She gave one last complicated glance, and turned to the door. Denyse and Justle followed her without comment. Soon the sound of footsteps receded into the distance.

The door still leaned against the far wall, the bed beneath it hanging outside through a jagged hole. Scuff marks covered the floor, and most of the sheets sported singe marks from all the lighting up that had been going on.

Penny sat down on the floor, her little frame trembling, her uniform drooping over her shoulders. She had had a rough time, August knew, so he decided to do something about it. He nudged Elyse with his mind. Elyse listened to his idea and smiled.

August got down on the floor next to Penny, and put his arm around her. He pulled her close against his side, her small frame fitting snug under his arm. Penny didn't protest, but instead buried her head in August's chest. "I'm sorry," August said. He made sure to communicate as much as possible his care for her situation, in those words.

"It's ok," Penny said, her voice muffled by August's shirt. "I'll be fine."

August gently pushed Penny away, enough so that he could look her in the eyes. They were swollen, tears streaked down her cheeks. "I have a proposition," he said.

Penny looked up at him as if he had spoken a different language. "Propo..."

"It means idea for you," Elyse explained for August, her tone slightly sarcastic.

Nice job, she thought to August.

I know you're just trying to help, August replied, grateful despite her attitude. It covered up something inside of her, August saw, but he didn't press it.

Thanks, thought Elyse, a little chastised.

August continued with his proposition. "I know you're having a hard time," he said, "and I want to help you."

Penny nodded, still looking into August's eyes.

"And so I have a question," August said. "How about you let us travel with you, for a little while, wherever it is that you're going? If it means helping you, than Elyse and I have agreed to go wherever you do."

Penny's eyes watered. "You'd really do that for me, Uncle August?" She pressed against his arms, leaning in to emphasize her seriousness.

"We'd both do it for you," August told her, "And just call me August."

Penny seemed embarrassed as she thought about it. "You promise? To help me?" Her larger-than-life eyes shone with an otherworldly glow that wanted to bind August to his word. August knew that anything he said would have to be carried out, all the way.

"I promise." August answered.

"As do I," said Elyse, still safe in her perch on the bed.

Penny pushed her arm out towards August, her fist closed except for the pinky, which stuck out straight up. "Pinky promise?" She said, in all seriousness. Her newfound tone of command was returning.

August inhaled sharply. Something magical shone in the air, and Elyse got down from her bed to sit next to August.

"Pinky promise," August said, as he locked his pinky with hers.

Penny held out her other fist to Elyse. Elyse looked at it for a moment, and then looked at August.

I'm stuck with you, she thought to him. "So why not," she said out loud, "Pinky promise." She locked pinkies with Penny.

A spark ran through their interlocked arms, emanating from somewhere deep inside Penny. When it had disappeared, she let out a satisfied sigh, as if a giant weight had been taken off of her.

"Thank you, Elyse," she said, taking her arms in both hands.

Elyse reddened, ever so visible through her moon white skin, like a blood rose tattooed on her cheek. Her rose colored eyes fought back tears. "No problem," she said. "I do this all the time."

From the windowsill, Koko stirred. "A most beneficial arrangement, Private," he said.

All three in the room were surprised to see him still there. They turned to face him.

"Your next mission is to report to General Stysh, at exactly 0500 Spherical time." Koko anticipated their next question. "In order to assist you inside the Capital time zone, I will now be obliged to provide you with the reward for your first mission."

The air in front of Penny shimmered, and then something slipped out of a pocket in space: a golden pocket watch, ever so intricately carved and tooled, about the size of an apple around. Countless gears spun about in absolute silence inside its beautiful curved shell. Three dials rested upon those countless gears: two gauges, that counted some unknown force; and one clock. Its hour hand pointed to 3, and its minute hand pointed to 48.

"That's twelve minutes!" Penny exclaimed. "We don't even know where it is!"

"That is not a problem," Koko answered. "The chancellor has many functions." With that cryptic remark, he hopped from the windowsill and left into the sky beneath the dome.

"The chancellor . . ." Penny examined her pocket watch closer.

August did so as well, leaning over her to see it in her hands. "There's a button, right there," he said, and pointed to a spot on the edge of a shell, where a small cylinder stuck out. "Try pressing it."

Penny pressed it. An arrow, made of light, materialized in front of the face. It fit nicely around the chancellor's engravings.

"Wow," Elyse said, her voice full of admiration. "A magical compass."

August and Penny gave blank stares.

"It's an automatic fortune-telling machine," Elyse explained. "A colleague of mine—well, he was a colleague—devised the mathematical spell to extract temporal data from the threads of fate and embed them in—"

Elyse stopped when she saw August give her a look. *And you scolded me for saying "Proposition."* he thought.

Elyse reddened. August felt her try to staunch her curiosity. *I do want to hear about it another time,* he said, genuinely interested. Elyse's mood brightened. *But you'll have to translate for me.*

I can do that, Elyse said.

Penny started from what looked to be deep thought. "So it points where I need to go?" She said, more of a deduction than a question.

Elyse and August exchanged glances. "Yes, that's exactly what it does," Elyse said.

"I'm not stupid, you know." Penny crossed her arms. "And I think we only have eleven more minutes to go where this watch tells us to go."

"You're right," August said, "But who's going to clean up after us?"

They all looked around the room. The bed through the wall was a particularly devastating touch.

As if in response to their question, a large sum of money slipped out of space, and into Penny's palm. *This is for the room,* a note attached to it read. *Koko,* it was signed. August put the money on the bed that had punctured the wall. Then, they all picked up their belongings, and headed out the empty doorframe.

Their journey through the Capital was a frantic one, with much racing and dodging and being sworn at by machine pilots and beast drivers alike. Penny led the way, holding out the pocket watch in front of her like a compass. Whenever they reached a street they needed to turn on, the compass snapped in its direction. In this manner they finally arrived at an empty lot in the warehouse district, where no one but the lizards in the streets took notice of them.

Penny looked at the compass, and then at the field of tall grass. "It says we should go here," she said. She moved the compass about, trying to see if it would change. It didn't.

August and Elyse stepped forwards first. Penny followed, a little frightened despite her newfound confidence. When the three reached the center of the lot, the compass froze in place, and then jerked the watch in Penny's hands until the arrow pointed straight into the ground.

"Underground?" Elyse said, the first to understand. Before anyone could respond, the earth opened up and swallowed them whole.

Down a cold metal slide they flew, arms flailing for support as welded ridges jumped past. Penny grabbed hold of August, and August grabbed hold of Elyse, so that the three fell together, and tangled together like a human snowball.

Surprisingly, no one screamed. Instead, Elyse let out a burst of glorious laughter, and then Penny began to scream with delight, soon followed by whoops and calls from August. Together they made quite the crazed trio, sliding down into darkness.

Just before they hit the ground, a magical force brought them to a halt like a bed of soft butter. They landed on the floor as one, collapsing into a heap of heavy breathing. No one moved for a moment.

A shadow fell over them, cast by magical white lights hidden in the ceiling. August looked up, to see a magical girl of about Penny's height looking down at them. She had on a black and orange dress, and possessed pretty enough features. Her stature resembled that of a statue: straight as a board.

"General Stysh requests your immediate attendance, Private Sharp," she said, without commenting about their state on the floor. She waited for a moment, while the three adventurers got to their feet. "If you would follow me, please." She turned on her heels and walked down the hall, her boots clicking on the stone floor.

August, Penny, and Elyse followed right after her. The hall they passed though grew wider, until it merged with a sort of underground boulevard, that bustled with commerce like Main Street in the capital. Only, every last person was of approximately Penny's height, and looked between the ages of 7 and 11. Those were the only two major similarities that August could see, though: it was as if a costume ball had been mixed with a military showcase during a children's festival.

From his vantage point one and a half feet above the crowd, August could see an entire spectrum made completely of magical girls: girls with long hair, girls with short hair, girls with hair every color; girls with big swords and short swords, blades and nijatos and shurikens, staffs and quarterstaffs and crowbars; he could make out dresses of every color and shape from pretty and short to voluptuous like a Victorian princess. All the colors boggled his mind. He didn't even know how to begin processing what he saw.

"You are unique, August Cerulean," said the soldierly girl who led them down the wide tunnel. "You are the first male to lay eye on our secret base in fourteen years."

August made a face involuntarily; his facial muscles just responded without him thinking. Elyse laughed out loud, and Penny chuckled.

You should see yourself, Elyse thought, her voice crackling with humor. *In fact, I'll show you.* She cracked a devilish smile.

August received an image, from Elyse's vantage. It was of him, and he couldn't help but be amazed. His eyes had opened so wide, they seemed to cover a quarter of his face. His jaw hung agape. August quickly closed it, but couldn't help but look stupefied.

Penny took August's hand, as much to steady him as it was to keep her feeling well in all the newness of the crowd.

Soon, they reached a small, unassuming door just off the main tunnel. The soldierly girl knocked once on the door, and waited. A magical ball lit up and a voice emanated from it, soft and sweet and steely as an iron foundry.

"This is General Emeralda Stysh's office, I am out or occupied at the moment, please try again during my open hours." The ball disappeared.

The straight-backed girl tapped on the door again, three times, and then another three times, as if it were all a part of the routine. A voice came from inside, this time. "Come in," it said.

The girl opened the door, and ushered the three adventurers in. Inside, Ruby, Denyse, and Justle stood in front of a desk. There, behind the desk, sat the Supreme commander of the Disciplinary force, Emeralda Stysh.

General Stysh: Smart, Cute, and Very, Very Dangerous

Emeralda was a little taller than the rest of the magical girls, but possessed the same ageless charm and picturesque features. She had short white hair, almost the same color as Elyse's, only a little more on the silver side. Her eyes burned with a fiery determinacy, and her posture echoed the office of command better than any male general that August could imagine. She wore a rainbow dress, the only one of its kind, somehow made tasteful, even beautiful, despite the vicious clash of colors. It drew the eyes of all who looked upon her. At her side she wore a single, white dagger, its almost tiny size attesting to the fact that she knew exactly how to use it.

From behind the desk, she levered a kindly smile at the three newcomers, and the one messenger. "Lieutenant Hall, you are dismissed," she said, her voice both cutting and caressing. The messenger snapped a quick salute, and then clicked her heels and left the room. The door closed behind her.

"Take a seat, August, Elyse," Emeralda said. "Penny, Ruby, Denyse, Justle, I know regulations require you to stand in the presence of a commanding officer while on duty, but I don't think we need to worry about that right now." She waved to a row of chairs in front of the desk, spaced out in a circle. There were six. "Take a seat," she said.

All the members of both parties sat down. When they had finished, Emeralda leaned her elbows on her desk and began. "I have called you here today to explain a most pressing matter, that has been troubling us, and the world, for a long time now. It has come to pass that the thing that we have defended against for so many long years has resurfaced, with new weapons and allies to bolster its cause."

Emeralda paused for a minute, to let it sink in. "For the benefit of those who are not familiar with true history," she looked at August, Elyse, and Penny, "I will start from the beginning."

"As you know," she said, "our world is flat. It is a proven fact. What many people do not know—most people, in fact—is that our flat world is three-dimensional." Emeralda paused, letting implication work its way into August and Elyse. "What this means," she continued, "is that our would is more like a disk than a slice of paper. And, on every disk, indeed on almost everything in three-dimensional space, there is an underside."

"Now that underside, being as much a part of this world as we are, is inhabited. Long ago, when humans first appeared out of the caves of monsters, the underside and the topside were linked by a gate called The Centrix. Just inside the edge of the sky, it sat for millennia, connecting the two worlds on either side of our great circular land." Emeralda paused for effect.

August marveled, at that moment, at her speaking ability. The General had a way with words. Her voice modulated at just the right frequency to create a pleasing tone that flowed off of her tongue.

"Trade flowed through the Centrix. Monsters on the underside and humans on the top cooperated together, creating things that can only be dreamed of now. The monsters then were noble, of the same stock as humans, as intelligent and enlightened. Only, one thing was wrong with the world: almost all the metal had for some reason been deposited on the human's side, out of reach of the monster's miners."

"Now, you may not know this, but metal is just as important to civilization as fire. Without metal, there can be no plows, but for stones that do little better than hands. Without metal, there can be no magic, for magic requires energy to function, and metal is the only possible channel for that energy. Do you understand what this means?" Emeralda looked August, Elyse, and Penny in the eye.

August thought he understood. Elyse understood, and supported August's reasoning with her own. Penny looked on with wide eyes.

Emeralda continued. "When the metal ran out, monster civilization teetered on collapse. Only the thin trickle of human trade kept it from disappearing completely. But human society is unstable, as all are, and soon a great human war began that stopped all trade in the world. No one remembers what it was about. All they remember is that it caused the collapse of monster civilization. Without food, magic, and metal, millions of monsters flooded onto the topside, filling the world with the sort of violence that desperation brews. Eventually, the humans were forced to close the Centrix forever, sealing it with a magic that could only be broken by metal."

"But where did all the metal go?" Penny asked the first question, her voice squeaky.

Emeralda simply smiled. "We theorize that several of the monster species of the time ate metal, and rendered it unusable."

Penny leaned back, satisfied.

Emeralda seemed happy to help her understand. "So, in the end, with monster civilization destroyed, most of the monster species eventually lost their ability to reason, which had been tenuous as best, as they were the lower classes of that society." Emeralda paused, realizing that she was about to go on a tangent. "You can ask me about it later," she said. "But in any case, the monsters we see today are the way they are because they ran out of metal. The ones on the topside are the descendants of the ones that poured out of the Centrix, thousands of years ago."

"And this brings me to my point. Monsters beneath us, on the underside, have somehow managed to rebuild their civilization, without using metal. Only, these monsters seek vengeance. We learned this when we captured a monster a decade ago, that admitted to communicating with the underside. They seek to destroy all human civilization, and wipe us from this side of the disk.

"I say this is a pressing problem now because we know that they have a plan, and we know that they plan to put it into motion very soon. We do not know anything more, other than that the monsters are capturing metal mines near the edgelands. And, of course, we know of their attack on you, Penny." Emeralda faced Penny directly, her gaze turned a little ways down, but still steely soft in a caring way. "Which leads me to my main reason for bringing you all here: You."

Penny seemed taken aback, and pointed at herself. "Me?" She asked, incredulous. "I thought Koko was kidding, like a cute way to get me to join, when he said I was important." Penny looked unsure of herself.

Emeralda nodded. "Yes, you, Penny Sharp, the most fated girl that has been born in the last thousand years."

August furrowed his brow. *Fated?* Beside him, Ruby cringed, as if someone had hurt her physically. Denyse and Justle looked at her with sympathy.

"Ten years ago, there was a twist of fate, so big, that it caught the attention of every magician in the world. Some believed it to be a result of an accident at the Royal Academy. We magical girls know better. It was the birth of you, Penny. We wanted to wait until you were eleven, but the monsters forced our hand. We had also wanted to tech you many things, many secrets only known to magical girls, that could have helped you on your journey."

"Journey?" Penny asked. "I suppose that's what this is all about?"

Emeralda nodded. "Very perceptive of you." Emeralda sat up straight in her seat and assumed a tone of total command. "I, General Emeralda Stysh, and the Disciplinary Force of Female Magicians, along with the rest of the guilds in the Capital, who I do hope agree with me on this, hereby appoint you to undertake the most important mission our civilization has ever seen."

August and Elyse leaned back in their chairs, Penny sat straight, Ruby fidgeted.

"You will travel to the edge of the sky itself, to the location of the Centrix, and you will put a hold on whatever the monsters from the underside are planning. You will then support our expeditionary force as it begins an assault on whatever has taken root in the foul surrounding regions. Due to the need for expediency, you may take with you only two companions past the last airship port before the edgelands." Emeralda turned to Ruby. "Major Ruby will train you until then, teaching you as much as possible before you must embark. She has requested this assignment personally."

Ruby's cheeks reddened, and she looked down. Penny smiled at her.

"Naturally," Emeralda continued, "Others will stay with you until you reach the edgelands. But once you are past the border, there will be no support. You will be on your own. You must be ready to face any challenge, to defeat any foe." She stood up from her chair, then, bringing herself to her full height. "You are the hope of our world, Penny, because fate has blessed you with the most gracious gift of all: luck."

Emeralda then surveyed Elyse and Penny, until her gaze fell onto August. "You, August Cerulean, and you, Elyse Marigold, have both been chosen by this fate to accompany Penny on her journey into the edgelands. It is not my position to question fate's decision," here Emeralda dropped into an undertone, "although you may lodge any complaints with the Office of Divine Intervention,"—she continued speaking normally—"and so I have authorized both of you to learn the secrets of the Disciplinary society, and made you honorary members."

Elyse smiled. August, however, leaned back in surprise. "Are you sure, General Stysh?" He asked, his tone somewhat fearful. "I'm . . . You know, a man."

Emeralda looked at August, her gaze kind, penetrating. "Desperate times call for desperate measures, and Penny needs all the help she can get."

August changed positions in his seat, a little miffed at being a desperate measure.

Emeralda turned back to Penny. "This mission is a quest, not an assignment. Meaning, you may choose whether or not to accept. The road is dangerous, and I cannot guarantee success."

Penny contemplated for a long while.

"Also," Emeralda added, "Be aware that your choice will effectively be your companion's choice, as they are bound to you by the law of promise."

August exchanged glances with Elyse. *There's no going back now,* he thought.

But it's not so bad, is it? Elyse replied. *Saving the world at least ought to be interesting.*

Penny looked up to August. August nodded. She turned to Elyse. Elyse nodded as well. She turned finally to General Emeralda. "I only understood half of that," she said, "but if August and Elyse are ok with it, than I accept this mission."

Sparks flew from Penny's dress, lighting on all the members of the meeting. General Emeralda nodded sagely, her pretty young face shining in the light. "Then by the powers invested in me through the order of magical deities, I hereby appoint you, Private Penny Sharp, as the hero to save the world."

Yeah! Save the World! So, Where do we Start?

Ruby now stood up from her seat, and glanced at Emeralda, who nodded to her. "We leave at 1200 tomorrow, on the Disciplinary force training vessel *Firebird*. Please use the time until then to purchase supplies and gather your strength for this mission."

"We will provide you with food and funds to purchase weapons and armor," Emeralda added.

Ruby nodded in assent. "Please do be judicious in your selection, a pony can only hold so much baggage. You will be using them eventually."

"You may sleep here tonight," Emeralda said, "and the capital have a very nice selection of shops. Perhaps you would like to walk about. In any case," here Emeralda stood up straight and saluted, "This meeting is over. You are dismissed."

The adventurers left the room, and then left the secret base, and began their preparations under the glow of an early morning Capital sun. Elyse dragged August to an ingredient and potion shop, claiming to be teaching him about her craft. Indeed, she filled his head with so many new words and ideas felt as if were about to burst. He had never had an education before, and didn't even know how to read, but enjoyed the act of learning new things.

Penny separated from them at the alchemist's shop, and took Ruby and her girls with them. August waved at them as they made their way down the street, towards the weapons district.

Next, Elyse took August to a tinkerer's shop, burdening him with several bags full of parts that weighed more than they looked. She then took him to a delicatessen for some preserved meat, and a lens maker for a backup lens and other more strange things, piling them on top of August until he could barely walk upright.

In this manner the adventurers prepared for the long journey ahead. When they had finished, they returned to the secret base of the Disciplinary Force and spent a restful night in a room in which August's head grazed the ceiling.

The next morning, at the skyship docks of the capital, Emeralda came to see them off. They were six: August, Elyse, and Penny; as well as Ruby, Denyse, and Justle. The ship they boarded looked much fatter than most skyships, for it had a large open deck that had been converted into a real training field, complete with an obstacle course and fighting arena. It seemed that Emeralda had thought of everything.

The crew was made exclusively of Disciplinary force sailors, all with regulation short hair and dressed in sailor's outfits that were as appealing as the normal dresses that most girls wore. Multicolored ribbons took the place of strings in their white uniforms, giving them a look of sprightliness.

August had a cabin all to his own, on the other side of the ship from the girl's. When Ruby mentioned it to him, the look on her face was one of disapproval. However, Elyse insisted on staying with August, until Ruby gave in with a sigh and a wave. She smiled and punched August on the shoulder. *Who knows what you would do in there, all by yourself,* she thought. *Someone has to watch you, and you didn't do anything to deserve such a big room.*

August didn't care either way, although it made him more comfortable, for some reason, when he knew he would never be that far from Elyse. Something about their aura entanglement made it hard for them to leave each other's sight. It was as if they instinctually knew that staying apart for too long would result in something very bad.

Penny embraced Emeralda just before climbing aboard the *Firebird*. Emeralda grew red, and gave her a squeeze as well. "Take care," she said, before she stepped back. Penny boarded last after everyone else had gone aboard. Emeralda finished it off with a wave.

The *Firebird* cast off from the dock and joined the clutter of ships floating in and out of the wooden piers, which stood atop tangled struts reaching down a hundred feet where they anchored in solid stone. The real sun was a welcome change from the sickly capital light, and everyone in the party had high hopes for the future.

And so the monster hunter, the genius lasher, and the chosen one—all entangled by fate—began their journey to save the world.

It's a Dress! It's a Fairy! It's a Dress Fairy!

Ruby began their training the first day out of the Capital. All six members of the party stood in the middle of the ship's training field, Ruby and her girls facing August, Elyse, and Penny. The field looked to be about the size of a ball court, stretching over the side of the ship on the port side. Fences separated it from the rest of the ship, and the other training devices, of which there were many: wooden target dummies, an obstacle course, and magical energy absorbers, to name a few.

"You are now a magical girl," Ruby stated to Penny. She broadened her gaze to meet August and Elsye, who stood tall over the rest of the heads in the group. They had gotten used to it, though. "You are now members of our organization," Ruby said to them all, "and so you must learn our secrets. But," she paused here to draw a line in the ground, dusted to prevent slipping, "I must first judge your fighting and cooperating ability."

Ruby looked at Penny. "I will start with you, private. Step forwards, if you will."

Penny stepped closer to Ruby, and the rest of the party stepped back. They formed a wide boundary around the two short girls, who faced each other in the center. Ruby walked to a rack at the edge of the field, and pulled out two training swords, wrapped in blunt cloth. They still looked like they could hurt, though, definitely enough to bruise. Ruby tossed one to Penny and kept one for herself.

Penny looked frightened, her nervousness showing through her pretty features. Her magical dress seemed to shiver with her, as if it were gathering energy.

Without warning, Ruby struck. Penny, however, deflected it almost accidentally, as if she had just stretched her arms at the right time. She looked bewildered.

Ruby stepped back, as if she had expected it. She then tried a series of short and long jabs, and a slash, all deflected by Penny without so much as a hitch.

"It is as I expected," Ruby said, her voice calm. "Your fated nature had blessed you with an incredible amount of luck, so much so that hurting you has become next to impossible."

Here Ruby took a fighting stance and analyzed Penny with a critical air. "Try at me," she said.

Penny looked at her sword, and then at Ruby. Ruby motioned with her wooden blade. Penny swung down hard, her form wobbling, her entire body off-balance. Ruby moved to block. Penny's sword twisted in mid-air as if touched by an invisible gust of wind. Ruby's block was left empty. Penny dove in for the strike. Ruby twisted her feet around, quick as a cat, and stepped away from the sword. Penny staggered. Ruby struck her in the chest. For an instant nothing happened. Then Penny doubled over in pain.

"Ah!" She cried. She looked incredulously up at Ruby.

Ruby did not look smug. Rather, she looked contemplative. "A well trained warrior can eliminate luck in a battle," she said. "Even the luckiest person alive cannot survive a well-placed maneuver."

Penny nodded, her point taken. "When you fought me, last time, in the inn" she said, her voice thick with pain, "why didn't you do that?"

Ruby shook her head, her countenance suddenly changed. "I was not acting as a well-trained warrior, then. I was merely a babbling fool." Ruby looked at Penny. "Though it was lucky for you, for if I had been in control of my senses, I do not believe you would be alive now." Her statement was one of fact, which no one in the party questioned.

Penny stood back up, her hand on her ribs.

Ruby eyes her critically. "The first thing you need to know, to fight well as a magical girl operative, is how to bond with your . . ." here, she paused, and looked at August and Elyse. "What I am about to say is a Disciplinary force secret. It is the key to our power, the reason for our age, the thread of our very existence. If you tell anyone of this outside of our organization, we will be forced to eliminate you without question, and erase the memory of you from every person you have ever been in contact with. Do you understand?"

August swallowed, and nodded.

We're in all the way, Elyse thought. *No backing out now.*

Ruby turned back to Penny, but instead of looking at her face, she looked at her dress. "Gliss, you may come out now."

A sparkling appeared at the shoulder of Penny's dress, where her emblem would have been had she not been a lowly private. Then, seemingly out of the fabric, a little bug crawled into being, attached to the dress by a thin thread.

It's not a bug, Elyse noticed. *It's a fairy!*

August moved closer to look, and saw that it was true. It was a beautiful fairy that looked pretty enough to have been a princess had she been human. As it was, her countenance radiated not only light, but a sort of emotional happiness as well. August felt his entire being drawn towards her. Elyse felt the same.

The dress-fairy named Gliss yawned, stretching her tiny arms behind her head, almost touching her translucent sparkling wings. "I suppose this means we can all come out now, right?" She asked, after she had finished waking up. "Lester, Tamalda, Bliss!" she called, at Ruby, Denyse, and Justle. "The girls say we can wake up now!"

From the dresses of the other magical girls, three more fairies slipped out and perched on shoulders. There was one boy fairy, who sat on Ruby's shoulder, and two other girl fairies. They called out to each other like it was a reunion, chattering away about incomprehensible things.

Gliss, Penny's dress-fairy, fluttered in front of her face. Her voice carried out over the field, surprisingly big for one so small. "Hello," she said, "I'm Gliss, your dress."

Penny smiled and took it in stride. "Hello, Gliss," she said. "My name is Penny Sharp, and I'm a Private, I think."

Gliss fluttered about, dancing on the wind. "I know, Penny. I'm the one that found you. I've been with you since you were born." Penny's eyes opened wide, and Gliss laughed, a clear, magical laugh.

Fairy laughs make extremely good potions of magic energy, Elyse commented, her voice brimming with excitement.

Don't you dare, August thought. *Remember what Ruby said about elimination?*

Elyse turned her attention back to the fairy, ignoring August.

"We have a lot of work to do," said Gliss, her voice trilling with magical power. "I have many things to teach you."

Ruby cleared her throat. "Gliss is one of the most powerful fairies in existence, as a matter of fact." She shuffled about a little awkwardly. "She sensed your fate swirl even before the best of the human masters, and claimed you for her own. She was how we knew about you so early."

Penny took it all in, her eyes wide. "What do I do now?" She asked.

"You learn," Ruby answered. She cupped her own fairy into her hands. He seemed to enjoy it, and twirled about. "And we will teach you." She said.

August and Elyse watched for a little while longer, as Penny learned the basics of being a magical girl operative. Her class type, as Ruby called it, was spell caster, for she had an unnaturally large reserve of magical energy. The staff that was magically generated each time she called for it channeled that energy, its core made of the purest metal that could be made, covered with wood to keep it safe. As she learned to cast her first spells, she faltered often, and quite often blasted the magical energy absorbers into pieces. Emeralda, it seemed, had planned for even this, and there were plenty of replacements.

When August and Elyse became tired of watching the spell casting, they decided to try training on their own. Both of them were accomplished fighters; years of experience in the wilds had given them strong muscles and sharp reflexes. They chose a spot in the corner of the field, far away from the rest, where the wind whistled through fences that hung out over the land a thousand feet below.

August looked into Elyse's deep black spectacles. In the bright light, he saw her eyes behind it, locked on his. Their thoughts slowed, focused only on each other, the only distraction being an awareness of the battlefield. Elyse's shock white hair flowed with the blowing wind, the airflow that surrounded the ship.

August picked up a training sword. Elyse took a spare piece of rigging, just as long as Instrator. She hefted it in her hands, her eyes evaluative.

August attacked first. Elyse anticipated his attack before he even thought it, following his train of thoughts instead of his movements. August quickly changed his tactics to do the same. They danced across their corner of the field, August whipping his sword around in a dozen different directions as Elyse cracked her rope like a living thing. The sound of rope on wood was like a wet thunk, a hiss as the rope's cords ran over the cloth-bound edge of the training sword. However, neither of them could hit the other. They were too evenly matched, but, more important than that, they anticipated the other's actions before they had even come to pass.

They moved faster and faster, and read into each other's minds deeper and deeper, until they would have been seen as a blur from the outside. August had never known that he could move as fast as he did. It was glorious, while it lasted, but soon neither of them could continue. It was too tiring.

When they stopped, a clap echoed from the area where Penny trained. It was Ruby, who had halted her instruction to watch the two fight. "That was good, you two," she said. "You demonstrated a quite masterful evaluation of your opponents."

Penny clapped to this time, and smiled at them. "Ruby says you guys should come here. She has something to show you."

August and Elyse, both of them coated with sweat, walked over to where Penny stood with the three officers. Elyse looked the most miserable, underneath her thick black coat. August could almost see it steaming from where he stood.

Ruby raised her hand and chanted a spell. Elyse's body seemed to relax, as if new energy were flowing into it. She also seemed to dry out. "I'm a healer by class," Ruby said, anticipating their questions. "But I did call you here, so I could explain to you a few things about party combat."

"Party combat?" Asked August, mystified. "You mean, like fighting in a group?"

Ruby tilted her head sideways. "Yes, and no," she answered. "I'd be best if I show you." She looked at the fairy that sat atop Penny's shoulder. "Gliss, you may put together what you've been working on."

The little fairy princess flew up from Penny's arm, trailing three pieces of string, as well as the one that bound her to Penny's dress. She attached one to August's chest, one to Elyse's, and one between the two. The strings sparkled, and then disappeared. August's clothes felt a little warmer, then, like a magical energy had entered into it.

Like we really need more things binding us together, Elyse commented.

August only shrugged. *It's part of the job, I guess.*

Penny grinned. "Gliss says she can have it up and running for all of us."

August looked around. "What do you mean?"

Ruby spoke. "It's better if I explain it to you first." She reached into her dress and pulled out her chancellor pocket watch, and motioned to the three dials. "This watch measures three things: health, magic, and time." She pointed to the dials as she explained. "Health is your ability to fight. It includes you current stamina, your body's condition, and your alertness. It's measured in Vitality Points, 100 meaning that your body is in peak condition, 0 meaning that you are unable to fight. An operative should strive to keep her points above the ninety mark." Here she pointed to a green area on the health gauge. "And, if you ever fall into the red," she pointed to the twenty and below area, "Get healing or run."

August, and Elyse nodded, takin it all in. Penny paid attention too, having just learned about it a minute ago.

"The second gauge is a measure of your magical energy," Ruby continued. "A simple diviner rod keeps track of how much magical energy you can muster at any one time." Ruby pointed to a blue area on the dial, near the upper end. "Try to make sure that you always have an ample amount before entering combat. It's not as important as health, of course. Magical energy is measured in Magica Points, so the scale of your watch will change with your strength. Three points is about enough to lift a hundred pounds one foot into the air."

Meaning that healing a bullet wound will cost four points, a sword stab through organs will cost ten points, a fireball the size of my fist will cost two points, and so on, Elyse translated for August.

August nodded his head, still unsure as to why they needed points to keep track of things. He knew his own body well enough.

Ruby noticed his questioning look. "The point of these measures is not for the benefit of the one measured. Rather, it is for the benefit of the party that that operative works in, letting them know critical things about the state of the battle."

"But how will we be able to see her watch in the middle of combat?" August asked, perplexed.

Ruby nodded in the direction of Gliss, who had been flying about, doing fairy-like things to Penny's watch. "Gliss, is it ready?" Ruby asked.

"Yes ma'am," Gliss answered, her tiny voice excited. She placed a few more things into place on the watch, and then a flicker of light passed through the mechanisms.

August stepped back, surprised. In the upper left corner of his vision, floating there as if it had always belonged, was a list. Three names lined up one after another, with a red and a blue bar beneath them.

Penny, you, and me, in that order, Elyse translated for August, who could not read. August felt a little bad at not being able to do it for himself.

Penny's blue bar—her magica bar, August correctly guessed—was by far the longest. Their vitality bars were of about the same length.

August noticed that his own magica bar was only a fraction of the size of his two partners'.

Of course it would be, he thought. *I'm no good at magic.*

Ruby stepped back and faced the three adventurers. Her girls stepped back with her, blue-haired Justle on the left and fiery Denyse on the right. Ruby leveled her training sword at Penny. "We will now fight you, three on three."

Politics. Little Girls. Need More Be Said?

Emeralda

General Emeralda Stysh stood in the meeting chamber of the Capital city, where the guilds that comprised the world's governments met to discuss topics of importance. She had often stood in her position, as the spokesperson for the most powerful organization in the world, but she knew from experience that magical power meant little to nothing to those who did not wish to cooperate.

She had wished to gather all the guilds for the discussion; as it was, a two-thirds attendance rate really was all she could hope for.

Thick ornamentation proclaimed the room's importance. In the center there stood a circular table, voluptuous, shaped like the world. Miniature terrain covered most of it, and a raised dome mimicked the sky, with a gap between for viewing and conversing. Emeralda's seat was the tallest, to remove her height disadvantage, but she rarely used it, instead commanding the table with a steely glare while she stood in the highest place in the room.

Only Stebel Misermasher, head of the clockworker's guild, held a more imposing visage—and this was only because he was chosen for his grandiosity as a public figure, to be the head of city politics in name only. The guild masters that had come whispered to each other as they waited for Emeralda to start. Of the four night guilds, she saw three: the necromancer's, the vampire's and the werewolves'.

The master of the necromancer's guild looked just like any other human, a little younger than most in his position. Of course, he had looked that way for most of fifty years.

The werewolf's pack leader showed off his bifurcated form, half human and half wolf. His skin sported furry armor, his nails had been replaced with claws. A dog-like fervor burned in his eyes. Wolves were not the only creature that these half-monsters could change into, but they were by far the favorite.

Least noticeable of the three was the vampire brood-master, looking only a little pale in the room's bright light.

All three were considered to be civilized guilds, for the most part.

Missing from the night guild's section was the undead worker's union, who rarely attended any meeting despite their hard-won official recognition. Due to the affordability and versatility of undead labor, the necromancer's guild had been making a killing off of the trade; that is, until the undead went on strike and brought the necromancers back to earth. They were seen with mixed feelings, and hated by the necromancers.

Much of Emeralda's support lay in the night guilds. Their closeness to the world of monsters made them hyperaware of the goings on within. No doubt they had already found out about the monster's plan to take over the world from their own sources. The problem would be turning their support into resources.

From the High Guilds—the religious powers that colored much of daily Capital life—Emeralda only saw one: a representative of the Pantheon committee, a minor godling by the name of Justice. He was, in fact, a god of machine oil. Emeralda knew she should be thankful for even this token show of support. The gods did not often trouble themselves with politics. However, all she could manage to do was get infuriated.

Missing were the representatives of the Holy Church and the Monks of the Way; the church didn't involve itself in conflict, due to its strict edicts; and the Monks of the Way tended to keep to themselves. Elyse had met some extremely powerful monks in her long life, and wished that they had come. She had delivered the invitation personally, but wasn't even sure if it had reached their master.

All in all, the higher powers didn't seem very interested in her conflict. No doubt they thought they had more pressing matters to attend to. Perhaps they even did, something so big and mighty that lowly mortals could not deign to understand. Emeralda didn't believe it, though. *They're all just lazy,* she thought.

Next to the god's seats were the seats of the Mechanical guilds, the powers that kept the world running. Arguably, they were more powerful than the High Powers. No one had tested it yet, though, much to the world's relief. Emeralda saw two of the four in attendance: the Steamer's guild and the Dragoon's guild. The Dragoons held much of the world's conventional military power, and the Steamers had constructed much of the infrastructure. They had come only out of curiosity, Emeralda knew. She couldn't expect much from them. *Though, a dragoon army would be nice,* she thought to herself.

The Artisan's guild—representatives of industrial interests—and the skysteel guild—controllers of the world's airways—did not bother to come. Emeralda would have to provide logistics for her army on her own.

Overall, Emeralda did not hope for much from the Mechanicals. She knew where her support lay, and planned to use her time wisely.

Of the Day guilds, the alchemists, the chemists, the scientists, and the magicians had all come. They made it their business to know of everything new, but did not have much power outside their spheres of influence. Emeralda knew the best they could provide was perhaps some advanced technology to help her cause, and a whole lot of research. They did not have the resources to manufacture anything more.

The last three guilds of the city, the Green Bloods, the Monster Tamers, and the Worker's Guild all sat together. Their representatives talked to each other in undertones, probably discussing inter-guild logistics, as they worked together closely. Emeralda banked on pulling their support, as saving the world from monsters was certainly within their interests.

When she had finished surveying all of the assembled guilds, Emeralda pulled upright in her chair and clapped her hands twice. "I now call this seven thousandth, six hundredth and seventy-sixth meeting of the Capital guilds to order, requested by the Disciplinary force of Female Magicians to address the pressing matter concerning the monster's plan to reopen the Centrix."

The quiet whispering in the room died down. The pantheon's representative, Justice, tapped his speaking gavel. Emeralda tapped the assent hammer, given to the guild master that had called the meeting. It was old, with a handle that had seen centuries of use.

Justice spoke. "I propose you change the title, to something more interesting," he said, giving a knowing smile. The room rippled with soft laughter. Justice continued. "Something like committee to save the world from a big hole, and screw over the Capital in the process." Laughter, again, but suppressed.

Emeralda bit back her frustration. She tapped her assent gavel once more, to reply. "You point is taken, divine sir." She almost couldn't finish the formality. She squeezed the gavel hard. "However, my intent is entirely serious, and concerns all humans in this world and those who depend on them," with this, she stared straight at Justice.

Justice shrugged, and began to clean his fingernails.

Emeralda looked around the room. "Do we have any more comments, before I begin?"

Heads shook all around. The room's central light cast small shadows over the table's ornate model terrain. The room felt chilly, as if the air outside had just cooled considerably.

"Then I shall begin," Elyse said. She presented the problem facing the world, of the Centrix and the metal and the monsters taking over mines, but left out the part about Penny and her adventure. She needed an army, but she wasn't about to do anything that could endanger her quest. When she had finished, no one spoke. She could see that most of the guilds, outside the night guilds, did not believe her. If they did, they relegated her problem to the bottom of their lists. All, that is, except for the Green Blood Guild.

The Green Blood-master, Harl Studd, stood up, the traditional signal for support. He tapped his gavel. Emeralda responded with her assent hammer.

"What do you propose to do about this problem?" Studd asked. He seemed genuinely concerned, and Elyse could see that he spoke for his allies, the Monster Tamers and Workers.

The Worker's Union head, Samuel Briggs, tapped his gavel. Emeralda tapped hers. "I must add," he said, his voice thin and reedy in the big room, "I must ask another question. Why have we not known of this before?"

Emeralda waited for a minute, and then responded. "I'll answer your question first, Mr. Briggs. We in the Disciplinary force have known about the Centrix for some time, but only a few weeks ago did we find out about the monster's true intent." Briggs looked satisfied, but only just. Emeralda paused to think for a moment.

She planned to build an army, of course, but it was much easier said than done. She had not told them of her plan because she wanted to present all her reasons for it first, so that she would have the best chances of success. She faltered for a moment. *Do they really look like they want to field an army to fight against some unknown threat?* She asked herself. *Can I really make them believe?* Centuries of experience had taught her that in politics, words were cheap, and deeds were more valuable than gold. *First of course, I have to deal with the problem of information.* She decisively cut her reverie.

"To answer your question Mr. Studd," she said, "I plan to build an army." At her words, rustles of conversation jumped across the room, not all of them good. She continued nonetheless. "I plan to leave in two months, for the edgelands, and past them into the Centrix. The monsters have been building up there, undoubtedly to carry out their plan. I will fight them, and eliminate their presence." She surveyed the room, looking at each present member in turn. "I will take any support that I can get, but let me tell you this: the disciplinary force cannot do this alone."

More murmurs. Emeralda never admitted weakness in her organization. If she had just done it, than it proved that she was serious. Or so she hoped. She could not read any of the reactions, held as they were behind political facades.

The vampire's guild master, Viscous Nem, stood up. "My guild will offer you our help," he said. On one condition. You must help me move homes, as we have been asking you to do for some time."

Emeralda nodded. "I will think about that. Thank you, Mr. Nem."

Samuel Briggs stood up. "The worker's union will offer you our help if you can get the steamer's guild to raise our wages."

Emeralda nodded. She wrote down the request on a piece of paper, next to the guild and the name of the leader.

And so the rest of the meeting went, with Emeralda brokering various agreements with all the guilds that showed their support. Every guild offered their support, of course, as was custom; it was their request for return that showed their true intent. The possibility of the request meant more than the request itself. Eventually, Emeralda finished, having heard only one agreement she thought she might be able to complete: in exchange for her assistance in scouting and classifying new monster types, the Monster Tamer Guild agreed to supply beasts of burden and combat.

As soon as Emeralda had ushered the attendees out of the room, she slumped against the wall.

Now, for the hard part, she thought to herself. *Backroom dealing.* She still had a long road ahead of her.

Beat Up By a Buncha' Little Girls

August

Ruby, Denyse, and Justle faced off against August, Elyse, and Penny, on top of the airship *Firebird*. Air blew lazily around the training field, pushed aside by the ship's wind-blockers. Still, Elyse's shock white hair lifted a little, and Penny's pigtails drifted about.

In the upper left corner of August's vision, the party's status bars hung in the air. They moved whenever he moved, and could always been seen without even a glance. All of the bars were as full as they could be.

Ruby and her girls had the same technology, of course. Linked together, they felt different, more cunning. Ruby stood behind Denyse, the swords-girl, as befitted her healer class. Justle stood between them, off to the side.

All players held training swords, except for Elyse, who held a long piece of rope in one hand. Ruby had allowed buff spells, but no destructive spells. Stamina boosters were also allowed.

August's party waited for Ruby's mark, eyeing their enemies up and down.

I'll take the one with the red hair, August thought to Elyse.

And I'll take the one with the blue, replied Elyse.

August didn't think to communicate anything with Penny.

Ruby gave the signal: a slash down with her sword. The combat began. Denyse and Justle both charged at August, brandishing their swords. Ruby chanted something in the magical language, and their swords moved a little faster. Penny interrupted Ruby with a jab to the side, and began to dance around her return swings. Elyse cracked her whip at Justle, who deftly parried the heavy flinging rope. It was a free-for all, to the pain, until one side admitted defeat. The members of August's party each tried to close in on an individual target, but found that they couldn't. Elyse would find herself with no one to swing at, while Penny would meet the blades of both Justle and Denyse. Ruby darted in and out of grasp, her green dress fluttering as she twirled about; she attacked each of her targets no more than once before darting out and letting another girl take over for her.

Hard pressed to stay on their feet, August's party retreated closer and closer into a circle formation, facing outwards. It seemed as if the attacks were coming from all directions, all at once. August would aim his sword at Denyse only to find Ruby's sword blocking it. Ruby cast buff spells on her team-mates, pumping them up to the point where it was unnatural to fight against them.

Soon, the red bars that signified vitality began to drop. Penny's fell to two-thirds, and then to half, as she barely withstood a triple barrage. August and Elyse found themselves tangled up together, again and again. It was no use trying to communicate, there were too many things all at once. More often than not, Elyse's whip curled around August's shoe, or wrapped around his sword arm just as he was about to strike.

When August finally fell, it was because he tripped over Elyse's rope. He lay on the floor, unable to get back up. His entire body felt as if it had been though a landslide. On their own, Elyse and Penny didn't stand a chance. Soon, all three members lay in a heap, too sore to do more than stare at the sky.

Ruby stood over them. "You did fine, for what you are," she said, her tone that of instructor. "But I see that I have many things to teach you." She bent down to one knee. At this height, August could reach out and pat her head from his position on the floor. He might have, if he had been able to lift his arm more than an inch.

Ruby forced them all to stand. "You are done for today," she said. "Get some rest. No healing. Your bruises need to stay, to teach you how to properly handle pain and hardship."

August turned to his cabin, glad to get even a small respite. Elyse followed him, also at the end of her power. The two entered the room and closed the door behind them. They were too tired to do more than notice each other's thoughts, and soon fell asleep to the drifting motion of the airship.

The next day, August awoke feeling even worse than he had the previous day, if possible. However, his muscles were not as tired as they had been the day before, and with effort, he reported to the training field as soon as the sun had risen over the horizon. Ruby stood there already, with Denyse and Justle. Some of the sailors had come to watch the day's training, their white dresses fluttering in the cool breeze. Ruby wasted no time in beginning, once all three adventurers had arrived.

"Today," she said, "I am going to teach you about proper party combat." She tapped the ground with her training sword. "Individually, you three are powerful. In fact, you may be able to beat me and my team, if we fought one-on-one. However," Ruby lifted up her sword, "You will almost never get a chance to do that. If an enemy offers you one-on-one combat, you have already won." She pointed at each of the three adventurers with her sword. "In real combat, you are not a team." She paused to let it sink in. "You are a single creature, with one mind."

Penny raised her hand. "If we are all one thing, than how are we supposed to communicate?" She asked, voicing the question that August and Elyse had also held.

Ruby nodded towards her. "Good question." She began to pace back and forth in front of the three. "Did you notice me and my party saying anything, perhaps, while we fought?"

August thought about it. He had, in fact, heard them say lots of things, but had attributed it to cursing or grunting. Most of what he had heard was gibberish. "I think so," he said. Elyse and Penny nodded.

Ruby stopped in front of Penny. "Twist," she said.

Without warning, both Denyse and Justle darted forwards, coming in to place next to Penny. Denyse held her sword at Penny's neck, and Justle looked ready to defend her.

August and Elyse reacted, but too slow. The distance between them and Penny was too great.

"In party combat," Ruby began, pacing back and forth once more, "You must always have a plan beforehand. The most effective way to achieve this is with code words: pieces of otherwise meaningless jargon that signify a particular formation or target. You will know your targets, because your clothes-fairy will distinguish them for you, if you ask politely."

Gliss popped out of Penny's skirt-strap. "Yup!" She exclaimed. "If you'd just ask me, I can do lots of things for you."

"Like you'd really be able to handle three people at once." Lester, Ruby's clothes-fairy, stuck out his tongue at Gliss.

Gliss huffed and turned away. "I can do it, and you know it."

Ruby cleared her throat, and continued. "Gliss, if you will show them how it works."

Gliss twirled about, and fluttered, and did other incomprehensible fairy things. She also sparkled, though August wasn't sure that it was necessary. When she stopped, the overlay in Augusts' vision, that had until now been only red and blue bars, gained a new element. Above the head of every person around, there floated a crystal symbol, semi-transparent, not even affecting the light that should have passed through it. Over Penny and Elyse, they were green. Over the sailors watching the training, they were yellow. Over the head of Ruby and her party, they were blue. They symbols were meaningless to August, and even Elyse, who could read quite a few languages.

"You will learn the symbols on your own," Ruby said, once she had seen Gliss had finished. "I've scheduled a study session daily, after your individual training." She raised her sword and pointed near the top of her head. "I am an enemy," she said. "Gliss has labeled me as such, and has also judged my intent to be nonlethal. As such, I am blue." She pointed to them. "The members of your party are green." That much was obvious. "As a general rule, it is good to trust Gliss's observations of people. Fairies are much better judges of intent than humans."

Gliss nodded her tiny head. "That's right!" she said, relishing the praise.

"One more thing," Ruby said, as she turned about on her heels for the hundredth time that morning, "Your party needs a leader. A single person has to issue the commands, the one that has the greatest power of observation. This person must learn to be aware of their members at all times. They must learn how to effectively use them in a tactical situation."

Elsye and Penny looked at August, without hesitating.

Me? August thought. "Me?" He asked out loud. It didn't make sense, to him. Elyse was smarter. Penny was more powerful. He couldn't possibly lead the group.

You have more to you than you think, Elyse said to him. August could feel that she meant it.

"You're a great fighter, August," Penny said, looking up at him with a look of certainty.

"I think they made the right choice," Ruby said, stopping in front of him. August looked down until he met her eyes. "I would have recommended you myself, if they had not," she said. "It is no wonder, either."

August still couldn't believe it. "What have I done?" He asked.

"It's not what you've done," Ruby said, "but what you can do. You are very observant, for a human. Both of your party members trust you wholeheartedly."

August reddened, unsure of what to think. "This means I'll have to come up with all the stuff you talked about, right?"

Ruby shook her head. "That is a job for all of you to decide, on your own." She turned away for a moment, walked back, and then turned towards them again. "Your real training starts now," she said, and she meant it.

The rest of the day, the adventurers in August's party strategized, theorized, and practiced their respective fighting styles. They trained individually, and trained together as well, putting into practice the codes that they had worked out. Some, they found didn't work. Some went off without a hitch. Each time they thought they had it covered, though, Ruby would surprise them with a more complicated play. By the end of the day, August had a new coat of bruises to match the ones from the day before.

August sat on his bunk, in his cabin, reading a book that listed the marker symbols and their meanings. He picked out each letter, and asked Elyse what it meant, determined to try to read. It was slow going, and August soon saw letters swirling all across his vision.

He looked up from his book then, to see Elyse climb down from her bunk and sit next to him. She leaned on his shoulder, and nestled up against him. Her moon white hair fell across his arm, and her black spectacles pressed into his side from where they hung on her coat.

August said nothing, but held her close to him while he tried his best to read.

Secretary of the Gods

Emeralda
Emeralda didn't like what she heard. She stood in the office of the head necromancer, in the process of bargaining with him. She needed his necromancers, since they were the best healers, magical or otherwise, that could be found in the world. However, what he asked was a little over the top.

"You want me to break a strike?!" Emeralda exclaimed, her voice raising just a little. "How do you expect me to do that?"

The Head Necromancer, Jan Tross, folded his arms across his pristine suit. "If you won't do it, that's fine," he stated, with an air of finality. "I don't particularly need your services, and I can most certainly find someone else to help me. But you certainly need mine, do you not?"

Emeralda couldn't argue with it. It was true. That was how business was done in the Capital, one favor for another. As of yet, no one really felt the urgency Emeralda did about the coming monster storm. She supposed it was somewhat her fault for striking pre-emptively, before they did any real damage, letting the guilds and the masses get on with their daily lives like nothing were occurring. But, she knew it was different, this time. She had to stop it, no matter the cost.

"What else do you want from me?" Emeralda asked, looking into the Necromancer's eyes. She had long since learned to compensate for her height with a fiery gaze.

"I want you to investigate the disappearance of one of my company's copper mines," Jan Tross said.

The Necromancer's guild owned most of the dangerous industrial operations in the world. Anything from coal mining to pear diving to steel pouring, their twisted hands dug deep into wherever there was profit, using their necromancy to supply endless undead labor. Recently the undead had formed their own guild, however, and the necromancers were seen to be in decline—it was a source of many problems, including "terrorist" acts like mine sabotage.

"The mine just disappeared?" Emeralda asked. She knew who the head Necromancer suspected, but she was more inclined to believe that it was the work of the monsters, in their driving quest for metal.

The Necromancer nodded sagely. "We would appreciate it if you could uncover the truth."

Emeralda thought for a moment. She could most certainly find out more about the mine, but something smelled, the request seemed too easy. *It's nothing my girls can't handle,* she decided. *I won't get a better deal, anyhow.*

She looked the Head Necromancer in the eyes. "I'll break your strike, and I'll investigate your mines, if you agree to my requests."

Jan Tross steepled his fingers, each fingernail assiduously polished. "My guild would be happy to help you, to an extent."

As custom dictated, the person who was providing help presented their quests first. It was a finicky business, because the nature of their quests revealed the nature of their support: the more difficult their quests, the more support they intended to give, to a point. The system turned on its head when impossible quests were offered. Emeralda had had centuries of experience, though, so she knew what she could ask.

"I need a company of combat-ready healers, ready in a month to begin training," she said. Jan Tross looked as if he had expected it. It was nothing, really: every guild had their reserve of cannon fodder to do the dirty work. Her next request was a bit trickier. "I need a raid of summoners, skilled enough to participate in large-scale combat," she said.

The Head Necromancer clicked his tongue. "I can spare some summoners, but only a single half-raid."

A raid was a unit of warriors, trained together to perform medium-scale operations. They consisted of four groups of six warriors, each with a commanding officer. They were reserved for elite combat units; normal soldiers formed squads, companies, and battalions, all the way up to armies. The only size bigger than a raid was a full-raid: four groups of twelve operatives. A half-raid consisted of four groups of three.

"Are you sure you cannot spare any other raids?" Emeralda asked. "I know of at least two raids that are stationed in your reserve at this moment." She knew she would end up with the half-raid. In fact, it had been what she was aiming for. Her question was simply to put the Head Necromancer at ease, to make him feel as if he had won.

The Head Necromancer leaned forwards, a sickly expression on his face. "I cannot do that, my beautiful princess."

Emeralda shuddered. The Head Necromancer oozed cloying sweetness.

"I must keep some units in reserve," Jan Tross stated, "or do you expect me to empty my barracks, and my coffers, for your unknown enemy?"

"The enemy is very real and present, I assure you," Emeralda said, her voice steely. "But if you must, than I can accept a half-raid. However, be sure you do not thrust upon me some useless baggage of a unit." She turned her fiery gaze up a notch. "I want them well-trained."

"You are bargaining hard, for one who is making the request," Jan Tross said, "but do not worry. The necromancers are not so derived of honor as to sully an agreement." He reached into his desk and pulled out a sheet of parchment and a magical pen. "If you will, Miss Stysh."

"It's General," Emeralda corrected, before taking up the pen. She flicked it over the paper, tracing her signature into the smooth vellum, and rows of writing appeared. Her intent had been preserved legally.

"Very well, General." Jan Tross took up the pen, and signed his name. His hand moved with practiced flourish, ending with a twist that spat magical ink across the desk. The words on the page changed, combining Emeralda's intent with that of his own.

A magical envoy from the High Church, overseer of all contracts, flittered into being above the desk. He fluttered on two wings, somewhat like a fairy except for his ruddy construction and drawn-out stature. He held a ball of magical light in his hands.

"Ah, General," he said, facing Emeralda first. "I see you are still trying to build that army of yours."

"Indeed I am, sir Harl." Emeralda twisted her hand in front of her chest, making the form of a circle. It was the proper greeting for a messenger of the High Church.

"I am sure you two already know what you are getting into," sir Harl said, "so let us begin." He fluttered down and touched the paper, humming as he did so. "It all seems good," he said after a while. "No unknown intent has been declared."

Both of the men in the room fiddled while sir Harl conducted his rounds. Despite his stature, he had extreme power. Naturally, he was of divine origin, but even so his mortal power brought tension into all who fell under it.

"I think we're okey-dokey." sir Harl fluttered back up into the air. "You first, General."

Emeralda knew what to do. "I, General Emeralda Stysh, head of the Disciplinary Force of Female magicians, now agree to the terms of this contract with Jan Tross, head of the Necromancer's Guild."

Sir Harl simply nodded, and a little ball of light appeared around him. He turned and repeated the process with Jan Tross. When they were finished, he checked the contract one last time. "All right, I have the go-ahead from my superiors," he said. "Like always, be careful, and honor your contracts." He snapped up the paper in a whirlwind, leaving behind a dry, inked copy, written in the divine hand. Then, he disappeared back into oblivion.

Their business finished, Emeralda and Jan said their farewells. Emeralda left the office, and began to climb the deep staircase that led to the Necromancer's surface operations. When she finally opened the door onto the main street where the building stood, sunlight streaked onto her face and made her blink. Her dress-fairy,

June, fluttered awake for a moment to look at the sunlight and the bustling street with her.

"You did a nice job, Emerald," June said. She was the only one who called her by that name. "I'm sure, at this rate, we'll get that army in no time."

"We'll see, June," was all Emeralda said, as she stepped into the street. June disappeared back into Emeralda's dress.

Emeralda didn't get far before a figure with a long white cloak and crazy hair hailed her. "General!" She called, clearly in a hurry.

Emeralda approached her, and recognized her as the sub-head of the Scientists' Guild. "What is it, Scarlet?" She asked.

Scarlet took a moment to catch her breath. She had been running hard, it seemed. When she finally got up, she brought Emeralda good news. "Our guild has something for you," she said. "A present."

You Have Learned a New Spell

August

The day after their first day of party training, August, Elyse, and Penny stood before Ruby, in the center of the training field, ready to learn about magical combat. Until now, Ruby had only taught them how to fight with weapons. Just like with normal fighting, though, the basics of magical combat changed drastically in party-based combat.

"Magical potential is based on two things," Ruby said, as she tapped her sword on the dusty floor. The *Firebird's* crewwomen had made a habit of coming to see the adventurer's train, and some sat now in the rigging above the field. The colorful ribbons on their sailor uniforms flowed about like pennants. "The first thing," Ruby continued, "is intelligence." She looked at Elyse. "A person's intelligence is the speed at which their mind can process information. It is more than that, as well, but the only thing that direct magic usage requires out of your mind is the capacity to think fast and store information."

Elyse nodded her head. She already knew this, and Ruby knew it as well. Ruby's speech was for the benefit of everyone there: the subject was new to August, and to Penny as well, he saw.

"Magical spells are written, much like a book is," Ruby said. "They are complex, and all but the most practiced of mages cannot even hope to design their own spell. Instead, regular mages use spells that are imprinted in their mind, beneath their consciousness. These spells are 'unlocked', so to speak, with keywords that vary from mage to mage. A high intelligence allows a faster retrieval of spells, and thus a lower casting time; as well as the ability to store more spells. A low intelligence is a burden to the retrieval of stored spells, and puts limits on how many complex spells a person can store in their mind."

Elyse spoke up. "The method of spell storage was developed five hundred years ago, by sir Danievel Loris," she said. "It is the only reliable method of using magic in daily life, and far better than its predecessor, the scroll book."

Ruby nodded her head, following Elyse's explanation. "I see," she said. "It is always good to know the origin of your tools. Thank you, Elyse."

Elyse looked down. August felt her embarrassment at being praised.

"It's no problem," she murmured.

Ruby continued from where she had left off. "The second thing that affects magic usage is a measure of the amount of energy one can release from their body at any single instant. Since we are always releasing a small amount of energy to supplement out daily interactions with people, this measure is called Charisma. A high charisma allows people to release more energy into day-to-day interactions, and thus become more successful at communicating. As you probably have guessed, a good ability to release energy is also critical to the use of magic."

Ruby paused, to let what she had said sink in. "Unlike intelligence, which is fixed, Charisma can be increased through training, just as muscles can increase in strength when used."

Elyse spoke up again. "Intelligence can also be raised, with the right potions," she said. "I know of one that can do the trick."

Ruby nodded to her. "Again, thank you, Elyse. If you don't mind, I would like to see this potion sometime."

Elyse looked shy. "Well, you see, the ingredients are..."

Ruby tapped the ground a little harder, irritated by Elyse interruptions. "We can talk about this afterwards," she said. "For now, let's get some things done."

Elyse backed away, chastised. August felt her, then, wanting to help and not knowing how to do it. *Hey*, he thought to her, *if you have anything you want to tell people, I'll listen.*

Thanks, Elyse replied.

"The point I am making," Ruby said, "is that you need these two skills to use magic properly. However, there is much more than just skills to magic usage."

Here, she said a few words to herself, and a white ball of crackling plasma appeared in her hands. "When in a group," she said, hoisting her arm up, "you need to learn how to cast as a group." The ball dissipated into little droplets that swarmed all around Penny, August, and Elyse. "I have just cast a spell of protection around you." She turned to Elyse. "I'll teach it to you now." She held out her hand, and a light emitted from it. Elyse held out hers as well, and the two linked hands. They both took on a surreal glow, Elyse's translucent skin lighting up from the inside. When the transaction was finished, they stepped away from each other.

Elyse looked at her arm. "Protection," she said, her voice cutting through the breezy air. A plasma ball appeared in her hands, just like in Ruby's. She released it into a million droplets. Instead of forming around August and Penny, however, they flew up into the rigging and coated two of the watching sailors.

They giggled and poked at each other. "You'll do better next time," one said, who had a green ribbon on her chest. The other just looked down and smiled.

Elyse sagged, disappointed. She had expected it to work out better.

"It's ok," Ruby said. "I am well aware of the fact that magic users often prefer solitude."

Elyse didn't feel any better, despite the consolation. August didn't know how to help her.

"The only thing you can do is try again," Ruby said, her voice sweet on the cool air.

And so Elyse tried again, and again, until she could cover exactly who she wanted with the protective little droplets. The instant she did, Ruby gave her another spell, and then another. She gave Penny some spells too: spells that healed, spells that made muscles stronger, spells that made feet faster. They both worked and worked until their energy had been completely exhausted. August watched as their blue magica bars dwindled down to nothing.

"I'm going to give you a spell too," Ruby told August.

"I'm not good at this," August said. "I don't think I have a high Intelligence or a high Charisma." It was no use protesting, though, for Ruby stood in front of him, her feet planted, looking up at August with demanding eyes that brokered no argument.

"All right, I'll try," he said, as he called out the keyword. It was a heal spell, minor, that didn't draw too much of his magical strength. On his first try, the spell went out of control and healed every hangnail on the ship, and some of the paper-cuts. His second try was just as successful as the first.

Soon, though, he had the hang of it, and could heal some of his party member's ailments with just a word. He felt powerful, even though he knew it was just a small spell. Magic had always seemed like a far-off world to him. Now, though, he was a part of that world, and would make use of it to help save the world.

Ruby stood them in a row when they had depleted their energy. "Your energy will take time to recharge," she said. "In that time, I want you to come up with ten new strategy code words involving the use of magic, and have them memorized."

August groaned. Maybe knowing magic wasn't so terrific after all.

Science!

Emeralda

Geovanni Carlini—head of the science guild—stood with General Emeralda Stysh and Scarlet Mayberl in a laboratory near the Capital's center. Geovanni was bending his head underneath some huge contraption, that reached up to the ceiling and poked through a hole in the wall which looked as if it had been constructed with a hammer. It probably had, considering who built the thing.

After a long moment of shuffling and clinking, Guildmaster Geovanni backed out from underneath, his face covered in soot and oil. "Ahh, Emeralda," he said, as soon as he saw her standing before him. "I have something to show you." He puttered over to a table in the middle of the room, clean except for a strange looking hairband.

He was a tall man, made shorter by his hunchbacked demeanor and shuffling walk. He wore thick rimmed spectacles, and his hair had the same frizzy, shocked appearance that most active members of the science guild boasted. He wore a dirty white lab coat, almost black with white spots now. He had a kindly countenance.

"What is it?" Emeralda asked, looking closer at the strange hairband.

Guildmaster Geovanni pointed at it, looked as if he were about to say something, and then stopped. He turned to Scarlet, his second-in-command. "What did I decide to name it, again?" he asked. Clearly, he did not remember.

Scarlet sighed as if it were something she did every day, which it probably was. "The Extreme Telekenetter Chassis, sir," she said, biting the name audibly.

Guildmaster Geovanni nodded his head up and down in a bobbin-like motion. "Yes, yes, a genius name, if I may say so myself."

"Right, sir," Scarlet said, her voice betraying her true thoughts about it.

"Ah, Scarlet, where would I be without you?" Geovanni said, in a reminiscent tone. "My best student, I don't ever think I'll be able to thank you enough."

Scarlet reddened. "Sir," she said, her voice thick with embarrassment. "We have a visitor."

Emeralda looked almost straight up, at Guildmaster Geovanni. The Guildmaster looked around the room, confused.

"At your feet, sir," Scarlet said, now guarded.

Emeralda cleared her throat, a big loud noise that did not fit her image at all. Geovanni started, and then looked down at her. "Why, if it isn't Emeralda!" He exclaimed.

Emeralda was used to his antics, by now. Three hundred years of dealing with scientists had made her very patient. Scarlet rolled her eyes.

"I have something to show you," he said, motioning to the table.

Emeralda peered over the edge, her eyes just crossing the top. This time, she waited for him to explain.

"I call it the Extreme Telekeneter Chassis," he said, proudly. "It utilizes Finschneive's theory of auratical interfration to seize incoming Gronel waves and relate them into the Netherwata."

Emeralda waited for Scarlet to translate.

"He means it blocks mind control," Scarlet said, in a dead tone.

Emeralda's eyes lit up with a bright fervor. "Does it block all metal communication?" she asked, her interest now piqued.

"I suppose it does," Guildmaster Geovanni said. "It blocks a lot of other things too, including mether-infractions and glossery vibrations."

"Attacks by the metherwerry and the evil aura of night forests," Scarlet translated. She did her job well, though her voice just sounded tired.

"Is this your gift?" Emeralda asked.

"Indeed," Geovanni answered. "You may use the design as you see fit."

"But we do not have the capabilities to produce any more than a few," Scarlet added, "so you will have to contract with the Steamers, or perhaps the Artisans."

Emeralda nodded. That would be easy. Manufacturing contracts with those two guilds were common and cheap, making things being their sole purpose of existence. Some silver bullion would do fine.

"And what do I have to do for you, in return?" Emeralda asked, wary of the catch.

"Nothing!" Guildmaster Geovanni exclaimed. "Er, I think," he added. He looked towards Scarlet.

"This is a research project into telecommunications," Scarlet said, "So we need large-scale amounts of data. If you would be so kind as to record the performance of the device, and allow one of our researchers to accompany you..."

"That will be fine," Emeralda said, without hesitation. A crucial piece of battle armor for some research data was a good price.

The two scientists nodded, and looked at each other. "It's yours," Geovanni said, as he picked the hairband, gleaming silver, off the table and handed it to her. Emeralda took it and stared at it. It felt unnaturally heavy, as if it were absorbing all kinds of things that she couldn't even imagine.

"Here are the plans," Scarlet said, handing Emeralda a storage crystal. "They're in standard notation, so you should be able to translate this right into production. We've even come up with the manner of mass-production."

Geovanni nodded his agreement. "Parallel Doxman converters, combined with—"

Scarlet cut him off with a hand wave. "You have things to do now, correct?" She asked. Geovanni's eyes lit up, and he turned to his machine.

"My nethermeter!" he cried, forgetting all about Emeralda in his excitement.

Emeralda was content to leave then, with the hairband. Scarlet gave her an apologetic smile as she walked out of the room.

Back on the street, Emeralda fell to thinking. *What's the best way to bust a strike?* she asked herself, determined to fulfill the necromancer's contract. She filed away the hairband in her dress, making a note to tell her procurement officer about it. She would get it sorted.

Emeralda's vast hoard of experience included many things, but one thing it did not include was anything on the subject of strike busting. Complicating matters was the fact that it was an undead strike, led by the undead worker's guild. Since its formation 12 years ago, it had stirred up more trouble in the world than all the other guilds combined.

Emeralda could understand, of course. The years after the vampire guild split from the were-wolves' guild were troublesome, for a new guild was never truly welcome. That was 200 years ago, and this was now.

Emeralda stopped where she was standing, in the middle of a market street. More beasts than machines roamed about, telling of the area's low economic status. Street vendors prowled about on four-legged bucklers, the beasts' flat backsides supporting their wares. An ornithopter flapped past overhead.

I should go see the strike, at least, Emeralda thought to herself. She changed course and headed to the industrial district, near the edges of the Capital's circle. The brick and wood houses that lined the streets soon turned to stone and reinforced concrete. Smokestacks rose in the distance. The air grew heavy, and stung with each breath.

Industry was a relatively new thing in the world. When Emeralda had first founded the Disciplinary force—through a fiasco involving the Pantheon Gods—the world had been much more sedentary. Machines had not yet turned into the driving force they were, skyships had not been invented—or at least, the proper construction techniques had been long lost—and the Capital had still been open to the outside world.

It's all magic's fault, Emeralda complained, after inhaling a particularly heady aroma of burnt cinders and unknowable chemicals.

Magic had powered machines, and machines had powered magic, creating a cycle that changed the face of the land.

Emeralda came to a junction in the middle of the industrial sector, where hundreds of heavily-laden beasts and machines roved to and from filled with all manner of things. The air stank of sulphur and saltpeter and brimstone. Emeralda felt pity for those forced to work here, where the stale Capital air did nothing to remove the pallid miasma that hung all around.

Emeralda heard a commotion. The traffic on the road sped up, or turned around, clearing the center of the road. The battered dirt street soon stood empty, and the beasts and machines on the side of the road muttered and clanked and roared to produce a dissonant cachaphony.

From the direction of the magical sky, from the outskirts of the Capital's circle, there came a chanting and a stomping of feet to match that of any army. Emeralda felt the ground beneath her feet begin to shake, and then she saw the flags, flapping over the tops of the factories and between the pallid smokestacks. Written on them were slogans: "We are not Zombies", "Death do not us part", "Live free, die free", "Death is an illusion", and more things like that.

Then Emeralda saw the first of the marchers, undead workers who might have been the leaders, though it was hard to tell. They showed almost no decomposition. They had probably been resurrected with their entire brains intact, minutes after they died. Then, behind them, came more undead workers, the skilled ones, the ones that only somewhat kept their brains. Some of them had no arms, or walked on crutches, their usefulness having been stripped from them by industrial accidents. Emeralda saw bone through their stumps.   Only whole humans were raised by Necromancers, the ones broken afterwards cast aside like toys.

In the defense of the Necromancers, they really did theorize undead were like machines, until they began to talk back and protest. Emeralda didn't like to take sides on issues like this. However, she had a job to do.

As she called in for her support teams, the skilled laborers made way for the thralls, the undead that had been reanimated months after death. These could barely think for themselves, their brains mostly having been rotted away. They were still human, however, and acted like them. It was when all the brain was rotted that a reanimated corpse became a zombie, though the threshold was vague and hadn't been formally decided yet. Most of the time the undead were judged by how much they acted, as well as whether or not they were able to understand abstract concepts.

The thralls marched past, row after row, waving banners like spears. The working workers—both human and undead—stood at the side of the road and occasionally jeered or offered cries of support. For the most part, though, they stayed quiet.

Emeralda didn't like what she was seeing. The power contained within those angry dead men was enough to shake the entire city. Even with the power of her organization, she couldn't see how she could stop an army like that.

An idea came to her, then. *They want something,* she realized. *Every army wants something, and this army is no exception.* She thought for a moment, trying to see what it was. If the workers had been human, it would have been obvious. Food, shelter, higher wages, things that living people needed. However, with dead people, it was a little different.

Emeralda decided to ask. She walked up to the nearest marcher, and kept in step with him. She tugged at his shirt to get his attention, and her hand came away slimy. *Ew,* she thought, as she wiped her hand on her dress. She knew she would get it from June—her dress-fairy—later, but she didn't care.

The man took notice of her. He only had half of a jaw, and his eyes held a glazed expression. "What'owan?" he asked, his voice almost unintelligible.

Emeralda understood it to be "What do you want." "Do you know where your leaders are?" She said, in careful English.

The man nodded yes. Apparently, his ears had not been damaged. "E'oreare" he said, as he pointed towards the front of the long column, a mile away.

Emeralda thanked the man, who kept staring at her as she ran ahead of the marchers. She jumped up the side of a building with ease, and took to the rooftops to shorten her journey. Ahead, the marchers had turned at the end of the industrial sector, not crazy enough to try to march through the business district. Yet, anyways, and Emeralda was thankful for that.

Up and over the roofs she jumped, her feet pattering on the slate tiles that often topped the warehouses and foundries. She deftly dodged around the forest of smokestacks, blazing hot from the fires beneath them. Her dress billowed out as she vaulted over alleys.

Soon, she came upon the street where the front of the column marched. She ran alongside it, hopping over the side streets that joined with it, her long jumps made all the more impressive by her size. Soon, she had reached the head.

June popped up on her shoulder. The wind fluttered in her winds, and her hair flowed around her back like a pennant. "You have a call from Sergeant Lansey," she said, her high voice mixing with the voices of the protesters.

Sergeant Lansey was the Operative Emeralda had called in to assist her. Lansey had under her command three privates, and was quite young for an officer of her rank. "Patch her in," Emeralda said, still keeping pace with the head of the column.

Emeralda heard a hiss of magical static as the fairies connected. In her heads-up display, Sergeant Lansey's name and rank appeared, underneath a little animated talking face. June had drawn it long ago, and Emeralda had never gotten around to telling her to remove it. It just made sense, somehow.

"General," a voice said, as if it were right in Emeralda's ear. It was Lansey. "I've reached the point you pointed us towards, but I don't see you anywhere."

"I'm near the edge of the industrial sector, next to the business sector," Emeralda said. "I'm following the head of the marchers, now."

"Yes ma'm." Lansey stayed on call, but Emeralda knew she would soon arrive.

Now, she thought, *how to stop the column?*

She kept pace with them as she thought, now slowed down to a walk over the tops of the foundries. She surveyed the front marchers. Their eyes gleamed with intelligence, just like a living human. Most of them had minor injuries, but none of them sported gaping holes or conspicuous missing limbs like the marchers behind. Emeralda knew she should probably talk to one of the leaders in a more peaceable location, but the Head Necromancer had been clear: break the strike. There was no room for maneuvering. She had to stop the column, or forfeit her contract.

First, she tried communication. She jumped back down onto the street, taking a produce peddler and a tailor leading a giant silkworm by surprise. The silkworm spat out little bands of silk, startled. Emeralda apologized, and then ran apace with the column. When she leveled with the first row, she switched to her long stride, an effortless walk that matched the speed of even the tallest man. It had taken her years to perfect, one of the many things she was proud of.

The marcher closest to her looked down, noticing her. "May I help you?" He asked, his voice surprisingly gentle. The only thing that told of his death were the pallid bags beneath his eyes, and his ghostly skin.

"I want to talk to your leader," Emeralda said, grateful that she did not have to try to get his attention.

The marcher thought for a moment, and then looked down at her, without losing his place in the column. "You're speaking to him," he said, in a civilized tone. "I am Horis Meribed, master of the Undead Union. I will ask again: how may I help you?" He spoke as if he were addressing a fellow conspirator, an honored comrade.

Despite her guardedness, Emeralda was surprised. She did not expect the undead to be so civil. In contrast, the master of the Human Workers Union seemed crass. "I am looking for a way to stop this strike," Emeralda said. She had planned to wait for a moment, but the man's civility had led her to state her intentions. It was not as if she minded, however. It wasn't often that she got to converse with people that treated her with respect.

Stop thinking about that, Emeralda commanded herself. *You're not a little girl anymore! You're older than any of these people!* Even so, she became painfully obvious of the stares directed at her. A little girl in a dress conversing with undead strikers was not a common sight.

"I do apologize, miss," Horis said, his voice sincere, "but we cannot halt our operations, not while our goal is in sight."

Emeralda had expected as much. "What is your goal?" She asked. They wanted something, of course. But even with all the slogans around her, even knowing what she did, she did not know what it was. It was as if the leaders of the Undead Union did not want the world to know.

"Our goal is the integration of our society to contain those on both sides of the stelean chasm," Horis said, seriously.

A fine goal, Emeralda thought. He had even mentioned the Stelean chasm, named so after the burial monuments erected in ancient times, and coined by the Union. *But it's too vague,* she thought. Something like that was a long term goal, taking generations to complete. Emeralda had seen it before.

"I know you probably won't answer me," Emeralda said, "but I want to know what the goal of this strike is."

Horis seemed to contemplate, his head bobbing as he took ever-so awkward steps. "I think we would be content to be seen in a new light," he said, finally.

Emeralda came to a realization. *What if it's not that they can't tell of their goal?* She asked herself. When she thought of it, she became more certain. *What if they do not truly know, themselves?* They were not only a new guild, they were also a new life form, invented in the past century. The Human Workers Union also went on strike in their manner, with marches and slogans and banners. Perhaps they were only copying them? The turmoil involved in knowing that they were new in this world, that was so old . . .

"I can give you a purpose," Emeralda said, and almost regretted saying it. Almost. Her idea would probably change the face of the known world.

The Undead Union master stumbled a bit, finally interested in what she had to say. "And who are you to be claiming such, miss?"

Emeralda drew herself up to her full height, matching Horis's stride inch for inch. "I am Emeralda Stysh, General of the Disciplinary Force of Female Magicians," she stated, doing her best to be confident. Introductions were crucial, after all.

Horis took it in, turning it over in his countenance. He seemed to decide something. "Very well, Ms. Stysh. I shall listen to your argument." He reached into his pocket and pulled out a flag. It was red, small enough to fit in his coat, but on a long, telescoping stick. He waved it about his head, the fabric fluttering limply in the stale Capital air. Soon, the other head marchers had taken up the signal. It rippled down the column, until it disappeared around a bend. The marchers slowed, pell-mell, some bumping into those who stood in front. Soon, though, the marchers had stopped.

Well, that was easy, Emeralda thought.

"I wish to hear your argument now, Ms. Stysh," the Undead Union's master said. All around them, the throng of people, animals, and machines that had been halted due to the column started up again, skirting the edges. People did not linger long, for there were many things to attend to in the Capital.

Emeralda head a voice in her ear. It was Lansey, calling to report in.

"We've found you," she said. Emeralda spotted a girl in a red dress darting though the crowd, followed by two girls in blue dresses and one in a bright pink dress. They made quite a show, pushing their way through marchers and spectators. They soon stood next to Emeralda, panting had after their flight. "We await your orders, ma'am."

Emeralda felt sorry for them, as she realized that she no longer needed their help. Unless the column started again, which she hoped to prevent.

"Ms. Stysh?" Horis interrupted their rendezvous.

"Right," Emeralda said, and turned to Horis. Quite a few people, and quite a few marchers as well, stared in her direction. She felt the pressure building.

"Have you ever considered being warriors?" She asked, wrapping her hands behind her back.

Meanwhile . . .

August

A week passed by, after August and his party learned about magic, in which they did nothing but train. Ruby was creative with her regimen, thinking up crazy ideas to force them to bond together as closely as possible. She locked them in August's bunk, one day, and forced them to sit and listen to each other's breathing for three hours. She made them hold each other out over the side of the airship, with only their own strength and faith keeping them from a doom three thousand feet below. She fought them with her own party, again and again. August's entire body protested at the beating.

His mind did as well, what with the massive amounts of learning that Ruby crammed into his head. Being the leader, he had to memorize all of the code phrases, know where they should be applied, and think up new ones, all while learning how to read and cast magic. It was a nightmare that he only survived through Elyse's help. She became a part of him, almost as much as he was himself, and he felt empty whenever they would get too far away from each other. Her sarcastic observations and dry sense of humor were never far, and August enjoyed it.

Penny took to the training like a fish to water, especially the team-building exercises. She soon knew the exact dimensions of August and Elyse, and everything there was to know about their movement patterns. She used the information well, as she cast spells that amplified their strengths and supported their weaknesses.

On the tenth day out of the Capital, the crewwoman in the mast spotted a large column of smoke. The captain talked with Ruby, and the two decided that they should investigate. The three adventurers bustled about their morning training with vigor, as it would be the first time in over a week that they had stopped.

In his cabin, August polished his skysteel sword, marveling at the jade glimmer that it gave off under light. Elyse sat in her bunk, above August's, and watched him, her hand supporting her cheek. Her pink eyes glowed softly in the lamplight.

It's been nice, you know, Elyse thought, breaking the comfortable silence. Of course, the only sound in the air was still the scraping of August's grindstone.

What do you mean? August asked. His entire body ached. His mind had felt as if it would burst at any minute for some time now.

I mean, you're getting stronger, right? Elyse nursed something beneath her words, something aching.

Yes, I guess so. August couldn't deny it. Lately their matches with Ruby's party had gone from total mismatch to simple overpowerment. Not that it was much of an improvement.

And, you're getting to know us better, Elyse thought. She was hinting at something, but it was so subtle, that August couldn't pick it up.

You and Penny, right? August thought. *I'm pretty sure I can tell you two apart from anyone alive by your sounds, scent, even the way you breathe.* Elyse's scent was a little like a spice of some sort, perhaps paprika, dampened by the thick leathery aroma of her coat. It stuck to her, even when she undressed, which was seldom.

I once drank too much of a strength potion, which had some paprika in it, Elyse explained. *It kind of just stuck, and now even my sweat smells spicy.*

August had never thought to ask. *You are an interesting person,* he thought.

How interesting? She asked. The question felt very important. August could feel her eyes on her, even though he faced the wall.

Do I have to say? August replied. *Interesting enough for me to enjoy being with you.*

Elyse's mood brightened at his reply, but something still searched within her. *I . . .* She held back something. August could feel it, in the deepest part of her mind.

I love you, you know that? Elyse spoke it all at once, a torrent breaking through a dam. She caught her breath. August heard it as well as if it had been a train whistle. Her breathing patterns were imprinted in his mind.

August stopped sharpening his sword, and placed it gently back on the table. He took out his scabbard, checked it for rips, and then placed it next to his sword. He turned to Elyse and met her gaze. She wore only her undershirt, her coat shed in the humid atmosphere through which they had been traveling for the past few days. She held her arms wrapped around her knees, in her high bunk, her shock white hair falling around them, the bright red streak over her left side. August saw that she was pretty, then, like a picturesque drawing.

He gazed into her rose red eyes. *I love you too,* he said, and he meant it.

Elyse smiled.

Nothing else was said in that room for a while longer.

It's Got a Gutter. On Its Back.

On the ground, August took a look at the scene that surrounded him. A village, that surrounded a mine of some sort. The houses stood empty, deserted, half of them still burning from what must have been an invasion. However, not a single soul could be seen. Carts full of ore sat untouched, left where they had been dropped by their pushers. Only one body lay on the ground, in the middle of the courtyard, next to the water pump. He looked to be a miner.

August, Penny, and Elyse walked through the wreckage, taking everything in. Behind them, Ruby and her party circled the other way around the village, while a party of four sailors searched the area around the ship.

"This must be one of the metal mines that was taken," Ruby said, through her fairy-comm. Gliss had managed to patch August and Elyse into the system, literally. They each wore a piece of fairy-dress, sewn into their shoulders. They had also acquired ranks, since becoming members of the Disciplinary force, and the patches would have displayed them, if they had not been lowly privates.

August had mixed feelings about it all, but didn't complain. It worked. "I don't see any monsters here," August said in an open channel, "but there should be, considering the fact that they took the mine for the metal."

"Maybe there's a different explanation," Penny said, her voice cheerful despite the desolation that surrounded them. "Maybe it wasn't monsters."

"You could be right," Elyse said. "There aren't that many bodies, after all. You would expect more after a monster attack."

"But remember what happened to Penny's village," August pointed out. "There were no bodies there, either."

"True," Ruby said, "But in any case, be on your guard."

That much was obvious. August entered a house, no more than a hovel, really, and searched it for clues. No dice. He moved to the next one, joining the others in a systematic search. Nothing else was revealed, no bodies other than the one in the courtyard, only evidence that the place had been left in a hurry. In one house, a meal sat, undisturbed. In another, a bathtub still held warm water, mine dust floating in it as a reminder of the person who had been using it until recently.

When they had finished checking the houses, they gathered in the courtyard, around the body of the miner. Ruby examined it, having trained in necromancy sometime during her 200 years.

"It's fresh," she said, "no more than a few hours old. I could resurrect it to interrogate him, but I fear that whatever killed him might have damaged the brain beyond repair."

It was true, the man had died from a blunt object to the face. His broken teeth gazed out in a wicked smile, underneath what was left of his face. Bits of broken skull poked out near his cheekbones.

Penny turned away, and threw up onto the floor. Elyse almost followed her, but kept herself together.

I'm an adult, I'm an adult, I'm an adult, Elyse repeated to herself. August put his arm around her, unable to do anything to help her.

Ruby did not so much as blink. With a sigh, she closed the body's one intact eyelid, and looked towards the airship. "I don't think we—"

A harsh, guttural cry cut her off. It came from the direction of the mine, just off the center of the village.

Everyone turned, to see a pair of gutterbacks crawling out of the entrance, surrounded by ganglers. Two miners followed them, linked together by crude wooden chains.

Gutterbacks were humanoids of epic proportions, head and shoulders taller than a tall man, and utterly stupid to boot. They got their name from the jagged plates of armor that sprouted from their backs and chests, that were said to smell worse than a gutter in the Capital on a hot day. The ganglers that surrounded them were much more nimble, and numerous.

Nothing moved for a split second, in which both sides surveyed the other. Then, the ganglers began to run. The gutterbacks followed, their footsteps pounding the hard packed earth.

August reacted instinctively. Above each of the monsters, an icon floated, colored a deep, crimson red. Gliss had deemed them hostile. They were listed as monsters 1-11, with the gutterbacks being first. August took this into account as he prepared to issue commands. He needed to react in a split second, as the tides of battle changed. Penny and Elyse were depending on him. His first command was to separate from Ruby's party, in order to split their opponents into two groups. Ruby made the same decision, and soon they faced the monsters at an angle.

Monsters 1, 3, 5, 7, and 10 charged at August's party, their icons keeping pace with their movements. The gutterback's footfalls brought up tufts of dirt waist high.

August spoke a series of codewords. To Ruby's credit, they were put into effect instantly. Penny cast a layer of protective spells, Elyse brought out Instrator. They both stood their ground as the monsters approached.

"Stand your ground if you can," Ruby had told them, when speaking of fighting. "The more still you are, the less likely the charging enemy will be able to change course when you suddenly move aside."

August saw this put into practice, and as he curved around the side of a charging gangler, sword raised, he reflected on the wisdom. He brought it down with a slash. Number 7's icon flickered, and then disappeared.

August had not lost track of Penny and Elyse. Using all of his senses—the sound of their breathing, what he saw of them, their footfalls, the warmth of Instrator and the slight flutter of Penny's dress—he surveyed the battle as he participated in it. Elyse lashed a gangler in half, but not before catching her arm on its spear. She stumbled, biting through the pain. August noticed the change in her breathing, and gave Penny a code-word. Penny, jolted out of her duel with the gutterback, flipped under its feet for a moment and cast a healing spell. A second later Elyse rejoined the fight. Instrator cut through yet another gangler. 3 and 5 had fallen, leaving only 1, the gutterback, and 10, the last gangler, one that looked a little tougher than the rest. It carried a stone axe, unlike most of the monster monkeys.

August gave the codes: kill the gangler first, avoiding the gutterback for now. Penny he told to keep it occupied. He knew that it would require all three of them to kill.

Penny, reaching only up to the gutterback's knees, cut an almost comical figure as she rolled around, trusting her luck to keep her from being stepped on. The gutterback became more and more frustrated, as it tried again and again to stomp her into a pancake, only to fail at the last minute.

August slashed at the last gangler. It defended itself well, though, using its axe to make crude parries. However, it couldn't defend against two fronts. Elyse looped behind it and sliced its head off with a masterful flick of her whip.

She stood still for a moment, and smiled at August. "We're doing it," she said.

August nodded. At that moment, a crash erupted from behind August. He turned to see Penny and the gutterback rolling about inside the wreckage of a hovel.

"Help!" Penny cried, forgetting to use the code-word for distress. August and Elyse ran to her aid. The monster's icon twirled about in the wreckage, almost as if it were a part of the monster itself. August saw Penny's vitality bar take a hit. Luck was no good, if you were crushed underneath a half-ton of flesh.

August glanced at Elyse. They needed no code-words to form a strategy. Elyse lashed Instrator at the gutterback, but instead of attempting to cut it in half, she caught it around the middle. The fiery whip sizzled as it fought with the gutterback's foul armor. Elyse yanked with all her might, and the gutterback whipped up into a standing position. Penny appeared in the rubble beneath it, dazed, but okay.

The gutterback gripped at Instrator, clawing at it even as it ate through its massive paws. It howled with rage, and charged straight for Elyse. August was prepared, however, and jumped in front of it. The monster did not slow down. Just as it was about to hit him, August sidestepped and gripped a piece of its foul-smelling plate. It was hard, and yet spongy. A disgusting thing that could not have made a better handhold. August gripped its back, and, as it chased down Elyse, plunged his sword into its neck. His arms struck against Instrator, the fiery tendrils singing them with a hiss. He felt no pain, at first. Then his world exploded into a cachaphony of noise.

He fell off the gutterback just as it plowed into the ground, shouting every curse word that he knew. The place where he had touched the whip was charred black, like overcooked steak.

Elyse ran to his side, spouting apologies as she pulled a potion out of her coat. "I'm sorry, I'm sorry, I'm sorry!" she shouted, pressing the potion against August's lips.

August almost couldn't drink it, his arms hurt so much. His teeth gritted involuntarily. But, once the magical liquid reached his stomach, his blood felt as if it were made of liquid gold, and the burn pain gradually subsided. Soon, his arms looked as good as new, albeit a little pink.

"Whatever that stuff is," August said, as he inspected his arms, "I think I've fallen in love with it."

Elyse kissed him, dropping down to the ground. "Of course you have," she said, when she came back up. "I invented it."

Ruby and her party finished off the last of the ganglers just then. It hit the floor with a wet thwack, its crude stone spear rolling out of its open hands. The body of the gutterback that they had fought lay half in the town well. The other half hung over the cobblestones, covered in layer of fine frost. The rest of the gangler bodies lay strewn about.

The miners that had been held captive huddled in a corner, between two hovels closest to the mine. They flinched when August and his party approached. Ruby's party entered the mine, to search for more monsters, and if possible, survivors.

August looked over the miners, but stepped back in shock when he saw that they had both been mortally wounded. Gaping holes had been torn in their shirtless bodies, pieces of flesh hanging off like ripe fruit. One of them had a hole in his cheek though which his teeth, surprisingly white, showed. Their eyes widened as Elyse and Penny moved closer.

They're just undead, Elyse thought. *Nothing to worry about.*

Right, August replied. *Just undead.*

He took another look at them and realized they were much more afraid than he was. This eased his tension a bit. He squatted down next to the one with the hole in his cheek. "I'm August," he said, "And this is Elyse," he gestured at her, "And Penny." Penny nodded and smiled.

The undead miners' eyes flickered from person to person. August did his best to look non-threatening. "What happened here?" He asked.

The other undead worker, who had pieces of flesh hanging from his chest, freshly torn, responded. He seemed a bit more in control of himself. "They were taking us prisoner," he said. "I don't know why, but they didn't kill anyone but Rill over there." He motioned to the body.

"Was Rill alive?" August asked, and regretted it when he got a harsh scolding from Elyse.

Be polite, she said. *Undead are alive too, technically.*

August saw his mistake. However, the undead seemed not to have noticed.

"Rill was one of us," the calm one said. "The monsters bashed him right in the head, they knew how to put him down, right after he started going crazy. Babbling on about the end of the world or somesuch."

August took it in without flinching. It was part of the end of the world, after all. The monsters were going to create some sort of machine to bring about doomsday. It had to do with metal, August knew, but he couldn't understand why they needed undead miners. He was sure there was some monster that could mine metal at a hundred times the rate of the miners—though he was certain he would never want to face it in combat.

"Do you know where they were taken?" Elyse asked. She seemed to be thinking about something.

"I don't," the undead man said, "but I'm sure they left plenty of tracks."

At this moment Ruby and her party came out of the entrance to the mine, towing another undead miner between them. Ruby led him to where the other two huddled, in front of August's party. She turned to August.

"I've gotten into contact with Emeralda," she said. "She'll be here any minute, now." On her shoulder, Lester the clothes-fairy sat with his wings folded. His face twisted in concentration, and he did not move an inch.

August raised his eyebrows at this, but said no more. The magical dress-fairies were full of surprises, it seemed.

Lester opened his eyes and let out his breath. "Contact has been made," he said. From his back, almost invisible, a thin spider-web caught the sunlight. In front of him, a light appeared, and then grew until it was about the size of a melon. It hovered in place at first, but then moved to face the assembled adventurers.

A voice emanated from within it. "Hello," it said. It was unmistakably Emeralda's.

August leaned closer, impressed.

"The ball isn't really there," explained Ruby. "It's just projected onto your fairy tactical display, like the markers above monsters. But Emeralda really can see us, as if she were really there."

"Indeed I can," Emeralda said, through the plasma ball intermediary. "I see you have been training together, August, Penny, Elyse." She said this as if it were expected. Which, in a way, it was: she had ordered it.

"They have been making good progress," Ruby said, "but still have a long was to go." She switched topics like switching gears. "We discovered a mine that had been attacked by monsters, Ma'am."

The plasma ball that was Emeralda hovered for a moment. Then, it spoke. "Take me in," Emeralda said.

This is Going to Take a Whole Lot of Paperwork.

Emeralda

Emeralda stood inside her office, in the chair she always sat in for long-distance fairy communications. Her entire vision was filled with what the other side saw. Only a small window to her right showed her reality.

She surveyed the village, reflecting on her good fortune. The Head Necromancer had asked her to investigate the disappearance of his mines, and here she was, right in the middle of one of them.

Ruby excused herself after Emeralda had taken a survey of the village. August and his party followed. It was to be expected, for they had a long journey ahead of them, as well as much training to do. Ruby left behind three girls: Corporal Denyse, and two sailors that could be spared. They were to help Emeralda dig deeper into the mystery.

As she floated around the scene, she controlled the motion of the viewport with a glove, sewn from the same fabric that comprised the dress-fairies. Her intentions were communicated perfectly though the wire.

Corporal Denyse saluted to her. Emeralda saluted back, even though she knew all that they saw was a ball. Formalities were a major part of command. Denyse then led Emeralda into the entrance of the mine itself.

It was dark, and Emeralda assumed it was cold as well. One of the two sailors lit up a werelight that suffused the rough stone walls with a bluish glow.

"What's your name, sailor?" Emeralda asked, to the girl with the werelight. She wore a standard uniform, white, with blue ribbons that turned even bluer in the eerie light.

"Mary James," the sailor answered, her voice betraying her nervousness. It was to be expected, when Emeralda held such a position.

"You've done well with the light," Emeralda complimented. She hadn't thought about bringing a light into the cave.

"Thank you, ma'am," the girl said, her voice wavering.

Emeralda decided not to torture the girl any longer. "Where are we going?" She asked, to Corporal Denyse.

"We're going to go see something you need to see," Denyse answered. "We'll be there shortly."

Emeralda stayed silent, and watched the cold walls pass, broken by wooden struts and the occasional magical lantern.

Eventually, the mine branched off into several channels, one leading down on a steep grade. Denyse took it, her footfalls sending pebbles scattering down the slope. Sailor James brought up the rear, with the other sailor in the middle. The blue light gave their faces a gaunt look.

At the end of the slope, Denyse stopped suddenly, her posture wary. "Did you hear that?" She asked. Emeralda didn't, but she saw Mary and the other sailor nodding.

Denyse drew her oversized sword. Her dress-fairy popped out of her shoulder, and began to whisper things into her ear. The two sailors also prepared for battle. They walked down the cavern with their weapons raised.

They walked past an open tunnel, on the right side. Like a flash of lighting, something darted out, and then darted back in, taking Private James with it. The blue light disappeared. In the darkness, Emeralda heard bones crunching. Crunch, munch. There was also something much wetter in the sound. Tearing flesh? Emeralda analyzed the sounds impassively, shielding her mind from their implications.

Denyse lit another were-light, this one green. The tunnel lit up again, but there was nothing to be seen.

"I'm sure we checked it all," Denyse said, her voice shaking. The sailor that stood next to her held her hands over her mouth.

Emeralda addressed them calmly. "Eliminate it," she said, her voice full of steel. "Do not let it taste flesh without a price."

"Aye, ma'am," Denyse said, as she began to approach the side door. In the green light, she looked as if she were about to retch. Perhaps she really was about to retch. Emeralda had seen girls do so at much less.

"You'll do fine," Emeralda said, as her orb followed Denyse. It was fine for her to say, of course, because she wasn't really there. She had her doubts, but she kept them to herself.

Denyse took the lead, the blue were-light bobbing each time it went under a cross-support. They searched the tunnel to the end, where it turned into a solid rock wall. There was no monster, and no sign of Sailor Mary, except a stain of fresh blood on the floor.

Emeralda turned her orb around. "Show me what you intended to show me, Corporal," she said, determined to keep control of the situation.

Denyse and the sailor obeyed without question, but not before thoroughly checking the tunnel. As they left, they turned their heads to look behind them more than once.

When they rejoined the main tunnel, the surviving sailor leaned against a wall, and began to cry softly. "Why," she said, her voice low and full of fear.

Emeralda had had more than six lifetimes' experience consoling the friends and family of those who died, but it never got easier. At least in the case of her soldiers, their families had been long dead almost as a rule—being immortal had its downsides, the death of everyone mortal you knew being one of them.

But, to compensate, immortality formed deep, strong friendships. Some of her soldiers had been friends for centuries. The distancing of death somehow made it all the more real when it happened, and the loss of so many years was crushing.

Which is why Emeralda found herself at a loss of words. Corporal Denyse took the lead for her, wrapping her arms around the sailor, who now sobbed openly. Two dress-fairies also fluttered about them, unsure of what to do.

A third sat on the floor, on top of a green scrap of cloth. *I didn't do it, I didn't do it, I didn't do it,* she repeated, again and again. Her eyes had a haunted, starved look.

Emeralda reminded herself to reassign the fairy as soon as possible. A new partner almost always pushed away the memory of the last.

"We should get going," Denyse said, her voice still gentle.

The crying sailor nodded, and then followed Denyse as she walked deeper into the tunnel. The dead sailor's dress fairy trailed behind, hanging limp like the piece of cloth she held in her hands.

Denyse led Emeralda and the girl deeper into the mine, with much more caution this time. At each branching tunnel they stopped. Denyse held up her hand, and the were-light would enter the tunnel. She peeked in behind it, and signaled clear only when she saw that it was safe.

Soon they came to a branching tunnel that appeared smaller than most. It did not follow the ore vein, like most of the tunnels had. Instead, it jutted straight through it, and right out into solid rock. Denyse shone her light into the tunnel. She gave the signal for all clear, and then entered it. The last sailor followed, trailed by Emeralda's sphere.

The tunnel was short, leading deeper, but not by much. At the end there opened a room filled with all kinds of broken metal things. Mine carts, tracks, big lumps of slag, all piled on top of each other. The pile looked as if it had been recently shifted, the dust broken around a spot near the top where a rotted support beam poked out of the bottom of a hollow mine cart.

Denyse seemed surprised at this. "There was something there," she said, climbing the junk pile to look at the place. "The workers said that they dug it up a week ago, and tossed it here. It looked to be ancient, part of some gigantic machine. I think it was what the monsters were after." Now she lifted the rotted beam and peered under it. She dropped it back, disappointed. "Maybe they really did take it."

"How do you know this?" Emeralda asked.

"We interrogated the survivors," Denyse answered, "And they all said that the monsters had come to this room first. We found them here trying to move the part with a pair of gutterbacks."

Strange, Emeralda thought, as she surveyed the room. *There are no bodies.* "Did you kill them?" Emeralda asked.

"We did," Denyse said. She looked around the room, at a few spots here and there, her face puzzled. "The bodies were all here, last time we checked, it couldn't have been more than fifteen minutes."

Emeralda had a sneaking suspicion in the back of her head. The monster that had attacked them, the lack of bodies, the disappearance of the object, they all pointed to something. It had to be a monster of some sort that had taken the part. But what?

Denyse crouched low, sensing something. She said the code word for "caution, underground assailants," her switch to combat mode mirrored by the other sailor.

Emeralda could hear it, but could not feel it. A low rumble, setting the pieces of junk all around to clanking. She wondered why they had not noticed it the first time the monster had attacked. Soon, she got her answer. The room fell silent. The only thing that could be heard was the breathing of the two girls. It felt like the eerie calm before the storm.

Denyse closed her eyes, and stamped on the center of an overturned mine-cart. The disturbance traveled down the pile of junk, amplifying, until the entire room rang. A shuffling sound, like someone shoveling dirt, came from the corner where the sailor girl stood. She let out an "Eep," and then rolled away from the sound. The ground erupted into a fountain behind her, just where she had been standing. Out of the fountain came a black, shining carapace, bristling with spiny appendages, like an oversized beetle.

A carapecian! They rarely showed themselves in the civilized world, and were feared throughout the land for their cunning minds and rock hard shell. Incidentally, the shell of a carapecian was worth enough to purchase a mansion on Capital Main Street.

Emeralda had other worries, though. Even though she could only see, hear, and issue commands, she did her best to assist her sisters in arms. Two against one was hardly fair against a carapecian. If she were a betting girl, she would have placed her money on the monster. She wasn't, so instead, she coordinated Denyse's attacks with the sailors.

"Leftin!" She called, the universal code word for healing assistance. She followed with "Alf," meaning party member two. The words were specifically designed to be unintelligible to anyone that did not know the code, which is why they sounded harsh to most ears.

Denyse, party member one, extricated herself from the grip of two legs. Pieces of carapace flung everywhere as she hacked away. On the other side of the beast, the sailor lay on the floor, having torn something in her leg when she made her desperate dive. Emeralda could see that her vitality was bleeding out slowly, as she gave in to her pain.

Just as the beast rose up to strike the incapacitated sailor, Denyse snatched her up and jumped aside. The bug plowed into the ground, continuing until it disappeared like a fish into water.

Emeralda saw it all, from her vantage point on high. She had moved her sphere to the roof, where it hung, looking down.

Apparently, the girls in the room were not on the monster's objectives list. A rumbling sounded underneath them, and then grew fainter, as the bug tunneled away through solid stone.

"Do you think it was carrying the part?" Emeralda asked, as soon as Denyse had healed the sailor. The sailor's eye flipped open, and she coughed.

"There could be more," Denyse said, "But, probably."

"I have a mission for you, Corporal," Emeralda said. She knew she was asking a lot, but the world could be at stake.

"Yes ma'am?" Denyse sounded excited, despite the situation. It was not often that someone only in the middle of their first century got a mission straight from Emeralda—Penny being the exception to the rule.

"I need you to follow the monsters that raided this village," she said. "I want you to find out all you can about them, and what the object means to them."

Denyse saluted. "Yes, ma'm," she said, her voice crisp.

"You may take the crewoman with you," Emeralda said, cursing herself for not asking her name, "And you are authorized to use Disciplinary Force funds and contacts for your mission."

"Yes ma'am," Denyse said. She understood. The crewwoman she had saved sat up, and looked at where Emeralda's sphere hung.

"That is all, Corporal," Emeralda said. "I trust this is all I need to see?"

"Yes ma'am," Denyse said. She turned to her dress fairy, and spoke to her.

Emerada hear June's voice in her ear. "Disconnecting," she said, as Emeralda's vision flickered.

Emeralda soon saw nothing now but the inside of her office. She reached her arms into the air, stretching the tension out of her body. She had things to do, and an army to build.

Ice Cream Kiss

August

August, Elyse, and Penny spent another week in training, and then another week, and then another. The days all blended into one, their destination never seeming closer. It was as if time were frozen, right where they were, and they would continue to train until the world ended. Each morning, they awoke to individual drills. Elyse practiced her battle-magic, Penny learned swordplay from Ruby, and August alternated between studying and sparring with Justle, who had a surprising talent for swordsmanship. The loss of Denyse had put a hold on their party combat training, but it did not stop their learning. They practiced three-person drills on an empty field, again and again, until they could do it blindfolded, muffed, and half-asleep.

August's body became hard, like a coiled spring, and Elyse's body lost some of its softness. Her white skin glistened with a healthy sheen, and her hair sparkled, a dazzling sight in the bright sunlight. Penny, however, stayed how she always had been. It seemed becoming a magical girl had suspended all visible change within her—although she got stronger as well, it seemed.

August and Elyse became close with Penny as well, and they spent many nights together in August's cabin, talking and laughing and having a good time. Elyse and August grew even more attached to each other, each never venturing far from the other. Their personalities gradually bled into each other, until Elyse would say what August would, and August would say what Elyse had.

Ruby kept up her driving force, as she pushed them harder and harder. However, she remained friendly, and sometimes joined the party in their revels, dragging Justle with her.

On the first day of the second month of the voyage, Ruby called them all to the training field.

"We're going to land in the city of Elderdale," she announced, in the presence of the whole crew. "We need to take on supplies," she explained, "and we'll be refitting, as well. So, we'll be staying here for a while, perhaps three days."

Elderdale was a walled town, just under the size of a city. The granite that surrounded it had been quarried out of a hill on its skyward side. The hill itself formed part of the wall, the quarry creating a steep grade that rivaled that of the man-made part. Hovels clung to the outside like barnacles, the tiny figures of people stringing in and out across the narrow streets. Inside the wall, the houses increased in splendor, until, in the center, there stood a magnificent palace. Smaller than the Royal Academy in the Capital, it still dominated the land around it.

Being the last big city skyward towards the frontier lands, in this wedge of the world, it was built to withstand heavy assault. Monster raiders, and human raiders, often tried to make a go at sacking the city. They had never once succeeded. The wall's turrets bristled with cannon and ballista, aimed at the sky. Huge trebuchets sat in the middle of the outer city blocks.

The *Firebird* landed in their skyward port that jutted out of the top of the hill like a big tongue. Dozens of other skyships berthed alongside them, moored to the wooden spires that stuck out of the port. Trade bustled, seamen carried barrels of all sorts, sails fluttered in the brisk wind. August, Elyse, and Penny stepped off of the ship, and marveled at the sights. They followed the dock into the city, past the dock gates. Inside, the streets bustled with frenzied activity. Everything seemed to be happening at once, not unlike in the capital. Except here, things felt brighter, lighter, and much less serious.

August stopped next to a street performer, who spun magical balls in the air and made them dance through the crowd. A pair of them turned into people, and started dancing around the air while the performer played the flute. When he finished, the crowd applauded, and filled his hat with coins.

August added a few coppers to the pile, and moved on. Elyse and Penny waited for him at the next intersection.

Come on, Elyse told him. *We're going to show you something.*

August followed the two, down the street and into a shop that looked as if it sold sweets. Elyse walked up to the counter, and the man behind it looked up from his newspaper.

"What will it be?" The man asked.

"Three ice creams, please," Elyse said, placing the money on the counter.

The man reached into a gigantic contraption behind him, covered in frost, humming with magical energy. He brought out three bowls, in which was a pasty substance that looked a little like cottage cheese.

"It's not cheese," Elyse said, as she took one of the bowls. She handed the other to August. "It's iced cream."

August stared at the freezing glop in his bowl. Elyse and Penny ate the stuff with gusto. August thought it looked too much like puss, the way it collected in the bottom of the bowl when it melted.

You mean, you've never had ice cream? Elyse asked, her eyes incredulous. She shook her head, and then leaned over to August. She grabbed him and kissed him, right on the lips, with a mouth full of the stuff. August, too surprised to resist, simply leaned back, while all around him people laughed.

August could feel blood rushing to his face, but he also tasted something else, cool, sweet, and really quite good.

He supposed it was the ice cream.

Is this really necessary? He asked Elyse, after he had tasted the stuff off her tongue.

"Yes, you doofus," Elyse said, as she broke away. She smiled at him, a winning smile, and then turned back to her bowl. August wished he could see her eyes behind those black spectacles.

"It's a crime not to like ice cream," Elyse said, as she shoveled more into her mouth.

"Mph!" Penny voiced her assent.

August sighed, and began to eat his ice cream. He enjoyed it, really, but he wished Elyse wouldn't be so...

Forward? She asked, catching his train of thought. *But you like it, don't you?*

Truth be told, August did. But it was something about the way people were looking at them, that made him nervous. Maybe it was because they looked so weird together. Maybe it was just himself.

Fine, Elyse thought, a little hurt. *I'll save it for when we're not in public.*

August continued to eat his ice cream in silence. *Well, maybe not always,* he thought. He looked at the milky stuff in the bottom of the bowl, left over from the solid stuff.

If that's what you want, Elyse thought, as she drained her bowl like a cup. Penny did the same.

August sighed, and realized what he had just agreed to. It wasn't that bad, though. He copied Elyse and Penny, and drained his bowl of ice cream. When he was finished, he leaned over towards Elyse. He lifted up her spectacles, so he could see into her rose red eyes. *Just promise not to be too embarrassing, ok?* He asked, not blinking.

Elyse grinned. *Not embarrassing, right.* She thought.

August saw a smear of ice cream above her lips, and wiped it off with his finger. He scowled, and then leaned back in his chair. He was happy, though. "So," he said, as much to himself as to the others. "Where to next?"

"I want to see the castle walls," Penny said, right away. She had been looking at them with admiration ever since they had arrived. The globe of the Capital was big, but it was more of a backdrop than an object. More like the sky than a mountain. Of course, it was also the strongest physical barrier in the world, but that part of it was all magic. Invisible.

The big, imposing stone walls of Elderdale made a picturesque scene, against the high hill that formed part of them, and the forests around them, and the houses inside them. August wanted to see them, as well, so he didn't complain. Neither did Elyse. They left the shop and headed towards the wall.

They entered through the bottom of a gatehouse, its massive metal doors open to the outside world, letting in droves of people, tamed monsters, and machines. Penny showed the man at the door to the stairs her magical girl seal, the proof that she was part of the

Disciplinary Force. Ruby had given it to her as they left the ship, for this reason. The gateman let them through, but not before staring at the three assembled before him.

It was no surprise, really. A pale girl in black spectacles and a coat with shock white hair that had a red streak running through the center; a ten-year old with fiery eyes and a deadly looking staff; and a monster hunter with a massive sword across his back had all just come calling at his door.

He let them through, though, and soon the party began to ascend a tall spiral staircase. They reached the top, and August pushed open a heavy trapdoor. Wind howled around the opening. When August stepped out, he felt as if he were on top of the world. Fifty feet below, the houses on the ground seemed like mere toys. The spires of the palace reached higher than him, but their spindly lengths only added to the sense of aloneness. Elyse and Penny came up behind him, and moved to either side. They all three faced over the edge, staring out at the mountains beyond, and the sky beyond them. That was not the direction they were heading, however. Their destination lay behind them, where the city's hill raised up in a gentle slope before cutting off in a steep drop; where the *Firebird* lay berthed. In that direction, the sky felt closer, tighter, as it came down to meet the earth.

A commotion broke the party out of their reverie at the top of the world. A solder ran past, his head turned out away from the city, his armor clinking as his feet pounded the stone floor. Another soldier ran past, and then another.

A bell tolled in the center of the city, from above the capital. It rang, and rang, and then rang some more, as if it would never stop. The rest of the bells in the city—the church bells and school bells and shipyard bells—all joined the chorus.

"What's happening?" Penny asked, voicing the questions of the others.

A passing soldier stopped by them. "You should be getting down, civilians," he said. "It's not safe for you up here." He sounded pressed, and nervous.

From where they stood on the wall, August and his party could see nothing but the blue sky and green earth. All the soldiers, however, had been running towards the hill, the skyward-most part of the city.

"We should join them," Elyse said, ignoring the soldier's warning. August and Penny agreed.

They ran along the side of the wall, all around the city, passing soldiers arming ballista and shoving cannon balls into big iron cannons. In the streets, people flowed like a river, returning to their homes. The gates, still open, admitted floods of life, people, tamed monsters, and machines all jostling with each other. The city had an air of barely contained panic.

When August and his party had reached the halfway point, right above the clockwise gate, the panic broke through the crowd. One man began to run. A walker, steaming along on three legs, followed him. Then all hell broke loose. The runners trampled through the streets, all trying to get as far away from the gates as possible.

In the distance, August heard a low rumble, like a thousand roars mixed together. He didn't like it, and neither did Elyse.

An army? Elyse theorized, hoping that she was wrong.

August said nothing, and increased his pace. Penny kept up, using her magical strength to propel herself further than anyone her height had a right to.

As they approached the part of the wall carved from living stone, the stone quarry came into sight. Behind it, August saw a massive monster army.

Are They... Edible?

Emeralda

"I had no idea they would come so fast," Ruby said, as Emeralda looked upon the army approaching Elderdale.

Emeralda watched from her fairy-link, her orb hovering just above the hill wall. She saw everything.

Squadrons of beaterbats—giant bats with a vicious venomous spit—and groups of alzoths headed the army, flying in clouds above the heads of marchers. Grandshrooms, massive walking fungi, could be seen towering over the heads of the foot soldiers. On their shroomy caps, the monsters had built siege engines, and devices to scale walls. Tiny figures climbed up and down their stalks, communicating with the foot soldiers.

Of the foot soldiers, there were multitudes: at least a division--10,000 soldiers—Emeralda estimated. She knew that Elderdale kept only a battalion in reserve. That meant the city was fighting ten-to-one odds. Elderdale wouldn't fall that easily, though. Her walls were thick and her gates strong.

As to how the monsters had managed to hide such a force, Emeralda had just learned. They had used wave interference to get rid of their magical aura, massive as it was, and simply killed anyone who had spotted them. Not that many people lived skyward of Elderdale, anyways.

Emeralda cursed herself. If she had only sent Penny and her party off sooner, then they could have warned of the battle. Which led her to remember: it wasn't their main mission. Emeralda hated to say it, but she needed the party to continue with their journey, siege or not. It was too important.

As to her army, she had just recently finished negotiations with the Necromancer's guild, and had received the news that her order of special hairbands was finished. The monster-tamers had supplied their monsters, like promised. The Green Blood Guild had even given up a corps of volunteers.

Emeralda knew she should be thankful for what she had, but she just couldn't. Not when the size of the enemy stared her in the face. Her only repose was her new-found force, rivaling even the power of the Disciplinary Force: the undead army. Surprised as she had been that no one had suggested it earlier, Emeralda had still been able to negotiate a contract with Horis, the undead guildmaster. If they would fight in her army, she would provide them with military equipment and training. They had the potential to be the most effective army in the world, with their almost invincible soldiers.

The Necromancer's guild had balked, of course, but they couldn't pull out of a divinely witnessed contract. Emeralda had stopped the strikes, and investigated the mines—a dirty business, a result of which she had promoted Corporal Denyse to Sergent. She deserved it.

"General?" Ruby asked, turning to face Emeralda. "Are you there?"

"I am, Major," Emeralda said. Lost in her thoughts, she had almost forgotten the matter at hand.

High above the castle, squadrons of flying machines scrambled. They zipped overhead, heading towards the massed beaterbats and alzoths. The flying monsters circled, their movements full of menace.

The grandshrooms' footsteps increased in pace. The ground rumbled, amplified atop the high wall. Emeralda could hear the individual cries of the ground monsters: ganglers and gutterbacks and many others beside. She knew that between them, the more dangerous monsters lurked: Meriwethers, and dangermuffs, wigglers, and carapecians.

She forced herself to turn away. "Major," she said, about to drop a heavy order, "You are to continue on your journey as soon as possible."

Ruby blanched, but knew better than to protest. Emeralda had thought it out, after all. It was the only logical choice. Penny needed to reach the Centrix.

Explosions sounded in the distance. The trebuchets on both sides began to swing their massive loads, their targets now in range. Elderdale's tall walls could withstand any beating, but it was not so for the houses within. A great big boulder fell out of the sky near where Ruby stood, squashing a whole block beneath it. Sharp screams of pain cut through the sound of splintering wood and stone.

"Dismissed," Emeralda said, unable to watch any longer. Her army was due to leave in two days, but she had one problem: she didn't have enough airships.

She did have one thing, though: a crisis.

Whalegirls' Doing Some Wranglin'

August

August stared at the giant mushrooms, as they marched steadily closer. Underneath them teemed thousands of monsters, of all sorts, and above them Elderdale's air defense force faltered. From the edge of the hill, running towards the gatehouse, August watched the town navy lift off from its pier. Several Drummonds, a sloop, and a war galley, as well as a scattering of smaller ships. Together, they might have had 20 or 30 cannon.

They looked formidable, against the puny alzoths and beaterbats. But then, the aurawhales showed up: ten of them, riding a downward thermal out of a high altitude cloud. Their long, sleek bodies had been coated with wooden slats, creating floating platforms equal to the human's airships. On the platforms, scores of gangler archers stood ready to unleash volleys of fire. The aurawhales themselves flipped the air with three huge tails, big enough to reduce a ship to splinters. The navy didn't look so powerful then.

From the castle walls, the archers began to fire at the monsters skirmishers that approached the wall. The main body of the army still marched about two miles away, just outside the range of a trebuchet, slowing down as they made camp. The army spread out around the city, looking like a wave of water fanning around an invisible line. They burned the surrounding forest and villages as they went, the cries of the people who had not evacuated hanging thin on the air.

August felt the pit of his stomach open up. He had never seen such destruction before. He wanted to go out there and pummel the monsters until they all were nothing but dust, but knew that it would be futile. Three against ten thousand was not even in the realm of possibility.

"There you are!" From the spire of the skyward gatehouse, where the downward staircase hid in a cleft of rock, Ruby came out onto the wall. She ran to August's party, her long hair twisting in the breeze. "I need to talk to you," she said, as she huffed from exertion. The wall was tall, and there were many stairs.

August ripped his eyes from the battle before him. "What of?" He asked, certain that he would be called upon to fight.

"We need to get to the ship," Ruby explained. "We're casting off in an hour."

"But look!" August exclaimed, glancing at the huge army surrounding the city. "The city's in trouble!"

"Pretty obvious, don't you think?" Elyse said, her voice dry. "But I see her reasoning."

Penny hunched her shoulders, knowing what was coming.

"Penny needs to get to the Centrix," Ruby said. "That mission is more important, and may stop the monsters for good."

"This is only the first of their invasion," Elyse added. "We know that they haven't even opened the Centrix yet. All these monsters are local to this side of the world."

"But, there's so many," August protested, looking for an excuse to help the city.

"Aye," Ruby said, "So many that three extra warriors won't make a single difference."

August leaned out over the wall and cursed, aware that they were right. Still, he looked out at the burning villages with fire in his eyes, and listened to the terrible screams coming from within the city. He had it in his mind to do something.

"I know what we can do to help," he said, his teeth gritted. "And we won't stray from our mission."

"What?" All three girls asked him. They looked at him as if he were crazy.

"We hijack an aurawhale." August stated.

Ruby looked at Elyse, and Penny adjusted her pigtails. They seemed to be thinking it over.

"All right," Ruby said, after a long pause. "But how do you plan to do it? The monsters have anti-ship weapons mounted on their grandshrooms, not to mention the aurawhale itself. How do you expect to pilot it?"

August stood up to his full height. "I'm a Green Blood, remember?"

Understanding dawned on Elyse. "You really want to capture one, don't you?"

August nodded. The paltry city navy didn't stand a chance against ten. It was the least that they could do to help.

"You know that won't turn the tide of the battle, right?" Elyse asked, prodding August to make sure he was serious.

"I'm aware," August said. "But we have to do something," he continued. "We're powerful, and will be able to make a small difference, maybe enough to give this city more time to get help."

Ruby looked out at the battle, at the magnificent aurawhales floating in the sky. They stayed afloat with the help of gas bags, perched underneath their thick frames. The platforms on their tops were open, with no sails, and no guard rails. From where they flew, it was a long way down.

Ruby nodded her head. "We can try," she said, "though what good it will do, I don't know."

At this, August lightened, and Elyse looked at the aurawhales, in truth a little bit excited. Penny walked behind them without a word, as they returned to the port.

They found it under attack by a squadron of beaterbats. Several ornithopters and one gyrocopter zoomed around overhead, attempting to keep the monsters on the outside side of the wall. None of the monsters paid any attention to the figures running down the pier beneath them.

Ruby called all of the *Firebird's* sailors through the fairy-com, as well as Justle. In less than five minutes all of them had boarded, and the *Firebird* was ready to lift off.

Ruby gave the command. "Full sail!" she shouted, just as a beaterbat collided with an ornithopter overhead. The screech of metal clashed with the squeaking of the bat as it fell to earth in a burning fireball.

The *Firbird's* sailors armed themselves with rifles, ready to shoot down any monster that journeyed to close. Those that could use magic readied their fireballs, their icicles and thunderbolts.

Ruby took the helm, steering them towards the nearest aurawhale. It was locked in combat with a city schloop, the airship's cannonballs tearing big holes in its side. The aurawhale responded by ramming its huge head into the side of the ship, splitting it in two and spilling all of its contents to the ground, a thousand feet below. The pieces of the skyship still attached to the engine shot straight up, dropping all manner of things out of their open holds. A few parachutes opened up beneath the *Firebird*.

The aurawhale turned, its drivers noticing the *Firebird's* approach. They were ganglers, all of them, armed with short bows and crude knives.

"Clear its deck first!" August yelled, as they got closer to their target. The aurawhale bled out of several holes, but still appeared intact.

August, Penny, Elyse, Justle, and three sailors piled into a lifeboat. Its tiny skysteel engine glowed as it started up, with Elyse at the controls.

Ruby brought the *Firebird* up hard, so that it angled over the path of the aurawhale. Right as they passed over the whale, about a hundred feet above, August and Justle pushed off from the hull. The lifeboat staggered, but stayed upright. It drifted gently down, guided by Elyse's masterful manipulations. It was her engine, after all.

The thunk of arrows hitting wood shook the lifeboat. The ganglers' arrows flew up, all around, and arced back to earth a few seconds after. One of them poked its stone head through the bottom of the boat, scaring one of the sailors into jumping up with an "eep!" She wore purple ribbons on her uniform, and her badge declared her as a private, first class.

August hadn't gotten to know any of the sailors, and regretted it now. The three with him had trained as a team, of course, but it would have been nice to be able to coordinate with them like he did Penny and Elyse.

Above them, the magicans on the *Firebird* opened fire. Meteors of energy, in all forms, rained down upon the deck of the aurawhale. The sound was not unlike a barbeque in the summer, the screams of the ganglers almost like the sound of sizzling meat.

August shook the thought from his head. Every gangler killed was one less he had to fight. The lifeboat leveled with the aurawhale. In the distance, the other aurawhales pitted themselves against the city's navy, swarmed around by flying machines and monsters. Explosions of energy lit up the mid-afternoon sky from all sides.

The lifeboat hit the aurawhale's planks with a clatter. The platform was about the size of the training field on the *Firebird*, made of rough-hewn boards. Two dozen ganglers surrounded the seven that had come aboard.

"Lighting them up," Gliss said, as icons appeared over each of their heads. She numbered them 1 through 23.

Three to one, thought August. *Not bad.*

The barrage from the *Firebird* petered out in order to avoid hitting the boarders. The planks showed evidence of the attacks that had stopped, charred bodies lying within blackened circles.

August surveyed the monkeys, and then angled towards the place where a gangler held the ship's reins. Seven monsters stood in the way. Justle and the sailors faced away from August, preparing to clean up the rest of the platform.

August gave the code word for a wedge formation, best used against an overwhelming number of opponents. August stood in front, Elyse to his right, Penny to his left. They formed a sort of triangle, never straying far from its center. They had practiced it again and again, bound to each other by ropes, and Ruby's exclamations.

Now it was time to put it into practice. August and Elyse traded places first, in order to give Elyse the longest reach possible. Penny fired up a lightning spell. Two ganglers fell, numbers 6 and 19. Their icons flickered out as soon as they hit the floor.

August watched the magica bars carefully, in the corner of his vision. When the magic ran out, they would have to close with weapons right away.

Another gangler dropped to the floor, its chest impaled with an icicle. A lightning bolt fried two more. That left two ganglers on their side of the platform.

An easy battle, thought August.

Don't get cocky, replied Elyse. *We're not done yet.*

From overhead, three beaterbats broke through the *Firebird*'s markswomen, and headed straight for the aurawhale's platform. Two of them dove at August's formation. August gave the code-word for flexibility, meaning that for the moment, they should all watch themselves.

The beaterbats clawed the boards as they landed, beating their furry wings. Their emaciated bodies seemed ridiculously small inside of all that fuzz.

Elyse finished off the last gangler with a slash of Instrator. The two charred pieces hit the boards and rolled.

At that moment, the aurawhale banked hard. The platform tilted, until August could see the ground rushing over the port side. Everyone grabbed holes in the planking. Up where a gangler had held the reins, a skirmish unfolded between two sailors and three ganglers. Each time the gangler holding the reins dodged a strike, the aurawhale jerked, tossing loose bodies into the air. Each time, August came back down with a grunt. His fingernails dug into the wood, burnt from a magical attack. The crumbly charcoal broke off around his hand, forcing him to grip ever harder, or else risk falling to his doom.

The sailors finally dispatched the last of the ganglers. One of them grabbed the reins, and tried to pull on them, to right the whale. No matter how hard she tried, though, the aurawhale did not respond.

August reached out to the mind of the aurawhale. He felt a surprisingly small consciousness, barely cognizant, like that of a cow. It wasn't at all corrupted with evil. From what he saw, the whale had just been doing what it was told to do. He tried to soothe it. Calming his body, despite the protesting from his hands, he murmured thoughts of reassurance.

A beaterbat made a dive for him, as he concentrated, but Elyse swung over and kicked it away. The bat screeched in annoyance, dodging a magical fireball from the *Firebird* above.

Elyse and Penny surrounded August, doing their best to form a wedge, hanging 1000 feet in the air. August dove deeper into the giant monster's consciousness, reaching a point where he knew he could convince it to help him. He finally reached it. The whale responded with a shudder, almost breaking August's grip.

The rest of the adventurers on the whale didn't comment, too busy fighting their own battles. The ganglers, with their home-turf advantage hanging from the planks, had come back to fight ferociously. Only five remained, giving more trouble that the last dozen or so. The beaterbats only made things worse.

"Got it!" August yelled, when he had convinced the aurawhale to listen to him. The girl holding the reins pulled up, hard. The platform righted, tossing everyone into the air. The five gangler-monkeys scrambled about on the now-flat ground. Elyse and August dispatched them in a pinch. The last beaterbat spiraled down towards the forest below, trailing smoke and pieces of singed fur.

August dropped down onto the deck, dead tired. His red vitality bar sat at half-full, reminding him that his strength had been disappearing at an alarming rate. Elyse's and Penny's fared no better.

With the aurawhale captured, the sailor with the reins angled back towards the city of Elderdale, the *Firebird* trailing behind. As they approached the pier, giant ballista turned on them, but held their fire once they noticed the waving humans up top. They whale docked in a merchant's berth, conveniently just the right size.

The captain of the guard ran to them, waving, his heavy plate clinking as his feet hit the stone floor. He stopped in front of the crew and stared at the aurawhale before speaking. "What did you do?" He asked. A curious crowd of soldiers gathered around them.

"We have a present for you," Elyse answered. She gestured towards the aurawhale. The whale moaned, a long, keening sound that carried all across the city. The crowd of solders stepped back.

"Thank you," the captain of the guard said, his voice thin. "We, ah, appreciate it."

"Don't mention it," said August. He stepped down onto the pier. Some of the solders looked on him with awe, though he couldn't tell why.

I think they respect you, Elyse said, her voice a little caustic. *You managed to capture an aurawhale, with only girls for help.*

August pursed his lips, but didn't say anything else.

It's not that bad, Elyse thought. *We did get the job done.*

Sure, August thought. *And now we have to leave.* He glanced at the massive army that surrounded the city.

Ruby stepped up to the aurawhale, having disembarked from the *Firebird*. "We're leaving as soon as possible," she said, facing up towards the aurawhale, "as soon as we can come up with a plan."

Sing to Me, Softly

Denyse

Denyse had traveled for two weeks, now, and had just about reached the wilds. The trail that she followed had been more like a road, carved out of whatever it went through by hundreds of monster feet. Kelly, the sailor who had left with her, kept up for most of the journey without complaint. They had seen nothing, in the two weeks since they had left the mine, except for a few towns where they had purchased supplies. No one had seen a group of monsters traveling nearby, so Denyse knew that they must have traveled by night through the civilized lands.

Her job wasn't to catch them, of course. It was to follow them, and to watch what they were doing with all of the human and undead prisoners that they had taken.

On the first day of the second month since Denyse had left the capital, just under two weeks since she had left the mine, she stopped to make camp near a river, at the edge of the border between the wilds and civilized land. The wilds were a sort of grey zone between civilized land and the edgelands. While not as dangerous as the infamous edge, they still held their fair share of traps for the unwary.

As they made camp, Kelly sat down hard on a log, and looked as if she were thinking. Denyse looked at her for a long moment, and then decided to ignore her. She had long since proven unsociable after the death of her friend.

So, it surprised Denyse when Kelly spoke to her of her own accord. "Why are we immortal?" the girl asked, staring at the hem of her dress. Her dress-fairy, Jan, fluttered sadly at her side, the dead sailor's fairy having since been reassigned.

It was such a strange question, that at first Denyse thought that she had imagined Kelly asking it. She continued to try to light a fire, in the way that she had been taught at scout camp. Build a pyramid, put the tinder underneath, light a small piece with the sparkler. Only, she couldn't do it. *It must be too wet,* she thought. It had rained some in the past few days.

"I mean," Kelly continued. "If we're all just going to die one day, than aren't we not really immortal?"

Denyse gave up, and lit the fire with a blazing fireball. Dangerous, the scout guide had said, because of the chance of an explosion. Denyse didn't care, though, as she thought of an answer to Kelly. It was a hard question, especially for someone in her position.

"I think the problem is, is that we're not immortal." Denyse finally answered. She paused for a moment. "We're just ageless." After another moment she added, "and very powerful."

Kelly seemed to mull over what Denyse had said, her face scrunched up in concentration. She was a pretty girl, attractive in that farmer's daughter type of way, like all magical girls. She wore a green ribbon through her sailor's uniform, now browned and beaten by two weeks on the road. Her dress-fairy mirrored the condition of her dress, battered and limp.

Her eyes were big, even for a magical girl. They possessed a sadness in them, and had even before her friend died.

Denyse couldn't blame the girl. After only fifty years of being immortal, her experience only extended as far as an old woman's. But Kelly, at 107, had lived twice as long. It was rare that a magical girl died in combat, or died at all. They were too powerful.

And so, Kelly's shock was understandable. A century of living without fear of death had made her painfully vulnerable to the harsh reality of mortality.

Denyse chuckled to herself, despite the morose subject. She had never known that she could wax so poetic. Maybe it took a crisis to bring it out.

All the while, while the two girls thought, the fire crackled merrily, and then calmly, and then died down to a bright glow underneath two logs. The dusk turned to night, and the nocturnal creatures made their presence known.

"It wasn't your fault," Denyse said, when the moon had just risen above the trees. "There was nothing you could have changed. We were on a mission, and that mission had its hazards."

Kelly looked up at Denyse, her eyes breathing in the moonlight. "I . . ." She looked down at her hands, and then at the fire, her internal turmoil etched onto her countenance. "I know." She finally said, her shoulders slumping down, as if she had finally stopped fighting. "I know."

Denyse got up, and sat down next to Kelly, on her log. She put her arm around her, and looked up at the moon, and began to sing softly.

gently, gently, father Time said,
the world is full, and you are young,
for since I made this moon go round,
the life of me has dawned,

look down, look down, at your small bed,
and know that when you are done,
your ears will perk up at the sound,
when the life of me will dawn,

I walk throughout the world at wide
and see the cities, hue and cry
but every time I look at you
I remember the dawn, too

Denyse's voice drifted off into the distance, joining with the chorus of frogs and crickets. Kelly buried her head into Denyse's arms, and cried, softly at first, and then deeper, as if she were digging into her pain, until her entire body shook. Denyse held her tight, caressing her auburn hair, twisting her green ribbons in her fingers.

They stayed like that for a long time, and when the moon reflected off the leaves and the fire died down, it was not two little girls, but two wise women that sat on a log, in each other's arms.

Just Being Careful

Emeralda

Emeralda walked through the streets of the Capital, on her way from a meeting with the head of the Skysteel guild. She had an army, with enough fighting power to match the army marching on Elderdale, and beyond, but she only had enough skyships to carry her own men, not to mention the huge amounts of supplies an army that size would need. Of course, undead didn't need very much, but she still had a battalion of monster riders, another battalion of Green blood volunteers, a corps of healers and a half-raid of summoners. In combination with her own forces, totaling a brigade of about 3,000, her total number of troops was over 7,000.

She cursed the head of the Skysteel Guild again, for being such a selfish pain in the neck. Elderdale was operated by the artisan's guild, but the Skysteel Guild owned a rival city, Chortop. Those two cities competed with each other for control of the rim trade in that wedge of the world. The Skysteel Guild saw the siege as a way to seize the competition and form a monopoly, and would never willingly send aid. Of course, the head hadn't phrased it that way. He had simply declined Emeralda's request.

Arrogant politicians, Emeralda thought, her mind seething.

She bumped into a man as she passed an open alleyway, hitting her head on his arm. It happened far more often than she would have liked, due to her cursed small height, so she thought nothing more of it.

As a result, it surprised her when the man hailed her. "Miss!" he cried, tapping her on the shoulder.

Emeralda turned around. She faced a perfectly ordinary man, in a perfectly ordinary suit. He held out an envelope towards her.

"I think you dropped this, miss," he said, his eyes locking with Emeralda's.

Emeralda took it, too stunned to resist. She almost opened it, but then paused. It was too suspicious: it might be a curse, or a magic bomb. She decided to open it in her weapons lab. Still, the danger didn't do anything to dissuade her curiosity, no more than did the sudden disappearance of the man who had given it to her, vanished without a trace.

She hurried back to base, the envelope clutched tight in her hands. She entered through the clockwise entrance, an elevator hidden at the back of a candy shop. Clever, because no one ever thought it strange that so many little girls came and went from within.

Down she went, deep underneath the capital. The doors opened, and she stepped out onto her base's main boulevard.

The Disciplinary Force base wasn't so much a fortress as it was a self-contained economy. Emeralda purposely did not order much when it came to construction, finances, and other civilian things, trusting the individuals under her command to make do and prosper. There were two major operations that the Disciplinary force undertook to supply financing: weapon-smithing and tailoring. Both under front companies, of course. Emeralda took pains to not become too publically acknowledged.

Individual magical girls had a talent for battle, and an uncanny strength. They also had an eye for fashion and design. Centuries of experience didn't hurt, either. As such, the weapons and clothes produced by the girls were always of superior quality.

Emeralda walked down her base's main tunnel, admiring the view in the shop windows. All around her, girls snapped salutes, pausing as she passed.

When she reached the door to the weapons lab—far down a side alley, out of sight—she pulled out a magical crystal, and waved it over a gap in the door. The door clicked, the mechanisms inside unlocking. She entered into a wide, open room, filled on one side with all sorts of magical and mechanical gadgets.

In the center of it all, Emeralda's head scientist, Grisela, stood over a desk. She worked on something small, too small for Emeralda to make out at her distance. Parts scattered around her.

"First Lieutenant," Emeralda called, to Grisela.

Grisela looked up with a start. "Oh, General," she said, the surprise in her voice obvious. "Can I do something for you?"

"I need help opening a letter," Emeralda told her. She brought out the parcel that had been given to her, as light, long and wide as a regular letter.

Grisela studied it with interest. "It seems you got mail," she commented. "How do you want me to open it?"

Emeralda looked towards the explosive and magic safety arms. They hung from the ceiling, and used magical power to pick up dangerous items and manipulate them. Half of the room had nothing but bare steel flooring to do this on. Clear blast shields lay scattered around the other side of the room.

Grisala noticed Emeralda's motion, and walked to a table half embedded in the wall, full of knobs and dials. "I take it you want me to preserve the letter inside?" Grisala asked, as she pressed a few buttons. The mechanical arm flexed.

Emeralda placed the letter in the center of the empty area, above a magical force field emitter embedded in the ground. The letter stayed where she left it, four feet in the air. Locked into place, it didn't budge when the mechanical arms wrapped around it.

Grisela worked the controls, her face scrunched up with concentration. "You'd better get behind a blast shield, just in case," she said.

Emeralda hastily took her advice. From behind the clear wall, she saw the letter sliced open by a thin knife that protruded from the mechanical arm. She cringed. Nothing happened.

Grisala shut down the arm. "It doesn't look like it's trapped, general," she said, as the whirring of machinery died down.

Emeralda approached the letter, reaching out to take the slip of paper from inside. On it were two things: a set of polar coordinates, and the words: *Tonight. Alone.*

The great escape

August

As night fell over Elderdale, the monsters spread out all around the city, until every foot of space around had been occupied. They stayed outside of the range of the city's trebuchets, and soon had all but destroyed the city's navy and flying machines. The city's air defenses—cannon that shot hundreds of small steel balls into the air—kept the flying monsters out. They had reached an impasse: a real siege.

August, Elyse and Penny, however, had to leave as soon as possible. They loaded the *Firebird* enough supplies to complete their journey, a gift for capturing the aurawhale. The whale moaned sorrowfully when it learned that August had to go. August told it to behave, and listen to its new masters.

Ruby's plan was simple, yet decisive: fly low, lower than the tops of the grandshrooms, upon which sat the monster's massive fire ballista. Down near the ground, they would have to contend with arrows and flying monsters—not much against the solid hull of a skyship. Or so Ruby hoped.

The actual thing was a little different. Flying just above the trees, any disturbance could send them crashing into the top of a pine. It would be a tough ride, one that would take all of them to get through.

The *Firebird* had three main sails: one on each side and one jutting up from the main deck. Each of these unfurled just as the sun disappeared beneath the earth, and the moon shone brighter in the sky. August stood at the prow, the fence of the training field behind him. Elyse and Penny both hung in the rigging, ready to fire magical missiles at incoming monsters. Sailors scrambled about on deck, making final preparations.

Near the gangplank, Ruby faced Justle, the last member of her party. She said something to her, and Justle stepped back, clearly surprised. But, she saluted anyways, and walked back down the gangplank and onto the pier.

"Where is she going?" asked August, walking over to get a better look. Justle had with her another sailor, and the two now talked with the captain of the city guard.

"I ordered her to stay and help arrange the castle's defenses," Ruby explained.

August nodded his head. "So you did feel the need to help them after all."

Ruby turned away from August for a second, hiding her embarrassment. "I can't disobey orders," she said, "but I do have a little bit of authority. Justle and Iris won't be missed, much. Iris is just a cabin girl."

"Iris is her name?" August asked, as he looked at the sailor.

"She volunteered," Ruby said, and left it at that.

When the preparations had finished, August took his place at the prow. Unable to produce more than a small flame on his own, and a horrible shot with a crossbow to boot, he had been put in charge of the group to repel boarders. The monsters that made it through the markswomen and magicians in the rigging and on the decks would have to deal with him.

He missed having Elyse at his side, though. He felt better when someone was watching his back.

I am watching your back, dummy, Elyse thought. She lay crouched in the rigging, on a platform designed for shooting from. *I'll make sure you don't screw up too bad.*

Thanks, August thought, although he still felt alone. It was just him, on the deck, as if he were an afterthought.

The monster's line of defense grew closer, the grandshrooms towering over the tallest pines. Between them and the trees, a gap just large enough for the *Firebird* opened. The monsters spotted the ship, several groups of fliers taking off from the ground.

The monsters had made campsites all through the forest behind their lines, so that in the dark, they looked like reddened stars. As the *Firebird* approached the gap, more campfires lit, beacons to signal the defense.

Atop the grandshrooms, a commotion brewed, but it was all for naught. Soon, the firebird was below their reach. The first of the fliers surrounded the ship. Alzoths, perhaps a dozen. The marksmen and magicians in the rigging opened fire, sending the reptilian creatures into a deadly dance. Bolts of magical energy—lightning, fireballs, icicles, high-speed bubbles—spewed from the *Firebird* like popcorn out of a hot pan. The smell of singed meat filled the air, and alzoth corpses rained down past the rails, wings smoking, or frosted, or covered in a soapy sheen.

August shifted on his feet, leaning with the motion of the *Firebird*. The magicians seemed to be handling things. The massive stalks of the grandshrooms grew ever closer, until they towered overhead like turrets in a castle—oversized ones, at that.

From places all over—the tree tops, the fungal caps, from platforms hanging on the stalks—a rain of arrows headed towards the *Firebird*. Most pinged harmlessly off the hull, but some flew dangerously close to the women in the rigging.

A sailor magician rectified that. Her yellow ribbons flying in the wind, air flowing though her straw-colored hair, she called out a few code words that cut through the battle's noise. A thin bubble appeared around her, and then extended around everyone on the ship. Other magicians joined her, layering her defense with more spells of protection. Soon, the volley of arrows arching towards the ship could do no more harm than a volley of pebbles.

Just as they passed the stalk of the first grandshroom, right over the monster siege line, August spotted a bright light ahead of them. It looked to be on the forest floor, emanating from a single solitary figure.

"Watch out!" August called, able to do nothing but watch. The ship's crew, all too occupied to listen, ignored his warning. Only Elyse dropped from the rigging, hitting the ground with a roll. Just as she got to her feet, lighting arched up from where the enemy magician stood, striking six girls in the rigging, including Penny. One sailor dropped down to the deck, smoking. Another lay motionless in her perch.

Small fires had started where the lightning had missed its targets. August and Elyse scrambled to put them out, following the sailors' lead. The *Firebird*'s course veered.

The bright light appeared again, closer underneath the flying ship. The arrows still rained down, and the beaterbats and alzoths circled ever closer. The *Firebird* tilted as Ruby, at the helm, attempted to drive it away from the magician.

Another light lit up the sky, this time from a different direction. Ruby banked the *Firebird,* hard, heading for the gap between them. A pillar of fire erupted out of the night, right where the ship would have been. The figures in the rigging cast a strange silhouette, against the magma-red backdrop.

Just as the pillar dissipated, four beaterbats came diving in from behind, carrying underneath them a huge figure.

A gutterback! August realized, as he drew his sword. An arrow split the plank floor just to his right, but he ignored it. A piece of flaming wood flew past his shoulder, off the ship, chucked by a sailor. He ducked, and faced the beaterbats. One of them jerked, sprouting a quarrel from its face. It fell, pulling the others with it, but not before they had reached the *Firebird*'s deck. The gutterback launched itself with a roar, and landed right on the training field with a force that yanked the stern up and the bow down. Elyse stumbled, catching hold of a rope to keep from sprawling.

August kept his feet. He leaped over a fallen section of the training field's fence, and issued a challenge to the gutterback. "You pig-faced brute!" he called, distracting the monster from an injured sailor. "I bet you can't even touch me!"

The gutterback steamed, not understanding his words, but still understanding his intent. It roared, a grating sound that shook the ship, and filled the air with a foul odor. August drew his sword, and strapped on his shield. The gutterback charged, all nine feet of it headed straight towards August. The world disappeared around him, until all he saw was in the moment.

August danced around the gutterback's first charge, swinging down with his sword. It bounced off the creature's natural plate with a protesting clank. More foul odors swirled into the air. August surveyed his enemy, closer this time, looking for an opening. He remembered the last gutterback he had killed with a blow to the exposed neck. However, that neck was eight feet in the air, and August stood less than six feet tall. He couldn't hope to reach it, unless he had a plan to get it on the ground. He didn't.

He couldn't rely on anyone else. They were all too busy: fighting fires, tacking the sails, shooting at the flying monsters that swarmed about. Penny, unscathed by the bolt that had stuck her, had run out of magical energy, and now fired a crossbow into the darkness. Elyse scrambled about the ship, using water spells to put out the fires that sprung up all over.

August traded a blow with the gutterback. The plates on its arm curved to form a crude club, capable of smashing in even the toughest skull. It took all of August's strength to parry. The gutterback growled, and raised his arm again. August ducked to the side, the club smashing the plank floor where he had been standing. The gutterback paused for a moment to rip his arm out, and August got an idea. With the gutterback's neck now just reachable, he aimed a blow. Too late, though, for the gutterback lifted up at the last second, and August's sword rebounded with a wet thunk.

August stayed on guard, unfazed. Now he had a plan. He taunted the gutterback again. "Ha!" he called. "If that's the best you can do, your mother was a gangler!"

The gutterback seemed to take real offense at this. If it had been angry before, now, it was furious. With twice its previous speed, it swung its club-arm down with enough force to split the plank floor in two, just as August passed underneath. The jagged edge clipped August's arm, leaving three bloody trails.

Now firmly stuck in the floor, the gutterback yelled mightily. August ignored it, and sliced its head off with a quick, clean blow. The body slumped down, the decapitated head rolling away, falling off the ship though a break in the railing. Just as it fell, August saw into its eyes, and met a hard, cold gaze filled with what could only be resignation.

August dropped to his knees, his entire body shaking with the aftereffects of adrenaline. The last of the grandshrooms passed behind them, and the only enemies left were the fires, easily fought with water and frost spells.

Elyse dropped to the floor next to August, staring up at the sky. *We made it,* she thought, full of relief and roiling with loosed fear.

Aye, August said, looking around at the sailors who had fallen, and the wounded, and the damage. *We made it.*

Little Girls Alone in the Forest

Denyse

Just after crossing into the wilds, Denyse and Kelly stopped near a clear lake, surrounded by tall pines. The place had a pristine air, as if no one—no human, at least—had seen the place in a very long time. The monster's tracks led around the lake, and back into the forest, where they disappeared beneath the shady trees. The two girls, however, had been traveling since the night before: almost a full day. After what had happened that night, a dam broke, and Denyse and Kelly became fast friends. Sometimes, it seemed Kelly forgot all about what had happened.

The moon and stars reflected off the surface of the water, creating two skies that stared at each other with countless eyes. A fish jumped. Ripples spread across the water, mixing across the sky.

Because they had entered the wild-lands, Denyse had decided not to build any fires. Instead, the two girls drank potions of cold resistance. They were standard fare for long journeys, but weren't cheap, and tasted like foul urine.

Denyse sputtered a bit as she drained her glass bottle. Sitting on a log next to her, Kelly wiped her mouth and burped, the loud noise startling a frog that had been sitting nearby. When they had finished, they placed the bottles back into their packs, afraid to do anything to sully the clean landscape.

Kelly leaned against the trunk of a tree. "Tell me a story," she said, as she stared out at the stars. They really were beautiful, as if the entire sky were lit up with white fire.

Denyse lay down on her log, thinking for a minute. She didn't have that many stories, being as young as she was. There hadn't been any great conflicts since she had been born, the last one being the war between the Green Bloods and the Werewolves, almost a century ago. That one had lasted for a decade, and almost destroyed the capital. She was almost sorry she hadn't been there to see it. Life was dull as a combat specialist when the world was at peace.

She had gone on one adventure, though. She finally remembered it as she played with the leather strap of her sword. She smiled.

"I won my sword in a bet with a skyship captain," Denyse said. Kelly stirred, but said nothing. "He was really drunk when he made it," Denyse continued, "and I was maybe nineteen, looking for an adventure. The man said that a customer of his needed some special ingredients, and when I offered to help, he laughed so hard that he fell off his chair."

Kelly chuckled a bit. "I take it you made the bet with him then?"

Lying on her back, on the log, Denyse reflected about how long it had been. "Yes," she said. "I challenged him to a bet, where I promised to get all the ingredients faster than he could. I think he was under the impression that I was just an ordinary little girl, and was just kidding around. 'A little warrior like you needs a big sword,' he said. I thought it was a great idea."

Denyse smiled at the memory. "He was so surprised when I came back with the raptorbeast claws that he actually honored his bet, and let me keep the sword."

"You killed a raptorbeast alone?" Kelly asked, her voice full of admiration.

"I sure did," Denyse said, proudly. "It was hard, and I almost lost my arm, but I managed to lure it underneath a rock wall and use magic to cover it with a landslide."

Kelly stayed silent for a minute, thinking about her story. "I wondered why someone as young as you was so high up," she said. "Now I think I know."

Denyse blushed a little bit. *Kelly admires me?* she thought, a little incredulous. She was used to admiring, not being admired. It felt a little weird.

Suddenly, her entire body tensed. Her dress-fairy, Tamalda, popped out of her shoulder-strap just as she bolted upright.

"I'm sorry to interrupt your little chat," the twinkling fairy said, "But it seems that several large humanoids are approaching us."

Denyse closed her eyes and listened. Sure enough, she head three sets of footsteps. Most worryingly, they were loud and announcing, as if the ones who made them had no intention of staying concealed.

Kelly and her fairy, Amber, picked up the two packs that had been lying on the pine needle carpet. She tossed one to Denyse, in case they needed to make a quick escape. Denyse drew her sword, its blade almost as tall as herself. Kelly brought out the cutlass that she fought with. Its sleek, unadorned design seemed almost a part of her, extending out of her hand.

The stomping came closer. Voices carried across the forest. Denyse wasn't sure if it was good, or bad. They were definitely human, but here in the wilds, that could mean anything. The two backed up against each other, watching all sides. Denyse's battle display fired up. A green icon appeared over Kelly's head, and she saw their status appear in the upper-left corner of her vision.

Since they hadn't practiced as a party, they had only the universal code words to work with. Against monsters that wasn't so bad, but against another trained party, it could be dangerous.

The rustling and stomping grew closer, and closer, until the trees in front of Denyse parted, and a tall man carrying an axe stepped out of the forest.

He looked kindly enough, wearing overalls and high work boots. He had a beard, long and black as pitch, and he wore a cloth cap. Upon seeing the two girls, his eyebrows shot up. "Oy!" He called out, turning his head behind him. "I found something!"

Two more men with axes appeared out of the underbrush. They stood together and looked down at the two heavily armed little girls in dresses.

"Identify yourself," Denyse stated, determined to take the initiative.

The man with the long black beard paused, taken aback by Denyse's challenge. His eyes opened wide, as if he were seeing a pig fly. Clearly, they had never heard of the Disciplinary Force, or of magical girls.

"What are you doing out here, young miss?" The man asked, after a long pause.

Denyse didn't answer. *I still have no guarantee that they're not hostile,* she thought. "I'll answer that when you tell me who you are, sir," she finally said.

The woodsman contemplated this, and then seemed to relent. "I'm Hank," he said. He motioned to his comrades. "The one with the blue shirt is Bill, and the one with the long hair is Charles."

The two men he pointed to grunted their greetings in turn. Denyse looked them over, and didn't see anything off. Above their heads, yellow icons floated, which meant that Tamalda had identified them as neutral. Denyse relented, trusting her fairy's judgment.

"My name is Denyse," Denyse said, forgoing the formalities. She was a sergeant now, but she doubted that it mattered to these men. "This is Kelly," she said, motioning towards the sailor. Kelly nodded, though she kept her cutlass unsheathed.

Hank looked from Denyse to Kelly, and then back to Denyse. "I don't suppose you would care to answer my question now?" he said.

"We're here tracking a group of monsters that attacked a copper mine centerwards from here, about two weeks ago," Denyse answered.

Hank and his men seemed genuinely surprised by that, staring harder at the two girls. By all accounts, Denyse and Kelly were indistinguishable from normal girls of ten or eleven, except for their expressions and deadly weapons. In fact, it could be said that they looked even more innocent, like an ideal of the form.

"I have a daughter your age," Charles, the one with the long hair, said. His face read a mixture of emotions, confusion and concern winning out.

Denyse decided to play along for the moment, and see where these men had come from. Perhaps they knew something about the monsters they had been tracking. "I would like to meet her," Denyse said, in her nicest little girl voice. She sheathed her sword, causing an audible breath of relief to come from the standing men. Kelly followed suit.

"We live not far from here in a small town," the man said, "but we don't get very many visitors."

It was true that some humans lived in the wilds. However, they were often considered to be the dregs of society, cast off and unable to live in the settled world.

These men looked nice enough, however, and Tamalda had gauged them as neutral. When a fairy decided someone's intentions, it was without a doubt right.

"Take me to your village," Denyse said, doing her best to tone down the command in her voice. The men looked unsteady, as if they could not believe what was happening. Kelly followed her, and soon the group of five headed skyward, deeper into the wilds.

Armada of Blue Steel

Emeralda

Outside the capital, the night burned dimly, the stars hidden by the bright lights hanging from the pillars that supported the city's giant dome. Emeralda passed through the suburbs quickly, and soon capital Main Street became no more than a dirt track. She checked the note, again, against a map of the capital and the area around it. Satisfied that she was headed in the right direction, she folded it and put it in one of the folds of her rainbow dress.

Even at this hour, the streets were not empty, the occasional pack beast or transport walker interspersed with a steady stream of travelers on foot. About a mile from the city wall, Emeralda turned clockwise. In front of her, glowering in the night, there stood an ancient barrow, long since stripped of anything worth looting by the inhabitants of the capital.

Emeralda climbed up the steep, grassy side, until she reached the very top. She checked the coordinates, and then checked the magical compass. She was there.

Only, not a soul could be seen. The capital dominated the centerward horizon, and the pathways with streetlamps made glowing trails through the mud and grass, but up on the top of the barrow it was as desolate as if it were in the middle of the wilds.

It could be a trap, Emeralda thought. She drew her combat knife, the short point knife-sized even for her. Down one edge, sharp ridges created a serrated pattern that whirled and looped like flames. It was the only decoration on the otherwise plain blade.

"Hello, General," a voice said, form directly behind Emeralda.

Emeralda twisted at full force, swinging her knife in a twirling uppercut. She sliced thin air. In front of where she had struck, the same man that had given her the letter stood, in all his peculiar ordinariness. Emeralda had not heard him approach, and neither had her dress-fairy, June.

"Sorry," June whispered in her ear. "He has some sort of power that I can't detect."

Emeralda stood up to her full height. "Why did you call me here?" she asked.

The man smiled, as if he knew something very secret, and was about to tell. "You are in need of skyships, yes?" he asked, his voice level.

Emeralda nodded, surprised by his question.

"I have something for you," the man said, reaching into his pocket. He pulled out a crystal, but one unlike any Emeralda had seen before. An ordinary crystal was translucent, like clouded glass. They were used to store information magically, and were quite common. But this crystal, the crystal that the man held, didn't look at all like the normal ones. In the same shape, it seemed to suck in the light around it, and give off a peculiar metallic sheen. Two straight furrows, like blades of blue light, divided the crystal into four sections.

The man let down his hand, but the crystal stayed where it was. After a second, it floated down, towards Emeralda. Emeralda caught it in her palm, a look of wonder on her face.

"This is the key," the man said. "Use it wisely."

Emeralda was about to say something, but stopped short, as she stared at empty air. It was if the man had never been there. The key still hovered in her palm, pulsing with a clean energy.

Behind where the man had stood, the entrance to the barrows loomed tall. It was in ruins, but in the dim glow from the capital, Emeralda could see that the material had once looked similar to the key she held. She entered the barrow, holding the key out in front of her. As she went lower, the key seemed to take on new energy, and even began to rotate in her palm. It was warming up, but for what, Emeralda couldn't tell.

At the last floor of the barrow, deep underground, Emeralda met with a dead end. She stood for a moment, contemplating heading back up and checking the barrow again. She was about to turn around when the key threw the room in a deep blue light, and zipped out of her palm and into a barely noticeable crevice in the wall. The wall did nothing for a moment, looking purple in the light of the key. Then, beams of light, just like the furrows on the key, traced through every surface around her, lighting her in a castle of blue lines.

Behind her, the blue lights traced their way all the way down the hall, and up the stairs, and out into the barrow beyond. The door in front of her came apart, into big, metallic squares, and folded into the wall until it disappeared. The corridor ahead of her was dark.

Emeralda stepped over the threshold, and saw dimly a forest of shapes, huge, inside of a cavern that looked as if it could swallow the entire capital whole. She wondered where she was, in relation to aboveground. Not anywhere she had heard of, before.

The blue furrows of light rushed past where she stood, and began to climb up the walls, tracing a simple, abstract design, that was more elegant than the richest of tapestries. Around her, the big shapes she had seen lit up as well, with the same blue lines.

Emeralda gasped. Her eyes went wide. All around her, filling the entirety of the massive blue-lit room, were row upon row of skyships.

Old Man + Little Girl =

Denyse

Their village was no more than a cluster of hovels, surrounded by a crude wooden palisade. Hank led them through the gate, under the watchful eyes of the guards. Their weapons were simple farming implements, and they wore no armor to speak of. Denyse wondered how they had survived, out in the dangerous wilds. Kelly walked beside her, both of the girls walking in front of Charles and Bill. When they had all entered the village, the doors shut with a creak.

A little girl the same age that Denyse looked to be ran out of a hovel against the skyward side of the wall. Her golden hair shone in the moonlight. Upon seeing Denyse and Kelly, she began to skip happily. "You brought friends, Da!" she called out to Charles.

Charles scratched the back of his neck, unsure of what to do. He looked to Hank for guidance, but got only a shrug in response. The little girl stopped in front of Denyse, and looked her up and down critically. "My name's Mary. What's yours?" she said, her face inviting.

When she told her name, Kelly froze. Kelly's eyes opened wide, as if she were experiencing what had happened all over again. Denyse rushed to her side, and caught her just as she stumbled. Kelly's face showed real fear, and extreme distress, as if her life were in danger. The villagers that had gathered around them saw, and began to murmur amongst themselves.

Kelly began to struggle against Denyse. Denyse held her fast, not knowing what was happening. Kelly became more violent, kicking, scratching, and even biting Denyse. She screamed out short, unintelligible words. Her eyes stared a million miles away.

Kelly paused, and remembered her cutlass. Denyse saw the motion before it began, but was too late to stop it. The sword flashed out, shining bright with starlight, and whipped around Kelly. Denyse jumped back just in time. Kelly yelled at the top of her young voice, and stabbed at the air, and then into the ground. She stabbed it again, and again, and again, until clots of dirt flew up all around her. Denyse could do nothing but watch. The three woodsmen who had brought them moved to restrain her, but Denyse cut them off with her own sword.

"She's all right," she said, not believing it herself.

Kelly froze just then. She looked around herself, at little Mary, at the sword in her hands, at the village. She seemed to realize what had happened. She dropped to her knees, her face contorted with an expression of deep suffering. She buried her head in her knees and dropped her cutlass.

Denyse approached her then, and put her arm around her. Kelly didn't resist.

"You're ok," Denyse said, in her most soothing voice. "I'll protect you, you're safe with me."

A voice carried across the courtyard. "I've never seen battle-mind as bad as that," it said. It was old, and strained, as if the man who spoke it had to fight to get the words off his tongue.

Denyse turned to see a wrinkled figure, hunched over a crutch, with silver-white hair and only half of one leg. He moved with purpose, despite his evident debility, and none of the villagers moved to assist him. They kept a respectful distance, dead silent as the man approached the crouching girls.

"You must have seen something terrible," the man said, stopping just above Kelly and Denyse.

When Denyse stood up, she found she could almost look him eye to eye. The man didn't flinch. Instead, he looked as if he were gazing into her soul.

"You are older than you look," the man said, after a minute. "Much older." He lifted Kelly up from her position on the ground, using his free hand to gently pull her arm. Kelly looked the man in the eyes, her countenance dead.

The old man scrunched up his face. "And you, my girl," he placed his palm on her face, and closed his eyes. "You are older than any of us, older than we can imagine."

Denyse nodded, surprised at the man's perceptiveness. Kelly sniffed, and her eyes gained a little spark.

"The monsters you are looking for stopped their journey not far from here," the man continued, "but I would not want to face them in the condition you are in." He pulled Kelly up to her full height. "Stay here for a while," he said. "The monsters are more than it seems, and it would be best if you were to see them in full health."

Denyse nodded dumbly, too muddled to make much of it. It seemed that a day going hard without sleep was finally taking its toll on her.

The old man silenced the protesting mutters from the crowd with a piercing glance. "They are my guests," he said. "And I will have them treated as such."

Burial at Sky

August

It took two whole days to finish the repairs to the *Firebird,* in which Ruby did not train them. August spent most of his time repairing broken floorboards, especially where the gutterback had smashed through the deck. He regretted his plan often, as he bent his back under the harsh sunlight for hours on end, hammering, sawing, and fitting.

Two sailors had died during the escape, one from the lightning bolt, and one from an arrow that made it past her magical defenses. Their names were Orine and Bess, and the ship's captain read them a eulogy as they were prepared to be buried at sky.

This meant that magicians would attach plank to some skysteel, and strap the body on. They would angle it up, and light it on fire, so that the heat of the burning wood—and the burning body—would give the skysteel lift.

August watched as the two flaming piers lifted up, and went higher, and higher, until they disappeared into the clouds. He reflected on his own mortality, and how close he had come to them, but quickly shoved away the thought. It was not something someone on a dangerous adventure should be thinking of.

With two sailors left behind at the mines, one left at Elderdale, two lost in combat, and two more injured, the *Firebird* was a few hands short. And so, Penny and Elyse learned how to fly a skyship, under the instruction of the captain. Her name was Francine Jules, but everyone called her captain Freyjay. As her name implied, she was an easygoing captain.

Just as August finished the last of the deck repairs, the flat forest that they had been traveling over before rose up atop rolling hills. They were approaching the mountains of the sky, the border between the wilds and the edgelands. They would need to pass through on foot, using an ancient network of tunnels that led to the Centrix. What was behind the mountains, only the deities knew—and they really didn't like sharing information.

August looked over the side of the ship, watching the hills rolling past, thinking of what was to come. He had started on this adventure because he wanted to help Penny, and because he didn't have anything better to do. Not the best reasons for risking his life, sure, but so far it had been quite a ride, and he certainly wasn't bored. But now that the goal was in sight, the edgelands, he felt himself more invested in what was happening. The army of monsters that had attacked Edlerdale came from somewhere, and if there was one, there might be others. His instincts as a monster hunter told him that something huge was afoot.

Elyse came up to the rail beside him, and rested her head on his shoulder. Her shock white hair flowed to the side with the wind, her black cloak puffed about, her black spectacles gleamed. August looked at her for a while, wondering. She was beautiful, yes, but not in the normal way. She looked too strange for that. It was something in her bearing, her mannerisms, that made her who she was, and also gave her such a subtle attractiveness.

It's beautiful, isn't it? Elyse thought, speaking of the mountains that passed by. She had heard August thinking, of course, but that sort of thing went unspoken for the most part.

They look like old warriors, August thought. *Ready to fight at any moment, but standing there proud, all the same.*

It's certainly something to look at, Elyse added.

In front of the *Firebird*, skyward, the tallest mountains hid in the distance behind purple veils. At any one time, they seemed as stationary as solid, unmoving stone, but if August forgot to look at them for a moment they would creep just a little bit closer. The *Firebird* had a tailwind, and had had one for a while. The sky brought air currents towards itself, towards the junction between it and the ground, almost as if it wanted the *Firebird* to come.

Ruby, seeing that the repairs had been finished, entered the training field. "Penny, August, Elyse!" She called, tapping a practice sword on the ground. August groaned, and turned away from the scene that rolled by.

When they had assembled before her, Ruby walked back and forth, just as she had on their first day together. "As you have noticed," she began, "My party is now scattered about the world. Since you must continue your training nonetheless, I have decided to drill with you, instead of against you, as a party of four." She stopped, a little color showing on her cheeks. "I hope that we can continue to improve, and that we will have the best possible success."

Penny smiled, and walked up to her, wrapping her in a big hug. Ruby cleared her throat, embarrassed, but hugged her back. "So you've decided to join us," Penny said.

"It's just for training," Ruby said, her face reddening even more. "Until . . ." She broke off, and then disengaged from the hug.

August and Elyse both smiled at her. "Well, someone with your expertise will certainly do us good," Elyse said.

Ruby stood up straight, this time addressing them as part of a circle. "Today we will be practicing basic four-person drills," she said, back to her usual business tone.

August looked at Elyse, and the two smiled. Penny hopped from on foot to another, and it was almost exciting when Ruby took out the targets.

The Little Girls are Coming!

Emeralda

The ancient barrow was a skyship dock, complete with auto loading machinery and launching mechanisms for the near 600 skyships that sat within. There were more than enough ships for Emeralda's army, including the ones needed for the transport of supplies. With the power of the ancients, Emeralda could finally hope to face up against the monsters.

The only problem is that she was sure the monsters had found something similar. Everything pointed in that direction. However, she pushed the thought out of her mind, as she supervised the loading of her army.

All around the barrow, curious crowds had gathered, held back with a ring of undead soldiers and magical girls. Every guild in the city had either threatened her or tried to bargain with her, only to receive a simple rebuttal. There was no time to build a bigger army, and of course, it was no use trying to threaten somebody with one. However, that didn't stop the civilians, and the reporters, from trying their best to bring a halt to her operation.

As she broke through the ring to reach the barrow, coming back from a meeting with the head necromancer, dozens of reporters swarmed all around her.

"Miss Stysh!" They all cried. "Where did you find these ships? How do you feel about the invasion of Elderdale? Are you really planning to go on the offensive?"

Emeralda stayed silent, and made her way to the top of the barrow. When she had activated the port, the barrow's top-most layer had sloughed off, to reveal an entire skyship dock, that brought the ships up from storage on a massive conveyor belt. The undead soldiers were leading now, long columns leading down the barrow and through the ring of reporters, all the way back to the Capital. They saw her as some sort of saint, she believed, and almost worshipped her. Certainly they held a zeal for her cause, and it wasn't something she wanted to get rid of.

However, it was still disorienting when people called her "Holy," making her check behind her for any agents of the holy church. Apparently, they didn't care much for undead worshippers, but it still made her nervous.

The healers and summoners from the Necromancer's guild had come, better trained than she had asked for. The head of the guild, Jan Tross, had decided to back her full swing, now that she had a force behind her. Every other guild envied his position.

The Greenblood's volunteer corps had swelled to almost 3,000, with the publicity the ships had generated. Emeralda wasn't sure how many of them could hold in a sustained battle, but she wasn't about to turn away able warriors. She certainly had enough ships.

On the other side of the ancient pier, monster-riders from the Monster-tamer's guild loaded onto barge ships. The barges, just like every other ship in her armada, looked as if each one could take on the whole world.

Emeralda made it to the top, amid the bustling of supplies and soldiers, and approached the flagship, the *Amshfisht*. Its name, almost unpronounceable, came from the ancient lettering on its side, written out in the glowing blue lines that covered most of the technology.

Emeralda climbed aboard, and met with a tall woman, young and fit, that had a certain air of immateriality to her. She was the ship's magical intelligence, a real person that was part of the ship, as far as Emeralda could tell. When she described it, it made as much sense as all the other things behind the mysterious ships.

"Hello, Amy," Emeralda said, as she stepped across the grey metal deck. Her real name was Amshfisht, just like the ship, but since no one could pronounce it, they called her Amy.

"Hello, General," Amy said, her voice as sweet as a normal woman's.

Emeralda walked up to where the ship's control house jutted out of the deck like a cube on top of a flat table. Amy called it a bridge, but Emeralda couldn't see why that would be.

In the bridge, magical girls bustled about, moving things with crystals just like the one that had unlocked it all. The controls were intuitive, and even an undead could figure it out. As Emeralda entered the room, all activity stopped, and a dozen sailors gave salutes.

"At ease," Emeralda said, after a second. The activity continued.

A girl in a red sailor's jacket, with a matching blue dress, walked up to Emeralda and saluted. "Loading is on schedule, and our operatives are preparing to begin boarding."

That would be Emeralda's portion of the army, 3,000 soldiers. Each and every one was a highly skilled warrior, but it was quite a small amount when compared with the massive army the monsters had fielded.

"When will we be ready to leave, lieutenant?" Emeralda asked.

"In 12 hours," The lieutenant replied. "Add another five if the reporters keep slowing us down."

Emeralda nodded, happy with the reply. She was fielding a large army, and it was quite much to ask for expediency.

Outside the windows of the bridge, Emeralda noticed a disturbance in the civilians and reporters. They turned away from the pier for a moment, towards a column of figures marching out of the Capital.

Emeralda had never brought together this many magical girls before, and the effect was truly astounding. The individualistic nature of the girls showed obviously when they marched in column, their high flexibility and long experience enabling them all to march in lockstep, even without training. In just a few days, the Disciplinary Force had gone from shadowy operation to full-fledged fighting guild, with only a few hitches.

Of course, an army of 3,000 highly skilled warriors that looked like ten-year old girls was sure to catch the eye of anybody anywhere. Emeralda smiled, and remembered when she had first been given her power, when she had had no more than her group of friends with her.

Most of them had since died or gone on their own paths, but Emeralda still remembered the spirit with which they had begun. "To save the world!" they had said, "and protect it from evil!"

And so, as the ships loaded, and the sun went down, Emeralda's army prepared to help save the world.

A fix

Denyse

They left the small, nameless village at dawn, two days after they had come during the night. The old man—who had never given his name—had spent most of that time sitting in the courtyard, staring at the sky, with Kelly right next to him. They both stayed motionless from dawn to dusk, having a conversation without words, between like souls. By the end of it, Kelly had cheered up to almost her former self, with only the slightest tinge of sadness and fear hidden behind her eyes.

Denyse couldn't say how it had happened, but it had happened, and for that, she was grateful. While Kelly sat, and healed, Denyse busied herself playing with the children of the village, at first like a mother with kids, and then after a little while just like one of them. She let out things that she had been holding in, too, ever since her selection for the service. It was as if time reversed, for two days, in which the two girls lived out their dreams.

But, all good things had to end, and so the pair prepared to travel out into the wilderness beyond, as the sun rose on the third day. The woodcutters, and the old man, and Mary and the kids all watched them go, waving at them, having laden them with plenty of delicious preserved food.

Once on the road, Denyse took out the map the old man had drawn for her. It seemed that the monsters had stopped, just before the two had stumbled on the village, and begun to do something that the man who had seen it had not understood. He had said they were "Playing with solid light." Denyse had her suspicions, but she saved them for when she saw whatever it was.

Cutting through the forest on a thin deer trail, Kelly pulled up close to Denyse. "I wanted to thank you," she said, passing underneath a branch that would have hindered a grown man. "You helped me," she said, "and I hadn't done anything to deserve it." She sounded serious, as if this meant a lot to her.

Denyse chose her reply carefully. "I would have helped anyone in your situation," she said, just a little bit embarrassed.

"I know," Kelly said, "which is why it makes you so much more amazing."

Denyse almost cringed, and then caught herself. *What are you worried about?* She asked her internal voices. *She's just . . .*

"I feel safe, now," Kelly said, her voice happy, and calm. "So, thanks."

Denyse nodded dumbly. "I feel safer with you, too, Kelly," she said, as she stepped through a thorn bush. Her magical fairy-dress protected her from most of the pointy ends, but a few still scratched her hands and cheek.

Kelly stayed silent for a moment, and the awkwardness only grew in proportions. "It's just," Kelly finally said, swatting at some buzzing flies. "No one ever saved me before, and everyone I know would have probably run, or done something like abandon me when I needed them most."

Denyse held back a lump in her throat. "I take it Mary protected you, too?" She asked, because if felt like the right thing to ask.

Kelly said nothing for a while, and Denyse concentrated on the path in front of her. It was becoming more difficult.

"Yes," Kelly said, after a good long while. "I . . ." She huffed. "This is hundred year-old history, but my dad wasn't the best."

Denyse had almost forgotten that people like her had fathers. She hadn't seen hers since she became a magical girl, more than forty years ago.

"And then Koko came and found me, one day, after I had run away from home, when my parents had a big fight." Kelly talked faster now, as if she were desperate to get things off her chest.

Denyse understood, and stayed silent.

"I thought it was a rabbit at first, but when he started flapping his bunny ear wings, I almost died of shock. But then he was so cute, that

I couldn't help but like him." She lingered for a moment. "I never said goodbye, and I never saw them again. Mary became like my family, after I met her. I became a sailor because she did."

Denyse shook her head. She had thought they were fast friends, but from the looks of it, it seemed that they were closer than that. Magical girls weren't supposed to feel love, but . . .

"If you ever need a friend, I'll be here for you," Denyse said, after a while.

Kelly stayed silent, as if she were waiting for something. She traveled behind Denyse, so all Denyse heard were her footsteps and her breathing, getting harsher as they climbed over rough terrain.

A chasm opened up in front of them, and the two stopped. The deer trail led down the side, twisting around boulders and little green shrubs. Denyse checked her map, and confirmed it: the monsters were hiding somewhere in this chasm, probably in a small cave of some sort.

Kelly huffed again, and threw her arms around Denyse from behind. Denyse, who had been thinking of tactics, yelped in surprise. Kelly held on for a moment, and then let go, after Denyse said nothing. "Don't leave me, ok?" She said, her voice soft.

Denyse sighed, and turned to face her. Kelly's eyes burned with a vigor that she hadn't seen in them before. It was almost as if she were a new person. This person, Denyse also saw, would probably fight much better than the old person. And, if she ever needed help, she saw that Kelly would come after her, no matter the situation, no matter the circumstances.

And, of course, it didn't hurt that she was cute.

"I won't," Denyse told her, holding her gaze. "I pinky promise." She held up her pinky.

Kelly lit up even brighter before, and seemed almost to be beaming. She held out her hand, and locked pinkies with Denyse. "Pink promise," she confirmed.

The lightning came out of their dresses, and twirled around their forms, turning two into one, that shot off into the sky in a pillar of energy. When it was over, the two girls' hair floated back down into place.

"Let's get going," Denyse said, as she turned back around. "We have some monsters to find."

You Don't Gotta Look Tough to be Tough

Justle
Justle stood on the counterclockwise wall of the frontier city of Elderdale. The sailor that had disembarked from the *Firebird,* Iris, stood next to her. The two cut a picturesque figure, against the horizon, marred only by the ugly purplish caps of the monstrous grandshrooms. Justle had been put in charge of coordinating the inner city defense, to protect the city in the event of a wall breach.

At first, the very notion that a girl like her could command soldiers had put the guardsmen into hysterics. No matter what Justle did, she couldn't get them to take her seriously. That is, until Iris challenged their champion wrestler to a duel.

That day, the dust from the city streets had clouded up and now powdered every open space. The fighting arena, packed tight with civilians that were bored from the siege, seemed to drink in the heat, and the harsh sunlight.

Murmurs of astonishment went up as Iris, in the corner of the ring, ripped off her dress, exposing her bright cloth underclothes. Even Justle had been surprised, but she didn't comment. She knew that women fighting in the arena often wore almost nothing, and was grateful for Iris's protection.

The crowd, growing ever bigger as news of the spectacle spread through the city, leaned in their chairs to get a better view of the contestants.

Iris seemed minuscule, like a tiny doll, when put across from her opponent, Gurren the Powerful. One time world champion, he had since fallen from glory, but still possessed the muscles of a pure fighting spirit. He towered over even ordinary men, his features resembling that of a gutterback, ever so slightly. He smelled nicer, however, and his skin shone a clear bronze.

He wore a loincloth, and nothing else. His furry chest heaved with each breath, although he seemed a little hesitant to do battle. From what Justle heard, he had daughters, three of them.

Iris stared him down, not even flinching. The skin of her arms, a thin, pasty white, reflected sunlight almost like a mirror.

If Justle were a betting person, she would have put all her money on Iris, even before she knew the outcome. She felt sorry for the men and women that lost their money that day.

The match began when a man swung at the massive gong that hung over the entrance. Iris and Gurren circled each other, Iris barely topping the man's thighs. She stared, unafraid, and it was actually Gurren that showed the fear in his heart.

The crowd began to jeer, and taunt, and catcall. The arena seemed to take all the sun that landed on it and focus it into the fighting pit.

Iris made the first move. She dived at Gurren's knees, attempting a knockdown. Gurren dodged, just in time, and Iris rolled under and popped up on the other side. The crowd oohed, and Gurren turned his heavy body around. He made a lunge for Iris, half-hearted, that she could have just ducked under. Instead, she kicked off his thigh, shot through the gap between his arms, and, dancing on his grasping knuckles, pulled a backflip across his back and down to the floor.

The crowd silenced. Not a person spoke. Then with a boom that would have made an armada proud, they erupted into violent noise. Cheers, jeers, curses, cries. More money changed hands, and the betting offices filled to the brim.

Justle smiled. *So Iris is a show-woman at heart,* she thought.

The match continued in the same way for almost an hour, each clumsy attempt at catching dodged by Iris in the most amazing fashion. Iris twirled, and spun, and seemed more than magical as she tried to bring the massive man down.

Finally, at near an hour after they had started, Iris managed to land a hold. She flipped off Gurren's bent knee, and, twisting in mid-air, landed right on his shoulders, his head between her legs. She twisted, just enough to bring the man to the ground. They hit the dirt with a thump. The stadium grew quiet. Then the announcer began the countdown. The audience joined on the second number. Soon, the place had been whipped into a frenzy, men standing up and climbing over each other to scream into the air.

At the last moment, with seconds to spare, Gurren somehow changed the tide. He pulled a contortionist's twist, and somehow, Iris ended up directly underneath him, now pinned to the ground.

The stadium went silent again, and then went even more wild. The countdown started. Then, it faltered. Slowly, steadily, Iris was pushing Gurren right up into the air. One foot went up, and then the other, and then both arms, until she held Gurren up completely in the air. The man scrabbled for purchase in the dust, but found none. With a grunt that still managed to sound cute and womanly, Iris flipped the man over like a hamburger on a grill. She was on top again, holding the man's arms down in the most painful of fashions. Sweat dribbled from her body like a waterfall, visible even from the stands.

When the countdown hit 0, it was as if the entire world broke underneath a wave of sound, the stadium goers shouting so loud that Justle wondered if the monsters thought for a minute that they had lost, somehow. The shouting about that couldn't possibly have been any louder.

And so, through a strange series of events, Justle was put into control of the city's inner defense, and was obeyed more solidly than any other commander in the city's history.

A short swim

Denyse

The cave they found was a small opening underneath two brown shrubs that looked as if they had seen far too much wind. Narrow at the entrance, it soon widened considerably, until it was as hollow as a cathedral. The monster tracks led in further and further, ending at a river that rushed though, from darkness, and back into darkness, the red circle illuminated by Denyse's werelight roiling with white foam.

Denyse searched the area, and, upon closer investigation, noticed a small dock carved out of the rock. Denyse thought for a moment, and then called up her dress-fairy, Tamalda. Amber, Kelly's dress fairy, came out as well.

"How much material can you make?" Denyse asked, without preamble.

"About enough for three dresses," Tamalda answered, confused. "The stuff takes a lot of magical energy to maintain. It's woven out of pure light, you know."

Three dresses, two fairies, six square feet per dress... Leaving a square foot for each of us, for waterwear... She looked at the rushing river. "We're going in," she said, certain of herself.

Tamalda flittered around her face. "What do you mean, you're going in? If you do, you'll get cold-sickness, and who knows what else—"

Densye cut her off. "Me and Kelly aren't actually going in," she explained. "You are."

Tamalda paused, and then looked at the water. "Huh?" she said.

Denyse explained her plan to them. Tamalda and Amber would join forces to create a boat, that Kelly and Denyse would ride in, down the river. It was simple, and elegant. The only problem was one of cloth. Tamalda did the calculations. They had enough, they even had extra. Denyse, however, insisted on waterwear.

"If our clothing gets soaked," she explained, "It will be heavy, and cold."

Tamalda agreed with her logic, and soon the two girls had stripped down to tops and bottoms.

When the boat had been completed, Denyse drenched the boat in water, and then, when it was wet, cast a spell of freezing. The boat hardened, not even slippery, as the ice formed between the cloth's weave. Tamalda shivered involuntarily on her perch next to Denyse's ear.

"It's cold," she said.

Denyse placed the boat into the water, and held it with one foot. She let Kelly board first, her bare feet splashing as she waded into the river. Denyse tossed her a potion of cold resistance, from her pack on the ground. She then took the pack and froze it over too, so that the ice formed a waterproof casing. She did the same for Kelly's pack.

When they were all set, Denyse stepped in, and lodged herself firmly between the boat's sides. She created two paddles out of ice and fabric, and tossed one to Kelly. Kelly took it, the expression on her face showing admiration at Denyse's resourcefulness.

The boat moved slowly at first, the current rushing past the icy sides. Stalactites hung down over the tunnel they were about to enter, and a few ordinary bats fluttered past, screeching in their peculiar language. The werelight above Denyse lit up the water for a few yards before them, but after that, a wall of darkness blocked everything from sight. More stalactites came out like so many bared teeth. The walls closed in around them, and soon, they traveled at the speed of the water.

Kelly stared out of the boat, at the wonderful patterns that formed on the walls, like waves made of living stone. Thin curtains of white lime hung down in between the stalactites, the red light giving them an unearthly pinkish aura. The boat drifted peacefully. Denyse kept it on course by pushing at the walls with her makeshift paddle.

A new sound became audible, like the rushing of a distant waterfall.

"Hold tight," Denyse said, as she formed some handholds out of solid ice. She gripped them tight, the oar across her bare stomach. Kelly wrapped her arms around her, warming her back, catching some of the spray that now tossed forth from the river. The river widened, and the boat entered a current in the center of it all. It headed down straight as an arrow, towards the source of the noise. The water chopped up, and all around, freezing into little droplets when it sprayed onto the boat's interior.

With their potions of cold resistance in full effect, neither of them felt the cold. Denyse was sure that if they had been uninsulated, they would have caught cold-sickness. As it was, she shivered involuntarily when waves water washed over her body.

The river sped up. They now hurtled down the tunnel, stalactites disappearing behind them at an alarming rate.

The monsters made it, Denyse thought, to reassure herself. She hoped that they hadn't used some sort of unknown trick to go over the falls, or maybe gone down an unseen tributary.

It was too late for decisions, though, and the cavern soon filled with a fine misty spray. The waterfall sounded in both of her ears, simultaneously, but different, the cave mixing up the echoes into the noise of rushing water. Swirls the size of their boat appeared all around, almost close enough to catch them. They stayed safe in the center, as safe as one could be while riding a frozen boat down a subterranean waterfall.

The cave opened up, without warning, popping out of the dark like a surprise party. It was massive, as tall as a mountain, which led Denyse to believe that the river had taken them very deep underground.

And then, they were in the air. They stayed motionless for a second, and Denyse let go of her handholds for a moment and felt as if she were flying. Then, they fell. The water rushed all around them, spilling into the boat, spilling back out, drenching them from head to toe. Denyse thanked the gods that she had remembered to put on waterwear. The pantheon probably had nothing to do with it, but it was safer to make sure.

And then they hit the water, the boat ripping at Denyse's arms, as she held fast to her handholds. Her hands froze into place, as they went deeper underwater. Kelly gripped her hard, barely hanging on through the turbulence. Denyse felt the smooth strands of her hair, as it went in all directions.

The boat popped back up, brought to the surface by the ice that constructed it. Denyse gasped, and almost hit her face on the prow. She tried to move, realized she was frozen into place, panicked, and lit the boat up with a fire spell.

Too late, she realized her mistake. The boat collapsed into water and fabric, drenching them both again. Thankfully, they both could swim, and soon they lay on the shore, panting, beads of water dripping off their skin, their hair plastered to their faces.

Denyse got up first, and looked up, just to see where they were. She froze into place as soon as she saw what hung above them.

An underside, to a massive structure, larger than a city, with legs that extended far out to the sides of the cavern, and out of sight: a mechanical walker, of epic proportions.

On closer examination, it appeared that droves of figures walked about, all through the scaffolding that surrounded the massive walker. Denyse knew, even from here: they were monsters. She rolled over and looked at Kelly, who also stared upwards, on her back.

"What should we do?" Kelly asked, her voice exhausted and full of fear.

"First," Denyse said, determined to be practical, "we need to get dry." She spoke not for herself or Kelly, already drying in their light clothing, but rather for the two dress-fairies. The fabric of the boat lay sprawled across the stone floor, on top of which Tamalda curled, not moving. The water had affected her badly. Amber dragged her tiny body towards Kelly, her wings stuck to her side.

Denyse scooped them both up, and deposited them on her shoulder. They sat without complaint, barely holding on.

Kelly stood up as well, and the two girls worked together to fold the fairy-cloth up into a neat pile. Later, when the fairies had regained their strength, Denyse expected them to return the cloth to its original state. For now, though, Kelly added it to her load. Their packs had survived the fire spell, in their place at the back of the boat. They had frozen solid to the sides, and only now melted back into soaked cubes of fabric. Denyse checked inside her pack. Almost no water had gotten in.

Their packs shouldered, the two girls headed towards the closest thing that looked like shelter. As they were obviously in the middle of some sort of monster secret base, it was no good lighting a fire in the open. They were lucky enough that no monsters had noticed the boat, or Denyse's panicked fireball spell.

That closest thing was a collection of stalagmites that reached up ten stories, surrounded by smaller stone spears, so that the whole gathering resembled a forest. Several of the stalagmites had grown together, in whatever way they grew, and had created a small cavern that was just big enough for the two girls to sit in comfort, with perhaps room for a fire.

Denyse entered first, and, seeing that it was small, ushered Kelly in. Kelly dropped to the ground as soon as she passed the threshold. She unstrapped her pack, and it clanged on the stone floor. The cloth she had been carrying unfolded some.

Denyse had another idea. Taking the cloth, and without asking the two dress-fairies, she hung it over the entrance like a rug door, breaking little hooks out of the thin curtains that traced the walls. Later, she would ask the fairies to camouflage it, but for now, it worked well enough. As long as no monsters got too close, which seemed unlikely. They had not seen any patrols on the ground.

Denyse formed a small fireball, using the same spell she had used to melt the boat. It hovered in her palm, consuming just enough magic energy to stay lit. She placed it near the ground, being careful not to touch it to anything. It was quite dim, but warm all the same. Denyse set a werelight in the far corner of the cave to supply a constant, brighter light.

Soon, it felt as homely as could be, underneath a superweapon far beneath the ground and surrounded by monsters that wanted to kill them. Which is to say, good enough.

Denyse leaned back, and, trusting the fairies to keep watch as they dried out, drifted into a doze.

Just before she fell into a deep sleep, she felt Kelly curl up against her, and she felt a small piece of cloth come over them both. She smiled, feeling strangely safe for the first time in ages, and fell all the way to sleep.

How *do* you pronounce it?

Emeralda

Emeralda's army left 6 hours behind schedule—instead of the estimated five hours. Near 600 skyships, of all sorts, lifted off from the barrow, filled with near a division of soldiers, plus enough supplies to keep them going for half a year. It was a grand exit, one that would probably live on in the memories of the capital for centuries. They sky shone clear, the few clouds that puffed through the sky seemed cleaner than normal, and the wind blew nicely.

On her flagship, the *Amsfisht,* Emeralda looked over her armada. They traveled in erratic bunches, each one piloted by her own sailors. The controls, intuitive as they were, had made airwomen out of all of them.

Or course, it helped that each ship was a living being, like Amy, with their own wills and personalities. Or so Amy claimed. They were all female, because, "In all of history, and in every language, humans have referred to airships and naval vessels as *she.*"

Amy seemed so proud, when she said it. Emeralda couldn't see why she would be, but then, she couldn't understand most of what Amy said. She doubted that anyone else did, either.

Amy had also mentioned the fact the ships had no weapons. They were built for the purpose of transportation. Anything more and the builders would have created something far too powerful.

The *Amsfist's* navigator, Warrant Officer Charlie, stepped up beside Emeralda to give her report. She clicked her heels together. "Warrant Officer Charlie Davis, reporting," she said, her voice clear as a morning sun.

"How long until we reach Elderdale?" Emeralda asked, watching the trees flit by underneath her ship.

"Amy can tell you that, ma'am." Charlie said.

"That I can, Captain." Amy materialized next to her, like a spectral-type monster, her form jagged instead of fluffy.

Emeralda hadn't gotten used to it yet. She jumped a little. "So how long is it?" She asked, hiding her reaction.

"Elderdale is located at the coordinates two-four-five-six, fifty-seven, forty-nine, fifty-eight, correct?" Amy asked. That meant 2456 miles away from the capital in a straight line, at an angle of 57 degrees, 49 minutes, and 58 seconds measured from the Capital axis, along which Main Street ran in one direction and Main Avenue ran in the other, centered on the Royal Academy. The world had a diameter of exactly 10,000 miles, with the center of the capital being 5,000 miles away from all sides.

"Correct," Emeralda confirmed.

"With current weather predictions," Amy said, "and accounting for the improvement of the relationship between your crew and their ships, it will be at least seventeen full rotations."

Emeralda cursed to herself. Elderdale might be able to hold for 17 days, but then again, it might not. Emeralda turned towards the bridge. "Make it faster," she said. "show me what these ships can do."

"Right away, Captain," Amy said, disappearing into static.

Emeralda sighed, and then saluted to Officer Charlie. "You are dismissed," she said, in a half-hearted tone. She had got everything together only to be late for the party.

"You have an incoming call," June said, appearing over her shoulder. "It's from Sergeant Denyse Lilly."

"Patch her in," Emeralda said, suddenly excited. Denyse hadn't reported in for a while, and she had been wondering what had happened.

Denyse's name appeared in Emeralda's field of view, right under a talking character smiley face.

"General, is that you?" Denyse's voice came from somewhere close to her, yet this time, it sounded far off, distorted at the edges.

"The thread is weak," June said, fluttering around Emeralda, checking her dress up and down. "I don't think it's me."

"Sergeant Denyse," Emeralda said, relieved to be hearing from her. "Are you calling to report?"

"That," Denyse said, "And, I think there's something you might want to see." Denyse said it as if it were the greatest understatement in the world. Her tone gave Emeralda shivers.

"All right," Emeralda said, as she turned to a hatch in the deck of the ship. "Hold on while I find a place to sit."

Denyse waited, the only sound a strange, hollow reverberation, like the sound of a vibrating string. Emeralda climbed down the hatch, entering the ship's barracks. A few sailors walked the halls, blue crystal icons above their heads, as Emeralda's fairy-display did its job. More blue lights, this time those furrows of blue energy that were so prominent all around, traced unknown paths through every surface. They never turned, only split at perfect right angles.

Emeralda walked down the hall, getting salutes from the airwomen she passed. She stopped in front of a door that looked just like all the others: almost a part of the wall, outlined in blue lighting. She took a crystal from her pocket, like the one she had used to open the docks. The crystal hummed, and lit up, and the door disappeared into the wall in an orderly folding of blocks.

Emeralda stepped in, and the door closed behind her. Her room lit up brighter, the single window separating the stateroom and the outside made from a mysterious humming energy.

Emeralda sat down on her desk that she had brought from her own office. "Connect me," she said, to both June and Denyse. Denyse would be forming her magical orb about now, she imagined.

"You're connected," June said, as Emeralda's vision filled with darkness. "Correcting for low light," June said, and Emeralda saw the world outlined in a soft red.

Denyse appeared in front of her, as well as Kelly, who stood a little ways back. Emeralda could see that they were both in a small cave of some sort, with a blanket hanging from one side. A little fireball burned on the ground, and a red werelight explained the world's reddish tinge.

"General," Denyse said, getting straight to business. Kelly saluted, from behind Denyse.

"Sergeant," Emeralda replied, saluting from her chair. She turned the orb with a flick of her fingers and looked around. "So what is it you want me to see?" She asked, curious.

Denyse said nothing, but lifted up the blanket that hung on the wall to reveal an opening.

Emeralda followed her out, into a massive, dark valley. Emeralda frowned, because it should have been day outside.

"We're underground," Denyse explained, as she turned her head up. "Look up."

Emeralda rotated her orb up, and then froze, as she saw what Denyse had been looking at. It looked to be the same technology that powered her ships, only it was red, and far, far bigger than anything she could have imagined. The legs alone could have crushed a capital block, if ever they were so unlucky to be walked on.

"I take it this is what they were building," Emerald said, though she already knew the answer.

"They stole parts from various metal mines across the world," Denyse explained. "That's the reason why they were attacking! They're using human slaves to operate the machinery, because for some reason, they can't."

Emeralda nodded, impressed with what Denyse had discovered. "Are you safe where you are?" She asked, a plan forming in her mind.

"We think so," Denyse answered.

Next to her, Kelly nodded. "I don't think the monsters have spotted us, yet," she said.

"Good," Emeralda said. "I want you to stay here for as long as possible, and watch the machine. From what we know, it might start moving any day."

"It seems to be missing a critical piece," Denyse said. "A while ago, it started up, but then stopped after a few minutes. We heard a lot of commotion, and assumed it had broken somehow."

"Do you have enough supplies for a long wait?" Emeralda asked, checking practicalities.

"Yes, ma'am," Denyse said. "We resupplied at a friendly village not long ago."

"In the wilds?" Emeralda asked, raising an eyebrow.

Denyse simply shrugged. Kelly looked down at her feet.

"Is that all?" Emeralda asked.

"We have nothing else to report, General," Denyse said, and then saluted once more.

"Cut me off," Emeralda said, to June.

"Cutting you off," June replied, as Emeralda's vision flickered back to reality.

Now, all she had to do was get to Elderdale in time.

Wait—Did You Say *Dress* Fairies!?

Justle

A week after the monsters had surrounded Elderdale, the citizens began to settle down into the routine of a siege. Justle, now in charge of inner city defense, made good use of her time, forming a militia out of every able bodied man not already in the army, as well as quite a few women. Iris helped her with this, becoming almost a symbol for the people of Elderdale. Her mere presence lifted the spirits of those who fell into depression, and she spent most of her time surrounded by loyal fans.

Justle smiled, whenever she saw Iris swarmed with presses of people. Even then, the crowds were respectful, wary of the prowess she had demonstrated.

Arranging the militia into blocks, in which each was stationed in and defended a part of the city, Justle began to drill them in the art of war with ruthless efficiency. Since very few people had real jobs to do, now that they were stuck inside, Justle could train them all she wanted to.

The city of Elderdale was circular, not only because the world was circular, but because circular walls deflected missiles better and were harder to damage. The wall's curve made the effective thickness at each point more that what the wall really was. Added to this was the fact that the city's walls curved downwards slightly, so that when one stood on the highest edge, they had about a foot of open ground beneath them. All in all, Elderdale was a very well planned city.

On the outside, at least. Houses sprawled through the inside with little regard for defensiveness. Some of the houses near the wall toward over all the others, using the city's wall to chill wine in peacetime, easily capture archer platforms in wartime. The streets were sprawled out in an unintelligible mess, except for the four gate streets, that ran straight to the keep without so much as a trap. Meaning, the defenders would have difficulty coordinating against two fronts, and the monsters would just have to run straight ahead.

Justle planned to compensate for this, though. As well as training the militia, she set up activated traps all across the city, especially in the main avenues. Lever-activated fire pits, oil cauldrons, arrow launchers, even anti-air ballista that she commandeered and pointed straight down the main roads. Most of the citizens disagreed silently. They said nothing to her face, all the while nervously looking at Iris.

That seventh day, Justle and Iris sat in a café near the wall, eating rice porridge, watered down to conserve the city's food supply. The baron of Elderdale, Johnathan Ilsith Darov Elder, (the first), walked into the shop without so much as a glance around, and headed straight for Justle and Iris. Every patron in the café went silent, keeping a respectful distance from the man.

He wore a pristine suit, embroidered with gear-like patterns all over. On his head sat a top hat, that sprouted all kinds of brass and copper mechanisms. He had a handlebar moustache, and, to complete the image, he gripped a copper pipe walking stick with an emerald the size of a fist embedded at the top.

"Justle Lin, Iris Alworthy," he said, his voice cultured. "I have come to personally invite you to a ball, tonight, at eight o'clock sharp, in the grand dining room of my kingly castle." His voice brokered no refusal. "There will be entertainers, and a seven course meal. If you would please to grace my presence with yours, I will gladly welcome you." He bowed, crossing his stick over his chest.

At the mention of seven-course meal, the citizens in the café began to murmur amongst themselves. Justle almost joined them. *What do you mean, seven course meal?* She shouted at him in her head. *There are people starving already, and this siege has just started!* She hid her unpleasant thoughts behind a smiling mask, however. There was no refusing a baron, who had come to invite them personally. She wondered what he was getting out of it. *Money? Power? Respect?*

In any case, the man needed a reply. "We would be happy to join you," Justle said. She got up from her seat and curtsied. Iris looked at her as if she were crazy. Justle shot her a withering glance. Iris got up and curtsied, as well.

The baron seemed pleased enough, and turned to go. "Don't be late," he called. "You wouldn't like what happens to those kinds of people."

It sounded vaguely like a threat. Justle seethed inside, and she almost felt Iris's anger. The two looked at each other, realizing what a formal ball meant.

Clothes.

The two spent the rest of the afternoon with their dress fairies, Bliss and Stacy, coordinating their outfits. Justle tried for the minimalist look first, with a V-neck and short skirt, but decided that it just didn't look right for the occasion. Bliss rotated through a dozen color schemes, but Justle rejected them all with a shake of her head.

Iris, before another mirror in their city apartment, tried on several pairs of pants, settling on tight, black stockings. Justle pointed out to her that it was a traditional ball, and Iris changed into a dress with a groan.

Justle tried frilly dresses next. She put on one that fluffed up at her shoulders, and came down in three layers around her feet, and liked it. However, she couldn't find a color pattern that would go with the occasion.

Iris decided on a plain dress almost immediately after she relinquished her pants. "It's too airy," she complained, looking under the fabric. "What happens if a sudden breeze picks it up?"

"We'll be in a closed room," Justle answered, exasperated. "There'll be no breeze. And, that dress is not a formal dress. Find something prettier."

Iris gave an exaggerated groan. She was only 23, almost a fifth Justle's age. She was still fighting the mental battles that an ordinary human fought, which is why Justle cut her slack when it came to things like this.

Justle finally decided on a derivative of her battle uniform, a simple, straight short skirt topped with an upgraded version of her combat blouse, in subdued reds and greens. On her hair she placed a black hairband, and for earrings, she summoned her staff and pried out the jewels, hanging them with little strings ornately tied by her fairy.

Her staff was always losing jewels in combat, so it didn't mind Justle borrowing them. Justle then applied makeup, with a light touch, just enough to make her shine, and finished it with a touch of mascara.

She turned to look at Iris, who still switched between dresses. Each time they changed, the room lit up, like it did when they called their dresses during combat. Stacy, Iris's dress fairy, fluttered about, making adjustments.

"I like that one," Justle said, when she saw a two-layered dress with one shoulder strap appear. Fishnets completed the look, giving her a mature, yet rebellious air, still managing to be formal. "Choose black," Justle suggested, and iris did just that. "Blue hair ties and laces would be nice," Justle added. "Make them deep colored," she said to Stacy. Stacy nodded, and set about it. When she was done, Iris looked beautiful, instead of the cute that she, and all other magical girls, usually looked.

Justle nodded. Iris looked to her again, expecting her to say more. "Some eyeliner, and maybe some colored lipstick," Justle said, after inspecting her face. "But keep the base to a minimum. Your skin is almost perfect as it is."

Iris beamed a little, and then began to apply her makeup. When she was done, she turned to Justle. "How's this?" She asked.

Justle stifled laughter. It was horrible. She looked like a zombie monster, or maybe an undead worker. Justle didn't comment, however, and picked up a wet cloth from her table.

"Let me do that for you," she said. Iris didn't resist as Justle wiped her face clean. As Justle applied the makeup, with a century and a half's expertise, Iris squirmed.

"It tickles," Iris said, batting her eyelids. Justle continued without comment, applying the eyeliner with a liberal, yet focused, brush. She put a little powder down, and then added a touch of blue lipstick to match her ribbons and laces.

When she was finished, she stepped back. Perfection. Everyone in the room would either want to be Iris or kiss Iris—on the cheek, as a father would kiss a daughter. Or perhaps kill her, but they would have to be suicidal to think it.

Iris looked at herself in the mirror, and gasped. The clock chimed 7:30, and both of the girls turned to the door. Their coats materialized over their dresses as they stepped out into the night air, and headed towards the palace.

Elderdale's keep towered over the center of the city, its five spires grasping the sky like giant fingers of stone. On the outside, it seemed no less ordinary than the rest of the castle, solid curved stone walls reaching up on a slight tilt. Justle had surveyed the tower, when she had been preparing the defenses, but she was not the one in charge of defending it. That fell to the captain of the palace guard.

They entered through the main gate, the gateman waving them through after a single glance. He turned his head to watch them walk away, whether from envy or infatuation, Justle could not tell. Perhaps both.

They walked through the inner curtain wall, and out into the palace's subsidiary buildings, the kitchen and the royal stables and the keep's skyship dock. The mechanic's workshop and blacksmith's forge were not in sight, in their place behind the keep from where the two girls entered.

The palace itself rose up in a single cylinder that narrowed until it was only one spire, the other four spires jutting from the wall that surrounded it. Flags that bore the crest of Elderdale, a half-hill on an orange background, proclaimed to all who was in charge.

When Justle and Iris approached the palace door, the two guards who stood watch crossed their ceremonial polearms. They wore plumed helmets and ornately tooled breastplates. Every inch of cloth on them, and there was much, was in rich, royal scarlet.

"Who are you to approach the palace of Johnathan Elder," the one on the left said, "seventeenth of the line of Elders?"

Justle stood up straight. The outside breeze picked up her skirt and waved it around low. "I am Sergeant Justle Lin, of the Disciplinary Force of Female Magicians, and this is Private First Class Iris Alworthy, of the same."

After a regal pause, the man on the right lifted his polearm, followed by the man on the left. "You may enter," they stated, together. The doors opened with a rumbling and a grating of gears.

Behind it, there opened a magnificent hall, decorated with all sorts of mechanically inspired furnishings. It was an artisan's dream: a pipe chandelier the size of a bus, tapestries made of woven metal strands, bannisters that had teeth like gears, intertwined with more parts and baubles than Justle could count.

Interspersed among the strange furnishings, groups of regal looking people gathered and talked in low voices. Justle stepped off the threshold, followed by Iris, and counted almost a hundred people.

From behind, the voice of an announcer startled Justle, loud and clear over the low hubbub. "I present to you Sergeant Justle Lin and her entourage, the champion Iris Alworthy!"

Justle saw Iris's conflicted emotions, caught between called an entourage and a champion at the same time. Justle smiled, and took her arm, and the two walked into the mess of people.

Justle saw that all the ladies wore gloves, so she whispered to Bliss, and soon it was fixed. Gloves appeared on her hands, in matching colors. Iris followed suit. As soon as they did, however, a crowd of curious nobles accosted them. Justle saw the captain of the guard, the captain of the army, and the navy admiral. She wondered why they were all here. If they were here, they weren't watching the city, which could be attacked at any time. That left no one in charge outside. Justle was sure the baron wasn't a dullard, but it took one to arrange something like this. Perhaps it had been one of his servants.

In any case, Justle and Iris spent their time before the meal in a flurry of conversations, meeting all the important figures in the city and then some. Everyone wanted to get a glimpse of the beautiful fighting girls, who looked like porcelain dolls. Justle got more than one coo from young and old ladies alike, that she barely tolerated.

I'm five times your age, you old coot, she screamed in her head at an old lady that wouldn't stop rubbing her hair. Iris saw her and laughed, but was soon after accosted by a trio of giggling teenage girls.

For a moment, the world turned a little bit darker, around Justle, and she found herself staring at the fixtures in the walls. *They're certainly abstract,* Justle thought, as she surveyed the toothed patterns. *They would make great cover in a battle.* Her thoughts were turned aside by the attention of another lady of minor nobility, who fussed at her dress and complimented her on her makeup.

It was a relief when the crier finally made his way to the corner stage, and began the call for dinner. The guests streamed out of the main hall and into a dining room that was perhaps even larger than the room before. Justle wondered how it could be that it all fit within the walls.

The table that spread across the center of the room was empty, except for the settings, which were many. Each seat boasted a name card with the name of the person who was to sit there, as well as five forks, three plates, two spoons, two cups, and a napkin. Justle had eaten fine food once or twice in her life, but Iris stared at the silverware with an amazed expression, as she passed over the name cards looking for her seat.

The two girls were seated quite close to the baron himself, after only the captain of the guard and the admiral of the navy. Again, Justle wondered why the baron chose to honor the solders at this time. They had important duties to attend to. A siege wasn't exactly the best time to be partying.

When they had all sat down, Baron Elder raised his glass to a toast, full of before-dinner wine. The table followed. "To our brave defenders," the Baron said, his voice clear and ringing. Even at the table he wore his mechanical hat.

"To our brave defenders," the table chanted, clinking and then drinking.

Justle stayed her hand on the wine, knowing that it took only a small amount to get her very drunk, light as she was. She pushed Iris's glass back down, just as the girl was about to drink. Iris shot Justle a killing look, but to her credit, she moved her glass away.

Soon, the conversation became more lively, tongues loosened by the excellent drink. It flowed freely, and even those who did not normally drink were soon red-faced.

The baron rang a bell, and legions of servants appeared out of hidden crevices in the wall, that opened up like so many gears grinding. Justle stared hard at a servant, convinced that something was wrong. Then, she saw. The servants were not human: rather, they were clockwork imitations, cunningly made and dressed so that it looked almost a deception. The other guests noticed as well, and gave their compliments to the baron for having such an interesting house.

"I apologize for the drab fare," the Baron said, when all the silver platters had arrived, "but with this siege, it is the best I can do for you." He opened his own plate, and sampled the first dish, a succulently cooked bird that steamed when he cut into it. He chewed, exaggerating his pleasure. He opened his eyes. "It is good!" he pronounced.

And the guests dug in. There were roast pigs, roast calves, whole roasted duck and quail and goose; there was a brilliantly fried beaterbat, that tasted like solid honey and melted on the tongue; there was cinch-root stew and gold-bird egg tamago and fiery lettuce bread; potatoes and onions by the bushel; even potions of major weakness, that were prized for their delectable smoothness, and their almost heavenly taste—if one could get past the weakness part.

Justle ate almost nothing. Something made her nervous, though she could not tell what. Perhaps it was the way the servants had suddenly appeared, out of the wall, where there had been no doors before. Perhaps it was the Baron's joviality, a little too strong, as if he wanted to put everyone at ease. In any case, a single slice of roast calf was all Justle ate. Iris ate meat, lots of it, but avoided everything else. Her manners were petite, almost comical compared with the pile of veal, bird, and pork on her plate.

The man next to Justle was a minor nobleman, who engaged in conversation on his other side. Every now and then he would shoot Justle and Iris a nervous look.

Iris made fast friends with the captain of the guard, who sat next to her. They talked of pleasantries first, but when Iris surprised the man with her knowledge of battle, the two talked shop in the way only two warriors can.

They were in the middle of a heated argument about the effectiveness of a halberd when Justle felt the need to relieve herself. She got up from the table without comment, and went in search of the latrine. She reasoned that it would be somewhere close to the walls, where it could drain into the keep's moat.

She wandered out of the hall, through the main door. She found a human butler in the middle of the hall.

"Excuse me, sir," she said.

The man looked surprise to see Justle's petite figure, dressed up like a doll, approach him. "Yes, young miss?" he asked.

Justle ignored the young part. "Where would the latrine be in the castle?"

The man looked around, as if something were amiss, and hunched his shoulders. "The baron says that no guests are to leave the dining hall," he said, his protest feeble.

Justle paused. Again, something felt off, though she couldn't put her finger on what it was. "Why not?" she asked the man.

The man, now even more nervous than before, hesitated before answering. "No one is to leave the dining, hall, Baron's orders," he said, almost to himself.

Justle wondered what was wrong with the man. It was almost as if he had battle-mind, or something like that. His twitchiness certainly resembled it. "If you can't tell me, that's fine," Justle told the man, holding back the pressure building in her bladder. "Can you tell me where I can relieve myself?" she asked instead.

The man looked perplexed, and then his eyes lit up. "You can do it in the dining hall," he said.

This man is clearly crazy, Justle thought to herself. *I should just go and find it on my own.*

And so she did, leaving the crazy butler behind, who simply watched her as she walked further down the hall. *Hrmph,* she thought to herself. *Some orders.* As she walked down the hall, the ornate mechanical decorations began to be replaced with traditional tapestries and cloth, like how a palace should have been. Justle wondered if all palaces were like this, multiple styles clashing all over, following the whims of the owner.

She spotted a low door to the side of the hall that looked somewhat less grand than all the others. She picked it, reasoning that lavatories weren't very good at being grand. Still tall for her, it was a little less imposing, the size of a normal door on a normal house. Justle knocked, got no answer, and then walked in.

Inside, it took a while for her eyes to adjust. The light here shone from torches, in sconces on the wall, instead of from bright magical lights. They flickered when the door closed behind her. She saw that the room was simply a staircase that went down into the depths of the hill the palace sat upon. Aware that it probably wasn't a bathroom, she decided to take a look anyways.

Down, down, down she went, spiraling and twisting as the staircase followed some unseen path through the earth. Soon, Justle regretted her decision to explore, as the pressure on her bladder steadily increased. She bit through it, though, and made it to the bottom, where a single door stood at the end of a short hall.

Justle tried the door, this time without knocking. It creaked open, unlocked. Justle crept around the edge, peering into the darkness beyond. She waited for her eyes to adjust, and then recoiled in horror.

Behind the door, around a strange, metallic object, five ganglers ambled about, crude stone tools in their hands. A man lay wrapped on the ground beside them, bound and gagged with thick hempen rope. His face could not be mistaken: he was the Johnathan Elder, Baron of Elderdale.

The Baron is a false person

Justle armed herself, not bothering to change clothes. Her staff swirled out of the ether and into her hand, the two jewels that hung in her ears still missing from its top. They were non-functional, though. Just decorative. It was a very pretty staff.

Justle tensed her body and prepared to enter the room. As she did, Bliss fired up her fairy battle display. The ganglers gained red crystals above their heads, numbered 1-5. They hadn't noticed her yet, peeking through the door. The Baron saw her, though, his eyes opening wide. The crystal above his head turned orange, meaning that Bliss had decided he needed rescuing.

As if I didn't already know, Justle commented, in her mind. Bliss didn't hear. Fairies weren't mind-readers, thankfully.

Justle breathed in, breathed out, and kicked the door wide. It hit the wall with a bang, rebounding with a half-hearted creak. As every head turned to her, Justle cursed herself for being so noisy. Spending a week with Iris had changed her.

Too late for any more second thoughts, Justle leapt into action, twirling her staff around her body. It was a magic enhancer, cored with solid silver. The silver meant that it also worked wonderfully as a club.

Justle channeled her energy through the staff, and, just as she reached the center of the room, she let out a lightning bolt, aimed at all five ganglers. The bolts swerved in mid-air, however, all striking the strange metal object that lay in the center of the room. Red lines of light became faintly visible through the dull metal.

The ganglers, more than a little annoyed, closed in from all around her. Her main strategy exhausted, Justle flung her staff around and pointed it at a single gangler. Number 3. She fired a bolt of ice this time, certain that it would hit. Just like the thunderbolts, though, the icicle veered into the metal cube in the center of the room. Again, read lines of light traced faintly over its surface.

Whatever the thing was, Justle decided that she hated it. She twirled her staff some more, keeping the ganglers at an uncomfortable distance. Gangler number 2 lunged, gripping a stone-tipped spear. Justle dodged, and, grabbing the shaft as it swung by, ripped it out of the monkey's hands. The monkey stared for a moment, and then shrieked. Justle swung her staff down hard on its head, just as she spun the spear around and stabbed a gangler that had gotten too close to her back.

The remaining three ganglers backed up, wary of her. Justle eyed them, looking for an opening, when all of the sudden a shout pieced the air, coming from the prone form of the Baron. The ganglers, surprised, jumped up and began hooting. As they glared at the Baron, Justle caved in the skull of one with her staff, and kicked the other against the wall, where it slumped down, its back broken.

The last gangler jumped from foot to foot, hooting and waving its stone axe. Justle dispatched it with clean swipe to the neck. She felt dirty afterwards, like her hands were covered in filth.

"You saved me," Baron Elder said, having wriggled out of his gag. He breathed heavily, as if after much exertion.

"I only did what anyone else did," Justle said, still a little confused. "Although, I thought you were up in the dining hall."

The Baron sucked in air through his teeth. "You see," he said, his voice subtly different from the baron Justle remembered, "I got replaced by a false person. I've been here for who knows how long, as those monsters did who knows what."

Justle looked back at the stairs, her mind racing. *The diners!* All of the military head, in one place, under the complete power of a monster! "Bliss, patch me in to Iris," she commanded, taking decisive action.

The Baron jumped slightly when Bliss appeared over her shoulder. "Ah, a fairy," he said, his voice questioning. "You must be of the Disciplinary force."

"You are correct," Justle said, listening to the fairy network's dial tone, like a bunch of guitar strings plucked out of tune. Then, they formed a chord, and Iris's voice sounded in Justle's ear.

"Sergeant?" Iris asked, the sound of the dining hall loud around her.

"Iris, did you drink any wine?" Justle asked, without preamble. "Did you drink any potions of weakness?"

"No, I don't think so," Iris said, her voice full of confusion. "You told me not to drink, so I didn't."

Good girl, Justle thought to herself. "I want you to be on guard," Justle told her. "Pull up some protection spells, nothing visible."

"Why?" Iris asked, even more confused. "We're in the middle of the palace."

"I have the Baron of Elder right here with me, underground somewhere. Is there a Baron at the table?" Justle needed to confirm, first.

"Yes," Iris said. "He just proposed another toast. Why?"

"I have reason to believe that that Baron is a false person," Justle said, making sure she said it clear.

Iris said nothing for a while, and all Justle heard was the babbling of voices. "All right," Iris finally said. "I'll watch him."

Justle disconnected without another word, and then turned to the real Baron. "What's this machine?" she asked, motioning to the thing that had sucked up her magic.

The Baron looked at it for a second. "I don't know," he said. "It's been in our family for generations, since before the fall of the underside."

Justle whistled in admiration. The Elders really were elder. "The monsters wanted it," she said. "Do you know why?"

"I don't," the Baron said. "They got in about a day after the siege, wrapped me up in here, and started tinkering with the thing. I don't think they got anywhere, because nothing happened." The Baron paused. "Until you shot your magic in here, that is." He held out his arms. "Can you cut this for me?" He asked. Ropes bound his feet as well.

Justle picked up a stone spear, and began to saw at the ropes with its tip. Soon, they unraveled and fell to the floor. Justle released the Baron's feet in the same way.

When his bonds had been cut, the Baron tried to stand. He stumbled, before he made it halfway up, and leaned against the wall. "Sorry," he said, "But I've been lying here for almost a week."

Justle looked at where he had been seeing, and noticed that what he said was true. The awful smell in the room wasn't just from the ganglers. Justle helped the man get up, although he was forced to crouch to accommodate her height. When they reached the stairwell, away from the magic-sucking cube, Justle cast a spell of increase strength. The Baron seemed to fill with vigor, and soon, he climbed the stairs beside Justle like he had never been a captive. The two climbed with determination, knowing that anything could happen before they made it to the hall.

When they were two-thirds of the way up, Iris's voice sounded in Justle's ear, full of panic. A boom sounded over the fairy-comm, and reverberated through the entire castle.

"He's killing them all!" Iris cried, the sound of some sort of battle almost covering them up. The clanks and clashes resounded through the halls, and back down the staircase which Justle and the Baron climbed.

The two increased their pace. "Hold them off for me," Justle said, her voice full of an experienced calm. "I know you can do it."

"He's turning into a monster," said Iris. "I don't know if—"

Justle cut her off just then, knowing that further contact would only panic her more. She and the Baron rounded the last curve in the staircase, burst out of the door, and slammed into a crowd of screaming people.

Bloodied, battered, and mostly incoherent, they streamed away from the door to the grand ballroom, from which a great clashing and pounding emanated. A roar, completely inhuman, reverberated through the hall, pushing the crowd into even more of a panic. Justle heard Iris's voice, clear as a bell, over the roar. She seemed to be fighting it, whatever it was.

Justle and the Baron pushed their way through the people in the hall and headed towards the disturbance. Justle noticed blood spattering clothes and faces, and wondered who had already been killed. Once they pushed out of the last of the running people, they sprinted towards the doorway. Grand entrances passed on their left and right, and the hall turned back into a gear palace, toothed circular patterns replacing the soft Victorian velvets.

A monster flew out of the open doorway and slammed into the wall, impaling on a bench that bore the spikes of a giant cog. Iris launched out after it, finishing the monster off with a punishing blow to the face. Iris fought without a weapon, her specialty being unarmed combat. Her fists dripped with blood, and one of her shoes lay embedded in the side of the monster.

It was a tigeresque, Justle saw, capable of moving unseen through even the most populated of areas. They were almost mythical, with their reputation for ferocity. Iris wiped her hands together when she saw Justle and the Baron approach.

"I need your help," she said, motioning back into the room, where something clanged against the stone floor. She faced the Baron. "Sorry about your house," she said.

"It's nothing, my dear lady," the Baron said, as he bowed, an eminently courtlier act than the ones that the fake Baron had attempted. This Baron seemed almost suave, with the way he moved, with confidence.

Iris reddened a little, and adjusted the hem of her skirt. She turned back to the doorway to the grand hall. "The fake Baron isn't going to wait forever," she said, slapping her knuckles into her palm. She stretched her neck with the airy confidence of youth.

Justle followed her. The Baron did as well, despite his lack of armaments. Justle didn't protest, and Bliss changed the icon floating above his head to green. His status—vitality and magica—appeared in Justle's upper left corner of vision, next to Iris's status. His magica bar was surprisingly large, indicating significant magical prowess.

They had no time to discuss it, however, as they stormed into the room behind Iris. Inside, surrounded by tigeresques, the fake Baron of Elder hung suspended from his hat, poised over a slaughterhouse.

Justle took the lead, shouting the code word for a coordinated attack, on the fake Baron. The fake Baron noticed their entrance then, and, turning upon the spindly metal legs that held him in the air, stared straight at Justle.

"Welcome to my real party," he said, motioning to the bodies around him. "I have already taken care of the rest of the important ones," he motioned to the bodies of the military commanders, mauled and broken, "and I was just about to go looking for you." He smiled, an inhuman smile that stretched further than possible on a normal face.

Justle paid no attention to him, and pulled her staff high above her head. "Firebolt!" She cried, creating a ball of flame that shot from the tip of her staff. It changed course mid-flight and spiraled around the fake Baron's spidery hat-legs, exploding far above him.

Justle grimaced, and jumped on top of the table. Iris followed her lead, china dishes clattering to the floor and breaking into shards. She moved towards the baron.

Bliss had numbered five tigereques, each with a red icon showing where they were at the moment. Without her, Justle doubted she would have noticed them. They blended into their surrounding unnaturally, taking on the pattern of whatever they happened to be against. Iris and Justle waited for a split second, and then put their code-worded plan into attack.

Iris ran towards the fake Baron at top speed, her feet finding purchase between the dishes, food, and bodies that covered the table. Justle broke to the left, running across another table that ran parallel to the one they had been on. A tigeresque pounced at her, but she ducked, and the creature went wide. Another jumped into her path, growling in a low, catlike voice. Justle steadied herself, and them at the last moment, vaulted over the creature with a spin. The tigeresque batted at her dress, ripping three claw-shaped pieces off. Justle landed unsteadily on the table's bench, and then continued to run.

The fake Baron, seeing two girls charging him at once, tried to swipe at them both as they got closer. His spindly metal hat-legs doubled as arms, and could probably take off a limb or two if they connected. The girls made sure that it didn't happen, though, Iris sliding just underneath one swinging metal poles, and then popping up again in the same motion.

When they were no more than a yard away from the baron, the attacks stopped. They were underneath the spider-legs now, jumping over bodies and pieces of bodies left from the fake Baron's slaughter. His body hung over them like a church bell, suspended from the center of the spider, his top hat. He cried something to his tigeresques, as the girls prepared to jump at him, and they responded with frightening quickness. One of them slammed into Iris's chest, sending her flinging to the ground. It prepared to swipe a killing blow, but forgot to check its back. Justle slammed the butt of her staff into the base of its skull, sending a resounding crack through the air. The beast slumped, and lost all of its unnatural color.

Two more tigeresques approached, with the other two circling the fake Baron's legs. In the close quarters between those legs, Justle thought hard about her next move. The tigeresques prepared to pounce, leaning back, their fur bristling and their lips pulled back. One sported the image of a disconnected arm on its side, among broken dishes. Another had pictures of blood spots mixed with real blood spots all tangled together in its fur.

Justle and Iris backed up against each other. Iris held up her fists in a fighting stance, and Justle prepared to cast a spell of instant freezing, that would cover them all in deep frost.

And then the table opened up and swallowed the tigers. They fell without a sound, as silent as stones, before the table closed back up over them. The other two tigers also fell into crevices in the floor, that slid open like the sliding window shutters. Nothing happened for a second. Then, the fake Baron, hanging over their head, lurched to the side. One of his spidery legs caught in the holes, as more opened all around. Then another caught. Soon, the false person had been immobilized, like a ripe apple waiting for the picking.

"I told you that you would regret impersonating me," the real Baron's voice called, from somewhere above. Justle searched for the source, but could not find it.

"Do you like it?" The real Baron asked, pride in his voice. "I had it built not long ago. To get rid of unseemly guests, but it seems the contractors took me a little too literally." He chuckled a little, a soft sound that seemed fitting for a drawing room, coming from a mouth holding tight to a cigar. "Lucky for me, I suppose."

The fake Baron lurched again, as another of his metal hat-legs dropped down a hole. It caught at one of its knees, and jerked sporadically as if it were a living thing.

"You humans think you're so powerful," the fake Baron said, his voice full of power. "You'll get what's coming to you."

Then, without preamble, his hat exploded into a million pieces. Justle threw up a shield spell just in time, as pieces of shrapnel cut through the air. Iris held on to her, underneath the cloudy barrier. When the steel rain stopped, Justle looked at the body of the false person. It didn't look human. It didn't look like any creature, in fact, more like a blob of goo than anything living. It held together for a moment more, and then dispersed into a puddle, draining down the holes that had caused its death.

"It seems that you're now in command of the city, Miss Lin," the real Baron, Johnathan Elder, said from his cubbyhole somewhere. "Being the last ranking officer alive, and all that."

And just then, Justle realized that she still had to pee.

More evidence that Denyse is awesome

Justle had the job of addressing the citizens of Elderdale, to tell them what had happened in the palace. As the new temporary captain of the guard, it was her duty, one that she undertook with a heavy heart. 25 people had died in the gruesome attack, including all of the defense's command structure. Justle would address that at a later point, but as she stood over the walls of the keep, on the proclaiming balcony, she felt smaller than she had ever felt before. A day had passed since the incident, in which its vividness had faded some, but the images still haunted her, of that bloodied ballroom, those ever-changing tigers.

Justle cleared her throat, holding the speech she had written in front of her. Baron Elder, the real one, stood to her left and back, towering over her like so many people did. Iris by her right hand, officially appointed as her guard.

"Good citizens of Elderdale," she began, trying to be as expressive as possible. "This siege we are enduring is of the utmost affront to civility, and we hope that it may conclude soon, and well for all those involved. I regret to inform you that last night, during the royal ball that, it was said, our Baron himself had hosted, it was revealed that the man who claimed to be that Baron was not him, and in fact, an imposter, working underhandedly for those monsters that are laying siege to our city."

Justle continued in this fashion for several more minutes, reading out in a clear voice, but still troubled inside. When she had finished, the crowed stayed silent, with not a whisper carrying over the gathering. Then, with sullen expressions, they began to disperse, off to do the things that people in a castle under siege do. Not one person stayed behind, and soon, Justle stared down at an empty courtyard. The sound of the monsters surrounding the city, like an ever-present river filled with legions of pebbles, drifted over the lonely stone.

Justle and the Baron left the balcony, Iris following behind, and made their way through the keep's tangled stairways. The two girls parted with the Baron after they reached the doorway.

"My humblest apologies, my lady," the Baron said, bowing to show his sincerity. "If I had known that you would have gotten mixed up in this, I might have tried harder to escape."

"It's not your fault," Justle said, not sure of anything. "We all did the best we could."

"Then we must hope to do better in the future," the Baron said, standing up. "I'm placing my hope in you."

Justle reddened, aware that Iris was looking at her as well. "I will do my best," Justle said. She turned away and began to walk down towards the walls of the keep, Iris trailing behind her. As she exited, she passed the anti-air ballista that she had repurposed to defend the main street. It sat undrawn, sheathes of flak-arrows piled by its side. Each flak-arrow was about the size of a dart, with small grooves on their side to fit into the machine's loading mechanism. The ballista itself had 42 strings, each with room for five flak-arrows. Designed to combat flying monsters in swarms, the machine predictably worked well against ground soldiers, as well. Justle just wished the city had more of them. Out of 12, she had only been able to take 4 from the walls. While the others were needed to defend the city's airspace, Justle really didn't have many other options when it came to defending the city's long, straight, and perfectly chargeable main streets.

"Did you ever see anything like this?" Iris asked, as they passed an armorer's shop.

"You mean, what happened last night?" Justle asked, as she thought about it. She had had her fair share of adventures, during her 163 years as a magical girl. Being a century and a half old had exposed her to almost everything there was to see, the good and the bad.

However, she couldn't remember ever being in a situation like the one she was in now.

"I don't think so," Justle answered. "I have had a lot of other experiences, though."

"Tell me about one," Iris said. She looked off into the distance as she said it, her eyes far away.

Justle searched her memory. *There's when I was trapped in a cave at the peak of mount Gorn,* she thought. But, that didn't have much to do with what was occurring at the moment. *Or, should I tell her about the time I was in a major battle of skyships?* It was certainly upbeat, and had a happy ending—for her, at least.

She decided to tell her about something good, instead. "I think I'll tell you about the time Denyse tried to make ice cream in the middle of a battlefield," she said, "with nothing but a bottle of milk and magic."

Iris smiled, anticipating what would happen. "And?" she said, prompting Justle.

"So, me, Denyse, and Major Ruby were all hunkered down in a bunker somewhere far one-seventy from the Capital. It was the middle of the Groundhog wars, when the monster tamer guild got angry at the steamer guild for some reason I can't remember."

Iris nodded her head as Justle spoke.

"The steamers won, of course, but at the time, we were there to try to stop the war. Our mission was to disable a capital steamship. This was before skysteel engines, so the thing had these huge smokestacks, and belched a ridiculous amount of smoke."

"But what about the ice cream?" Iris said, stopping Justle from going off topic.

Justle thought for a moment, and then continued. "So Denyse had a jar of milk. We were in a bunker, with nothing to do for a while. So, Denyse comes up to me and says 'I want some ice cream.' I told her, 'are you crazy, we're in a war!' I was pretty uptight back then, I guess."

Iris murmured about it, and Justle shot her a killing look. "So Denyse picks up some sand, and lights it on fire. Ruby had noticed, by now, and asked what she was doing. Denyse kept burning the sand, and said 'I'm making a bowl.' By now the sand had turned to glass, and we both just sat there and watched her. It was like the things came out of nowhere, out of thin air or something. By the time she was done, she had a bowl, a spoon, an ice-cream maker, and a mixer. She pulled some rations out of her pack, and before we knew it, she had sugar and salt too. Then, she froze over some water, broke it into shards, pushed them into the maker, mixed it with salt, and poured the milk into the churn."

Justle paused. "And then it exploded," she said.

Iris chuckled at this.

Justle continued. "It wasn't fiery, or anything, but I got a piece of sandy glass in my arm, that I had to get out using a healing spell. Ruby was so mad, we thought she was gonna blow, but it turns out that the glass had just ripped her dress, and she doesn't like that at all. So we didn't complain, and just let her do her thing. Denyse promised to fix it later."

Justle paused for a moment, reveling in the feeling of that moment. "And then," she said, "When we looked at the broken maker, all in pieces, there was the ice cream, as nice as if you had bought it in the store."

She licked her lips. "It probably wasn't that good, in retrospect, but it sure was the best ice cream I've ever tasted."

Iris clapped her hands when Justle finished. Justle curtsied, cheered up from her sullen mood. She began to look around her, at the houses, and then stopped. Something about Denyse's improvisation had triggered her, and as she looked at the jury-rigged stone-fall trap that she and the militia had set up, and remembered the Baron's pitfalls, she had an idea.

"Iris," she said. "We're going to need a lot of stuff."

Firing Up the Ol' Tower Defense

The people assembled in the square looked as if they had all seen better days. With rations being given with the mind to preserve food, they all possessed a sort of gaunt look that Justle knew would only become worse. Justle stood on a stack of barrels, high over the crowd, for once. All the upturned faces made her a little nervous, from this close. She had come knocking on their doors, a selection of metalworkers, woodcarvers, blacksmiths, and other assorted citizens, selecting them based upon how resourceful she thought they might be.

"I have a proposition for you all," she said, sweeping her eyes over the crowd. The crowd murmured, but did nothing more. Justle saw a few children dart through the assembled feet.

"The monsters have us outnumbered," she said, stating the truth. "And they might have us out-armed." A few mumbles swept through the men and women assembled. Of course they were outmatched. Of course the monsters were more powerful.

"They may be strong," she said, as the call of a grandshroom floated overhead—like the keening of a dog mixed with the churning of earth—to punctuate her point, "but," Justle said, "we have them beat in one place: Ingenuity."

The crowd rippled. Now she was getting somewhere. This small girl, who looked no older than ten, might actually be on to something.

"Who has seen the ganglers hold anything but the crudest of weapons?" she asked, getting into the full swing of rhetoric. "Who has seen the monsters devise any but the most simple of contraptions, only far after we humans invented them? I doubt that a single one of those monsters, if faced against you in a contest of wits, would do more than flop and make weird noises." There were some exceptions, of course. Like the false person—who was dead, fortunately.

Justle continued on. "We have what they don't," she said. "We can do what they can't, we can make what they can only copy, we can conceive of things that they will never even dream of, if they do dream at all."

Some of the heads in the crowd began to nod.

"We have an advantage, where they don't. So my proposition to you is: let's make use of that advantage. Let's take our ingenuity, our human drive to create, and let's turn it on them."

More of the heads nodded, and some saw where she was going, their faces lighting up.

"What can we make that the monsters can't? Machines. Things that do things for us. Things that can pull things, things that can drive things, things that can fly things. Things that can kill things." With this, Justle pulled down her fist.

The crowd stayed still, almost all of them mesmerized by her performance.

"And for every thing that kills a monster, another one of us is free to build more, to kill more, to spend our precious time defending that which we find most important. For every monster killed by a thing, there is one less monster trying to kill you."

The crowed stared, transfixed.

"Who can build these things?" She asked.

No one answered.

"Is it just the machinists, the steamers, those with power?" She paused again.

One head nodded.

"No," Justle said, "it is not just steamers, or mechanics—people that are higher than you all—that can build these things. We all possess the ability to create things, and, when the things we love are threatened, is it not a good time for that ability to show?"

More heads in the crowd nodded. Some smiled.

"So what I say is: make these things. Find ways to destroy those that threaten those you love, using that human thing called ingenuity." Justle breathed deep.

The audience breathed deep too.

"So I tell you! Fire up the forges! Start spinning the spinning wheels! Get thinking, get planning, get building! You, who cannot fight on your own, can make things to fight for you!" Justle swept her arm with each statement, addressing the whole crowd. Her voice carried far, father with every word. More people crowded into the square, to see the girl on the stack of barrels.

"We can do more than just help. We can support. We can build. We can fight." Justle lowered her voice, so that the audience had to lean in to hear.

"We can do something about this siege, you, them, I," she looked all around. "We can turn our houses into weapons." She stepped back a little. "We can turn our streets into weapons." She stood up as straight as she could go. "We can turn our carts, out barrels, our windows, our walls; we can take the things we have and forge them anew, so that any monster that dares to step inside this city will *rue the day*!" At this, Justle stopped, sweat covering her arms and face, breathing heavily.

Nothing happened for a moment. And then the crowd cheered, a little at first, but then as the infection spread, they cry was taken up all through the square, and was carried across the city.

"Trap the houses!" They called, as one voice. "Spike the streets! Bring out the powder!"

Justle looked at what she had done, and smiled. She sat down on a barrel that smelled of fish.

Iris climbed up next to her. "I didn't know you were a speaker, Justle," she said, looking at her with a new respect.

"Neither did I," said Justle, as she wiped her forehead.

Trouble Aboard the *Nonelstch*

Emeralda

"Captain, the *Nonelstch* reports a disturbance, that I thought you might want to hear about." Amy, the *Amshfisht's* magical intelligence, stood before Emeralda in the bridge. Her capital ship headed the fleet of near 600 skyships, that had all been found underneath a barrow close to the capital, and were all loaded with the men, women, and materiel that comprised Emeralda's army.

Emeralda straightened herself up, sitting in her captain's chair. She had taken a liking to Amy, in the week since they had set sail—or rather, simply flown, as Emeralda still didn't know how the ships moved—but she still made sure to appear professional.

"Who's the Captain of the..." Emeralda paused, trying to remember how Amy had pronounced it. "Noon..."

"The sailors call her Nanny," Amy helped.

"Nanny," Emeralda said. "Find me her name." All of the navy's commanding officers were magical girls, under Emeralda's command, both because they had had much more experience than ordinary humans in the line of battle and because they were all connected via fairy-comm, which made for excellent communication.

Emeralda only had to give orders to her Colonels, and they would take care of the rest. Magical girls were independent and individualistic as a rule. The structure of the army accommodated this, allowing for the maximum amount of freedom while still retaining some element of command. It was rare that magical girls disobeyed their superiors, as relationships between people were prioritized and fostered by centuries of interaction. It was hard to hold a grudge for more than a decade, much less ten.

That meant that as old as she was, Emeralda had never once had to come down harshly on those under her command. They respected her, and revered her, as she was the oldest of them by far, and therefore the most wise and experienced. In fact, she was one of the oldest semi-immortals in the world, next to a powerful necromancer that had once unlocked the secret to immortality on his own, and a man that had discovered the fountain of youth. Neither of them had shared their secrets as of yet.

"Her name is Juvia Richard," Amy said, after a while. "She is one-hundred and ninety-three, rank Second Lieutenant. The *Nonelstch* suggests that you contact her."

Emeralda nodded, again marveling at how Amy managed to know so many things. She could recount the names of every single person in her army, on command, and knew their exact position at all times. Emeralda's opinion of the ancients, those who had lived before the closing of the Centrix, and had created these ships, rose steadily higher.

She called to her dress-fairy, June. "Contact Second Lieutenant Juvia Richard for me," she told her.

June appeared on her shoulder. "Aye-aye, Captain!" she said, giving an exaggerated salute. She had been on a naval kick for a few days now, after spending time with Amy.

Emeralda heard the fairy-comm dial tone, and saw Juvia's name appear under the talking head. Soon, here was a buzz, and a sweet voice sounded in Emeralda's ear.

"General!" Juvia said, evidently surprised. "To what do I owe the pleasure?"

"My ship says that your ship has a problem," Emeralda said, looking at Amy. Amy nodded.

"Ahh," Juvia hesitated, her voice changing a little. "I suppose we do."

"Elaborate," Emeralda asked.

"Well, you see, we have undead and necromancers on this ship, at the same time, and they kind of . . ." she drifted off for a moment, "got into a fight and killed each other."

Emeralda let out a breath, confounding herself for not fixing such an obvious mistake. She must have lost track in all the commotion, and the boarding. "How many killed?" Emeralda asked, bracing herself.

"Just one," Juvia said, although she had made it sound like more when she had said it before. "A necromancer," she added, "a healer."

Emeralda was taken aback. She had expected an undead to be the victim. Still, she wondered if it were some sort of plot. Necromancers weren't such to be taken lightly in a fight, but if it were more subtle, perhaps a martyr for some goal, than it would make sense. "How did it happen?" she asked.

"It would be best if you came and saw, General," Juvia said, her tone a little dark.

Emeralda turned to Amy. "Can we do that?" She asked.

"Aye," Amy answered, "the *Nonelstch* says she can accommodate an in-air docking with me."

That was good, Emeralda supposed. The Army would continue on schedule. "Then take us to her," she said, facing the rest of the bridge.

Amy walked to where the ship's bridge crew, three of them, sat in cube-ish chairs around a simple, elegant control panel that projected a white magical image of the *Amshfisht* inside of a bluish sphere. Below it, the current terrain flowed past, slow in a window so small, and the ships that traveled the *Amshfisht* around lit up in deep green. There were many of them in view, as the scope of the window extended far.

All it took to control the ship was a stroke of a blocky pen, lit up in the same blue lines as everything else. The navigator, actually an experienced airwoman, charted a plot to the ship Amy had marked as the *Nonelstch*. The *Amshfisht* tilted, as its altitude dropped to level with the *Nonelstch*. The two ships closed, the *Amshfisht* staying in the center of the display. When they were almost right next to each other, the two ships jolted, and then the sound of the ship's block-material moving sounded from outside, on deck.

When Emeralda exited the bridge, she saw the *Nonelstch* flying beside her flagship, almost half its size. Its blocky shape stayed locked in place next to the *Amshlisht*, attached by bridges that had extended from both ships. Emeralda saw a girl on the deck, next to one bridge, waving her arms, and assumed that it was Second Lieutenant Juvia. She was right, and as she boarded the *Nonelstch,* Juvia approached her, her face scrunched up against the wind.

"He's down below," Juvia said, shielding her eyes against the glare of the sun. Emeralda nodded, and followed her across the deck. A tall, stately woman appeared next to them, and Emeralda saw that she was Nanny, the *Nonelstch's* magical intelligence. None of them spoke until they had stepped below-decks, into the ship's common room.

Necromancers and undead warriors filled the area, about the size of a large cafeteria. The Necromancers stayed on one side, and the undead stayed on the other, the tension evident in the room. All eyes turned on Emeralda, Juvia, and Amy, as they stepped out of the sunlight.

Emeralda saw several more of her magical girls, interspersed through both sides. They were talking to the men, trying to calm them down with soft words. Emeralda felt the stares she got as she followed Juvia into the ship's main corridor.

"It happened in the mess," Juvia said, as she led Emeralda through an open doorway.

Emeralda inspected the room, and sucked air through her teeth. She had a tough job ahead of her.

In the center of the mess, the dead Necromancer lay, a knife sticking out of his chest and blood pooled on the floor. The room looked thrashed, as if a huge fight had taken place, but Emeralda did not see any other wounds on the man, nor any other blood. It was as if he had been stabbed in the middle of another tumult.

"Do you know who did it?" Emeralda asked, fearing the response. If she did, she would have to execute him, for the penalty for murder was death, and she had the authority to do such things under military law. In fact, she would be forced to. There was no way the necromancers would allow this to pass unpunished. But, at the same time, executing an undead could start a fomentation in their ranks, and perhaps give some of them second thoughts. That would also be bad.

She weighed the advantages and disadvantages of the two sides. The necromancers, numbering just over a hundred when including the elite unit, were vital to her living soldiers. Their healing powers would not only be able to get wounded on their feet, but would be enough to get them fighting again. It would mean that only deaths would truly affect her men. They were great for morale, as well, and gave men bravery where otherwise they would fear to be wounded.

On the other hand, the undead had become a formidable fighting force in the small time she had been training them. Some of them worshipped her, it was true, but more of them fought simply because it was something to do, something that their superiors told them to do. Those were the ones with barely enough brain to be considered human. If the higher-ups among the undead were to become incensed, or get uneasy, that it would mean the loss of the core of her army.

Emeralda was still weighing the two options, when a third option presented itself, out of the blue. The man was dead, of course, but he had been living not long ago. That meant he could become undead.

Having decided her course of action, Emeralda looked no more at the scene. It would become obsolete, with the man himself to tell her what happened. She turned to Juvia, who stood at her side.

"Take me to the strongest necromancer you have aboard," she commanded, to excited to level her voice.

Juvia nodded, awed by Emeralda's presence, and obeyed without question. She led Emeralda down the hallway and back into the common room, where the undead stared down the necromancers.

"Attention," Emeralda said, not waiting for Juvia. "Any necromancer that knows the spell to raise undead and can use it, please step forth."

The room stayed silent for a minute, as the undead and alive digested what she had said. Then a tumult broke out. People on both sides shot up, and began to yell at her.

"Are you crazy?!" one necromancer called. "You can't do that to him!"

"We don't need another, your holiness," one of the undead said. "Do not bring upon us this curse!"

Emeralda put her arms over her head, breathed in deep, and shouted at the top of her tremendous voice. "Silence!" She called.

She got silence. Every eye locked on her.

"I asked, do any of you necromancers know the spell of raise undead, and if you do, can you use it." Emeralda repeated the words slowly, biting each. It was time to get serious.

One necromancer parted from the others, getting nasty looks from all sides. He seemed a reasonable fellow, more so than those that surrounded him. "I do, ma'am, and I can," he said, adjusting his shirt.

Emeralda beckoned him forwards. "Come with me," she commanded. The man did not complain, and followed her down the hall, and into the mess.

Emeralda pointed to the dead necromancer. "Can you raise him?" she asked, her tone brokering no argument.

"The raise dead spell has a thirty percent success rate, ma'am," the necromancer said, trying to be as polite as possible.

Emeralda shook her head. "I asked, can you raise him?" She cut through him with a fiery gaze. Her rainbow dress caught in some unsourced light and appeared for the moment godly.

"I, I suppose ma'am, I do have some potions of luck with me—" Emeralda cut the man off.

"Than do it," she said. She planted her feet and crossed his arms.

The man took a potion out of the satchel that hung at his side, a blue one, with a glittering sheen, and downed it in one gulp. He eyed Emeralda as he did, as if he were looking to her for assurance. When he had finished, he wiped his mouth. He moved over to the body, and held his hand out over its forehead.

"Raise dead," he said, and a light appeared beneath his hand, and traced a pattern all across the corpse. For a second, nothing happened. And then, in a sudden jolt of motion, the dead man became undead.

A Divine Slip-up

"Whoozawhatit?" The newly undead necromancer cried, as he looked around the room. "What happened? Why does my head hurt so much?"

Emeralda looked at the undead necromancer, evaluating his appearance. He looked just like he had as a corpse: white, creamy, blood spattered on his clothes. The knife that had killed him still stuck out of his chest. "What's your name?" Emeralda asked the newly undead man.

The undead necromancer hesitated, as if he were flinging his thoughts over a chasm. "Alek Hurnt," he said, his eyes regaining some glow.

Emeralda face the live Necromancer. "Is that true?" she asked.

The live necromancer nodded his head, but said nothing. He continued to stare at Alek.

"What am I doing here?" Alsek asked, his voice a little raspy. He tried clearing his throat, but it didn't seem to work.

"You've just become undead," Emeralda explained to him. "From what I heard, you've been out for about an hour." She looked at him critically. "Enough to have lost quite a bit of brain matter, I'm afraid."

Upon this revelation, Alek the new undead looked at his arms, his knees, and the knife sticking out of his chest. He stared at the necromancer who had raised him, his gaze pleading. "What did you do?" he asked, his voice full of sorrow. "I finally found peace, it was so nice, down there. Why did you bring me back?"

The man's words gave Emeralda pause. If anything, she would have expected the man to be grateful for being given a second chance. Even if it were sub-class, she had considered undead better than all dead. Now, she gave her ideas second thoughts.

"What was it like?" Emeralda asked, her curiosity getting the better of her. The investigation could wait.

"I don't remember how I got there," Alek said, "but I knew I went through some sort of gate."

Emeralda nodded. That would be the gate to the underworld, presided over by the parliament of death. Some of the members were acquaintances of hers. All who passed through were given a draught of powerful forgetting potion—meaning, the soul forgot everything. The body still remembered things, stored in its brain, which is why after-life interrogation was possible. However, a blank soul meant a lot of things. It explained a lot of the undead union's prerogatives, their lack of purpose.

"Do you remember anything at all?" Emeralda asked, continuing to sate her curiosity. The necromancer who had raised Alek also seemed to be thinking deeply.

"It was . . . It was . . ." Alek dropped off, obviously trying to search for the word.

"Sublime?" Emeralda offered. "Amazing?"

"How about deep?" The live necromancer offered. "Sepulchritudionus?"

Alek shook his head. "No, it was more like . . ." and then he released a word that rang like a clear bell, a crystal sound that reverberated through the room. All around the ship, the blue light strips that formed intricate patterns over every surface lit up with an intense brightness, for a split second, and Emeralda could have sworn the heavens were opening.

In fact, they were opening. A shimmering veil of pure light, as tall as the room itself, opened into a white vortex. The ship itself seemed to be drinking the energy contained within, as if it too were of the same stuff—or at least powered by it.

And then a goddess stepped out. She wore a black robe, and was stunningly beautiful, holding in her hands a long, pointed scythe. Despite her divine appearance, Emeralda thought she looked a little frazzled.

"Ahh, I'm so sorry, I didn't mean to do this," she said, looking around the room. She muttered to herself. "The potion was two milligrams short . . ."

Emeralda stared, as did the other two in the room. It was not something that happened every day, an agent of death arriving at their doorstep.

"Again, I'm so sorry," the goddess said, to everyone and no one. "You weren't supposed to hear that, so I'm so sorry, but I'm going to have to erase your memories of the past few . . ." she pulled up a stunningly bright ball of light, and the ship seemed to kick into overdrive, jolting the room about. "Two minutes and three seconds," she said, after looking up.

She looked at Emeralda. "I'm sorry, I'm so sorry," the goddess said, repeating it like a mantra. She brushed back her hair with the handle of her scythe. She took one last look about the room, and then nodded. A blinding ball of light surrounded everything, and then the room returned to its original state.

Emeralda sat staring at the undead necromancer, surprised that the raise dead spell had worked so fast.

As it turned out, the stabbing had been an accident, although there had been a riot in the mess hall at the time. It was over the usage of food: the necromancers thought that they were the only ones that should eat, because they were the only ones that had to. The undead that still had taste buds wanted to eat too, though, even though they didn't need it, and tensions had been high for a while.

The necromancers that had been friends with Alek soon realized that he was the same person, and actually got along with him quite well. The undead also accepted him as their own, and soon, the two opposing factions within the ship began to mingle, spurred on by Alek, who was of both sides.

Emeralda only learned this later, though. Immediately after the incident, she had to explain her decision, and extract the information from Alek, all while fighting her suspicion that she was forgetting something important. She had presented him to the people assembled in the common area, and proclaimed that since there was no precedent for an accidental non-killing that resulted in questionable damages, she could not, in good conscience, give an edict. They would have to sort it out themselves.

As the *Amshfisht* detached from the *Nonelstch*, Emeralda took in a wide view of her floating armada. The skyships, with their blocky, abstract designs, looked for all the world like a collection of floating buildings. The lines of blue that traced all through their grey metal sides reflected the sunlight, in deep contrast with the ship's otherwise dark tones. The green land, beneath them, rolled by with steady rhythm, and the wind tussled Emeralda's short, silver hair as it swung to and from beneath the motions of her skyships.

Amy appeared next to Emeralda, on the deck of the *Amshfisht*. She leaned over the side and spread out her arms, so that her hair—silky blond and smoother than real hair—flowed out beautifully in the wind.

"I can see why they put you in charge," she said, looking down at the ground below. "I wouldn't have come up with an idea like that, myself." She leaned back, and then put her finger on her lip, a pensive expression on her upturned eyes. "But then again, I don't know much about death." She looked at Emeralda. "Say," she said, "do you think I can die, too?"

Emeralda was surprised by her question, and couldn't help but show it. "What do you mean, die?" she asked. She was unsure of who, or even what, Amy really was. Was she a part of the ship? Was she a creation of the ship, dependent on it for energy? Was she the ship itself, operating from some hidden brain?

Amy spread her arms out again, and assumed a childlike expression. "I mean, what would happen if my subroutines were to return null? Would I go to the underworld, like you humans do?" She looked back at Emeralda, her eyes large and questioning. "Do I even have a soul?"

Emeralda tried to wrap her mind around Amy's quandary, but couldn't. It was hard enough, answering these questions as a human, especially an immortal one.

Amy didn't seem to care that she got no answers. She seemed to enjoy asking questions, and letting them float around. "How do you feel about dying?" she asked Emeralda, as she leaned to one side and tilted her head.

"I don't know," Emeralda answered. "I haven't died yet." She paused for a minute. "I don't think I will, anytime soon. It's always a possibility, but I've always been able to get myself out of situations where I might have died." She thought about it some more. "Usually without that much effort, as a matter of fact."

Amy leaned in, appearing to inspect Emeralda closely. "It's true," she said, "your aura is very strong, even for one who does not age."

"I've been told that before," Emeralda said. "Only, I'm not sure that I know what it means." She looked over the side of the ship, and Amy followed her gaze. "Everyone loves to talk about auras, and how they're people's souls, but I think that they're something separate."

Amy raised her eyebrows and leaned closer to Emeralda. "Oh?" She asked. "I don't have anything in my programming that mentions this."

"See," Emeralda said, "for some reason, I get the feeling that auras and souls are different. You can see people's auras, pretty easy, if you have the right training."

Amy nodded her head. "Indeed."

"And since, I've been living longer than pretty much everyone else on the world who has an aura, I'm the only one who remembers certain things." Emeralda leaned on the railing. "Even the royal academy claims that the aura is the soul. But I just feel as if it were different." She looked at Amy, for once in her life hoping that another would understand her, the things she thought about and knew about and had stored up after three centuries of being alive.

Amy smiled, and looked up at the sky. "So, what your saying is, maybe I do have a soul, even though I don't have an aura?"

Emeralda smiled, and nodded. "Perhaps," she said.

It's Drifting. Alone. In the Middle of Nowhere. Sure, Let's See What's Inside.

August
12 days after their escape from Elderdale, the crew of the *Firebird* spotted a derelict skyship, floating between two cliffs that rose up like the jagged teeth of a giant.

During the time since they had made their daring escape, not much had happened to August, Elyse, Penny, and Ruby. They spent their days training, working as sailors on the *Firebird*, and sitting around and talking. It had been a long journey, and though they were nearing the end of the skyship ride, it still felt to August as if time had long since stopped moving. Even though every day, he grew less sore, and handled Ruby's training better, and even though his face hardened and changed into one filled with fighting spirit, August found himself imagining that he would be on the *Firebird* for the rest of his days.

Every day, at sunset, he would sit on the prow of the *Firebird* and hold Elyse close to him, while Penny and Ruby sat in the rigging above. Each morning, at dawn, he would wake up Elyse a little early, or she would wake up him a little early, and the two would watch the sunrise together. There was nothing hidden between them now. Even Ruby commented on the effectiveness of their teamwork.

That day, the day that they spotted the derelict skyship, Ruby ordered the *Firebird* to pull abreast. They had long since entered the mountains of the edge, which grew higher with every passing hour. It was a rare sight to see anything having to do with humans. And so, when they pulled up aside the dead ship, aptly named the *Rotter*, painted in large, unwieldy lettering—over another name, it seemed—August found himself looking with both curiosity and annoyance upon it. The ship meant that the real world was out there, somewhere.

August, Penny, Ruby, and Elyse boarded first. The *Rotter* was a freighter, nearly twice the size of the *Firebird,* and seemed to have a full storage of crates. What was in the crates, August could not tell. When Ruby opened one of them, all they found was a black, powdery substance that felt as liquid as oil. Ruby let it fall out between her fingers as she stood in the above deck cargo hold.

"Something is strange, here," Ruby said, her voice measured. "I feel like someone is watching us."

"I do to," said Penny, who looked around with a wary expression.

August didn't notice anything, and neither did Elyse. The two stayed close together, behind Penny and Ruby as they entered the ship's main stairwell. There was no light inside the dark downward corridor, and so Penny lit a green werelight, that followed her, floating just above her head. Through his fairy battle display, August saw Penny's magica almost imperceptibly drain.

The stairway was short, and so Ruby entered the floor below just as August stepped in from the top. Ruby stopped where she stood, half in the door and half out, her expression frozen into place. Then, she let out a groan, a mixture of disgust and surprise. A terrible smell wafted up the stairway, like that of rotting meat left to float in brackish pond water.

August, filled with a morbid curiosity, hurriedly followed Penny and Elyse down the stair. He felt Elyse's reaction before his own, an almost overwhelming sense of terrible dread. When he reached the bottom, coming out of the stairwell to stand beside Elyse, Penny, and Ruby, he saw why, and he covered his mouth and nose with both hands.

The cargo hold of the *Rotter,* that ran the length and breadth of the ship, was stacked from floor to almost ceiling with dissected, rotting, human bodies.

Ruby walked down the aisle made of flesh that ran down the middle of the hold, looking from side to side, her eyes wide with horror. She leaned in closer to one body, and then gave another gasp, tortured and twisted as she sucked in the foul air.

Penny vomited on the floor, the stench of the contents of her stomach just barely adding to the malevolent odors that filled the room to bursting. August fought back bile himself, and Elyse gagged several times.

"I think," Ruby swallowed hard, "I think this I've seen this uniform before." She shook her head, as if trying to clear it.

Penny closed her eyes, plugged her nose, and ran for the surface. Elyse followed after her, only half to keep her company. August, however, moved up to where Ruby stood, next to a pile of what seemed to be the corpses of miners. August realized he had seen the uniform, as well. It was of the mine that the *Firebird* had visited before, where they had left Denyse, and where all the humans except for a few had vanished mysteriously from. Though the mystery had been solved, August did not want to know, and wished he had never known.

Ruby turned to August. "The monsters did this," she said, sure of herself. "Look," she pointed to the body of one man, half hidden under a pile of parts—and, most disgustingly, organs—motioning to wound in his side. "Bite marks," she said, and August noticed that they did indeed look like so. Now that it had been pointed out, many of the bodies had bite marks all over, too many for it to be coincidence.

"And look," Ruby pointed, to another wound in the man's side. "This hole is too big for a sword, or any metal weapon that I know of." She reached into it, causing August to turn away for a moment. She pulled out something, her hand coated in crusty red ooze. She examined it. "A stone fragment," she announced.

"Like the ganglers use?" August asked.

Ruby nodded. Her face twisted in what must have been a hundred emotions. "If I had known," she said, her voice low, "I would not have spared a single monster, of that army." She tossed the stone fragment away, and looked around once more, an expression of deep sorrow on her face. "And yet we left, while killing so few."

August certainly felt the same way she did. However, one thing bothered him. *Why did the monsters put them in a ship, and place them all the way out here?* He asked himself.

Good question, Elyse thought to him, from above decks. *I think you may want to come up here.* She sounded urgent, with a barely suppressed element of panic.

August turned to the stairway, and, calling for Ruby to come with him, left the storage room as fast as his feet could take him.

When he came out onto the deck, the sun blinded him, and the sweet air made him feel heady. He breathed deep, and then noticed Elyse, who stood in the middle of the deck, looking straight up.

August followed her gaze. What he saw horrified him. A worm, a giant worm the size of a city street, that poked its massive head out of the mountain above—through solid stone—and stared down at the *Firebird* and the *Rotter,* as they floated between the two jagged cliffs.

I think it wants its lunch, Elyse thought, still managing to find humor despite the situation. It was of a drab, morose kind, however.

Ruby came out of the stairwell behind August, and followed his gaze. Upon seeing the worm, she burst into action. "Lester!" she called, waking up her dress fairy. Lester popped into existence above her shoulder-strap. "What, Ruby," he said, and then drifted off as he saw the worm. "You want me to fight that?" he asked, his voice incredulous.

Penny, seeing Ruby's example, called up her dress fairy, Gliss. Gliss sparkled as the sun shone on her, and immediately went into action. August saw his battle-display updated, with one huge red icon that hovered over the worm's body. The worm undulated back and forth, as if confused about the second skyship that had broken into its lunch. August hoped it stayed that way, and didn't realize that it could eat them, too.

"Fireball!" Penny called, as she cast a fire spell. The flaming missile flew up towards the worm, until it disappeared. August thought it had, at least, but was proven wrong when a tiny flower appeared on the worm's side. Then, he realized how truly big it was.

"Run!" He called, not even bothering to use a code-word. The worm finally seemed to decide on something, and August didn't like it, from what he could sense of it. The worm's mouth opened wide, revealing a hundred sets of teeth that must have been the size of people.

August was the first back onto the *Firebird,* ahead of everyone else. Just as he hit the ship's deck, the worm began to drop down, out of its hole in the wall, towards where the two ships floated. Penny jumped over next, and then Ruby.

The *Firebird*'s sailors had already thrown up the rigging, and let out the sails, and so the ship began to move as soon as Ruby stepped on board. Elyse, seeing this, jolted to a halt on the edge of the *Rotter*'s deck. The gap between her and the *Firebird* widened more every second. The great worm bore down upon them, forcing the *Firebird*'s hand. They weren't going to slow down.

August, his body bursting with adrenaline, leaned over as far as he could over the *Firebird's* deck, his hand just brushing Elyse's fingertips as the *Firebird* rose into the air. The sunlight disappeared, as the worm's shadow grew ever larger.

"Throw me!" Penny called, running up beside August. She jumped onto the railing and balanced there precariously, for a moment. August grabbed her without question, and threw her down, making sure to keep hold of her ankle.

His grip slipped. Penny stopped in mid-air, and the whole world seemed to freeze. Then, moving fast even as the world slowed down, Ruby jumped onto August's back, launched herself into the air, and grabbed Penny by the waist, rope spilling out behind her. Penny, in the split second since August had let her go, managed to just reach Elyse's outraised arm. August caught Ruby's rope just as the last inch flipped over the rail. His entire body lurched as he held on, braking the three's fall. If it had not been for his training in the past few weeks, August probably could not have held on. As it was, he just managed to support the weight of the three. They swung downwards like a pendulum, first Ruby, then Penny, with Elyse on the end. The worm bore down a foot behind them, swallowing the *Rotter* whole, pushing a massive front of putrid air that spun the three like rag dolls.

And then, the worm disappeared, leaving only a hole in the mountainside. August relaxed, and almost lost his grip, as the weight of the three bore him down. He felt the arms of one sailor, and then another, wrap around his chest, and saw their hands grip the rope with him.

Elyse's clear voice rang through the mountain air. "WHOOOO!" she screamed, washing August with a wave of uncontrolled ecstasy. "Let's do that again!" Her laughter bounced back and forth against the echoing walls, pure and lovely like the sound of liquid sunlight.

A Reason to Start the Hatin'

Denyse

It was surprising, how little happened beneath the monster's massive war machine, deep underground. The only excitement that Denyse and Kelly had had were in the few times the monsters had run the machine, its red lined shell casting everything into glimmering pinks. Each time, though, it ground to a halt, as if something critical were missing in its construction.

So, Denyse and Kelly passed the time playing cards with a deck that Denyse had cut from fabric and sewn numbers on with a needle she kept in her pack. Tamalda, her fairy, objected strongly, but couldn't find any real reason against it. Amber, Kelly's fairy, had simply laughed at the idea, and provided Denyse with better thread.

Eight days and five hundred and sixty seven games of rock poker later, Denyse and Kelly sat in their cave, sitting among what almost looked like the comforts of home. Denyse had built a shelf out of fairy-cloth, on which their packs sat, neatly tucked in case of an emergency. They played on chairs Denyse had carved out of stone, keeping the flame spell on low to avoid attracting attention, using a table that she had made the same.

Their beds, filled with a springy cotton material Denyse had made out of the fabric by ripping and fluffing it over and over again—another action that her fairy strongly objected to, but could not prevent—looked as comfortable, if not more comfortable, than their beds at home. And the door, of course, had been cunningly camouflaged, layered to prevent light from getting through and textured grey like the rock around it.

All in all, it was a nice, quiet job. Until, one day, Kelly came back from the river with bad news.

"Denyse!" she called, leaning half in through the cloth door.

Denyse turned from the rock oven she had been working on, letting her practiced version of the 'fire' spell dissipate from her hand. "What is it?" she asked, not sure what to expect.

"I think they're doing something," Kelly said, her voice deadly serious.

At this, Denyse grabbed her pack, and tossed the other to Kelly. She grabbed up anything that was not made of stone or cloth, and turned to face Kelly at the door. "Show me," she said, ready for anything.

She wasn't ready for what she saw, however. After perhaps a half-hour of climbing over rocks, they reached the opposite side of the cavern. Here, a natural tunnel, perhaps large enough for an airship to pass through, sank into the wall. Where it went, Denyse didn't know, although a cold air vented from it.

Beneath the tunnel, a strange scene played out. A line of humans, some undead, some not, lined up in front of another human, who looked quite dapper in a coat and top hat. The man's appearance filled Denyse with a sort of incredulous feeling, giving everything a dreamlike quality.

"I've gathered you here today," the man in the coat and hat said, "because you have not been behaving."

Around the assembled men, ganglers held spears up high, at least three for every human.

"We have been very nice to you," the man with the coat said, "we have fed you, sheltered you, and given you a purpose to exist."

"Some purpose," a man growled, from the front of the rows. He glared at the man in the suit with terrible eyes, his face gaunt and drawn out like that of a ghoul's—though he was very much alive.

The man in the nice hat simply looked at the man. A gangler stepped out of its line, and calmly stabbed the gaunt man in the chest. The gaunt man looked at the man in the top hat, his eyes burning defiance even as the life fled out of them. He died with a gasp, his body falling limp on the spear.

"Anyone else care to comment?" The man in the hat said, surveying the hundred or so humans that were assembled. No one moved. "Very good," he said, evidently pleased with himself. "Now, I will tell you right this minute, that we are good hosts." He looked around. "We do not like to keep our guests in the dark." The way he said 'dark' seemed very sinister indeed.

"You will not die without knowing the reason why, I assure you," the man in the hat said, as if that in and of itself were assurance. "Now, I know you have been naughty, and that is part of the reason why I have assembled you here. Another part," here he paused, as if or effect. "Another part of the reason that I have assembled you here is because our friend, the wymagler, is hungry." He looked over the assembled crowd. "Does anyone know what a wymagler is?" He asked it seriously, with just a hint of ridicule.

No one moved. On man coughed, and without the man in the hat even looking at him, a gangler speared him through the chest. As he died, he coughed violently, again and again, as if to spite those who had caused his suffering.

The man in the hat looked annoyed, but said nothing about it. He waited a little longer, as if he expected someone to answer.

"What *is* a wymagler?" Kelly asked Denyse, from their hiding place in the surrounding rocks. Until now, they had both watched with a growing sense of horror and dread.

Denyse thought for a minute. "I think it's a legendary monster, a giant worm that is said to burrow though the living rock of mountains." She cringed as she remembered something else. "It is said that its favorite food is humans."

Kelly looked at Denyse, her eyes wide. "That that means—" she stopped mid-sentence, as if she were scared to complete it.

"I think it might be," Denyse said, as she looked back at the lined up humans, "that these poor souls are about to become worm food."

"No?" the man in the hat said, after a good long while looking at the assembled men. "I had thought better of you. Mayhap you humans aren't as smart as you think you are, after all." He seemed to beam when he said it, as if he enjoyed it to the fullest of his capacity. "But in any case, you will see soon enough." He looked comically sad, all of the sudden. "Or rather, you may see. Because, look at it this way. How many of you like to eat?" He asked.

No one answered.

"Well I know you undead don't," the man in the hat said, "but I had expected you living to say something. Perhaps that means I must make an adjustment to the feeding schedule . . ." he drifted off, tapping his foot against the ground.

Still no one said anything.

The man in the hat threw up his arms, as if he were exasperated though and through. "You are such a dull crowd," he said, his voice still smiling. "The last group I talked to was so much more fun."

He stopped, and then dropped his arms to his side. "Well then if you must," he said, his voice low. "I'll cut the theatrics." He cut one arm through the air, the motion sudden and harsh.

The ganglers that surrounded the crowd pressed inward, their spears lowered in a deadly pattern. The assembled men realized what was happening, and began to panic, fighting with each other to get somewhere, anywhere that was safe, but it was not to be, for the ganglers surrounded them all, and pressed them in, one by one, until they all lay on the floor, motionless.

Denyse caught her breath, and didn't realize it until it was over, and when it was, she noticed tears streaming down her cheeks. Kelly leaned over and wrapped her arms around Denyse, burying her head in Denyse's shoulders.

"Why . . ." Denyse asked, her voice low, and caught with tears. She looked again at the open area, where big two-legged monsters with multiple mouths piled the bodies all neatly into stacks, where the ganglers began to dissect them.

Kelly held back a gag, and Denyse held her tighter. They stepped away from their hiding place, and headed back to their base.

I need to report this, Denyse thought, just as a skyship appeared out of the tunnel in the wall and anchored by the killing field.

She wasn't looking forward to telling anyone.

Theory of Relativity as Projected in a Fantasy World

August

Two days after their encounter with the *Rotter*, the *Firebird* reached the tallest mountain, which it could not go over. It was their destination, and had been since they had first set off, for underneath this mountain ran a network of caves that led all the way through and out the other side. It was a dangerous route, but it was the only one available to them, and they had to reach the Centrix.

The *Firebird* set down next to an enormous cave mouth, which went down and down until it disappeared into blackness. Emeralda had provided them with maps, but August could not see how they would be able to come out the other side. The mountain was big.

As August, Penny, and Elyse stepped off of the *Firebird* and onto the ground for the first time in two weeks, laden with enough supplies to last them at least a month, they waved goodbye to the ship's brave airwomen. The sailors waved back, their white uniforms rippling in the wind.

Ruby came down to say her goodbyes, or so she had said. When an airwoman tossed her a heavy pack, which she strapped on without hesitation, August could do nothing but stare.

"You're coming with us?" Penny asked, her voice full of admiration.

Ruby nodded. "I trained with you, after all, and my party is scattered through the world at the moment."

August nodded, remembering how they had left Denyse and Justle, at separate times. He wondered how they were doing.

"They're doing fine," Ruby said, answering August's question before he asked it, "fine enough without me, that is. I've decided that you need my help more than they do, and so I have decided to come with you."

"We will be honored to have one with your experience to guide us," Elyse said, remembering her manners. She curtsied.

Ruby raised her eyebrows at the gesture. "Very well," she said. "We should get going." She shouldered her pack and faced towards the entrance to the cave. Penny followed her, close to her side, with Elyse and August tagging behind.

As they entered the grand entrance, and the light grew dimmer, all three girls in the party lit werelights. Penny lit a green one, Elyse it a red one, and Ruby lit a yellow one, and it looked as if only white light came from above them all.

It's the fundamental rule of light mixing, Elyse explained, happy to answer August's question. *The primary colors are red, green and yellow, mixing to make white.*

Why is that? August asked, curious.

Well, she paused for a moment, *the theory at the moment is that it has something to do with the mixing of transmutable inanimate auras, but I don't agree with it. However, I haven't been able to find an alternate theory. It's as if I'm missing something very big, like I'm just feeling the edges. In fact, I'm developing a magical formula now, that relates light to the things around it, and I might just be able to find something.*

She poured symbols, figures, and concepts into August's head that might as well have been gibberish.

Space is relative, Elyse said, *but light isn't. Isn't it odd?*

August shook his head. He didn't know. He just enjoyed listening to Elyse muse, admiring her and feeling happy that he was with her.

I mean, Elyse continued, as she squeezed through a particularly tight passage in the cave. Penny and Ruby, who had had no trouble, waited impatiently on the other side. *Have you ever tried to chase after light?*

August thought about it. *What do you mean?*

I mean, Elyse thought, *have you ever even thought of it as possible?*

Light doesn't move, does it? August said, confused. *It just is, right?*

Elyse filled with that peculiar satisfaction she demonstrated when claiming some natural law as her own. *What if it does move?* she asked, her mind filling with even more imperceptible, eminently logical gibberish.

Penny and Ruby had moved on far ahead, so that they seemed small, and occasionally disappeared behind a bend. August didn't notice, however, absorbed as he was while contemplating huge ideas.

So, imagine you're in a skyship, Elyse thought, and brought up an image of the *Firebird* in her mind. August saw it too, the way she saw it.

This ship can fly as fast as it needs to, Elyse said, adding the effect of speeding terrain. The terrain began to blur, as the ship moved even faster, and then faster, until it was as if they traveled through a world of lines. And then, everything became weird. The world condensed into a point ahead of them, everything moved weirdly, August even felt strange. In the background he could feel Elyse's mind working at full power to put on the show. August concentrated on it fully as well.

Which is why, when Penny and Ruby turned down a side tunnel, August and Elyse didn't notice.

Little Girls Lost in a Cave, Alone.

Penny

"August?" Penny called, searching back from where she had come, Ruby at her side. "August, where are you?"

Penny's dress fairy, Gliss, hovered around her. "I can't find them," she said, her voice a little panicked. "They must be too far away, and we're too far underground."

They had been searching for what seemed like hours, backtracking and retracing until they were not certain where they were, themselves. The caves blended into a whole around them, dripping stalactites filling crystal clear pools and making a drip-drip-drip that could have driven Penny mad, if she had not had her friends with her. It was the first time since the monsters had come, and taken her parents—no, killed, after what she had seen on the *Rotter,* she knew it was killed, in her heart, although she hoped that it had not been painful—that she had been separated from August and Elyse. They had been like parents for her, had acted like parents, had even been together like parents, but now that they were gone, the hole in her heart had opened up and was clawing at her chest looking for a way out.

Penny staggered on a lump in the floor, half-mad with fear and grief. Ruby steadied her, keeping her from hitting the floor, enviably calm through Penny's distress.

"Penny," Ruby said, her voice level. "Penny, we can't keep looking for them, they can take care of themselves."

Penny pushed ruby away. "Well," she cried, "I can't! Where are they?! Why did they . . ." She collapsed onto the ground, at Ruby's feet, her face covered in tears. "They said they would stay with me. They said they wouldn't abandon me. They pinky promised." At this, a fresh wave of grief hit her, so long delayed by her friendship with the two adventurers.

"If it was a pinky promise," Ruby said, her voice reasoning, "they couldn't have left willingly. They loved you, I saw."

Penny pounded the ground, feeling nothing give underneath her feeble attempts to release her sorrow. "Which is why they might be in trouble!" she said, looking up at Ruby. "We need to help them." She sniffled, and wiped her eyes.

Ruby leaned down next to Penny, and put her arm around her. She held her tight, and rocked back and forth. "They loved you," she said, "I'm sure of it." She let Penny sob into her arms, caressing her hair, fixing the loose pigtails. "If it was a pinky promise," Ruby said, "they will come back for you, you can be sure of that."

Penny nodded, and sniffled again, swallowing the tears that had built up in her throat. She felt the long-held back emotions rolling, but they seemed calmer, weren't as sharp. "Are you sure?" She asked Ruby, desperate for the answer that she wanted.

"Yes," Ruby said, her voice soft. "I'm sure."

Penny took a deep breath, and cleared her mind. Instead of fighting the emotions, she let them free, painful as they were. They melted away, running to some hidden corner of her consciousness.

"Very good, very good," a voice said, not Ruby's, and definitely not one of their dress-fairys'.

Penny and Ruby both looked around, surprised, and suspicious.

"Who goes there," Ruby challenged, her clear voice echoing off the cave's smooth walls.

"Just an old woman," came the voice, nearer, and closer to the ground. Out of the darkness, from one side of the cave, a hunched figure crept out. Her hair reached the floor, dank and sweaty, and two huge warts wrestled for attention on her cheeks.

Ruby held out her hand, and swirling water condensed out of the air around it, condensing into her ice hammer. She held it at ready, her dress tinkling with a soft light as her fairy prepared it for battle.

The woman didn't flinch, simply smiled, showing her two black teeth. Penny stared at her with a strange wonder, drawn to the old woman with an inexorable force. It was as if she were connected with her, on some deep, fundamental level.

The old woman cackled. "Hello, dearies," she said, her eyes crinkling. "I'm Gsh, pleased to meet you."

At the mention of her name, Ruby dropped her arms, her hammer hitting the ground beside her. "*The* Gsh?" Ruby asked, her voice full of incredulity. "Gsh, goddess of fate, the lone goddess?"

Gsh cackled some more. "The very same, dearie. You're a quick one, for sure," she said, when she had finished. "I've come to talk to Penny here, if you don't mind."

Ruby shook her head, her eyes still full of wonder. Penny wondered what it meant. She didn't know anything about gods and goddesses, although she supposed they were powerful.

"Why are you here?" She asked Gsh. She looked at the wrinkled woman's face, and couldn't help but feel a little disgust.

"I'm here to finish what I started," Gsh said, tilting her head, "or did you think you could defeat the *Marlperl* as you are now?"

Penny hesitated.

"The *Marlperl?*" Ruby asked, obviously confused. "Is it some sort of weapon?"

Gsh smiled sweetly, or as sweet as she could with her wrinkled face. In truth, it looked like a contortionist's act. "You'll find out soon enough," she said. "Things have already been put into motion." She shrugged her shoulders. "By me, of course, but there are also others who wish to have a say in the goings on of the world."

Ruby looked at Penny, and then looked at Gsh. "So it was you who gave her such a powerful destiny," she said, sure of herself. "You were the one that started this all." She didn't dare be accusatory, but she still managed to sound outraged.

Gsh shook her head and clucked her tongue. "No, dearie, I didn't start it." She looked up at Ruby, her face deadly serious, a powerful glint in her eyes that told of raging strength, enough to make the world over if need be.

Ruby stepped back.

"Mortals—or semi-immortals, in your case—should not get too involved in the affairs of those with more power than you can imagine," Gsh said, baring her teeth literally and figuratively.

"I will be sure to remember that, ma'am," Ruby said, the utmost respect in her voice.

Gsh smiled happily. "I'm glad that we reached an understanding." She walked closer to the two, and placed her arms on them, one on each. Neither resisted. "I'll just be taking you," she said, as the world disappeared in a blink.

It Might Have Been LSD. Who Knows?

August

August bumped into Elyse, as she stopped suddenly in the middle of the tunnel. It had been several hours since they lost Penny and Ruby, during which they had searched with all their might, finding nothing. August's fairy battle-display had disappeared a little over an hour ago, without so much as a warning. He did not like to think about what it meant.

Elyse held up her hand, and turned to August. She waved it around, as if she were testing the air. "Do you smell something?" she asked, sounding a little droopy.

The walls of the cave moved in, and then moved out, as if they were breathing. A stalactite seemed to grow bigger, bigger, until it occupied half of August's vision, and then its lines blurred into green and red and black.

"I . . ." was all August managed to say, before the world swallowed him up. Just as he was about to close his eyes, he saw a short figure, in a dress, approach out of the shadows. *Penny?* He thought, as he went under.

Crazy things happened inside August's head then, which he shared with Elyse, connected to him even as he lay unconscious. When he woke up an unknown amount of time later, all he knew was that it had been colorful. He sat in a wooden chair, strapped down with thick rope, in a wood-paneled room that accommodated several hanging stalactites. Across from him sat Elyse, in the same condition as he was, her shock white hair frazzled and her coat hanging askew.

"Wha . . ." August said, his mind still reeling with the effects of whatever had put him under. It seemed as if his tongue were made of fuzzy string, and in the place of language he had swirls of red chocolate. Slowly, his senses sorted themselves out, and he stopped feeling loud, and thinking in colors. He groaned once he regained enough control. Elyse noticed his actions, and smiled at him.

I thinksh thish if welderwroot, she thought, her mind still twisted. In it she held a strange giddiness. *I'w awaws wanped to try it,* she thought, her mind snapping to attention as a sharp, noxious odor filled the room. August felt his head clear as well.

"Are we all better?" A pretty voice asked, that reminded August of all the magical girls he had met.

The owner of the voice stepped into August's field of vision, and he could see that she was, indeed, a magical girl. She possessed blond hair, and features that were a cut above average. Despite her beauty, or perhaps because of it, she also held an air of danger, of something about to snap. She looked into August's eyes, her gaze unflinching, and then looked at Elyse. August could feel Elyse's discomfort, and got a sense from her that things were terribly, horribly wrong.

Of course it is, August thought. *We've just been kidnapped, deep underground near the edge of the world.*

The girl stood up straight, in the corner of August's vision, just far away enough to cause him to strain when he looked at her. "I think we are," she said, rubbing her palms together. "Now that that has been taken care of, let us begin. I'll start with introductions. My name is Shauna." She looked at August. "Now, you with the muscles, your turn."

August complied, not knowing what else to do. The thought of trying to escape his bonds occurred to him, but Elyse sent him a frantic message, something hot on her hand, a little bit of pain. *Don't.*

August swallowed. "My name is August Cerulian," he said.

Shauna smiled, her white teeth glittering. "August, like the month," she said, rolling the name about her tongue. "Very nice." She turned to Elyse. "And what is your name, you with the white hair and," she examined Elyse closer, "whiter skin?"

Elyse smiled as nice as she could, and answered. "My name is Elyse Marigold," she said.

Shauna raised her eyebrows. "Not *the* Elyse Marigold, inventor of the skysteel engine?" She asked, her voice full of mocking. "But it is." She giggled, a maniacal laughter that gave August cold shivers. "Oh, I think this just got much more entertaining." She clapped her hands together. "So, you two, tell me something." She paused for a bit, examining August's face, and then turning to Elyse. "What were you doing, so deep down, here in my front yard?"

Don't tell her, Elyse thought to August. *We can't give anything away, there's no telling who she might be connected to.*

Well, can you think of a good excuse? August asked, desperately racking his brain for a plausible answer.

They must have looked into each other's eyes for a bit too long, for a slow smile crept across Shauna's face, crazed, maniacal, and all forms of nefarious. "Don't tell me," she said, her voice full of suppressed emotion, "that you two," she tapped her fingers against her dress, "might just be in love?" She broke out into a huge grin.

August tensed, and felt Elyse's panic. He turned his head to face Shauna, desperate to deny, knowing that something horrible was about to happen. Before he could open his mouth, Shauna shushed him, putting her finger over her lips.

August swallowed. "What does it mean to you?" he asked, sorry he said it the instant he saw the expression on Shauna's face. It was devilish, twisted, filled with fermented anger and hatred.

"Oh, it means everything, all right," Shauna said, as she reached behind her for some unseen object. "You'll see," she said, almost to herself, "You'll all see, you're all wrong, wrong-wrong-wrong-WRONG!" She whipped her hand around, her fingers gripped tight around a sparkling, glowing, cutting knife. Her eyes possessed in them a madness, an utter brokenness, dredged up from the unseen blackness of her soul.

August gulped, his body tingling all over. Elyse stayed still as a rock, a tiny pain near her wrist, where her bonds were, that she gave to August, to tell him: *hold on!*

I. Am. God.

Penny

There was only white. Nothing but white. There was no up, no down, no around, just clear, cold, solid, unbroken, bright white. Penny stood in the center of it, next to Ruby, her dress still intact, so very out of place in the world of nothing.

"Hello?" Penny called, hearing only the echo of her voice for a long while. Ruby turned on the balls of her feet, wandering away from where Penny stood, and yet seeming to go nowhere.

Ruby turned to Penny, a strange understanding in her eyes, and then she looked all around. "I think the goddess trapped us inside your head," she said, her voice a not little awestruck.

Penny tapped her head with her hand, confused. "My head?" She asked, looking at Ruby, at her dirty dress, and her brown hair, and her kind eyes. "What do you mean?"

"I mean that this is like a dream, but worse," Ruby said, looking at her own hands. She looked back up at Penny. "It means that you have ultimate power." She shivered when she said it, as if she had just realized something.

Penny scrunched up her nose, and looked around. "What does ultimate power do?"

Ruby shook her head. "It doesn't do. It's something that you wield."

"Does it mean that I can do anything I want?" Penny asked, suddenly excited. "Anything?" She thought of so many things just then, so many things to do with her powers.

"Err," Ruby looked as if she were afraid, truly afraid. She looked up, as if she were seeking guidance. "I guess I'll have to trust her," she muttered to herself, rubbing her shoulders. She looked at Penny. "Yes," Ruby said, "You can do anything."

Penny knew right away what she would do first. And, just as she thought it, it happened. Like wind out of a tunnel, her home village appeared, complete with everyone that had lived in it. Ruby looked nervous, as she watched, strangely out of place.

Penny's dress changed back to what it had been before the adventure started. She walked up the village gates, over the dirt path she had remembered, and saw her parents, in the courtyard, waiting for her. They smiled, and she ran towards them, oblivious of everything, as tears began to well from her eyes, and the thoughts of everything that had happened, from Ruby, to August, to the horrible things she had seen, it all disappeared.

And Ruby, behind her, watched with a sadness born of centuries.

Penny stayed with her parents for what seemed like a few hours. It was day until she decided that she wanted it to be night, and then it was night. At first, Penny thought of Ruby every other minute, and then she began to think of her every other hour, and soon, she thought of her only every other day. The days turned into weeks, as she lived with her parents, playing, talking, having fun and being the good girl that she had always wanted to be. There was no sorrow, no pain, no stubbed toes or dead baby animals or slaughtered pigs. It was as she had always wanted to be.

And then the weeks turned to months, Ruby having disappeared from Penny's mind entirely, thought of once in a blue moon—which Penny did make, really blue, like she had always wanted—and soon after, not at all.

The months turned to years. Penny lived every day the same. One day, however, she decided that she wanted to take a vacation. So she did. She went to a beautiful beach, and imagined that she were older, and more beautiful and it was so. She had the perfect body shape. The perfect face. One day, as she basked in the sunlight, a man, exquisitely muscled to perfection, but with such eyes the world had never seen, so soft, and wanting, appeared by her side, and she kissed him.

And the years turned into decades. Penny decided she needed a vacation from her vacation. She journeyed through the jungles with her muscled, handsome, kind companion. Her parents had long since disappeared from her mind. Though the jungles were steamy, her happiness was more. She loved, and liked, and saw, and explored. The bottom of the ocean. The moon. The stars. She saw dragons, and rode them. She had adventurous clashes with swarthy pirates, always rip-lashingly stunning, and never once did she get hurt.

And the decades turned to centuries. Penny found herself wanting, for the first time, as she flew high above her palace in the skies, surrounded by riches unheard of. She ignored it, and gave herself the most beautiful massage, and felt truly, utterly happy, like she had every single hour out of every single day out of every single week out of every single month out of every single year out of every single decade out of every single century, and she wanted more. More. More. The thought hounded her like a predator. She found she could not escape it, for more than a minute at first, but them it was as if she were cloaked in her desire for something more.

And then one day, as she held the moon in the palm of her hand, Ruby appeared, her form minute, tinier than tiny, but still visible to her as she presided over the universe.

"I had higher hopes for you, Penny," Ruby said, disappointment evident in her voice. "I . . ." She shook her head. "It's no use, anymore, I've tried to talk to you normally, but you just forget me. Every time."

Penny remembered. Tiny aberrations in her life of centuries, of happiness, but they were there. And when they happened, she felt something. Something that matched with her wanting like a puzzle piece.

Ruby shrugged. "I really thought you were my friend," she said. She looked down at the floor. Penny could see tears glistening in her eyes. "I think I loved you," she said, her nose wet. And then she disappeared.

Penny swallowed. The universe rotated around her, everything she had ever wanted, but she still felt it: pain.

And then, she began to cry. At first, her tears flooded whole planets, brought about the extinctions of species, but then as she cried more, and let out all the pain she had accumulated during her short, real life, as she embraced it, the pain that covered her and yet kept her feeling alive. Her tears created rivers then, which flowed over the whole planet, and gave life to all sorts of flora and fauna.

She took that pain that she had carried, even since her birth, and examined it. It was there, actually there, something that she could really hold on to. But, she noticed, in its presence, her happiness felt better. Like it was meant to be with the pain. Like it wasn't meant to be taken alone.

And so her tears watered a garden. Penny looked about her, and saw not what she wanted, but what made her happy. And she realized that the two were not the same.

And so her tears dripped into a bucket, filling it up to the brim. She looked about her house, and saw her mother and father for who they really were, just normal people, like her, that would be disappointed to see her long for them so much. And her pain enveloped her, and almost caressed her.

And so her tears dripped down her nose, as she stood in the whiteness of her own soul, feeling much better, and centuries wiser. Ruby appeared then, not as if she had come out of thin air, but as if she had been there the whole time, watching, waiting, and Penny had only just now seen her.

Ruby smiled, tears in her eyes, and embraced Penny tighter than anyone had ever embraced her before.

"Welcome back," Ruby said, her voice choked up.

And then the two girls were in the caverns, locked in each other's arms, with the feeling that all would be right.

"It took you a little while," Gsh's voice said, from somewhere not in the world. "But I think you go the message," she said. She cackled. "Being a god is a lonely job, you know, so you take it where you can." She cackled again. "And, just so you know, I made sure that a reasonable amount of time passed. Say, a few hours. Bye bye!"

And then like that, it was over. Ruby looked at Penny, and Penny looked at Ruby. Though they had not aged in the real world, they saw in each other's eyes the wisdom of many more centuries.

"Is dealing with a god always this . . ." Penny said, casting about for a word.

"Crazy?" Ruby said, breaking into a little bit of laughter.

Penny nodded, also giggling. "Crazy, yes," she said. "Definitely crazy."

And then the two of them laughed out loud, their voices echoing and rebounding across the cave's walls.

Say I Love You

August screamed. The knife hurt. It was like fire, but worse, entering his veins and filling his entire being.

"Say it!" Shauna screamed, her voice delusional.

"I love you, Elyse!" August cried, at the top of his lungs. The words bounced off the wood-paneled walls, that looked, upon closer inspection, to have been constructed from the frames of a thousand backpacks. An untold number of adventures had died to create it, at the hands of the lunatic that held them captive. Elyse sent August another image, through his pain, the feeling of *Instrator* cutting through hemp and skin. *I love you too,* Elyse told him, her mind a whirl of activity.

Shauna, mad with some sort of infernal frenzy, pressed the knife against August's leg, in a place that she had not touched before. August screamed, and bit his tongue, for the fifth time, the blood curdling in his mouth. It hurt, it hurt, it hurt! He almost gave in, almost let the pain take him over, almost gave in to Shauna's insanity, but was stopped when Elyse shouldered some of his own pain. He felt her writhe, fighting to conceal it.

Shauna laughed madly. "You don't love her!" She screamed, with righteous conviction. "You can't love her! No one can love her!"

August fought against his fading consciousness, trying to stay awake so he could keep her occupied for one more minute.

"What do you mean, no one?" He said, bracing himself. "I do!"

And Shauna plunged the knife deep into his hand, until August could feel his bones crisping, and the tendons in his hand curl in the heat. It was like no other feeling he had felt before, even since the torturing began, and he struggled madly at his bonds. Elyse came to him again, siphoning off some pain, just enough to keep August sane.

Shauna lifted the knife, to August's infinite relief, and breathed heavily. Her beautiful features had since twisted into a mask of horror, her hair resembling the fronds of moss that hung from marshy trees. "Why don't you listen?" She asked, her voice suddenly low. "Why don't you understand?"

She touched the knife to August's skin, half-heartedly, this time. August cringed, and bit back the still formidable pain, from that and his other gaping wounds. He wondered why he was still alive, and suspected Elyse of secretly healing him. *Smart of her,* he thought, *extending the time that I'm in pain so she can get out.* He shook the thought out of his head.

Shauna noticed the flicker in his expression, though, and gave a gristly smile. "I see you are beginning to see things my way," she said, her voice dripping with satisfaction.

August shook his head violently. "I love her, I swear," he said, finding his heart not behind the words. He began to falter. *Why isn't she working faster?* he thought. *She's supposed to be the all-powerful genius!*

He looked past Shauna, who stood in front of him, at Elyse, and saw something he had never considered before. Elyse was a normal person. Sure, she was abnormal in many ways, but underneath it, she was still human.

And then August's feelings began to evaporate, slowly at first, but then faster, as he desperately tried to hold on to them. *I love her, I love her, there's no one else but her that I love, she's the perfect, pure white genius that is beautiful and always knows what to do,* he paused. Shauna had been looking at him for the past couple seconds, licking her knife. It was the longest break that August had gotten from her.

Across the gap, Elyse looked at August, her eyes showing pain. She had heard everything, of course, and stopped her efforts to escape. She didn't continue.

You said you loved me, she said, her voice longing. *I thought,* she paused. *I thought that you would protect me.*

I did, August said, desperate to salvage the situation. *I still,* he hesitated, but just for a moment, *do.*

Elyse noticed his hesitation. Her rose red eyes burned into him with fire in them. She took a jagged breath. *I did too,* she said, *I loved you too.*

August felt that it was true, that when his feelings had evaporated, hers had gone with them. It was as if someone had opened a box, and all the air inside had escaped. August hung limply in his chair.

"So you both are seeing things my way," Shauna said, her voice gloating. "I'm glad that I could have been of service to you."

Elyse spit, a crude gesture that was unlike her. She stared at August. "I don't even know what love is, anymore," she said, ignoring their situation.

Shauna gasped, and then smiled happily. "So you really do understand!" she cried, suddenly giddy like the little girl she appeared to be.

Elyse nodded. August stared at her, uncomprehending. "I thought that he loved me, that we were in love, but now I see it's all just an illusion."

Shauna clapped her hands, her face returned to its former beauty. "Tell me, tell me," she pleaded.

"It's just something the gods invented to trick us, isn't it?" Elyse said, turning in her chair. She seemed not to even care about escaping anymore. "Isn't it?!" she cried, looking straight up. She got no response.

August lay limp, his entire body aching from his wounds, wondering what it all meant. He had been happy before, he thought, but maybe Elyse was right. Maybe it really was an illusion.

I think so, Elyse said, her voice suddenly sad. *We were both fools, weren't we? To think that we had something special.*

August laughed a little inside, despite the situation. *Yes, and now we're paying the price for it.*

Shauna let out a breath, and looked towards August with a strangely sorrowful expression. "I know how you feel," she said, waving her knife to accentuate her words. "I loved a man once, too, or so I thought." She looked at Elyse. "But then even after I left the Disciplinary force, he left me, and said he fell in love with another girl.

A 'proper lady,' he said." Shauna was close to tears. "I fell for him even then, I chased him all over, and then he took me on an adventure and said that he wanted to show me something when he really just wanted to abandon me somewhere far away," Shauna brought down her knife in a slashing motion. "So I killed him!" She smiled, half lost little girl and half crazed lunatic.

Elyse nodded, taking in her story, listening to it. "I feel exactly how you do," she said, and August noticed a burning sensation in her palms.

I'm sorry, Elyse said, *but I had to deceive you.*

August looked at her, and realized that what had melted away wasn't the love, but rather his illusion of her. The real her, the flawed, human her, sat before him, about to pull off something awesome, that was not certain to succeed.

August smiled. *I suppose we should thank her,* he said, exploring the new feeling that he had, that felt cleaner and more whole than before.

Elyse gave a wicked smile. *After she's dead!* She thought, just as she whipped her arm out of the chair and pointed Instrator at Shauna's heart. Shauna, who had been monologing her woes, fell to the floor, too surprised to speak. Her knife clattered across the cave ground, hitting up against a small stalagmite.

Elyse prepared for a killing blow.

"Wait!" A voice called, from the room's doorway. Penny stepped into the room, panting. Ruby followed.

"Don't kill her," Ruby said, holding up her arm. "She's a wanted ex-magical girl, and needs to be tried by our court" she gasped, holding her side. "I knew she was here, I just didn't expect to run so close to her." Ruby looked at Elyse, and then at Shauna, on the floor. "It seems I needed to hurry, but for a different reason," she said, looking at Elyse with a new respect.

Shauna struggled, underneath Elyse's knee. Elyse held Instrator close to Shauna's neck, and Shauna's movement stopped.

"Well, it seems everything has tied together nicely," August said, surveying the scene. He turned to Ruby. "But, where were you?" he asked, as Penny cut his bonds and Ruby cast a spell of healing. August's wounds disappeared, along with the awful pain.

"You don't want to know," Ruby said, sharing a secret glance with Penny.

August nodded, and looked at Elyse. "I know what you mean," he said.

Shoot the Shrooms! Aim for the Shrooms!

Justle

The monsters finally made their move on the 19th day of the siege, 12 days after their failed attempt to capture it by impersonating the Baron. That day was the day they finally completed their massive engines of war, put together by human slaves that the scouts reported had been streaming in for almost a week. They were sorry fellows, whom Justle did not envy.

She stood atop the clockwise wall, looking over the handiwork of the citizens, as the sounds of massive gears turning grew in the distance. They had done all they could in the time they had, turning each main street into a veritable death trap—for any monsters that might have happened by, that is. The citizens navigated by way of rooftop now, walking over easily movable boards to avoid the dangerous streets. It was possible to walk from one end of the city to the other without touching ground, a feat that Justle was very proud of.

And, the traps, oh, the traps. Justle had not even imagined some of them, which now lay hidden all across the city. There were the classic ones, many of those: spike pits and log rollers and tripwire arrows. There were nefarious ones: acid baths and cages of killer wasps and little spikes topped with castor bean poison. Those were the reason that the citizens used the rooftop walkways. Then, there were the ingenious ones: a cart rigged to roll down the side of the hill, with knives protruding from every side; clockwork spears that shot out of the house of one mechanic, who lived right on a main road, at irregular intervals; and a clever flour-based trap that exploded barrels over the streets and then lit the resulting cloud of powder on fire.

It was a marvelous feeling, to feel so secure inside of a city at siege. Of course, that was one of the main reasons Justle's idea had the

Baron's full approval: morale had skyrocketed after the citizens had begun booby-trapping the place. There was something about scheming your enemy's death that made him seem much less intimidating.

Justle smiled. Even though the forces of the enemy bore down on them hard, she expected to hold out, at least until Emeralda arrived with her armada of reinforcements. They were to arrive at any moment, within the next day, she was given to believe. Emeralda had seemed very sure of herself when Justle had contacted her—but then again, Emeralda was always sure of herself.

A distant rumble began, near the clockwise gate. The storming of the city of Elderdale had begun.

Justle ran across the rooftop walkways, darting in between scurrying citizens, and rendezvoused with Iris halfway across the city. Iris followed her without a word, the only sound being her harsh breathing and the patter of their footsteps against wooden planks.

When they reached the gatehouse, Justle grabbed hold of the ladder that extended down to the rooftops. It was attached only at the top, able to be kicked down at the slightest provocation to defend the inner city from enemies on the wall. However, that made it very wobbly.

As Justle climbed up, she thought about what she might see up top. The monsters had looked formidable at a distance, with their massive grandshrooms and flying aurawhales, but would they measure up close? Justle certainly hoped not. It would be better for her if they had more bark than bite.

However, she was disappointed. As she crested the parapet, she saw the monsters arrayed in full, and sucked in her teeth. Three huge siege towers approached the wall where she stood, with countless more coming from all sides, all pulled by the massive grandshrooms. Even they were dwarfed by the towers, standing 80 feet tall to just reach over the top of Elderdale's parapet.

Justle readied herself. Her staff appeared out of the mist, in her hands, and Iris clambered over the wall behind her. She bore no weapons, unarmed combat being her specialty.

Behind every crenulation, at least one archer shot at the approaching monsters, but it was not nearly enough. The boom of cannon came far too infrequently, and Justle saw a disheartening amount of flying monsters swarm over the anti-air ballista. She suddenly regretted repurposing four of them for city defense.

Some of those flying monsters approached her section of the wall, where there was a gap between firing ballista.

"Look up!" Justle called, jolting the archers around out of their concentration. The monsters storming the walls could wait; there was a squadron of beaterbats bearing down hard. The archers fired wildly, most of the arrows missing, and arching back to earth. A few hit their marks, though, and their targets spiraled back to earth on all sides.

"Bliss!" Justle called, to her dress-fairy.

"Aye, ma'am," Bliss said, lighting the beaterbats up just as they swooped overhead. An unlucky archer was caught in one's path, and fell screaming over the side, ripped from his perch. Justle steeled herself. There would be many more that night.

A beaterbat dived towards her, spiraling to avoid the arrows in the air. Her fairy-display marked it as beaterbat number 462, which made her wish it were not there.

Just as it was about to hit, Justle turned to the side, shouting the party code-word for Iris's assistance. Iris responded immediately, twisting around towards Justle and pulling a flying jump kick that slammed the beaterbat into the parapet.

"Thanks," Justle said, without looking over. She knew she would be called soon, as well. Such was the nature of party combat. And so she lost herself in the mechanics of defending the castle walls. She was so concentrated on her targets that she almost lost her balance when one of the massive siege towers landed its gate right in front of her. A dozen angry ganglers stared at her, and charged as one.

Justle and Iris cut through them, Justle flinging out magical bolts of energy, filling the air with the smell of frying skin, and Iris twirling around using all four limbs as deadly weapons. Several times, Justle suffered a wound, only to see it disappear. She provided the same cover for Iris, healing her whenever she would strike too hard against a stone weapon of some sort. Justle felt sorry for the ganglers, almost, not having the power they did.

That feeling evaporated as the first of the gutterbacks hit the wall. They shook the ground with each step, and swatted aside the ganglers and men that got in their way. One man pushed back against a gutterback, and the two cracked though the parapet and fell down to their deaths, 50 feet below.

It was looking bad, on the wall. Justle tried to keep track as best she could, as she fought against a gutterback that stood a foot taller than the rest, but could not help but lose time to battle-frenzy. She struck, she swung, she fried with lightning and fire and ice.

And then, her magica ran out. She tried to cast a fireball at a gangler, just as it jumped on a soldier, but got only a fizzle out of her hand. She knew she needed to retreat, then, but the wall was almost overrun. It had come to pass. Elderdale was about to be breached.

From all four gates, great booms sounded, followed by massive roars that came from the gigantic, one horned monsters that rammed into them with the force of a thousand tons of steel.

Any minute, they would break. A gangler sliced Iris's leg open, but she couldn't heal it, because she had no more magica left. There were potions of restore magic stored in strategic locations across the wall, but none of them seemed to be reachable. Soldier after soldier met his death at the hands of a gutterback, or at the end of a gangler's spear. The floor ran slick with blood, of all colors. Justle made a decision.

"Retreat!" she cried, her voice carrying over the tumult. "Fall back from the walls! Defend the city!"

All around her, the remaining soldiers took up the cry. "Retreat!" they called to each other. "Fall back!"

As Justle scrambled down the ladder into the city, holding Iris's weight with one shoulder, the clockwise gate finally burst open. A thousand screaming monsters poured in, only to face a thousand devious and explosive traps. The entire battle froze as all turned to watch the monster's utter annihilation. Spikes were flung. Strings were tripped. Explosions warmed the air and covered all other sound. The cart with the blades all over disengaged, pushed by two citizens, and did its job even better than expected. At least three dozen ganglers lost some or all of their body parts as the machine coasted down the hill, ending its journey in the chest of a gutterback, sending them both sprawling into a house.

The people of the city cheered, and then stopped, as the traps began to run out. Ganglers made it through, a couple at first, and then more, coming in a stream that seemed never to stop. The other three doors blasted open, and the process began anew, ending each time with swarms of monsters streaming towards the keep. Justle watched from a rooftop near the city walls, supporting Iris on her shoulder, as her anti-air ballista chewed through the monster's ranks like so much candy. And still, they kept coming. Justle estimated that over three thousand had been killed, perhaps more, by her traps.

She thought about it. There were over ten thousand monsters besieging the city. Three thousand was barely a third. That meant seven thousand were now going to assault the keep.

In the streets, the citizens took up arms, fighting with improvised weapons and tools. Justle cringed, as she watched the lack of training take its toll, the men and women that were lost because she did not do her job well enough.

"We should head to the keep," Iris said, biting though her pain.

Justle nodded, and tore her gaze away from the battle before her. Dusk approached, but the fires in the city made it seem like it was still day. Smoke filled the air. Several times, on the rooftops, Justle had to find her way around a conflagration that reached up towards the sky with burning fingers. They passed citizens running all around, panicking, not bothering to look at them, not even bothering to watch where they were going, some falling uselessly to their deaths on the streets below.

Justle fought back tears. She had known this was coming. She had known there really was no hope, they were too outnumbered. And yet, she had allowed herself to hope. Stupid, stupid, stupid, she thought. She was stupid to have believed that she could do something against so many.

As they approached the keep, the number of scurrying citizens dropped. Screams filled the air all around, as the monsters rampaged through the city. A few delayed traps exploded, pushing the fires away, and then calling them back, ever stronger.

Justle and Iris reached the wall of the keep, where above, the palace guard kept watch.

"Hey!" Justle called, to one of the guards.

The guard recognized them immediately, and threw down two ropes. Justle tied one to herself, and the other to Iris, whose injured leg seeped blood onto the rooftop.

As they were hauled up to safety, Justle felt sick. Elderdale had had a population of 15,000, before the siege. Most of them were civilians. Most lived in the main part of the city.

And most of them were probably going to die tonight.

Pep Talk

Emeralda

"Go faster!" Emeralda yelled, in the bridge of the *Amshfisht,* looking at the magical projection of their position. It was the wee hours of the morning, and they had been putting on top speed without a wink of sleep for almost a day now. Elderdale's main wall had been breached last night, as Justle had reported, and the survivors were holed up in there like gophers. They didn't have much time left.

The monsters were after the missing piece. Amy had explained it all to Emeralda, as soon as she had heard of the problem. That was two days ago.

"My creators built many things," Amy had said, her hair flowing in the wind. "We built many wondrous things," she motioned to herself, proudly, "and they built many terrible things."

Emeralda had listened to her with rapt attention, finally getting the explanation she had been looking for.

"Yes," Amy said, "some of my ancestors were what you call monsters today. But they were mostly second class-citizens, the underside of society. There was a civil war, long ago, that had nothing to do with any of these things. It had to do with metal. It was the war you call the war for the Centrix, when the creatures of the underside went feral and fought for the metal of the topside. It was in this war that I, and everything of them that remains, were created." Amy looked down, remembering a time long lost. "We were made so that only humans could control us," she said, "and it is sad that only we remain." She looked out, up at the sky. "After the war, the remaining ancestors destroyed all remnants of monster technology that remained, so the monsters would never again rise to power. They sealed the Centrix, the portal between worlds, with their technology. And they left the world forever."

Amy stood away from the edge of the ship, and paced around the deck. "But they forgot to clean up after themselves," she said, her voice darker. "They left one of their superweapons behind, when all were supposed to have been destroyed." She looked at Emeralda, her face deadly serious. "It's called the *Marlperl,* and it's the largest single machine ever made. Its parts were scattered, all across the world, many buried deep underground."

"That's strangely pronounceable," Emeralda said, rolling the name on her tongue. *Marlperl.* What Amy had said explained a lot of things, like the monster's capturing of mines, and their need to take Elderdale. "Can the monsters use the *Marlperl?*" Emeralda asked, just to make confirm.

"They cannot," Amy said, shaking her head. "But they have found a way around it, a clever one."

"Human slaves," Emeralda answered, knowing the answer already. "That's why they captured so many small towns and mines, keeping everyone alive." She thought for a moment. "That means, a good portion of them might be alive," she said.

Amy nodded. "Your obsession with living is strange, but I understand what you're getting at. They will be useful to you now, yes?" Amy asked, tilting her head.

And so the discussion continued.

Back in the present, racing towards Elderdale, Emeralda felt a strange tension in her chest, knowing that everything was at stake. Before Penny could do her fate-thing, before anyone had to suffer through more conflict, she could end it. She had to end it.

Suddenly, the small point of light that had been in front of them all night became more of an outline, and Emeralda realized that it was the city of Elderdale, on fire.

"That's it," she said, reaching out her hand as if to grab it from the sky. "We made it."

Amy stepped beside her. "Estimated arrival in ten minutes, Captain." She gave a naval salute. "I suggest you address your soldiers."

Emeralda nodded. "How can I do that?"

Amy stepped in front of her. "I can have my sisters project your voice in every ship," she said, her body distorting for a moment. "I have made the connections," she said. "Calculations show that with this amount of wind noise, your voice will be audible enough to show emotion."

"Patch me in, then," Emeralda said.

Amy raised her eyebrows at the phrase, but didn't comment. "Done," she said, after no more than a second.

Emeralda stared at Amy, wondering how she should start. "Solders," she said. She had the most distorting feeling of listening to her own voice projected out over the ears of seven thousand people. "Sailors," she continued, after a paused. "Men, and women," she said, letting the words ring.

I can do this, she thought.

"I have called you here to fight," she said. "And I ask of you again, will you fight?" Amy mimicked her motions, and Emeralda assumed that every other ship did the same. And so, Emeralda swept her arm across her chest. "I ask of you again, will you fight?" She stared hard out before her, sweeping her eyes, hoping that the rest of the ships followed her. "You have gathered here to do one thing," she brought her hand into a fist. "But I ask of you again: will you fight? Will you stand up for what is good, against those that wish the destruction of the innocent? Will you stand down, look down, away from the powers that come against you?" Emeralda turned her gaze up a notch, from fiery to flaming. "Or will you take up arms? Will you be the saving grace? The last line of defense? The deus ex machina?"

She motioned to Elderdale, now visible as a city, burning. "Because," she said, "to these people, these men and women and *children*, you are the last hope." She brought her hand down hard. "You are their ray of sunshine. You are the light at the end of their tunnel. You are the cavalry, the ones that come charging down the mountain to save the day."

Emeralda held out her hand. "These people need our help," she said. "Will you give it?" She dropped off, and after a while, Amy wavered, the feed cut.

"That was all right," Amy said, her voice dropping a little. "I think I felt something."

"I thought you said you couldn't feel anything," Emeralda said.

Amy smiled. "I was joking, of course," she said.

Emeralda frowned. "Ha ha," she said, her voice dripping with sarcasm. "Very funny."

And the city of Elderdale grew ever larger upon the horizon.

Last Line of Defense

Justle

Justle counted the number of times the hornbeast had rammed its head against the keep's gate. *One hundred ninety-seven*, she counted. Boom, went the gate, and the beast roared. *One hundred ninety-eight*. The gate cracked a little, and a jolt of adrenaline shot though Justle's body. It was time. They were coming.

The men on the ground ran to support the gate, pressing against it, barricading it with anything they could find. Justle stood on the walls of the palace, within the keep. Iris stood next to her, her wound having been healed after they had both restored their magica. They waited to defend the inner palace against the monsters. Justle knew what they were after: the piece, the strange magic absorbing artifact that the monsters needed for some nefarious purpose.

The Baron had placed it in the depths of his treasury, making room for it by dumping bars of gold and bags of jewels into the halls. Perhaps the most secure place in the entire city, the treasury featured an arsenal of traps that made the booby-trapped city look like a hole in the road. Even so, after watching how the monsters had charged the city, Justle found herself wondering how much good the treasury would do.

The gate nearest to her, the skyward gate, broke its bars and swung open an inch, held in place only with the efforts of three dozen royal guards. The other gates around the keep fared no better. Another boom sounded, and the skyward gate opened enough for Justle to see the great horned beast's eye, and a sliver of its gigantic ivory spike.

Justle came down from the wall, leaving behind a platoon of archers firing upon the invaders on the other side. She gripped the wobbly ladder with one hand, using the other to steady herself against the wall as she watched the gate. The next time it boomed, it opened far enough to spill a few guardsmen to the floor. They got up as fast as they could, in their ornate armor, but Justle could see that they were fatigued.

Iris ran out of the palace, her black hair flowing, and rushed up to support the men at the skyward gate. Justle moved in to help. Together, they found a spot in between two tall guards. Justle recognized one of them as one of the guards that had greeted them at the fake Baron's party. He made no sign of recognition, though, too busy pressing against the door.

It was not the skyward door that burst first, but rather the counter-clockwise door, the men who pressed against it flung to all sides like ninepins. The honnbeast bellowed mightily, legions of ganglers and gutterbacks streaming past its feet. The other three doors opened in quick session, as the men holding them turned to engage the coming foes.

Justle ran into the building chaos, determined to make the monsters pay for every square inch, every life that had been lost that night. She burned with a fiery passion, and her spells translated that passion into scorched meat and blackened monster carcasses.

It was utter tumult. As more and more monsters streamed into the small courtyard, space became short, and then it was impossible to move and not hit something or someone. Iris, taking full advantage of the close quarters, played off her own strengths to the fullest, jumping up gutterbacks like a mountain goat on a cliff and driving them through rows of ganglers like sheaths of corn.

Justle soon ran out of magica, but had been prepared, this time. She took a bottle out of her dress, shining blue in the flames of the burning city, and downed it as fast as she could. The little bar that measured her magical energy flashed, and then shot up. Justle continued to fight.

Slowly, the defenders pressed closer to the walls of the palace, the endless stream of monsters still coming through all four open gates. Justle pressed against a battered tapestry, singed and ripped, and slammed a gangler with her silver-cored staff. Another popped up in its place, seemingly out of nowhere. The monsters had been numbered in the thousands, by Gliss, and Justle found herself blurring the lines between number and monsters.

"Fall back to the palace!" a voice called, over the courtyard. It was the Baron of Elderdale, Joshua Elder. He stood on a bedroom balcony, his hands cupped around his mouth leaning over the edge.

The soldiers in the courtyard obeyed without question. Some of them, brave souls each, fought an opening around the palace's single door. The rest of the soldiers streamed between them, avoiding darting blades and stabbing spears, for the most part. For every man that made it through, another slumped to the floor, dead.

Justle and Iris passed through the ring just as the palace doors began to creak closed. Justle turned to take one last look at the ring of soldiers, that would undoubtedly be left outside, to be overwhelmed without question and slaughtered down to the last man. Her eyes locked on those of a young man, of perhaps twenty, with a lash down his face that dripped crimson blood.

"You're needed," he said, his voice desperate. "Go!"

Justle chocked back a hundred emotions, and ran through the doors just as they closed upon the courtyard and locked the solders outside into their dooms. She leaned against a wall, huffing with adrenaline and exertion. The last few minutes passed by her eyes as if they were still happening, the young solder's voice loud and clear in her mind: "Go!" he cried, again and again. "You're needed!"

Iris slumped down next to her, her breath coming in ragged gasps. "I don't think we'll last much longer," she said, surveying the pitifully small number of soldiers that had made it into the palace. Every one of them looked as she did, ragged, beaten and demoralized.

And then the palace doors shook, and every man and woman forgot themselves in the rush to hold them shut.

Emeralda Saves The Day.

Emeralda

Elderdale burned. The monsters, now mostly inside the city, could be heard even over the crackling of the blazing infernos that devoured entire streets. The air lit up as if it were daytime, the smell of smoke and charred flesh heavy on the air.

Emeralda ordered most of her armada to unload outside the city wall, clearing a path through the monsters left behind before they entered the city through the gates. She claimed a few ships, the one with the half-raid of summonses especially, and headed directly to the keep, where she still saw the flashing lights that meant magic.

As Emeralda's ships flew low over the walls of the keep, she was just in time to see Justle dart into the palace doors as they slammed closed. The ring of men that held the monsters at bay folded in at that moment, and they came together right in front of the two huge slabs of wood, defending them to the last. Emeralda did not come in time to save them. She dropped over the courtyard in her flagship, the *Amshfisht,* airwomen tossing ropes over the side, just as the massive hornbeast took its position against the door. Every monster in the courtyard froze and looked up then, their faces reading the most pleasant surprise. To Emeralda, at least. To them, it must have seemed like the gods had come out of heaven to rain fire upon their heads.

The half-raid of summoners, twelve necromancers in four groups, set to work immediately. Two phoenixes, a sylphan dragon, and a black bear formed from the mist, and rampaged through the ranks of the monsters in the courtyard. Emeralda's magical girls slid down the ropes they had thrown from her ship, hitting the ground and wreaking havoc. Emeralda flinched, hard, when she saw one of the girls come down hard in front of a gutterback, that promptly smashed her against the cobblestones. Emeralda tasted bile.

It's war, she thought. *There will be casualties.* It still did not make it feel better. Emeralda drew her knife from the side of her rainbow dress, and grabbed hold of a rope. "June," she salled, to her dress-fairy. "Light me up!"

"Lighting!" June replied, as Emeralda saw her vision fill with symbols, icons, and information. She sucked in her teeth. The monsters here were numbered in the 4-7 thousands. Then, she jumped off the ship, her gloved hands hissing down the length of rope. She hit the floor in time to see the hornbeast burst through the palace doors, a hundred monsters behind it. They did not appear like before, however, and seemed thinned out, if but just a little.

Small graces, Emeralda thought, as she made her first kill, a gangler with the number 4879. *Sorry, four-eight-seven-nine,* she thought, as she stared into its surprised face. *It's personal.*

A phoenix, flaming red and dripping molten sparks, carved a huge swathe to Emeralda's side. She could almost taste the singed meat and fur in the air. It had a flavor similar to that of well-marbled beef, albeit a little burnt.

Emeralda shook the thought out of her head. *Focus,* she thought to herself. *What comes next?* She looked at the open palace doors, hanging on their ornate hinges, and remembered. "The piece," she said, to herself.

And so she ran. She bounded across the courtyard in a couple leaps, darting through the doorway and into the palace. It was as if someone had taken a paintbrush filled with rainbow paint, and plastered every surface in the stuff. Ganglers hung, drooped, and squirmed in the strangest of places, among the bodies of the dead of both sides, like grisly decorations to top the macabre theme.

Emeralda held in her bile. Running into the main hallway, she heard clanking ahead of her, signaling that the fight still continued. She put on a burst of speed, heading towards where June and Gliss said that Justle was. Behind her, the first of her magical girls entered the palace, pausing in surprise when they met with the grisly scene. Some vomited.

Emeralda kept running. Doors flashed by. June labeled two magical girls ahead, Justle and the sailor that had been with her. Upon reaching a massive door that hung ajar on one hinge, that seemed to be covered in gilding, Emeralda saw the fight.

A dozen or so soldiers fought against a hundred ganglers and a handful of gutterbacks, closing in on the ancient piece, like a contracting ring. Justle and Iris fought among them, worth two soldiers each, still nothing against the waves that assaulted them.

Three more soldiers fell. Emeralda sprang into action. However, the monsters formed a solid wall, a barrier of putrid flesh that was as impenetrable. She watched as the rest of the soldiers fell, one by one.

She watched as the sailor died, her head swatted off by a massive gutterback like so much garbage. The sailor slumped to the floor, blood spurting from her neck like a fountain.

Justle screamed then, a scream filled with agony and pain, and most prominently, rage. She stood over the body of the sailor like a guardian statue, taking on a hundred monsters at the same time, singlehandedly.

All the while, Emeralda fought to reach her. *Please!* She cried, as she sank her knife deep into the flesh of a gangler. *Let me reach her!*

And then a gutterback brought down its club arm hard, too fast for Justle to react. In a flash of pulpy red spray, Justle disappeared.

Emeralda froze, her entire body vibrating, every sense on edge.

"You can't take them all!" June called, her voice desperate and pleading. "Please, Emeralda!"

Emeralda still did not move, as every monster in the room turned to look at her. There were seventy-four, including five nine-foot tall gutterbacks. Emeralda sobbed, and then turned and ran.

She ran into the hall, where her magical girls raced towards her, weapons in hand, too late to erase what she had seen. Emeralda cried out in rage, and then twirled out, pointing at the monsters, who now carried the piece out from the treasury, on the shoulders of two gutterbacks.

"Stop them!" she screamed, her voice cracking for the first time in two hundred years.

The magica girls, centuries old all, paused at the sound of her voice. Then, galvanized into action like no other thing could have done, they assaulted the group of monsters racing out of the palace with the piece in tow.

Ten ganglers fell. A gutterback tripped and did not get up, a hole ripped in its chest. The piece slid, one carrier short, but was grabbed by another gutterback, who promptly disintegrated into ash. Two more, the last two, grabbed the piece, making three that carried it. And so they went faster.

Halfway down the hall, there were only two gutterbacks left. Three quarters, down, one held it on its shoulders, its face contorted in a sort of indefatigable ecstasy, bearing what looked for all the world like the weight of universe on its back.

And it fell, its leg dissolving into a puddle of acid, dropping the piece only yards from the entrance.

Emeralda felt a cheer rising in her throat, that cut short half-way out. The piece rose up again. Underneath, ten ganglers held it up, their wiry bodies trembling with exertion.

How?! Emeralda thought, desperate, crazed. She threw herself at them with the full fury of her power. They were no more than wheat in the wind, before her and her magical girls.

And as the last gangler died, the piece slid out the door, bumping on the steps, and came to a rest in the courtyard.

And then Emeralda saw the beaterbats, hundreds of them, all swarming to the same place. She fell to her knees, knowing that there was no way they could stop that many. She watched ten of them disappear into the body of a great fiery phoenix. She watched countless fall to balls of magical energy, to arrows and thrown spears. In the distance, she heard the sound of her arms liberating the city, but she knew that she would stay there, where she kneeled, for a very long time, the liberation stopping just before her heart.

Four beaterbats gripped the piece, like gentle princes, cradling it in their gruesome claws. One sprouted a shaft. Another took its place, the dead monster flapping down the ground like an empty bag. The piece rose above the level of the walls. Beaterbats fell to the ground like rain. They rose above the skyships, and soon went out of their range, faster and faster as more held on to the magical piece, that so many lives had been lost to defend.

And Emeralda cried, the hot tears streaking down her cheeks and soaking her dress.

Getting warmer

Denyse

17 days after they had entered the cave where the massive machine dwelt, 21 days since Elderdale's siege began, the ancient superweapon finally began to move.

The first thing Densye and Kelly heard was a rumbling, like the entire world were shaking.

Earthquake? Denyse thought, looking around the room in which she sat.

Kelly had the sense to look outside, past the flap of cloth that comprised their door. When she tucked her head back in, her face showed a paleness like that first time she had discovered something, only worse. "It's moving," she said, her voice incredulous.

Denyse jolted upright, and immediately placed a call to General Emeralda. She had told them to alert her if anything like this happened. Now it was happening. Denyse tapped her foot impatiently as she listened to the dial tone, like a guitar strummed while out of tune.

Emeralda finally patched in. "Hello?" she said, her voice so haggard that Denyse jumped in surprise. It almost didn't sound like her.

"This . . ." Denyse paused, and tried again, her body filled with adrenaline. "This is Denyse, I'm reporting movement, the walker is moving!"

Emeralda didn't reply for a while, and when she did, the sorrow in her voice was thick enough to grasp. "I know," she said. "Thank you for telling me."

Denyse swallowed. This wasn't the Emeralda she knew. This had to be someone else, absolutely without a doubt. "Where's the General?" Denyse asked, hoping for the answer she wanted.

"Right here, Denyse," Emeralda said, her voice hollow. "I'm right here." She sighed, the sound of her breath like the sighing of the wind. "I want you to board it," she said, her voice taking on the tiniest bit of her former aura.

Denyse shook her head. Whatever had happened, it had been bad enough to shake up the unshakeable Emeralda Stysh, strongest magical girl in the world. "I understand," Denyse said, as she picked up her pack and checked that everything was there. "We're going with it," she whispered to Kelly, who raised her eyebrows in response.

Denyse tossed Kelly's bag to her. "I want you to tell me about it," Denyse said, her voice taking on a softer tone.

"I . . ." Emeralda paused, and Denyse took the time to call up Tamalda, her dress-fairy. "Can you deal with the cloth?" she whispered, pointing to all the things she had made. Tamalda looked around, and nodded. Despite their call to action, after three weeks underground, Denyse didn't feel much excitement. Emeralda occupied all of her attention.

"I let them down, Denyse," Emeralda said, her voice dropping off at the mention of Denyse's name. "I . . ."

Denyse waited, for a long while, while she and Kelly prepared to move out. The rumbling in the ground grew louder. They had planned for this eventuality, of course, and Kelly had discovered a way in not too long ago while climbing about. The machine's legs, tall as they were, were not at all smooth. They were more like mountainous cliffs, scalable with the right amount of determination and skill. They had both.

"I told them that I would protect them," Emeralda said, her voice filling with grief. "I failed them, I let the monsters take the piece, I let them all die."

Denyse and Kelly were bathed in light as the dress-fairies recovered their material. The doorway, now more of a cave mouth, beckoned them.

"What do you mean, you let them all die?" Denyse asked, troubled. "If they died, I'm sure there was a reason for it."

Emeralda breathed in sharply, as if she were about to jump off a cliff. "I have something to tell you, Denyse," she said, swallowing.

Denyse adjusted her pack and headed towards the nearest leg, Kelly in tow. "What is it?" she asked, unsuspecting.

"Did you love Justle?" Emeralda asked, seeming to go around something.

"Of course I did," Denyse said, without thinking, using the past tense as well. "She was—" she realized what Emeralda had said, and froze in place, her pack banging against her back. "She's dead, isn't she?" Denyse said, filing with an indescribable sadness.

Emeralda said nothing, and Denyse knew that it was true. Denyse looked at Kelly, and suddenly, felt much closer to her. It was true. Something ate at her insides, now, that had not been there before. Something terrible. She wrapped her arms around Kelly, pulling her as close as she could, and she cried, the tears coming out without her permission, but still flowing down into Kelly's shoulders.

"Justle!" Denyse called into the air, thinking about all the time she had spent with her. All the adventures, all the close calls, all the times she had teased Denyse for the way she used magic. All of it gone.

"It's still there," Kelly said, knowing right away what had happened. "They're still there, they aren't gone," she said. "The memories you had with her. They're still there. All this means is that you can't make any more, and now you have to treasure the ones you have."

Denyse looked at Kelly, her eyes wide. "So she's not dead?" Denyse asked, grasping at straws.

Kelly smiled. "Not to you, she'll never be."

Denyse wiped her eyes. "Thank you, Kelly," she said, her eyes floating down. "I'll be fine."

She's fine

Once up the leg, Denyse and Kelly entered through a maintenance hatch, ducking into the dark machine's sinister insides. Every surface on the machine glowed with the lines of red light that traced abstract patterns and gave off a dim glow, just enough to see by. The two traveled though the low corridor, unsure of where they were, feeling the vibration of the hulking monstrosity beneath them.

They passed a small grille, presumably to exchange air, and peeped into the room beyond. Human slave workers, gaunt, malnourished, and looking to be at the ends of their strings, operated some sort of magical control panel. Behind each human was a false person, in their true forms, their blobby membranes vibrating in tune with the walker.

Denyse turned away. *I'm sorry,* she thought. *We'll rescue you soon, I promise.*

They headed further down the tiny corridor, crouched down low even at their heights. If they had been normal sized, they would not have been able to enter at all. They passed another grille.

Denyse looked out, and gasped. A field, with a roof so tall it seemed open to the air, teemed with thousands of monsters, marching, drilling and training under the lashes of more false people.

Are the false people the ones who are in control? Denyse asked herself, *or are they simply pawns too?*

They passed by the grille after taking a long look. The scariest thing was that there could be quite a few more fields throughout the walker, filled to the brim like the one they saw. The walker was certainly big enough.

Denyse held out her hand, the signal to stop. She listened carefully, and then tapped the wall to her side. It sounded hollow. She pressed her hand against it to steady herself, wondering what it meant.

And then the wall disappeared from underneath her hand, sending her sprawling. Denyse scrambled back to her feet, ready to fight anything, and then realized that it was an empty room, with only a single control panel of some sort embedded in the far wall.

Denyse walked inside, still wary. No traps activated. Nothing happened, except for a blinking that occurred at the control panel. The room's red lines lit up a little brighter when Denyse entered, and the console beeped faster. Kelly followed behind.

Denyse leaned over the console. It had three pictures: a sort of cube with a circle protruding from it, a tree, and a door.

Denyse touched the tree. The wall to her side lit up, causing Denyse to panic for a moment. She stared, uncomprehendingly, at the quick passing of a dank cave wall. It looked to be outside. Denyse reached out her arm, attempting to touch the solid rock rushing past, but her hand ran into an invisible barrier. Ripples, that seemed to exist in only in space, radiated outwards from her point of contact.

"It's a magical window," Kelly guessed, walking up to it. "Quite convenient."

Denyse nodded, and turned back to the console. She wondered what else it could do. Just before she touched the door symbol, she stayed her hand. *Who knows what will happen?* she thought. *I should be grateful that I'm safe, and can see outside.* She turned to Kelly. "We're staying here," she said.

Hello, I'm a Serial Killer Who Likes to Torture People, and I'll Be Your Guide for Today.

August

In a strange turn of events, Shauna, the magical girl that had tortured August and Elyse, became their guide, her magical abilities and strength held back by a spell cunningly woven by Ruby. Even with the restraints, it seemed that having someone to talk with had calmed down Shauna's insanity some, until she became almost agreeable. August marveled at the change, ever wondering when the crazy girl would return. She never did.

It was a good thing, too, for the caves under the mountains of the edge were twisted, dark, and not well mapped, or not mapped at all. The maps Emeralda had given them turned out to be worse than useless, showing paths where there were none and missing all the important tunnels.

The three werelights, red, green, and yellow, combined to make white, and August was sure he was the only one that appreciated it. Down in the tunnel, the hours blended into days, and August found entertainment wherever he could.

One day, as they were passing through a particularly twisted section of tunnel, the walls suddenly opened into the most beautiful cave any of them had ever seen. It was as if it were the hiding place of the sculptor of the gods, where he put his most treasured possessions.

They made camp underneath a hundred-foot high ceiling, next to a formation that looked like a ballerina reaching up towards the stars, up above. And such stars! Elyse said that they were actually worms, but they looked for all the world like twinkling stars on a clear night sky, arrayed for the pleasure of any who looked upon them.

Around them, deep pits tunneled down into foreboding blackness, far beyond the range of werelight. August doubted that those rocks had ever seen light before, let alone the stunning white light that surrounded them. They shone in protest, glistening with incredibly smooth sides that looked to have been made of melted and reformed cheese.

And the echoes! August clapped his hands and counted no less than seven claps returning to him, and when Elyse sang, a sweet song about wonder and love, her own voice joined her for a cannon in harmony.

Shauna spoke of the whole place as if it were hers, and August half believed her. She was the only living thing—large living thing, at least—that they had encountered underground.

Penny also seemed a lot older, but August had a hard time telling the age of magical girls, so he thought nothing of it.

Shauna regaled them with tales of her lost lover, who she still mooned for after more than a century of exile, even after she had killed him with her own hands.

And so the group of four adventurers and one psychotic serial killer made their way towards the Centix, and a resolution to their story.

Breakneck Speed

Emeralda

She would go faster, she promised herself. She had not gone fast enough before. She needed to push her army, her sailors, herself, to make up for the time she had lost.

It helped that the army thought that it had been a total victory, the monsters routed without much resistance, the survivors rescued, the day saved. Emeralda knew better—the monsters had retrieved the last piece of the machine that would bring them ever closer to their goal.

After the battle, Emeralda had wasted as little time as possible performing the necessary after-battle activities of cleaning up, counting casualties, and accepting the hordes of volunteers from the liberated citizens. Their fervor surprised her, especially after they had heard of Justle's death. She had been something to them.

Her army had lost a little over two hundred, low losses for a conflict of this size. The necromancer healers had helped tremendously, making those two hundred the only real casualties at all. Fifty-two of her magical girls had died, each one like a blow to Emeralda's heart. She had pushed them, she realized, and their deaths were entirely on her. They had followed her without question. And now they lay stacked in the hull of a barge, row upon row of little bodies, to be sent back to the Capital and the Disciplinary Force's honorary graveyard.

Her army increased by 1000 that day, despite the losses. And still the magical ships held them all, and more. Emeralda had to thank Amy, for without her and the other ships, she wouldn't have made it remotely in time. Elderdale would have been a smoking ruin.

And so the armada took off once again, heading towards the jagged peaks of the Edge Mountains, that looked no bigger than Emeralda's fist from the distance they were at. However, it wasn't really that far, as Amy had pointed out. It would be a little over a week, and then they would be there.

The blocky ships caught the sunlight, their grey skin drinking it, their blue lines reflecting it. The wind tussled Emeralda's hair, as she sat at the prow, awaiting her destiny.

Arrival of Team One

August

27 days after their escape from Elderdale, although the adventurers had long since lost track of time underground, August finally came out of the side of the mountain, and took in the view he had been heading towards for months: the Centrix.

The Centrix was not so much a thing as an abnormally flat valley, between the ridiculously tall edge mountains. It looked to be perhaps 15 miles in diameter, the far edge ending abruptly in mountain. It was, of course, a perfect circle. The first to arrive, August and his party clambered down the side of the mountain rocks tumbling and announcing their presence to no one. Shauna followed them, having attached herself to them during their stay in the cave. She had said that she was "looking for a second chance," and August almost believed her.

After being so long in the dark, the sunlight was blinding, but not so much as it would have been without the bright werelights. August stepped into the grass that covered the Centrix, and then wondered.

What do we do now?

He was not long in wondering, for over the peak of the tallest centerward mountain, breaking off boulders the size of cities, the massive walker *Marlperl* forced its way towards the ring of green grass.

Arrival of Team 2

Emeralda

They had been confined inside for a day. Amy had said the conditions at the altitude they were traveling at would kill a human in two minutes. Emeralda believed her, looking out at the shining, thin, blazing atmosphere. They had reached the Edge Mountains two days ago, and traveled since in a day what had taken August and his party a week.

Finally, after a long month of waiting, and traveling, and learning, Emeralda watched the Centrix appear beneath the tallest mountain. And then she gasped, seeing the *Marlperl* for the first time. It was even larger than she had imagined, towering over Centrix on its massive, solid legs. It looked to be alive, pulsing with veins full of red blood.

And on the other side of the Centrix, Emeralda saw a collection of dots, almost too small to make out. *Penny!* she thought, her spirits soaring. *She made it!* In some twist of fate, it turned out that Emeralda hadn't really needed to send Penny out first after all. If only Emeralda had known before, she wouldn't have had to go through so much trouble.

But then a small voice in her head said *it was meant to be,* and then disappeared.

Emeralda shook her head. She had a battle to fight, a war to win.

"You have a call from Sergeant Denyse," June said, fluttering on Emeralda's shoulder.

"Patch her in," Emeralda said.

"General!" Denyse said, her voice appearing in Emeralda's ear. "You came!"

Emeralda gave a wan smile. Not all of her had come. She had lost some of herself back in Elderdale. "What's the status of the *Marlperl?*" Emeralda asked, getting down to business.

"The thing has got armies on it," Denyse said, her voice thin. "I don't know how many, there must be tens of thousands, of all kinds."

Tens of thousands. If Elderdale had been overwhelming, than this was meant to be much, much more.

"You have a call from Major Ruby," June said, while Emeralda still talked to Denyse.

"Patch her in, to our conversation," Emeralda said. "And get Penny, August, and Elyse on the line as well." Emeralda turned to Amy. "Set us down on the other side of the Centrix," she said, "next to the group of humans."

Amy did so, the ship feeling weightless for a minute as it dived down the steep mountain sides. The Centrix was big enough for her armada and the *Marlperl* both, with plenty of room between them. As the last of her ships landed in the field, Emeralda surveyed the battlefield. It was going to be an interesting day.

The Big Bad

Densye

The *Marlperl* kept going, after it landed on the Centrix, heading for the very center of the wide swathe of land. Denyse and Kelly stood in their room, as bare as when they had entered it a week before, and watched the green grass crawl by. The *Marlperl* tilted with every step, but the two girls had long since gotten used to its motion. They had been in hiding the entire time, always watching for the monster that would fine them out, but it seemed as if the *Marlperl* was built for a much bigger crew, as they only caught sight of monsters twice during their stay. Both encounters ended in nothing but a hike in Denyse's stress level.

"We should do something," Kelly said, looking at Denyse.

Denyse thought for a minute, aware that Kelly was right. "Do you have any suggestions?" she asked, after a while.

"We could try to sabotage the machine," Kelly said, giving a shrug.

Denyse shook. In their crawling about the *Marlperl* on the inside, the two girls had discovered many things of interest. However, every single one had a legion of guards surrounding it. There was no way they could possibly affect the ship, alone.

There was one thing they could do. "Do you remember where the engines were?" Denyse asked, thinking of a plan. At least, they had thought they were the engines at the time. They were big, and contained in an empty room as tall as the *Marlperl* itself, full of crackling lightning and human slaves doing things. They had looked very important, at least.

"Yes," Kelly said, "I do."

"Good," Denyse said, having decided upon a plan of action. "Because we're going to lead the army straight to it."

Kelly's eyes widened. "But how?" She asked. "It'll be a full battle. There's no way they could climb up the legs like we did."

"Then we find another way in," Denyse said, pulling up her pack. "Come on," she waved at Kelly, "we have a job to do."

Plans of Mice and Men

August

August stood with the assembled army, facing Emeralda, as she stood atop the deck of her flagship, the *Amshfisht*. A pretty young lady stood next to her, of normal height, her hair waving in the breeze.

"We have a job to do," Emeralda said, to the assembled army. "We have a world to protect."

The army murmured amongst themselves. This battle, coming down on them like an advancing sunset, was the thing that they had all prepared for. It was the end of the line, and for many of them, it would be the last day they saw alive.

And still, they held fast. Something about Emeralda kept them on course, a sort of vigor that lent power to her cause. The approaching battle had brought it out of her like impurities out of molten silver.

"We have a fight to finish, and we're going to win it." She waved at the *Marlperl*, as it advanced towards the center of the Centrix. "Let's show those monsters who's boss!"

Ragged cheers sprouted from the crowd, and then the army dispersed, out to make preparations for the coming battle.

In the distance, the *Marlperl* stopped, right in the center of the flat, grassy valley. It bend down low, as if to disgorge something, and gangways the size of streets appeared out of each leg. From inside, columns of marching monsters appeared, their clanking and braying audible even from several miles away.

Some soldiers paused their preparations, their digging of fortifications and sharpening of weapons, and looked with awe at the army spilling out of the underside of the giant machine. Most, however, went on with their business.

"You have a call from the General," Gliss said, to the assembled party. Shauna was not there, having been transported to a ship for holding until the battle was over. She didn't mind, however, as she soon fell in love with a tall necromancer that worked on the ship. August shivered when she thought about what was in store for that man.

"Patch us in," Ruby said, speaking for all of them.

"August, Elyse, Penny, Ruby," Emeralda said, forgoing the formalities. "I need you to report to me on the bridge of my flagship, immediately."

The party did not hesitate, crossing across bustling traffic to reach the side of the *Amshlisht*. They walked up the gangplank, getting a closer look at the ship as they did so.

"It looks like ancient technology," Elyse said, as they stepped over the railing and onto the deck. "These ships are made with fully integrated magical circuits," she said, examining a line of blue light closer. "It looks to be some sort of skysteel alloy that the magic can move with exact precision." She looked around, filled with awe. "I was only able to make the crudest of motions with my engine, but this . . ." she waved her hands around at the ship. "This is awesome."

August stepped into the bridge, a squat cube that stuck out of the deck, quite out of place in all the flatness. Elyse stepped behind him, and Penny and Ruby followed. They stood together, facing Emeralda and the fair lady that had been with her as she spoke.

"This is Amy," Emeralda said, motioning to the fair lady. "It's short for the name of this ship, and I've been told that she and the ship are one and the same."

Amy curtsied. "Nice to meet you, fellow sentients," she said, her voice lilting.

Elyse's eyes lit up like a little child's. "A magical intelligence!" she moved up close, examining Amy with an exacting eye.

Amy seemed to enjoy it, but pushed Elyse away. "You may admire my craftsmanship later," she said, motioning to Emeralda, "but the captain has something to say to you."

Emeralda nodded. "I've called you here specifically because you, Penny, are needed to finish this battle." She looked Penny over. "I've been told that you acquired new power while in the caves," she said. "I would like to know more."

Penny shrugged. "There's nothing more to tell. It's power, plain and simple." Her words carried in them a deep wisdom.

"Can it destroy the *Marlperl*?" Emeralda asked, getting down to business.

"No," Penny answered. "It's not big enough."

"Can it destroy a part of the *Marlperl*," Emeralda said, "say, an engine? Something that will explode, and perhaps start a chain reaction?"

Elyse saw what she was getting at. *Magical circuits are volatile,* she said, *when massive amounts of energy are poured through them, more than they can handle. If an engine—a power source—were to be destroyed, the resulting energy surge would resound through the circuits and create a massive chain reaction.* Elyse looked at Emeralda. *I'm sure she realizes this.*

August frowned. "Won't an engine be deep inside the *Marlperl*?" He asked, uncertain. "Won't it be very well guarded as well?" He paused. "Do we even know how to get in?"

Emeralda pursed her lips. "To answer your last question, Denyse, who is currently inside the *Marlperl*, had found a hole that a small number of elite units will be able to enter through. A chink in the armor, so to speak." She looked around at the assembled party, sizing them up. "It so happens that that hole is the garbage chute."

"All of the garbage?" Penny asked, afraid to hear the answer.

"Yes, I'm afraid so," Emeralda said.

"So we're getting in through the sewers," Elyse said, her voice showing her disgust.

"It will only be for a little while," Emeralda said. "After you come up through the garbage chute, you will meet up with Denyse and Kelly, who will show you the rest of the way." She turned to August and Elyse. "In order to maintain security, we will need to create a distraction inside the ship, one that seems eminently more dangerous. And so," she said, looking August up and down, "You will carry a bomb onto the ship."

Elyse's eyes widened. "What makes you think they'll fall for that?" she asked. "From what I've seen, the *Marlperl*'s materiel should be invincible against conventional attacks."

Amy spoke up now. "I have requisitioned one of my sister's engine blocks, and primed it to overload on command."

Elyse whistled. "So we're the backup plan?" she asked.

All eyes turned to her. Emeralda nodded. "Yes, you are the backup plan."

August was used to being the backup plan by now, so he didn't complain. If anything, planting a bomb sounded a lot less dangerous than storming a heavily guarded engine room. "Where will we plant it?" he asked.

"Anywhere," Emeralda said, "Wherever you happen to be when Penny or Denyse calls you. Just be sure you remember the way out."

Outside, under the watchful eye of Emeralda's officers, the army had begun to form up. A small number of men and magical girls approached the *Amshlisht*, and climbed on deck.

"These are the soldiers you will be fighting with," Emeralda said, as the group entered the bridge. There were no more than twenty, and not all of them looked the part of elite operatives.

August walked up to a short necromancer, who glared at him with a practiced eye, as if he were thinking about how best to kill him. August shuddered.

"You will be taken to the garbage chute in one of the scout ships. That is all, you are dismissed." Emeralda paused, as if she were fighting against something. "I wish you best of luck," she said. She turned away, as if she could not bear to look upon them any longer.

A small ship docked with the *Amshlisht*, only as wide as the larger ship's deck. August climbed aboard, following Elyse and a magical girl with a single side ponytail, golden in the sunlight. Around him, Emeralda's army mustered, preparing to buy him the time needed to complete his mission.

And then the *Marlperl* shuddered, its violent vibrations carrying far across the valley. A gigantic drill appeared out of its underside, and touched the ground, right in the center of the Centrix. With a shredding noise and a fountain of dirt, the *Marlperl* began to rip the Centrix open.

Armies Are for Fighting With

Emeralda

Emeralda stood at the front of her army, arrayed behind her in rows and columns, as she faced the massive force of monsters across the field. There looked to be three for every one of her soldiers, and she knew her army could not hope to defeat them. Their only hope was to hold them off, just long enough to get Penny into the engine room, where she could work her magic.

It was much easier said than done, however. A hundred ships, all that the could be spared, circled around the one, tiny scout ship that contained within it their only hope. Across the field, standing higher up than the skyships, the *Marlperl* drilled relentlessly into the center of the Centrix.

The drill hit resistance, the barrier put up by the ancients. A horrible screech filled the air, like the sound of a file over slate. Sparks spewed out from the hole the drill had already made.

"March!" Emeralda commanded, determined not to show weakness in the face of the enemy. She had come so far, lost so much, and was not yet ready to give in. Her army followed her, slow at first, and then picking up speed, as the undead warriors moved their legs and the magical girls matched strides. Overhead, the skyships followed, heading with the army towards the massive machine burrowing into the ground.

In the sky above the monster army, thousands of points flitted about, flying alzoths and beaterbats all meshing together, almost looking to be smoke that rose from the blackness covering the ground.

Emeralda's army kept marching. Miles passed. Their pace slowed, as they fought to conserve energy for the battle ahead. The monsters turned from pinpricks to sticks to figures, arrayed in surprisingly well-formed blocks, ready to meet Emeralda's challenge.

Emeralda looked around herself. Her officers all held some sort of powerful emotion in their faces, be it rage or sorrow or fear, and the tension in the air rivaled that of the tension Emeralda felt.

The monsters got closer. The ships above closed on their goal.

And then, a ship exploded into pure red light, tossing molten fragments of metal about like rain. One landed among the ranks of undead, burning and sizzling. More landed among the monsters, tearing burnt streaks through their formations. Emeralda looked up, to see a magical weapon of immense power, mounted on the front of the *Marlperl*. It collected light towards itself, drawing from the red circuits that surrounded it, already powering up for another blast. Emeralda prayed that it would not hit Penny's ship.

The two armies stopped not a hundred yards from each other, doing nothing, saying nothing. It felt like an eternity, in which the world hung in the balance.

And then the arrows flew. The fireballs, the lightning bolts, the icicles, the spears of acid, everything happened at once, everyone running, and screaming, until Emeralda found herself in the center of a whirlwind.

"June!" She called and her battle-display fired up. She groaned involuntarily. They were numbered in the tens of thousands.

She faced up against a gangler, number 12468, and sliced a purple row all down its chest. The gangler looked at itself, looked at Emeralda, and hooted once, a sad sound that caught in its throat. And then it died.

Emeralda lost herself to the battle then, pouring all her strength, her sadness, and her rage into each motion, her knife flinging like a leaf in the wind, snapping, slicing.

The ground was already slick with blood.

It's Just Chance.

August

August watched as the ship next to his, the *Rufush*, disintegrated into molten plasma. Several small pieces landed on the deck of his ship, the *Yshl*, sparking against the ground as if they hated it. The ship's magical intelligence, Yain, cringed, as she watched her sister disappear in fire. August sympathized with her. Even though he knew she was a machine, he could not help but notice the expression of sorrow that showed on her face.

Elyse held on to the side of the ship, her knuckles white, staring down at the battle below. Stray bolts of magical energy flew up every now and then, as they passed over the main fray. Another ship exploded into plasma behind them. All around, beaterbats and alzoths closed in, kept away from the *Yshl* by the other ships, flying in a protective sphere.

And then they went under the shadow of the *Marlperl*. The light disappeared, replaced by the ruby glow of the machine's magical circuits. The sound of the massive rotating drill drowned out all else, dirt and sparks finding their way all the way up to where the *Yshl* flew, in giant clods and balls of shining light.

The *Yshl* dropped away from the main fleet, which stayed near the front of the underside, drawing away attention. Another ship exploded into bright light and sizzling sparks. Twenty more magical girls died, their small bodies vaporized in an instant.

August turned away, and looked instead at their destination, near the top of one of the stationary legs. It looked no more than an aberration, a pothole, instead of something that their entire plan hinged around.

The *Yshl* pulled up alongside the hole, and August saw brackish liquid flowing out of it. It really was a sewer. August wondered why it had to be dumped, when so much wondrous technology surrounded them. Although, he wasn't complaining. It was their way in. Elyse went in first, holding the bomb strapped to her back, followed by three magical girls and three necromancers. August went in last, holding up the rear. Penny's group stayed behind, to keep the groups separate.

And so August entered the *Marlperl*. It stank, of course, being a sewer, and the upward slope slipped in August's hands as his scrabbled for footing. From above, bits of sewage dripped onto his face, causing him to squint and sincerely hope that it would be over soon.

August saw Elyse disappear, and then the magical girls behind her, and then the necromancers, until only August looked up. He came across a square doorway—open—and passed through, stepping out onto flat ground, where the rest of his team stood looking at Denyse. She was at the meeting point like promised, surveying the dirty operative before her.

"There's a pretty important looking thing just down that corridor," she said, pointing in a direction away from the engines. "It's well guarded. You might make an impression if you try there."

Everyone nodded, as that was their goal: to make an impression, and draw attention away from Penny's group. August walked up beside Elyse, and squeezed her hand. Elyse squeezed back.

This is it, isn't it? August asked, his body broiling with adrenaline.

It is, Elyse replied, adjusting the weight of the bomb on her back. Around them, their six companions made similar preparations.

The first monsters they encountered were ganglers, walking through an otherwise abandoned corridor, holding several human prisoners. Two of them were female, and three were male: meaning that they had been stolen from some peaceful village, somewhere.

August and Elyse opened themselves to each other, and prepared to wait for orders from their leader, a magical girl named Cyress with deep, sea green hair and who fought with a wicked scimitar. Emeralda had appointed her for a reason, and August could see it as soon as her orders began.

August: Right, attack gangler 13, protect human 2, support Chris. All in less than two seconds. August did as he was told, attacking gangler 13, supporting the necromancer named Chris, and feeling like part of a well-orchestrated ballet.

The last gangler dropped to the floor a minute after the attack began. There had been no casualties. The freed workers looked at their arms, as Elyse sliced off their shackles using Instrator. One woman broke down and began to cry.

"August!" she said, her eyes welling up with tears, "have you seen my Penny? Do you know where Penny is at? Did you manage to save her?"

August stepped back, overcome with surprise. Of all the things to happen, this was the one he had expected the least. "She's doing fine, ma'am," he said, not believing what he was seeing. "I'm glad to see that you're safe too, Ms. Sharp."

Ms. Sharp nodded, rubbing her eyes. "I can't believe it's really you. Is Penny doing all right?"

Another woman that looked to be about her age comforted her, while the rest of the prisoners were told how to escape by Cyress.

"Penny's doing fine," August said. "She's helping to save you."

Ms. Sharp looked around, her eyes wide. "Really?" She asked, as Cyress pulled her up.

"Ma'am," Cyress said, "you should leave right now."

The woman who had supported Ms. Sharp pulled her along, following the rest of the released prisoners. Ms. Sharp looked back at August as she got further and further away. August hoped she would make it out of the ship alive.

Not likely, Elyse said, full of sorrow. *Even if they did reach our entrance, how would they get down?* She shook her head. *More likely they'll just get found and killed by monsters.*

August swallowed, and shook the thought of Ms. Sharp out of his head.

"We should get moving," Cyress said, as a squadron of ganglers rounded a corner in the hall. "I think we've attracted their attention."

A Hard Choice is Made.

Denyse

Denyse watched as Penny and Ruby climbed out of the garbage chute, covered in icky, slimy fluid. Penny put her hands on her knees and panted, but Ruby came up to Denyse and embraced her, sewage and all. Too surprised to resist, Denyse hung limp in Ruby's arms.

"I'm sorry about Justle," Ruby said, her voice close to tears. "I was the one who gave her that assignment, and so it's my fault."

Denyse shook her head. "If it's anyone's fault, it's the monsters that killed her," she said, feeling strange trying to comfort Ruby when she herself still felt so torn about it.

Ruby disengaged, leaving Denyse with brown smears all over.

Tamalda, Denyse's dress fairy, stuck her tongue out at Lester, Ruby's fairy. "You couldn't just stay dirty yourself, could you?" she said, her voice scolding.

Lester laughed. "Now we're all on the same page. The monsters that come at us will drop dead from the smell."

Tamalda gave a hmph, and disappeared back into Denyse's shoulder. Denyse wiped her hands on her skirt, turning to Penny. "Are you ready?" she asked, not sure what for. She still couldn't see how Penny was going to destroy the engine. In fact, only Penny seemed to know, possessing a calm air of confidence that seemed inappropriate, in the situation. Denyse wondered what was going on inside of her head.

"I am," Penny stated, with absolute confidence.

Denyse turned to the others assembled, the three necromancers and three magical girls, and addressed them. "Kelly will meet with us half-way, to show us through the door. She's keeping it open."

Denyse got a nod from the party leader, a necromancer with a balding head and fire in his eyes. "We're ready," he said.

And so Denyse led them through the tunnels that snaked through the *Marlperl,* avoiding monsters where they could. Sometimes, they had to fight, but it seemed that August and his party were doing their job well.

Kelly's voice sounded in Denyse's ear, over the fairy-comm. "They're here," she said, almost in a whisper. "They know someone's in here, they're guarding the door. I can't take them by myself. You might have to fight."

"Got it," Denyse said, turning to the soldiers that she led. "There's a fight up ahead, so prepare yourselves."

The magical girls brought out their weapons, and the necromancers summoned familiars, that would fight for them. Ruby brought out her ice hammer, Penny formed her staff out of air, and Denyse unsheathed her sword, its edges glinting in the ruby light.

They turned a corner, behind which stood their door, and met with Kelly, who hid in an alcove. Denyse held out her palm to the soldiers behind her. *Stop,* it meant. They stopped.

In front of the door that blocked the way to the engine room, a group of monsters stood. Only, half of them pointed inwards, leveling their spears at a group of human captives, bound and gagged against the wall.

Hostages! Denyse realized, becoming sick to her stomach. Whoever had come up with the plan had done their homework on humans. Kelly put her arm on Denyse's shoulder as she crouched in the alcove next to her.

"What should we do?" she whispered, her voice tickling Denyse's ear.

Denyse looked out at the scene. "I don't know," she said, truly at a loss. She turned away from the alcove, and made her way back to where the solders, as well as Penny and Ruby, hid.

"You," she said, pointing to the squad leader. "Ahh . . ." she searched for a name.

"Andrew," the leader said, his bald spot glinting ruby under the light of the magical circuits.

"Andrew," Densye repeated, "we have a problem. They have hostages."

Andrew appeared to think for a moment, and then called to his two squad mates, the other necromancers. He conferred with them for a while. When he was finished, he turned back to Denyse. "My men tell me that we can put up a temporary shield around the hostages," he said. "But it will not last long, so you will have to be quick."

Denyse nodded, and motioned to all the people in hiding. "We're going to charge," she told them, "on my mark. Be as quick as possible, do you understand? They have hostages, and we will be able to keep them safe for a short time."

Denyse got nods all around, as the warriors absorbed her message. Then, they followed her to the corner, around which the monsters stood guarding the door, hostages between them.

Denyse whispered the code word for assault all, barely enough to be heard. Kelly popped out of the alcove beside her, and, after hesitating a moment, joined the assault. The monsters didn't realize they were under attack until the magical girls were among them and the necromancers' familiars bit at their limbs. The ones in the center attacked the hostages, true to their intent, but found their strikes stymied. An invisible force wrapped around the helpless humans.

Denyse stabbed a gangler, slicing it almost in half with her wide sword. Her battle display lit up with information, as Tamalda updated the status of her party. Ruby, Penny, Kelly, and the three other magical girls all appeared on her display. Denyse fought her way towards the center of the confrontation, where the hostages lay, still under attack by several ganglers. There had been more than thirty at the start, but now, there were less than a dozen. They fell back on the humans as a last resort, desperately attempting to break the barrier, knowing somehow that if they did, it would give the attackers pause.

And they did, a gangler stabbing a helpless woman through the chest, its spear protruding from the other side. The other ganglers all grabbed living hostages, holding them at spear point and knifepoint.

Everyone paused. And then, to Denyse's utter horror, Andrew continued to attack, his two necromancers behind him. The ganglers screeched, and several more human hostages slid to the floor, dead, but Andrew did not stop. He and his familiar killed the monsters, one by one, slicing each as it were the last motion he would ever make. Purple blood muddied the room's red circuits, spattered far away from the battlefields. Red blood pooled on the floor, cast in a freakish light by the red all around.

Denyse said nothing, too surprised to even think, as Andrew cut down the last of the ganglers. When he finished, he wiped the knife that he had fought with, called back his familiar, and stared off into the distance. "It's clear," he finally said.

Denyse knew, deep inside of herself, that the man had made the right choice. Their mission was worth far more than a few human lives. But, deeper down, she was glad that he had been the one to make the choice, because now, she could place the blame on him, for what had happened. And yet her heart rebelled, and her body quivered, and tears streaked down her eyes, dripping from her nose and mixing with the blood on the ground.

Denyse swallowed. She walked up to the door, now stained with deep crimson and bright purple, and placed her hand on the opening mechanism, like she had done a hundred other times while living in the *Marlperl*. Only, when her hand came off this time, it was dirty. And when the blocks that formed the door flowed back into the wall, they left behind thick, crusting traces of where they had been.

Stress

August

"Watch out!" Elyse cried, as she dived to one side. Everyone followed her example, except for one magical girl, with strawberry blond hair and sad blue eyes, who just didn't move fast enough. The geyser of blue flame turned her entire body black, her dress disintegrating, her flesh peeling off until just her skeleton remained, which soon turned into vapor that smelled like bone soup.

Elyse gagged, and Cyress hunched over, breathing hard. The other magical girl, the one who survived, vomited black and red.

August averted his eyes. Elyse sidled up to the girl who had vomited, being sure to stay out of the field of fire, where a legion of monster magicians defended against intruders. It had been a stupid mistake, coming this way, but no stupider than heading anywhere else when hounded by the entire contents of a machine the size of a city.

Elyse held the girl close to herself. "What's your name?" She asked, her voice soothing, yet sounding as if it, too, were about to break.

"Naomi," the girl said, taking in a sharp breath.

Elyse touched her stomach. "You have an ulcer," she said, after watching how Naomi cringed. "Let me heal it," Elyse said, a healing spell beginning to form in her hand.

Naomi pushed Elyse away, shaking her head. Elyse's spell returned to where it had come from.

"The pain reminds me," Naomi said, "of what I need to do." She gritted her teeth.

Elyse held her close, a suspicion building in her mind. "She's not the first you saw die, is she?" Elyse asked, her voice thick.

Naomi shook her head. "I . . ." She stiffened, suddenly, and her eyes looked far, far away.

"You're in no condition to continue fighting in this state," Cyress, the party leader, said. She bore down with a harsh tone, no doubt covering up something herself.

Naomi cringed. "I can"—

Cyress cut her off. "You will get healed, or I will be forced to put you off of this mission." Her voice was unnecessarily harsh, varying a little too much in tone.

Elyse glared at Cyress. "She's hurting," she said, leveling her gaze with fire.

Cryess turned away. "She can't operate at full capacity," she said, her voice defensive.

Elyse stepped up to Cyress, bringing herself up so that even crouched, she towered over the magical girl. "You will let her continue," Elyse said, her voice biting.

Cyress lashed out at Elyse. "What do you expect me to do?" Her voice sounded almost hysterical. "If she dies, whose fault will it be?"

Elyse backed down, realizing Cyress's quandary. "I hadn't thought of it that way," she said, her tone simmering with emotion.

"I'll get healed," Naomi said, her voice tiny, broken. "I want to fight."

Elyse looked at Naomi, her expression haggard. "Are you sure?" She formed up a healing spell on her hand, the same as before.

Naomi looked up, with a new fire in her eyes, which suggested something more powerful than she appeared. Cyress stepped back, almost leaving the crevice, before catching herself. Seeing her pop out, the enemy magicians fired, their spells twining together to create a pillar of blue flame, which passed inches behind her.

Elyse healed Naomi's stomach then, as well as her other wounds, without another word. When Elyse finished, she looked around. "Are we all ready to go?" she asked, her tone serious.

August nodded, having been watching with rapt attention throughout the exchange. "I'm ready," he said, out loud.

Elyse nodded. "On the count of three," she said. "One," Everyone tensed, ready to jump back into the blast radius, and run as far as they could, hoping to reach the magicians before they could react with blue fire. They couldn't shoot more than one a minute, they had noticed. That gave them a tiny window of opportunity. "Two," Elyse said, and August felt his entire body stiffen like a board. "Three!" Elyse yelled, and every one ran out of the crevice they had been hiding in, faced the dozens of magicians, all linked together, energy pouring out of them as they prepared to launch another massive attack.

They were gildgales, the same type of monster that had fired upon the *Firebird* during its escape from Elderdale. The only monsters with the ability to use magic, they could link to each other like puzzle pieces, feeding off each other's magical energy, increasing the power of their spells exponentially.

It was a hard run, but they made it, just as the air in front of the monster's strange colony began to fizzle. It dissipated with a whizz as soon as Elyse sliced it in half, Instrator glowing with a fierce pride as it chewed through yards of flesh.

"This is for Clarisse!" Naomi yelled, the only one to declare her intentions to the world as she spun around the disorganized monsters, slicing them to bits with her bladed staff. "You monster bastards are gonna get what's coming to you!" She impaled a gildgale with more than enough force to come out the other side, its dripping gold carapace quickly losing its sheen as the creature beneath died.

August fought hard, harder than he had ever fought before, the next few hours blending into one hellish nightmare, as monsters of all types assaulted them no matter where they turned.

All Part of the Plan

Denyse

Penny opened the door to the engine room reverently, watching the blocks disappear into the wall with an expression of wonder on her face.

We made it, Denyse thought, the horrible last few hours of her life slipping behind her. *We're alive, and still fighting.*

After the incident with the hostages, Andrew had become more and more violent, lashing out at anyone that came near him during battle, even his own party mates. It was no surprise when he charged a gutterback, unsupported, and lost his head as he tumbled off of the bridge they had been fighting on. His decision to keep going, taking responsibility for the lives of the helpless, had taken its toll on him.

Since then, two more had died. One, a magical girl with short red hair and a purple dress, had simply been unlucky, and had fallen in battle to a wound to the head that could not be healed. Denyse had taken a liking to her, as a fellow red-head, but she regretted it with a passion, now.

The second was another necromancer, who, depressed after Andrew's death, had timed his strike just a little too low, when fighting against a colony of gildgales. He missed their joints, leaving them intact, and was blasted into oblivion.

But Penny, Ruby, Denyse, and three others had reached the engine room alive, and they were ready to finish what they had started. Just in time, Denyse remembered to place a call to August, who was still patched in to Penny's line.

"It's time to go!" she cried, hearing August's hard breathing over the line.

"I understand," August said, his voice hollow.

Denyse stepped into the engine room, behind Penny and Ruby, and wondered at something so stupid, she wished she had never thought of it. *How will we get out when the* Marlperl *explodes?*

The engine room rose the entire height of the ship, with walkways ringing the main power generator at every story. Each walkway led by bridge to a smaller walkway that ringed the engine itself. There, Penny would do her thing, and destroy the *Marlberl* forever. Only, Denyse couldn't for the life of her figure out how they were supposed to destroy it without killing themselves.

Attrition

Emeralda

The battle was going terrible. The *Marlberl's* cannon had picked ships out of the sky, one by one, until only a few remained, flitting about to avoid the massive beam of energy that hunted them. Underneath the *Marlberl,* the gigantic drill dug ever deeper, now flinging up pieces of molten rock instead of soil, that fell across the battlefield to land on soldiers of both sides.

On the ground, Emeralda fought as hard as she could, as best she could, but could not fight the fact that the battle was turning. Slowly, almost imperceptibly, her army was pushed away from the *Marlperl* by the masses of monsters that seethed all around. They left many dead behind, the necromancer healers lagging in their recovery, burning though their stocked potions of magica at an alarming rate.

Emeralda herself felt the cut of a blade many times, only to see it disappear soon after, as her personal guards did their job. Every time she saw one of her own fall, she desperately wished to help, to tell her guards to revive the downed girl, or man, but Emeralda knew inside that she needed to stay alive more than they did. And that hurt, more than any of the spear points that cut her with their jagged stone edges.

She fought, a losing battle, knowing that her only hope was thin, had been thin from the start, and was soon to be exhausted.

Extraction

August

"We're getting out of here!" August called, as soon as he got Denyse's message.

The ragged group of solders around him cheered, down three more after the loss of the girl in the fire. Naomi had lost her life holding a corridor, singlehandedly, creating time for the rest of them to escape to somewhere safer. Cyress had cried, then, tears streaking down her face as they ran away.

Now, only Cyress, August, Elyse, and a Necromancer named Juston were left, to plant the bomb where they stood and then get out of the place.

Elyse set the bomb down in a corridor, where it sat, drawing the attention of the monsters around them. It had done its job well, as word of the saboteurs with the bomb had spread through the *Marlperl*.

Elyse grabbed August's arm. *Do you know the way we need to get out?* she asked, deadly serious.

August paused. He didn't know, they had been running through the maze inside for so long that he had lost all sense of direction.

You really don't? Elyse asked, her mind filling with panic. If they were stuck, they would be inside when the *Marlperl* blew. They would be turned into vapor, into nothing.

August thought hard.

Cyress, noticing their hesitation, volunteered an answer. "We can walk down the gangplanks."

Everyone stared, not sure what she meant.

"The army had to leave somehow," Cyress said, "and we can leave that way."

Elyse nodded, understanding. "All we have to do in order to find it is to follow some marching monsters." They had encountered several such groups before, all heading down to the battlefield, but had avoided them because of their size.

August nodded. "It's a good idea," he said. "So let's go."

I Don't Want To

Denyse

"No!" Denyse cried, looking into Ruby's eyes. "You can't do that, there must be some other way!"

Ruby shook her head sadly. "I knew it would end like this, ever since I went underground with Penny."

Denyse pounded Ruby's chest with her fists, tears streaking down her face, wetting her dress, mixing with blood and dried sewage. "You can't!" she cried. She couldn't. Not another one. She couldn't lose them both. "I love you!" she cried, wrapping her arms around Ruby. "So please don't go!"

Ruby disengaged. "I have to protect Penny," she said, looking at the engine. "She won't be able to do this on her own."

Denyse's suspicion had turned into a horrible reality, where Penny and Ruby planned to stay behind to create the destruction and witness it personally. Meaning, they would become it, and disappear into so much vapor.

Denyse didn't want to live in a world like that. "Let me stay with you," she said, gripping Ruby's hands, "I don't want to do this anymore."

Ruby shook her head. "This is my job, and Penny's, and no one else's. You will go, that is a direct order." She stared at Denyse, her visage becoming hard, emotions by the dozens showing through the cracks.

Denyse choked up, and then felt arms wrap around her chest, and someone resting her head against her own.

"Please come with me," Kelly said, her voice low in Denyse's ear.

Denyse shuddered, and remembered a promise, made in the middle of a forest with a girl who had been wounded at the heart. She knew what she had to do, then, and accepted it.

She turned around. "We're getting out," she said, her voice hard. She almost couldn't finish the sentence. Her tears flowed on their own, without her even trying, still dripping as she walked away from Ruby, not looking back. Kelly held her hand then, and Denyse gripped it tight, and as the monsters finally began to enter the room, through the doors on all side, Denyse prepared to show them exactly how she felt.

A True Hero

Penny

Penny sat in front of the engine, meditating. She had been given a power by the god of fate, Gsh, and this is what she had been destined to use it for. No more, no less. Her hard earned lessons rebounded through her head, the memory of centuries spent as a god herself. Knowing that she could do so much more, Penny saw that there was only one thing she must do.

Ruby defended Penny, as Penny sat, and concentrated, becoming one with herself, calling upon the powers above to lend her energy. She touched the engine, and felt its magnificent rhythms pulsing underneath her palm.

She saw Ruby defend the walkway against wave after wave of monsters, ganglers and gutterbacks and gildgales, giving twenty times more than she received, and yet still falling behind.

Penny waited for a long while, as Ruby fought, and fought, and fought, and even when Ruby fell beneath a mountainous gutterback, and did not get up, Penny held her ground. She wanted to give her friends the time they needed to escape with their lives. When the ganglers began to stream towards her, stepping over Ruby's carcass like so much stone, Penny still held her ground. When a spear found its way straight into her chest, and came out the other side, she still held her ground.

It was when the world blurred, and the pain no longer threatened, but rather *meant* to black her out, that she finally released the power within her into the engines of the *Marlperl*.

Boom.

Emeralda
BOOM!

The entire world turned red. The heavens opened. Everything in existence suddenly meant nothing, the moment the *Marlperl* turned into the largest single firecracker in the world's long history.

As the glare died down, and the spots in Emeralda's eyes decreased in intensity, she noticed a small ship flinging drunkenly away from the explosion site, and she felt as if her entire body were squirted full of exultation.

"YES!" she cried, at the top of her lungs, as those around her did the same, the magical girls and zombie warriors and Green Bloods and necromancers, all raising their swords to cut down the monsters as they scurried away, routed. Emeralda laughed with feverish glee as she sliced open monster after monster, meeting no resistance, whipping through the enemy like wind through chaff.

And when she was done, when she saw the battlefield out before her, piled high with countless bodies and massive globs of congealed metal, the impact of what had happened finally hit her.

She had done it. Penny had done it. They had saved the world.

Epilogue

One year later

August walked down Capital Main Street, hand in hand with Elyse. On his finger, and on hers, gold bands of the highest quality shone with polished gleam. A present from General Emeralda.

Denyse stepped out of a side street, Kelly behind her, carrying a basket of fruit. "August! Elyse!" she called, her voice high and sweet over the tumultuous sounds of the city.

August stopped, Elyse with him, to meet the two magical girls as they weaved through traffic.

"I thought you might come," Denyse said, her face shining in the artificial Capital sunlight. She looked for all the world like an angel, some down to deliver a message.

August gave a wistful smile. "Today is the day, after all," he said, glancing at Elyse. Elyse smiled back, a sudden but quick storm crossing her face, and moving into August's.

"I brought you some flowers," Kelly said, reaching into her basket to bring out two bouquets. "For you," she said, "for them."

August took a bouquet, filled with sweet, magically grown roses and carnelians. They smelled like spring to him. They smelled like life. "Thank you," he said, looking Kelly in the eyes.

Kelly nodded. "It's the least I can do."

Elyse turned towards where they had been heading, before. "We should get going," she said.

August nodded, turning towards the great pillar gate to the outside world. "We should," he said.

And so they left the Capital, and came out into the natural sunlight, where the busy streets soon turned to dirt roads, barely traveled.

Denyse turned down a rough side path, which led towards a low green hill, topped with grey stones, like jagged, broken teeth. The air smelled like pollen, and bees buzzed around little clusters of flowers.

Denyse walked up to a gravestone, a little shorter than the rest, and laid her bouquet of flowers on top. She touched the top gently, as if remembering some long forgotten feeling.

Kelly watched her, her eyes misty. She turned then, and walked across the graveyard, to another headstone, indistinguishable from the rest except for its writing. She crouched in front of it for a long while, motionless.

August looked at Elyse, and the two knelt in front of the gravestones where Denyse stood.

Ruby Grandsham, one said, the one that Denyse had caressed. *May all who remember her remember her sacrifice.* Denyse had written the words.

August sat in the grass, the buzzing of bees all around, listening to the chirping of the birds in the trees, glancing at a stone next to Ruby's, with a single copper coin on top, as he listened to the rhythms of life.

Made in the USA
Columbia, SC
29 October 2018